BEYOND REASON

Elaine Evans Johnson

Elaine Evans Johnson

04/08

Published by
Aquarius Creations Publishing
P.O. Box 262641
Plano, Texas 75026-2641
WWW.AQUARIUSCREATIONPUBLISHING.COM
ACP@AQUARIUSCREATIONPUBLISHING.COM

ISBN: 978-1-928673-18-7

Book Cover designed by: Calvin Lee Hubbard

Photography by: Chris Wilson

Printed in the United States of America

10 9 8 7 6 5 4 3 2 1

For my ancestors who passed down the passion for storytelling and especially for Frank Johnson, Jr., Erin Evans, James Evans, Jr. and Aretha Ford.

In Loving Memory

In memory of my beloved, husband James Stanley Evans. When you left, I lost a part of me. You always allowed me to be me. You never judged me or tried to change me. I loved you with all of my heart.

In memory of my father Billy Hue Ford, my daddy. You were the best father that a girl could ever have. You were one of a kind, brilliant, loving, fun, and strict. I thank God for putting you in my life.

In memory of my only brother, Derrick Ford. I love and miss you and your contagious smile.

In memory of my maternal grandparents, Ressie and Mildred Hubbard. I thank God for you, for you created the best mother in the world. I loved you both very much.

In memory of my paternal grandmother, Pearlene Walker Lyons. I loved you very much and miss your laughter, your tenacity, and your love. You were awesome.

In memory of my paternal grandfather, A. C. Lyons, Sr. You were very special to me.

In memory of my many ancestors that have gone on before me. Just a few include Deborah Mixon, Jesse Lyons, and A. C. Lyons, Jr.

Last, but certainly not least, in memory of my Aunt Peggy Piggins, my earthly angel. I thank God for you. I miss you each day.

I thank God for having placed all of you in my life. You each played a special part in my life. I would not be who I am today without each of you. And, for this, I say THANK YOU.

Rest in peace,

Elaine

Acknowledgements

First, I give honor and all praises to my Lord and Savior for blessing me to be able to write this book.

I want to thank my husband who I love and appreciate for encouraging me. Many thanks to my children who laughed as well as encouraged me. I want to thank my mother for all that you have done for me.

A special thank you to my cousin Simbala Drammeh for pushing me to start writing the first line.

Blessings to my publisher Aquarius Creations Publishing, Adele Foster, and my editor Ronyea Dickerson.

Special thanks to the Ambassadors For Christ Drill Team ministry, Ralph Anderson, Bobby Arrington, Cheryl Barnes, Loretta Barnett, Seneca Calhoun, Bill Cotton, Deadra Courtney, Rev. Stuart Courtney, Lawana Durisseau Johnson, James Fields, Rita Frison, Tommy Griffin, JoAnna Harland, Mahasin Hazziez, Calvin Hubbard, Dal Jeanis, Charmaine Jefferson Lewis, James Johnson, Ricky Jones, Reginald Lewis, Lee Marshall, Sharon McDaniel, Kim McGee, Rev. Dr. Doris Miller, Regina Milton, Alia Moreland, Doris Nelson, Dr. Teresa Perkins, Karen Piggins, Rev. Robert Roberts, Stephanie Roberts, Emma Rodgers, Rev. Cecil Smith, Shirlyn Smith, Karon Thomas, Marie Walker, Loretta Ward, Margaret Ward, Deanna Wooden, and Rickie Wright.

So Amazing

"Driver, STOP!!!!"

The driver suddenly slammed on the brakes; the tires of the black stretched limousine came to a screeching halt; nearly throwing Charles and me towards the front of the vehicle. The young, petite, Latina female limo driver turned in a confused stare and asked, "Is there a problem, Mrs. Jeffrey?" She was wearing a black suit with a white button up shirt, black tie, with her hair pulled into a bun in the center of her head. She wore tiny rhinestone earrings and ruby red lipstick.

"Yes, I mean no. I mean yes. Back up please." I said trying to center my thoughts.

"Pardon me, Mrs. Jeffrey?" The limo driver asked again as if she misunderstood the request.

I turned to look out the back window. "It's Angela. Back up so I can see that marquee."

"Backup?" The limo driver asked looking confused once again.

"Yes, backup. It's okay. I need to get a second look at that marquee."

"Okay, but if I get a ticket." She stopped talking, sighed, and shook her head left to right as she proceeded to back the limo up.

I sat on the edge of my seat looking out the window. "You won't get a ticket. Go ahead." I gazed at the marquee with my hand over my mouth literally forgetting to breathe. My body began to shake seeing my name in lights. I mumbled to myself. "Wow, look at that, Everette/Jeffrey Wedding reception tonight." I turned to my new husband waving my hands in the air, "Charles, baby, get out and take a picture for me." I insisted with a huge grin.

Charles looked at his watch, "A picture Angela? We are going to be late."

I smiled and batted my eyes, "Pretty Please. How can we be late? It is *our* wedding reception. They can't start without *us*." Pointing to my chest really meaning they could not start

BEYOND REASON

without me. Go ahead and get the picture, baby, please!" I waved my hands for him to get out and carry out my requests.

He looked around for the camera "Angela, you are crazy. What are you going to do with a picture of a sign?" He gave me a slow passionate kiss before getting out of the limo with the camera in his right hand.

"It is not a sign, Charles. It is our ten minutes of fame, our name in lights." I followed him out of the car, still smiling.

The young, Latina driver rolled down the window and yelled. "Angela, are you always this happy?" She rested her chin on the backside of her hands.

"Yes, I am. What about you?"

The driver began. "Not really. I don't even know why I am here. I was not scheduled to drive tonight and I am not in a festive mood but…"

I interrupted her, "You know there *is* a reason you are here tonight." I walked around to her window and stooped in my gold, miraculous wedding gown next to her window. "Listen, I want you to come inside our reception and enjoy our night. Observe everything. Talk to people. Find out the reason you are here." I practically left no option.

"I guess if you insist." She replied, unenthused.

"Yes, I do insist." I turned toward Charles, "Charles baby, that's good. Let's go. It's show time." Charles and I got back into the limo and we rode to the entrance where the reception was being held.

The driver opened the door of the limousine. "Mrs. Jeffrey, let me assist you." She extended her small, tanned, hand to help me out.

BEYOND REASON

"Thank you, and don't forget what I said. Find out the reason you are here." I pulled my mink stole close and grabbed Charles's arm and we entered the reception hall. The Atrium Arts Center was simply grand. The ballroom room filled with forty-three tables elegantly adorned. Each table dressed with fresh calla lilies and fine linens. The lights in the fichus trees looked lovely. Everything was perfect!

We entered the ballroom, they announced, "Please welcome Mr. & Mrs. Charles Edward Jeffrey, II." Applause filled the air. Almost all the guests were standing. Charles was on my left dressed in a four-button forma, black tuxedo jacket with a herringbone style vest. We complemented one another. I must admit we were an item to see. I smelled the aroma from his cologne. He smelled and looked very good. I was proud to be his wife. For Charles to have been in his early fifties he was a very handsome, intelligent, and dapper man. He was about 6 feet in height and weighed roughly 230 pounds with a potbelly from the lack of sit-ups and maybe a beer or two, whichever one, it was there. He still had that glimmer in his eyes that melted my heart the very first time I laid eyes on him. His hairline had receded some with mingling gray along his temple, which only complemented his skin tone and confirmed his prestige. His beard and mustache were perfectly groomed with a deep dimple on his right cheek. At the center of the dance floor, Charles took me into his arms, dancing to K-Ci and JoJo's "This Very Moment." While taking in my surroundings and that very moment, I whispered in his ear, "Oooh Baby, don't start nothing up in here."

He smiled back at me broadcasting his beautiful smile. Just the touch of his hand caressing my back made my liver quiver. I looked in his eyes with love, adoration, and a smile on my face as large as the grill on a new Mercedes Benz. The joy inside me was bubbling up like a cup of piping hot chocolate. *Thank you Lord for my new husband, my Oooh Baby, My Boo.*

BEYOND REASON

My two-piece strapless gold iridescent gown whirled as we danced in each other's arms. I was no longer that petite young girl anymore, but felt real good with my sassy haircut, flawless makeup, and eyelashes. Draped over my shoulders was my Aunt's Victoria's mink stole. It had been in my closet ever since she passed away twenty-five years before. We danced until the song ended. Luther Vandross' "So Amazing" came on and our families joined Charles and me on the dance floor. All of our family members walked onto the dance floor in a large circle, hand in hand, swaying to the beat of the music. Charles danced with the women in the family and I danced with the men.

"Come on son, you are first." I said to my 16 year old son, Brandon Michael Everette. He looked so handsome just like his father with the same beautiful, white smile. He was quite slim and average height with a nice caramel complexion. I was so proud of him for putting on his good face for my special night. I knew deep down he was happy for me in spite of his own feelings.

Brandon chuckled. "Mom, this is not as cute as you think." He said as he rolled his eyes in a playful way as he often did.

"Sure it is. It's so amazing to be loved. And, why are you laughing?"

"Because you funny." He replied.

"Not funny, just joyful," I sashayed away to dance with my uncle. I reached for my uncle's arm asking him to dance, "Let's dance Uncle Bud."

My uncle held me in his arm and said, "You look beautiful Angie. I wish your father was here to see you."

I looked into my uncle's eyes and said faintly with a smile. "Me too." We continued dancing and I whispered to him, "I did not know you could dance like this Uncle Bud."

BEYOND REASON

He dipped me back swaying me from side to side. He then raised me up, and twirled me in the direction of my next partner. "There is a lot you don't know about me girl."

"I guess so."

"Let me dance with my step mom?" Charles' son, said as he glided to the center of the dance floor.

I looked up to Devin, "Show me what you are working with D."

Devin stepped close and whispered, "Angela, I am glad to have you as my step mother and I love the way you make my dad feel. He is so happy now." He paused before continuing. "Thanks for including everyone in the family dance; and just think you wanted to give up on the idea. This is wonderful! Welcome to the Jeffrey family." He bent down and kissed me softly on the cheek.

I looked to my left and noticed my mother, Autrice Franklin, dancing with Charles. She had such a radiant glow. Her silver hair was very elegant. I smiled at her. She smiled back, and mouthed, "I love you, so much." She was wearing a winter white suit with a faux fur collar. It looked beautiful against her dark skin. The both of us were stars.

Our moment was interrupted, "My turn." Charles' father said as he took my hand. "My son loves you very much. You truly make him happy."

"Mr. Jeffrey, I really love Charles and am happy to be a part of your family." *Thank you Lord.* I prayed silently.

Uncle Nate cut in, "Angie, I believe it is my turn." Uncle Nate was married to my Aunt Grace.

It was hard for me to remember that we were not blood related. There was no difference in the way I felt about Uncle Nate, than I did my blood uncles. I loved him that much. I raised my

BEYOND REASON

hands to dance with my uncle. "Uncle Nate, I love you and Aunt Grace more than you know. You are very special to me because you give my Aunt Grace the best."

"Angie, when I married your aunt, she told me just how special you were to her. I accepted you as my niece over forty years ago. I love you very much. Be happy."

The family dance ended and Brian, the husband of my dear friend Serena, blessed the food. Serena, my long time friend was wearing a long black velvet skirt with a gold chiffon blouse. For someone that could not do hair hers was always flawless with every stand in place. She had always worn her hair very short, which enhanced her oval face. Serena had long fingers, yet delicately small hands. Her nails were always well groomed usually with a natural buffed glow. We grew up together in North Dallas. We belonged to the same church and attended the same elementary, junior high, and high schools. I was a year older than she was, yet she was taller. We went to mission, Baptist Training Union (BTU), choir rehearsal, usher board, Sunday school, and congress together. On Sundays, we made tents in our backyards. I cherished her as my dearest and oldest friend. Serena married Brian Kendall. I really liked Brian; he was humble and sincere. I admired him as a man, found strength in him as a minister, and appreciated him as a great husband to my friend.

Brian was average height and average build. He had a quiet spirit that exudes respect. He often laughed at Serena and me when we greet each other. Whenever we see each other we both leaned back and reached toward each other and in exaggerated movements, we kissed each side of the other and then we both leaned back with a singing sigh. It was so cute.

Brian concluded the prayer and we moved to the receiving line where we greeted our guests. Leading the receiving line was Mrs. Thompson, "Hello, Mrs. Thompson, I am glad you could join us on our special day." Mrs. Thompson was a special person to me. I had always been able

BEYOND REASON

to confide in her and was honored she made our reception. She was a tall brown-skinned small framed woman. She usually had a cigarette as well as a cup of coffee in hand. When she talked to you, she tilted her head in the slightest way to get a good look at you. Her hair was long, black, and naturally curly. She was a beautiful woman and had flawless skin that made her look much younger.

Mrs. Thompson replied, "Now, Angela, you know I would not have missed this day for anything. You look beautiful and the ambiance of this place is stunning." She gave me a hug and kiss on the cheek before proceeding down the line.

"Hey Sis, let me have a kiss." While giving me a kiss, Rodney whispered in my ear, "You need to tone it down, or you are going to kill that old man." Rodney and his wife, Patricia, were just like family. Our families had always been close. We called each other brother and sister. Rodney thought he was the boss of me, since he was two years older than I was. He was tall, dark, and handsome. His wife Patricia, petite and sassy, was a supportive and loving sister to me. She was as sweet as they come. I loved them both. I stared in his hazel almond shaped eyes and shook my head from left to right, praying he was on his best behavior.

"Rodney, you are crazy. You better stop it before you make be mess up my makeup. I love you, now move it on down the line." I waved my hands for him to move on.

Next was Kayron, my hairdresser and friend. We grew up as neighbors. Kayron was very short, petite with a beautiful dark skin tone. She was wearing her hair in twists. She had hooked my hair up and transformed me into a beautiful swan. I raised my hand pointing to my head, "Kayron, does my hair look okay?" Without hesitation I asked, "And what about my makeup?"

Kayron looked at me, "Angie, you look fine girl. Keep smiling. There is a long line of guests behind me." She continued through the line.

BEYOND REASON

I greeted my next guest. "Hello Shari, I am glad you could come. Where is Don?" Shari was married to Don. Don and I met at work and became buddies.

"Eating," she replied.

"Oh, there he is. Hey Don." I waved to him as he passed me with two large plates in his hand. He was comfortable sporting his cowboy boots and his wrangler jeans. Don was a tall dark chocolate good-looking man with a shiny baldhead.

Don saw me but could not wave for fear of dropping the plates he held. "Hey darling. Congratulations." In the same breath he said, "Girl, these chicken wings are the bomb."

Shari continued through the receiving line to congratulate Charles.

I noticed my friend Raymond approaching. He gave me a long embraced hug and whispered in my ear. "You look good girl. But, I can't believe you married Ouch Baby." He stood back and looked at me before continuing. "I wish it could have been me." He said with a smile.

Raymond called Charles "Ouch Baby" instead of "Oooh Baby." I laughed and knew he cared for me as I did for him, but he was just a friend. "Thank you for coming Raymond."

"Oh, I would not have missed this for the world." Raymond replied as he shook Charles hand but still looking at me, "Treat her well man."

"I will." Charles replied as he placed his arm around my shoulder, marking his territory.

The last person came through the receiving line and Charles and I took our seats with our closest friends. I sat next to Cynthia. Cynthia grew up across the street from me. We went to school together from second grade through college. She had known all of the men in my life. Cynthia was a true friend. She was average height with long fine hair. She had a friendly smile and was fair skinned.

BEYOND REASON

Faye and Kenneth approached the microphone to speak. Faye was my dear friend, one of my best friends. She and I met in the summer of 1976 at our summer job. I had finished my sophomore year of college and Faye her freshman year. We hit it off instantly. I liked Faye and really admired her. Faye was what my husband called "good people." She was always up beat and positive. Her husband was Reverend Kenneth Preston. He told the funniest stories, even when he was not trying to be. I was happy when Faye found Kenneth.

Faye had a paper in hand and began reading. "Good evening everyone we are Faye and Rev. Kenneth Preston. We would like to tell you about Mr. and Mrs. Jeffrey, Charles and Angela." She paused for a second before continuing. "First, I would like to share my relationship with Angela Franklin Everette Jeffrey. We first met in nineteen seventy-six when we worked together at a local manufacturing company. We were eighteen years old. Angie and I were both college students but attended two different universities. We became very good friends and are still good friends to this day. I have four biological sisters and they are all here tonight. But, my adopted sister is Angela Jeffrey. Charles, her new husband, is considered her "Oooh Baby" and she wants to dedicate "My Boo" by Usher and Alicia Keys to him." Faye handed Kenneth the microphone.

Kenneth took the microphone smiled and began speaking. He did not have a paper or cue cards. He was supposed to introduce us but he was probably telling jokes in the foyer. Therefore, he was given another task. Kenneth looked around and smiled, "Good evening everyone. How are you doing?"

The crowd responded.

Kenneth continued, "I know you have never seen me before in your life and part of that is good." He smiled. "When I think about this couple; I think about "Songs In The Key Of Life."

BEYOND REASON

Life is a revolving door and 30 years is a long time for some of us, but in this situation thirty years is just a couple of days away."

He paused again, Kenneth turned and looked at Charles and elevated his hand. "I can see old Charles right now. The Isley Brothers were probably who he was hanging with at that particular time. Ya'll excuse the preacher." He said with a snicker.

Everyone laughed.

"He was probably listening to "Who's That Lady," and this was the question he was asking his friends, because you all know Charles is bashful. Also, when you look at the "Songs In The Key of Life," I have to look at Angela and think about Stevie Wonder's "Isn't She Lovely." These are just the words that I imagine Charles used as he made his approach. You know there is an approach and there is a landing. And this approach worked, but God had his hand in this union." He paused for a second and lowered his head. "There also had to be some "Amazing Grace." There had to be some "Old Rugged Crosses" and some "Rock of Ages" in this situation, but God does not make mistakes." Kenneth smiled and turned to look around the room.

"Yeah, Charles had to put down "Who's That Lady" and had to stop backing it up. Charles had to settle in. He said I am going to have to be the man of this household. She's a godly woman, and he's a godly man."

Kenneth looked down as he gathered his thoughts. "But I knew Charles before all of this and all we did was smile and move around, smile and move around again. I knew him over at Club R.J.'s by the Lake. That's alright, I wasn't preaching then."

The room filled with laughter.

Kenneth lowered his head still smiling waiting for the laughter to cease. "The Electric Slide and all that other stuff were out. I had just enough sin in me, but you... I mean... amen."

BEYOND REASON

Everyone laughed.

"Charles still has that smile on his face today. When I met my wife, she took me by Angela's and I became a part of the family. I love all of them. I had new friends, a smile on my face, and new victories. Charles has a new victory, a wonderful wife, and I thank God for this today. When Charles and I saw each other again, we made the connection."

Faye poked and nudged Kenneth to conclude. However, he turned to face Charles who was sitting behind him. "So I want to say. Charles, you know how to do it. You have been taught how to do it, and God is leading this train."

Faye was wearing a long brown velvet dress with diamond stud earrings leaned to Kenneth looking dapper in his tux and pointed to the paper for him to wrap up.

Kenneth looked at the paper, "Now, there is a song, but it's not "Amazing Grace," it's "You Are My Lady" by Freddie Jackson. Charles, Angela, we love you and may you share many happy years together."

Everyone laughed so hard including Charles and me. We could hardly stand.

We went to the dance floor. "My Boo" began and we danced. I sang to Charles, "There is always that one person who has your heart… Oooh Baby, you will always be My Boo."

After "My Boo" ended "You are My Lady" began and Charles crooned in my ear, "You are my lady…" We danced in each other's arms until, "The Electric Slide" began and everyone jumped on the dance floor. You know you cannot go to a black wedding, reunion, or funeral without doing the electric slide. That was when the real party began.

After several songs, Toni signaled for Charles and me to cut the cakes. Charles and I gathered at the south end of the ballroom where the cakes looked exquisite. The wedding cake was a four-tiered white cake with alternating layers of strawberry and parisene filling. The top

BEYOND REASON

tier of the cake had six perfectly shaped fresh cream roses adorned with baby's breath. Each of the layers below had the same cream roses all around the tops with a total of 42 roses.

Toni helped us cut the cake. Toni was a dear friend married to Vincent. Vincent and I worked together, at a major retailer. The two of them married shortly after we met. We all became good friends and had been through a lot together over the years. I did not know what I was going to do when they moved hundreds of miles away. I thought that was why Toni was not her usual self. Although Vincent and I were friends first, Toni and I became friends. Toni always said, "I love you. Mean it." I loved to hear her say it too.

Charles and I fed each other the wedding cake, which was delicious. Charles wiped my mouth before we moved to the groom's cake. The groom's cake was a three-tiered truffle with cascading chocolate dripping strawberries, topped with two strawberries to represent a bride and groom. I picked up the knife and Charles placed his hand on top of mine as we sliced the cake. We placed a small piece of cake in our hands to feed each other. The cake was decadent. Charles wiped my mouth and raised one of the strawberries to my mouth for me to taste. The strawberry was sweet and delicious for early January.

I glanced out the window to see the courtyard. The Christmas lights were still in all of the trees. It looked like a scene from a romantic movie. One I was happy to star in.

We moved to mingle with our guests. The party was really jumping. Everyone was dancing and having a good time. I chatted with several people. Sitting at one table were my lunch buddies and co-workers. I approached the table and said, "Hey y'all."

Everyone acknowledged me. I walked around the table to get a hug and thank each person individually for coming. I bent down to speak to Tommy first who was in his wheel chair. Tommy and I met several years before at work. I literally ran into him. I was rushing around a

BEYOND REASON

corner and fell in Tommy's lap. I was in such a rush that I apologized for the accident and rushed away. About two weeks later, he joined me in the break room. I apologized for my incident that occurred earlier and we began talking. We became instant friends.

Tommy was tall with a paper sack skin tone. He was very intelligent and a flirt. I think that was really, why we hit it off so well. Some say I was a flirt as well. Tommy gave me a kiss and said, "Congratulations, to you and Oooh Baby." Then he put his fist up to his mouth to hide his snicker with his shoulders moving up and down.

I looked at him and smiled taking hold of his hands, "Thanks, Tommy."

Lynette interrupted. "Come here girl." She began to speak fast. "You are working that dress, but you still got that butt." She turned to Tommy and hit him on the arm. "Quit looking Tommy." She turned back around to face me, "Angela, I am really happy for you."

"Lynette, I couldn't have made it without you." We hugged and I whispered in her ear. "You lean on me and I'll lean on you."

She nudged my shoulder slightly, "I know you're right."

"Get your 'A' over here girl so I can give my home girl a kiss."

I turned to face the loud deep voice. It was Big Daddy sitting on the other side of the table. I strolled to his side of the table, "What's up Big Daddy?" Everyone that heard me laughed. They all knew the story of why I called him Big Daddy. He hated for me to call him Big Daddy too. Howard was about 6 feet 3 inches and hefty in size. He had hands just like my father's. Actually, he reminded me a lot of my dad. Their language was similar and he loved his family very much. Big Daddy worked with young people and was a brilliant mathematician. He was a special guy.

BEYOND REASON

I noticed my cousin, Steve, approaching. "Steve, take a group picture of me and my lunch buddies. PLEASE!" Big Daddy, Tommy, and Don gathered around me.

Steve said with a chuckle, "Cuz, you eat with all of these men *everyday*?"

"Oh yeah," I responded. I put my arms around Tommy and Big Daddy and said, "Thanks guys. I appreciate you all. But, where is Gabe?"

Big Daddy laughed out loud, "Now you know his ass is going to be late."

"Yeah, you are right." I chuckled.

I heard Diahann clicking her fork to her glass for the toast. Charles and I made way to the center of the ballroom dance floor where Diahann was standing with her husband, Harold. Diahann was my girl, my best girl. Diahann did all of the coordination for the wedding. We met twenty-six years before when I was on an interview. She liked me right from the start. When we met I was not looking for another girl friend, but she proved to be a great friend. I loved Diahann and was proud to know she loved me as a sister. I described her as extravagant. She liked unique and expensive things; however, she was not at all materialistic. She loved and valued family and friends. However, she was very final. If you betrayed her trust there was no going back. Diahann was generous and although she liked grand things, she would give you the shirt off her back. In fact, she had done that very thing for me. I knew Diahann would do and give me anything she had.

Diahann's husband, Harold, was highly intelligent and very handsome. He had a dry sense of humor that we all mocked. Everyone liked to give him a hard time. He could not get anyone to be his partner to play bid whist and I am not sure why. He played well and was usually the butt of the jokes. But, I always took up for him. Diahann and Harold were married when I met

BEYOND REASON

them, and they had been married the longest of all my friends. Diahann looked a bit nervous to me. Most people did not know that she was shy, because she exudes such confidence.

Diahann began, "Charles, Angela, congratulations on your marriage. As we stand here tonight, we are happy to say you are our friends. You have been and continue to be a true example of love as you begin this new journey together called life. May you forever keep God in your hearts, stay in each other's arms, and always be as happy as you are now. As we raise our glasses, best wishes to you both. We love you. Cheers."

Dang, Diahann was good. I thought to myself. We raised our glasses to the toast and sipped. Charles gave me a soft, sweet, tender kiss. *Whew, I was ready for the honeymoon,* and hoped no one saw that last expression on my face.

Diahann handed the microphone to Willie. Willie, Charles' best friend raised his glass to us. "Charles, Angela, I want to say what a wonderful evening so far. Angela, you look elegant and Charles you look dapper as always. To the future Charles, I hope you stay together from this point on. Keep God first in your life. Me and my wife love you and look forward to many more years to come."

Charles took the microphone from his best man Willie and gave him a hug. Then he began to speak. "I'd like to thank everyone that came out and supported us tonight. It really has been a great day. You have made it even more joyful. Thank you all."

Charles then handed me the microphone after I told him I didn't want to say anything. I hadn't prepared anything to say, but I began to speak. "I am happy to see everyone tonight and I really appreciate all of your support and love." About that time the DJ put on Charlie Wilson's "Come On Home To Me" saving me from myself. I smiled and then sang, "Let's party." Everyone jumped back on the dance floor.

BEYOND REASON

Dancing continued while Charles and I took pictures. Eventually, the DJ announced for my sisters to join me at the photographer's area. Shortly, after the announcement my sisters arrived. They were not my blood sisters, but I loved them just the same. We all worked together with the youth at my church. The five of us posed in order by age. Gwen was the oldest married with one son. She was somewhat shy. Next was Irene. She was married with five children. Irene was also a counselor to anyone in need, rarely taking time for her self. Johnnie was the middle sister. She was divorced with two children. She kept us all in line as if she was the mother. I was in between Johnnie and Janice. Janice, the baby, was married with two children. She was spoiled rotten, just like any other baby sister. We finished taking pictures and I looked toward the entrance where Gabe was entering with his family. I raised my arm as if I was checking the time. As he approached I said, "Well, it is about time, Gabe."

"Now, I told you I would be running late." Gabe replied and gave me a hug and kiss.

Gabe, short for Gabriel, was another one of my lunch buddies. I shared most of my personal problems with him, because I valued his opinion. "I am glad you made it." I said to him.

"Well, where is the food?" Gabe asked immediately.

Before I answered, I spoke to his wife and daughter and then pointed in the direction the food was located. "You passed it in the foyer."

Gabe looked around, "Okay. I am going to eat." He walked away and I took it to the dance floor.

Eventually, the last song played "Reunited." Charles and I danced together. My night was coming to a close and I was not ready for it to end. I had a remarkable time. The song ended and I put my arm in Charles' arm and he escorted me to our limousine. I would never forget that night. *Thank you Lord, for blessing me.*

BEYOND REASON

***

The same Latina driver opened the door of the limo and said to me, "Angela, I noticed you tonight and wondered if you are really as happy as you seem?"

"Absolutely, I am more than happy. I am joyful." I said before getting into the car. As the driver got into the driver's seat I asked her, "What is your name again?"

She replied looking through the rear view mirror, "Mary. My name is Mary."

I leaned forward and asked, "Are you happy, Mary?"

She paused for a moment before answering, "Naw, I don't think so. I don't think anyone can truly be happy. I have been through a lot in my life, and I do not believe in that happily ever after stuff."

"Mary, you must believe that you can have joy in your life." I reached to touch her arm. "You know, I have so much joy in my life, not just happiness, true joy. There is a difference between joy and happiness, did you know that?" I looked for a response in her eyes before I continued. "Happiness depends on what is happening, but joy is independent of your circumstances. I count it all joy, and I find myself thinking about the song, "I've got a testimony. Do you know that song?"

Mary turned to face me. "No. I don't think so."

"It goes like this. As I look back over my life, and I think things over, I can truly say that I've been blessed. I've got a testimony." I paused, "There is a reason you were here tonight. Things don't just happen."

"They don't?" She replied.

"No, Mary, they don't. There is a reason and a purpose to everything in life. Listen while I tell you a story."

BEYOND REASON

REASON

The First Time Ever I Saw Your Face

It was the last week of August in 1974. I was eighteen years old. I had recently graduated from Berkner High School. I was petite, weighing about 110 pounds. Actually, I was skinny with a big butt. I hated my butt. I had been packing our car all that day to head to college. My boyfriend, Ricky, kept calling me, begging me not to leave him. I tried to convince him that I loved him, but there was no way I was going to let him stop me from going to college, in love or not.

Ricky was short in stature and built like an athlete. His eyes were a piercing light brown. He was a sprinter in Track and Field, a state champion in fact. His complexion was caramel. He was not bad looking just short. He was known for being a tough guy, in spite of his height. He was my guy and I loved him.

My parents were at work and told me to pack the car, so we could leave when they got home. I packed my entire bedroom as if I would never return home. It took me all day. Every time I came in the house, the phone rang. It was always Ricky.

"Don't go," he said.

"Oh yeah, I am going, but I will write you everyday."

This went on all day.

"I am going to kill myself if you go."

"Please don't do that. But, let me call you back." I said.

By three o'clock, my parents were home and ready to take me to college. They were both in the car, but I was in the house saying goodbye to Ricky. "I will call you as soon as I get to school. Bye. Gotta go. Luv you."

We left for Commerce not even stopping to eat. I was finally on my way to college, a day I dreamed of for many years. I could hardly sit still in the back seat of the car. I slid from side to side looking out of the window wondering what was ahead of me. I was so pumped. A whole new world was waiting for me. We could not get there soon enough.

I had never been to East Texas State University (ETSU) before, so I did not know what to expect. By the time we got to Lake Ray Hubbard, there was a flash flood warning and we were in it. My dad, Bernie Hue Franklin, could not see in the rain, and he was driving about five miles per hour. We drove for what seemed like an hour and a half in that storm. Commerce was only an hour away, so I thought we had to be close.

Finally, my mom insisted on driving. We were only about 15 minutes away from the house at that point. My mom took over, and we flew the rest of the way. Forty-five minutes later, we arrived in Commerce, and the sun was shining. I could see my dorm, Whitley Hall, from a mile away. The building was a 12 story pink brick with windowed stairways on each end of the building.

All of the other freshmen came that morning; I was the only one moving in that evening. I checked in and got my room assignment, room 1221, Whitley Hall.

We took the elevator to the 12th floor and walked down the long hall to my room. I was so excited I could scream. A poster outside of the door read, "Welcome Angela & Cynthia from Dallas." I was glad my new roommate was from Dallas. But, I knew it was not my friend Cynthia, because she was staying in a different dorm.

REASON

I opened the door. There was a large picture window that went to the ceiling facing the door. I went to the window and could see the entire campus. *"Wow, what a view. I am going to love this."* I whispered to myself. I stood there looking for a few minutes. I was the first to arrive, so I picked the bed by the large walk in closet, which had two sets of floor to ceiling dresser drawers. Across from the closet was the door to the shower and restroom. The sink was inside the room, not the restroom. The room was only about ten feet wide and twenty feet long. Both beds were built-ins, along with the desks at the foot of each bed. I sat on the bed to take it all in.

Mama said, "Do not sit down or touch anything until I disinfect this room."

"It looks clean to me." I responded and rubbed my hand across the naked mattress.

"You can't see germs, Angela. Just go downstairs and unpack the car with Bernie and I will clean the room and bathroom."

"Mama, they say we have maid service." I said to my mother still sitting on the bed.

My mom insisted that I help get the remaining items out of the car.

My dad interrupted and said, "Girl, are you going to help get the rest of your stuff or are you going to sit on the bed?"

I reluctantly followed my dad back to the car. He pulled suitcases, pillowcases, and boxes full of stuff out of the car, "Did you have to bring everything?"

"Yeah, I don't know what all I will need. I ain't been to college before." I replied.

"You could have at least put a pillow case on these pillows."

He was embarrassed because they were homemade. He did not want us to stand out as if we didn't belong.

REASON

Daddy, being of short stature, stood back looking at all the stuff with disbelief and said. "I can't believe you packed this stuff like this." He scratched his head and pulled his shirt up in the back. "Girl, I am not taking all of this shit inside.

"Why? I asked but decided to take it myself. I didn't know why he was tripping." My daddy would only take items that were packed in a suitcase. We argued over everything in the car. Although my dad complained about all the stuff I brought to school, he was proud of me. This was just as much his dream as mine.

My mom disinfected the room. She made the bed and helped put my stuff away. Once everything was done, we left the dorm and drove around to find something to eat.

While we were eating, my mom touched my arm, looked into my eyes, and said, "Angie, I am so proud of you."

I smiled back at her as I sucked on the chicken bone. "Thanks, Mama."

We finished eating and left to return to my dorm. As my parents were departing, my dad leaned over and whispered in my ear. "Don't take no wooden nickels, Angie." He turned to leave.

"What?" I said in a questioning tone.

"Don't take no wooden nickels." He repeated.

"Okay. I won't." However, I was thinking I wouldn't take any, whatever they were. I was beginning to get excited because they were leaving. *I'm in college! I'm in college!* I was so excited; I could hardly wait for them to drive off. I went straight back up to my room and started looking for my friends, Cynthia and Debra.

I knew they were staying in Smith Hall, and it had a curfew. My mom chose Whitley for me because of the private showers. She said there would be fewer germs without any and everyone using community showers. I called the Smith Hall office and asked for Cynthia

Moore's room. I dialed the number and Cynthia answered.

"Hey Cynthia, I am here in Whitley Hall room 1221." Without pausing, I asked. "When

did you get here? Where is Smith Hall? Can you come over here?"

She laughed at me like I was talking stupid or something, but she agreed to come right

over.

"I will be downstairs in the lobby. Okay?" I said to her before hanging up the telephone.

I went downstairs to wait for her. I was wearing purple hip hugger jeans that laced up in the

back and front of the crotch. I was dressed in a yellow seersucker puckered body suit. I wore

my hair pressed with curls, after wearing an afro all through my senior year. Although, my afro

was well shaped and showed off the natural curl in my hair. I wanted something different in

college. Last, but not least, I was wearing purple and yellow 4 inch clogs. You could not tell me

I was not looking good.

I went downstairs to wait for my friends and three good-looking guys were standing by

the door. One said something to the other. I could not hear them, but could tell they were

talking about me. Then one said, "You untie the front, and I will untie the back."

They were talking about my pants. I wanted to run and hide but decided to ignore them.

About that time, my homeboy, Dewey, came up. "Y'all leave Angie alone. She is my home

girl." Dewey said and gave me a hug.

"Thanks Dewey." I said to him, relieved and hugging him back.

"No problem, Angie. I got your back." He introduced me to the guys that had teased me

about my pants. The guys turned out to be the most popular football players at the school and they were always nice to me after that. All of them eventually became professional football players, including Dewey.

I went back upstairs and took those pants off vowing, never to wear them again. I hated my butt. It embarrassed me when people noticed it. I hurried to change clothes before my friends got there.

Finally, Cynthia and Debra arrived from Smith Hall. I asked them, "How long have y'all been here?"

"Since yesterday." Cynthia replied.

"Yesterday? The paper said we could not check in until today."

"They lied," said Cynthia. "We came by to see you, but we cannot stay. It is pretty late, and I think we have a curfew."

Debra chimed in, "Yeah, Angie we have got to get back." Debra grew up with Cynthia and me and lived on our street. They were best friends. We all had been friends since we were very young.

"Before you leave, what are we supposed to do tomorrow?" I asked.

Cynthia said. "We are supposed to be at the history building by 7:30 in the morning."

"Do you know where that is?" I asked.

"Yeah, it's. I mean. Girl, it's hard to say." Cynthia replied.

"Okay, I will find it."

"Bye Angela." They said in unison as they turned to leave.

"Bye, see you tomorrow."

REASON

I decided to go to the housing office and ask the girl how to find the history building. "Hi. Can you tell me how to get to the history building?" I asked the girl at the front desk of the lobby.

"Just get up and follow the crowd," the girl said with a chuckle.

Why can't somebody just tell me how to get there? I am good with directions. I went back upstairs and decided to knock on the door, across the hall from my room, to see if *she* knew where we needed to go.

The girl across the hall from me was Monica. She was from Arkansas. Monica was slightly taller than I was. She was dark skinned and was on a basketball scholarship. She was wearing an afro longer than mine. Some thought we favored one another. We had similar skin tones and the same grades of hair. We both had toothy grins. She was the niece of one of the professors. The two of us talked for hours that night.

She knew where the history building was so we decided to go to the freshman activities together the next day. After talking for a while, I went back to my room and wrote my boyfriend, Ricky, a letter.

August 26, 1974

Dear Sweetheart,

I made it to school safely. I am missing you already. Please don't be mad at me for leaving. I will never think I am better than you are. I promise not to look at any other guys.

Your sweetheart,

Love

A

REASON

I sealed the letter and went bed. The next morning came real early. I had to get ready in a hurry so Monica would not leave me. It was raining. "Dang, all this stuff and no umbrella, no raincoat *either*," I mumbled to myself. I grabbed a tablet and my purse. Monica and I walked the mile to the Student Union Building (SUB) in the rain.

The woman in the cafeteria told me I could not enter the cafeteria because I did not have a meal ticket. I told her I was with my friend Monica and was not eating. I went in anyway and took a seat. She tried to stop me, but it did not work. I took a seat, but she never took her eyes off me.

Finally, I asked, "Monica, are you done? I want to get to the history building."

Monica rushed to finish and we left. We walked in the rain to the history building on the other side of the campus. We took tests and listened to people give speeches. It was all quite boring. A professor said, "Look to the left, now look to the right. One of you will not be here in four years."

I thought to myself, it must be one of y'all because I am getting my degree. I just didn't know which one to tell bye at that time so I smiled to myself and slid down in my seat. I felt sorry for whichever one of them would not be there in four years.

We broke off into smaller group sessions. These white girls came in the room talking about rushes. What the hell were they talking about? I wanted to ask them if I could join their group. I bet they would have stop jumping around acting all perky then.

The next day was more of the same and still raining. My head was tow up. By the end of the week, they told me I read too slow and suggested I take speed-reading. I thought great idea and signed up.

REASON

Sunday morning, Monica's uncle came and picked us up for church. The church was in the Hole. This was the black community in Commerce. I was sure it was called the Hole because it was full of potholes on every street. You had to drive very slowly to get through the Hole. I liked the church. It was a Baptist church very similar to what I was used to in Dallas. The pastor was funny. I liked it when he would say, "Amen lights." I enjoyed the service and planned to go again. After church, Monica's uncle took us to the school cafeteria.

By the beginning of the second week, all of the upperclassmen arrived to register for classes. Registration was by last name. It was chaotic, long lines, and many short tempers. I had spent hours planning my schedule to find out most of my selections were closed. Eventually, I registered for English, business mathematic, algebra, history, speed-reading, and volleyball.

It rained so much that I decided to go back to wearing an afro. The new image of me was not working out. Now, nobody told me how to schedule my classes. My classes were all day long with long breaks in between. My first class was English. The teacher took attendance and let us go. I had an hour to kill. It was too far to walk back to Whitley Hall, so I went to the student union building (SUB) and stood in the middle of the hallway, leaning up against the cafeteria glass. It was wall-to-wall black people, and this was a predominantly white school. I decided to walk down to the post office and mail my Mama's birthday card. I had a good card for her but it was going to be late. Her birthday was that day and since it was Labor Day, she would not get the card for a couple of days. I did not understand why we were starting school on Labor Day and my mom's birthday, anyway.

I dropped the card in the mailbox addressed to Mama, without an address. "Dang!" That was the first time I hadn't just placed the card on the kitchen table. However, I was relieved no

REASON

cash was in the card.

I walked back to the front of the student union building and could not find any of my friends. I did not see anyone I knew. After what seemed like a lifetime this fine brother said, "You, here?" He had an island ascent and was pointing at me.

I found it odd that he was sitting on top of a bullet trash can and he had about five females standing around him. It seemed to me he thought he had it going on.

"You, here!" He said again.

"Me?" I pointed to myself.

"Yes you," he mouthed to me.

Damn. Don't say anything stupid, Angela. I thought to myself.

"Your name?" He asked.

"Excuse me?" I asked, wondering where he was from.

"Your name?" He repeated.

"Angela?" *Now that was stupid.* I sounded like I was asking him if my name was Angela. "And you are?" I stuttered out.

"Macias!"

"What?" I asked.

"Macias." He smiled and said, "Just call me Mac."

"Okay. Where are you from?" I asked.

"Ft. Worth." He did not take a breath. "Freshman?"

Ft. Worth, with a name like Macias. I thought he was from Jamaica or somewhere. "Yeah, I guess." *Stupid, what do you mean you guess.* I felt so confused, so I just stood there smiling, afraid to say anything else.

REASON

Mac introduced me to all of the young ladies standing there and as we were saying our hellos, my friend's brother, Sam, walked up.

"Hey Boo." Sam greeted.

As much as I hated him calling me Boo, I was glad to see a friendly face. "Hey, Sam." I said as he grabbed me and gave me a big hug. They were all surprised that I knew Sam. He was Mac's fraternity brother and one of the young ladies' fiancée. "Sam, what are you doing here? I thought you were in the service."

Sam smiled and said, "I am, but I came to see my baby, and I guess you too."

We talked for some time before everyone left to go to classes.

Since I was just passing time, Mac asked to walk me to class. We walked across campus, and it started to rain again. We stood on the porch of the journalism building for the longest time talking. I liked him. He was fine. Tall nice physique, long fingers, with small teeth. He was about 6 feet 2 inches with a cappuccino complexion. He had a small afro. He was different. Mac was fine and looked a lot like the young actor Boris Kodjoe. I wondered why he was spending all of his time with me, a freshman. But, I didn't care because he was so fine.

"What dorm are you in?" Mac asked.

"Whitley Hall, 1221."

"I will call you." Mac said and then he was gone in the rain.

I went to my class thinking how different Mac was. I was interested in him.

That afternoon, Mac came over to my dorm to visit. We sat out on the porch for hours talking. We both loved to talk.

Each day, Mac walked me to class. He walked me to English and picked me up at the end of class to walk me to volleyball. Mac taught me everything about college. He talked about

REASON

fraternities and sororities and even helped me with homework. We walked around campus, played ping-pong, bid whist, spades, poker, and he introduced me to all of his fraternity brothers. Most of his fraternity brothers were from Dallas, which meant I had a lot of homeboys. We listened to Barry White songs and talked about college. He talked about pledging and Greek shows. He explained every aspect of college.

About a month after school started, I got a letter saying, "Please pay additional funds for a private room or obtain a roommate." Monica got the same letter. Her white roommate had moved out soon after school started. Therefore, we decided to room together and since my room was facing campus, Monica moved in with me. Monica was a good roommate, but a lot of people found her annoying. A lot of people didn't like me because of her. I got used to it, and of course, I could care less.

***

One night Monica and I were walking through the tunnel from Smith Hall and a group of girls trailing us yelled, "BITCH."

I turned to Monica not even looking around and said, "Monica, they must be talking to you."

They yelled again, "BITCH from Dallas."

Monica said. "No, Angela, they are talking to you." She turned to get a look at them. She then turned to face me. "They look like girls from Smith Hall."

I stopped walking and turned to get a look at them, but did not recognize any of them. I looked at Monica and asked. "Who are they?" She shrugged her shoulders and I yelled to them, "Yo, Mama." I turned and strolled on.

REASON

Monica laughed, "You are always, talking about me getting you enemies. It looks like you have these on your own."

"But who are they?" I repeated. I hated having enemies and did not know who they were. How could I defend myself? This bothered me, but I kept walking.

***

By that time, Mac and I were sort of a couple, but not really. One day while at the fraternity house, he tried to move to the next level, but I only wanted to be friends. I had a boyfriend so that wasn't happening. We continued to talk and listen to music.

Eventually, I decided I would give him some since I was not a virgin. I mean, this was the seventies, free spirit, free drugs, and free love. One cool October night, I was on my way to Mac's place, in deep thought, I had decided to give Mac some. All of a sudden, I was startled by someone shaking me yelling, "Angela, Angela."

It was my cousin, Paula. "What is wrong with you?" She asked.

"Nothing." I said with a blank stare into her eyes.

With excitement in her voice Paula said, "I was hoping I would see you."

I put my hands in my jean pockets and asked. "What are you doing here?"

"I rode down here with my friend to see her brother. I just said to her, I need to find my cousin, and you appeared, but you are acting kind of weird."

"No, I am cool. Do you want to see my dorm?"

"Sure."

I thought to myself, Mac must think I was not coming, but I could not run my cousin off. Therefore, I took Paula to my room. We talked for a while before she left. After she left, I went to Mac's, and gave him some.

REASON

***

By mid October, I was excited about going home to see my boyfriend and to attend the Texas State Fair. Monica went home with me. While home, Monica, my friend Serena, my boyfriend Ricky, and I went to the state fair together. However, Monica and Ricky did not hit it off well at all, nor did Serena and Monica.

Serena and I had been the best of friends longer than I could remember. She was attending her freshman year at Bishop College in Dallas. We had been writing each other talking about all of the things that our freshman year had brought our way. So, it was important to me to see her as well as Ricky that weekend.

Monica wanted to go the parties, but Ricky wanted me to dump her and Serena so the two of us could be alone. Serena decided that Ricky and Monica were not worth the effort. Therefore, she went her own way leaving the three of us to argue. Monica and Ricky continued to argue all weekend. I felt like Silly Putty being stretched in two different directions.

Sunday night we returned to school and on the way back Monica said. "Angela, you need to drop that loser. How can you be so smart and date a jerk like him?"

"But, I love him. You just need to get to know him better."

"No. He is an ignorant jerk. Drop him!"

I was sad they had not hit it off, but I dropped the conversation.

Homecoming was a few weeks later. The game was during the day and Mac had attended the game with another woman. I was hurt when I saw the two of them together.

After the game, I went to the fraternity house to give him a piece of my mind. Well, he listened to me calmly as I ranted and raved about him being involved with someone else. I told

REASON

him I deserved better and would not be a part of this threesome. It was clear to me who called me a bitch in the tunnel. It was this girl and her friends all upperclassmen. Well, he so smoothly told me he had not done anything wrong. All he had done was attend the game with a female friend. Mac said, "Angela, have I ever seen you and not acknowledged you?"

"No." I said in a soft voice.

"Do you enjoy my company?"

I replied, "Yes."

"Then what is the problem?" Mac stopped talking for a moment and then said. "Angela, as long as you live you will be faced with competition. Even if we were married, I would still look. Now, the two of us have a friendly relationship and I want more. You keep saying that you don't. You even said you have a man in Dallas. Now, that young lady does a lot for me. She paid for the pizza we had earlier in the week. I would be a fool to get rid of her. Now, are you willing to do those things?"

"Do what? Give you money?" I asked with my eyebrow raised.

"Yes."

"Hell no." I snapped.

"Well, Angela, I really care about you and do not understand why you are upset. You should think about what it is you want from our relationship." He stood and walked me to the door.

I knew he wanted me to leave. He had said a lot. I had to think about how I felt about our relationship. So, I left the fraternity house and went back to my dorm.

Over the years, I realized how much crap he told me, and how we or let me say, *I* could have been so stupid.

REASON

Since I was pissed with Mac, I went to the homecoming carnival with Monica. The first stop was a gaming booth with black, white, red, and blue squares. The object of the game was to throw the dice onto the table, and the color it landed on was the winner. Well, I was pretty good at mathematics and the probability of the ball landing on either black or white was about 95 percent, blue only one percent, and red about four percent. I looked to the right and a fine, dark chocolate brother was standing beside me. He had a neat afro with long side burns. He was average height and build. His smile did something to me. "Put your quarter on the black," I said flirting with him.

He did and won fifty cents. He gave me a quarter. We did this for about six more times. We were up about one dollar and a half. He started losing and said with a smile. "I better leave, before I lose all of my money. See ya." He turned and walked away.

"I hope so." I mumbled to myself as he disappeared.

Monica asked, "Why were you flirting with that man? He was with a woman."

"He was flirting with me, and he was so cute." I thought for a second before continuing, "I didn't even notice the woman." I said to Monica.

"He was not that cute, and he was with a woman," she insisted. "How do you get yourself involved with guys that are already in relationships? You don't even notice the women they are with. What is wrong with you?"

I said to Monica. "If she was really with him, then why would she allow him to flirt with me in her presence? Did you notice that dimple on his right cheek?" I wondered what type of relationship the mystery man was in as we rode the Ferris wheel. We left the carnival and got dressed for the after party.

REASON

A graduate student had opened a new party house, called Spencer's Place, about a mile or two from the dorm. It was actually an old house. None of us had cars so we decided to walk. Everyone except me was dressed to the nines. Monica was wearing a green crushed velvet pantsuit, green leather boots, with a matching green felt hat, and large feather. I had never been to a college homecoming. I did not know what to wear, so I wore jeans. We arrived at Spencer's Place, and it was packed and very hot. My afro shrunk from six inches to a half inch. Spencer said to me, that I was the only one dressed for the occasion. Actually, I felt out of place because no one else had on jeans. I was bummed about my attire and my earlier conversations with Mac, so I went outside to get some air and think.

After sitting outside for a few minutes, the guy from the carnival came outside. He came over and introduced himself as Charles Jeffrey.

I responded, "I am Angela Franklin." But, he already knew who I was and had seen me around campus with Mac.

"Why are you sitting outside?" He asked.

"I am ready to go back to the dorm, but it was too far to walk by myself."

"I will take you back to the dorm." He said with a smile that revealed his dimple.

"Okay, but I need to tell my roommate that I am leaving." When I got back outside Charles was standing there with another guy that I had seen before. I thought the guy was crazy.

The carnival guy said, "Angela, this is my cousin Charles Jeffrey. He is the one actually driving tonight."

I tilted my head to look at Charles with disbelief and I said, "I thought you told me your name was Charles Jeffrey?"

"It is, and yes, we are cousins."

REASON

I paused for a moment. "Well, I don't know if I should go back to the dorm with the two of you by myself."

"We will not hurt you." Charles said.

The cousin Charles interrupted, "Girl, get in the car. I ain't thinking about you. Do you want a ride or not? I am trying to get my party on. Let's go."

I decided to let them take me to the dorm. They took me straight to Whitley Hall, but not before Charles, the dark chocolate one, got my room number.

Charles called me that night as soon as he got to his room. We talked until five in the morning. Now I was attracted to him immediately and after talking to him all night, I knew he was the one. He had a sultry baritone voice and was a senior. Charles was doing his student teaching in Paris, a small town in east Texas. Charles was the middle child among several sisters. I could tell from his conversation that he loved his family. One of the things I liked about him was he could talk just as much as I could. He was going back to Paris later that day, but would be back on campus next weekend for the Greek show. I wrote his name all over my books, while we talked into the morning, Charles Edward Jeffrey, II.

After we stopped talking on the telephone, I quietly sang, "The first time, ever I saw your face. I felt the sun rose in your eyes. And the moon and the stars were the gifts..." I just laid in my bed with a smile in my heart.

A week later, I saw Charles in the cafeteria. He walked up to me with his tray in hand and we stared into each other's eyes. We never spoke a word. Charles' cousin called for him and he left. Cynthia questioned me about my new friend. I told her I met him the week before, and I was in love. I never saw him again that semester, but he made a huge impact on me.

REASON

Charles Edward Jeffrey II was on the edge of all my books. I always found myself daydreaming and thinking of Charles Jeffrey, II.

***

That Thanksgiving while home, Mrs. Thompson, a family friend, came by the house to see my mom. She asked me how I liked college and if I had met some new guys. I told her I had met two, Mac and Charles. I went on to tell her I was still in love with Ricky, and one day we would get married.

Mrs. Thomson told me I would probably never get a degree or maybe I would get several degrees, but I would end up down in the projects. He would make sure I stayed pregnant and I would not have any friends because he was a jerk.

I told her that would never happen to me.

Mrs. Thompson replied sort of matter of fact, "Okay, keeping talking to him. You will see. And I will enjoy saying I told you so."

Basically, I blew her off. She was dead wrong. But, the thought of living in the projects made me crazy.

***

The semester was over, and I had done well. It was the day after Christmas; I was scheduled to have my wisdom teeth removed. I kept telling the dentist to give me another shot. I felt everything. I think I got about 16 shots. I heard my tooth breaking. It was an awful experience. I was high as hell from the gas when I left from the dentist. We stopped by the pharmacy to fill the prescription. By the time we got home, I was in excruciating pain. About 10 pills went down the drain with the blood that was flowing from my mouth. I put on an old gown, since my mouth was bleeding so much and went to bed. I was feeling horrible. My mom

REASON

tried to feed me some soup, but there was just too much blood. I tried to sleep in between pain dosages, but when it wore off, it was bad. Real bad!

The next day I heard my mom talking to someone. She was talking to Mac.

"Angela darling, you have company." My mom said.

I didn't say anything.

"You have company. Are you decent?" My mother asked.

"Wait!" I pulled the cover over my head. "No, I am not decent." I looked bad. My hair was in plaits all over my head. I had on a bloody gown and a man was at my bedroom door. I didn't even take company in my bedroom. What was wrong with her? She could have told him I was not at home or something. I pulled my blanket up and wondered whose idea it was to put my mattress on the floor? It seemed like a good idea at the time. "Okay, you can come in." I said.

It was Mac. "Hey Angela, I came by to see how you were doing from your surgery. Are you okay?"

I thought to myself, what do you think? What do I look like? And, why in the hell did you bring somebody with you. "I'm okay, Mac." I said trying to smile.

"Angela, this is my friend, Bruce." Mac said pointing to his friend standing in the doorway.

"Hi Bruce, it is nice to meet you." I said trying to shake his hand without letting him see the blood on my sleeve.

My mom came back with two folding chairs and said. "She has been real sick. So maybe you can cheer her up."

"I told you I was coming to see you after your surgery." Mac said.

REASON

"Thanks for coming." I replied. As I laid flat on my back in a blood dried gown and sheets looking like Buckwheat.

They stayed for what seemed like hours. Bruce commented about how friendly I was and I didn't even get up to put on any makeup. He was nice, but I didn't care what he said. I was too sick.

They finally left, but I was too sick to care that they came. It took awhile for me to recuperate after surgery. I was bedridden for at least two weeks. I lost about five pounds and did not spend any time with Ricky nor did he even come by to see how I was doing after my surgery. I recovered and was pumped up and ready to go to return to school.

REASON

Reasons

The spring semester of 1975, I returned to school. It was a cold January night prior to classes and I decided to go to a party at the Omega house. Mac was standing outside his fraternity house where we talked, until I noticed Charles in the courtyard of the Omega and Kappa houses. I abruptly ended my conversation with Mac and starting walking back to the dorm to conveniently run into Charles. Charles noticed me and approached. We talked for a few minutes but it was cold, so we sat in his car for some time talking. He told me he had finished his student teaching and would be on campus full time. Eventually, I got out of his car and walked to Whitley Hall. Charles followed me in his car as I walked the few blocks. We waved at each other as I walked to the dorm. It was all so sweet.

***

One Saturday morning, Ricky drove to Commerce looking for me. He found Monica and me walking to the cafeteria. He was in his mother's new car supposedly going to the store and came the sixty-seven miles to Commerce. It was raining and I got in the car to talk to him. He asked me to go back to Dallas with him, but I refused. He was angry with me when I got out of the car. I never understood why he thought I would stop my education for him. Anyway, I had to eat before the cafeteria closed. Because I never missed a meal.

***

One night I was sitting in the lobby of my dorm and in walked Charles. I was talking to Mac. Mac was dropping off a book and had not planned to stay long. As soon as he left, I approached Charles. "What's going on, Charles?"

Charles replied. "Not too much. But it looks like you are busy."

REASON

"No, I am not. What brings you over to Whitley Hall?"

"Oh, just hanging out with my cousin."

We chatted and what seemed like out of nowhere I said. "Do you have any children?"

Charles moved around in his chair and then said, "No."

His body language made me doubt he was telling the truth. Therefore, I lied, "I have a two year old son, Jansen." I handed him Jansen's picture that I carried in my meal ticket pouch. But, Jansen was my friend's son.

That was when Charles shared he had a five year old daughter named Tiffany. I knew I had read him right. I asked him was it so hard to tell the truth. Now, what I did not notice was the relief in his voice that I had a son. That did not seem like a lie to me because I knew it was a ploy to get the truth out of him. I never told him Jansen was not my biological child. We talked for a while and he said he would like to take me out sometime. After a while, he went on his way, I went to my room and wrote Ricky a letter.

February 10, 1975

Dear Sweetheart,

How are you doing? I miss you very much. School is so much fun. I have met a lot of people and am learning wonderful things. I wish you were here with me. That would make everything even more special.

I will be home this Friday for Valentines Day. I cannot wait to see you. One day we will be married and happy. You will see I do not think I am better than you are. Just wait. Please understand why I went to college. I have wanted to go to college since fourth grade, in Mr. Gray's class. It is going to be good for the both of us. You will see.

Did you get that trucking job? I hope you did. If not, keep trying.

Your baby,

A

PS. I love you with all my heart.

REASON

Each night after I prayed, I got in bed reminiscing about my day and wondered about my future. Monica noticed I rocked my feet from side to side before falling asleep. While rocking my feet from side to side all I could think about was living in the projects. I would show Mrs. Thompson, she was wrong because I was not living in the projects.

The next day Mac and I rode our bicycles to the city square to purchase Valentine's cards. I purchased three cards; a sincere loving one for Ricky, a funny one for Mac, and a simple one for Charles. After purchasing our cards, we rode our bikes all over town. Laughing and talking. It was a nice afternoon.

That night, I addressed Ricky's Valentines card. Ricky's card was loving and dripping with sweetness. I signed the card "With all my heart, A," and sealed the envelope with a kiss.

Before bed, I kept thinking about the projects. Living in the projects was beginning to consume my thoughts. I rocked my feet back and forth real fast. Until Monica said, "Go to sleep and stop that thing you do with your feet. All I can hear are the sheets going swish, swish, swish. Let whatever it is go. PLEASE!"

I hated when she called me on not being asleep. I had never noticed that I rocked myself to sleep until she pointed it out.

The next morning I woke up thinking about living in the projects. All day long, all I could think about was the projects. I began to think I should give up on the idea of proving Mrs. Thompson wrong. I worried over what I needed to do. It was as the projects were subliminally set in my mind and it was all I could think about. I had to do something or I would flunk out of school and live in the projects for sure.

REASON

Later that night I decided to write another letter to my high school sweetheart. It went like this.

February 12, 1975

Dear John,

I am writing you this letter to say it is over. It is over now. I realize we have no future together. I will not live in the projects. I do not think I am better than you are. I never have. I just want more out of life than you do. I wish you well.

Angela,

PS.   Note the correct spelling of my name. Do not call me. Do not write me. Do not contact me. Ever.

I felt good when I went to bed that night. No problem going to sleep. No swishing. I would never have to live in the projects. *Thank you Lord.*

Valentine's weekend, Mac was going home and I decided to ride with him to Dallas. He owned a bad 69' white Camaro that had two wide orange racing stripes down the top of the car with loud pipes. It was a nice car. We arrived in Hamilton Park around three on a Friday afternoon. We passed by Sam's house, Mac's fraternity brother, and he was standing outside. We stopped and talked to Sam for a while. After they finished talking, Mac took me home and he went on his way. I decided to go to "Project Boy's" house, to make sure he understood the Dear John letter. When I arrived, he was standing in the doorway. I got out of the car and approached the door. Once inside he went off, "How dare you write me an 'I love you' letter one day, a loving Valentine card the next day, and a Dear John letter today. Who the hell is John anyway?" He turned and walked to the coffee table where he picked up the cards and letters. He threw them across the room. He turned around and approached me getting in my face. His eyes were piercing through me. "I want you to know it will never be over. I love you too much to let you go." He snatched my purse out of my hand and went through it. "What is this shit in here for? You ain't nothing but a ho." He threw my panties and birth control pills on the floor. I snatched my purse from his hand and kneeled down to pick up my things.

While I was on the floor he yelled, "Who was the nigga in the camaro? I heard you came in town with him. Everybody is talking about it. Who is he? I am going to kill him."

I gathered all of my things making sure I had not left anything then stood slowly. I put my hand on my hip and pointed my finger to his face. "Well, I tell you what. If you so much as think about doing something to him. I will have my uncles and my daddy kill yo monkey ass! And you know all my dad needs is an excuse to get rid of you! Do not call me! Do not write me! Leave me the hell alone! Asshole!" I turned and walked away. I threw my purse over my shoulder and left abruptly deliberately slamming the door behind me.

Project Boy could not even spell my name. I realized from his letters he was illiterate. Technically, he should have been my first love, but I erased that section of my life never to think on it again. It is funny; I realized although I did love him, I did not like him at all. This was the first thing that my grandfather asked me. At the time, I thought that was the strangest question, but I didn't like him at all and have never mentioned his name since, only referring to him as Project Boy. I felt blessed we did not hook up. I was free and would never have to live in the projects. I drove away with a smile on my face. My next stop was Mrs. Thompson's house to say thank you.

The next day, Mac showed up on my porch ready to return to school. He had gone back over Sam's house and they went to a party. Mac never made it to Ft. Worth. He decided it was too late to continue home, so I got my things together and we left. We talked all the way back to school. Mac told me about an altercation with some guy the night before in my neighborhood.

REASON

"If Sam had not been with me I would have shot that little dude. Sam calmed him down and made him go on his way."

I knew exactly who he was talking about but did not comment on the incident. We talked about our dreams for our future riding back to school. Mac intrigued me, but something kept pulling me away from him.

He loved to touch my face, and every time he did, I flinched. He tried assuring me, that he would never hurt me. I was never really afraid of him, but I had seen him hit people before for no apparent reason. Deep down inside, I believed if we got too close, he would hit me too. If that were the case, I would have to get one of my uncles to take him out. He would only get one chance to hit me. I pulled away from him to keep him from getting shot. I learned what my dad meant by "Don't take no wooden nickels." One thing it meant was never let a man hit you. If it happened once, it would happen again.

***

One Sunday morning, Monica and I caught a ride to church in the Hole. Once inside, Charles came in and sat beside me. Since this was a college town, when the pastor went too long on his sermon, he would announce the students could leave to get to the cafeteria before it closed. Most of the people attending that church were students so it was a mass exit. I asked Charles before the minister made this announcement if he would take Monica and me to the cafeteria. He smiled and agreed.

Once outside the church as we approached his car, he told me there were others riding with him. It was not a problem with us. He opened the door of his two-door car and I flipped the seat down for the girls to get in. I told the three girls standing there to get in the back so Monica and I could sit in the front. The girls, all of which I knew, climbed in the back seat.

REASON

Monica and I got in the front. And, Charles dropped Monica and me off at the cafeteria and went on his way.

A few weeks later, in March, Charles came by Whitley Hall and asked me to go on a date with him. The date was to a high school basketball playoff game, for his hometown school. I agreed to go.

It came time for the date with Charles and I had decided not to go, because I had a better offer from Mac. Monica said I was crazy and began to compare the two. "Mac has another woman and I am not sure what his classification is. He is crazy, do you remember the time he pushed me down." She stopped talking and stared at me for a minute. "On the other hand, Charles is a graduating senior, nice, employed, and taking you on a real date."

Most guys did not take you anywhere while in college, at least not in Commerce. So, I decided she was right and agreed to go. Charles picked me up and informed me that his team had lost so there was no game. He offered to take me for pizza, but we ended up at his apartment. He played some jazz and we kissed. Soon into the night, he wanted to get some.

I looked at him as if he was crazy and said. "No. Are you crazy, Charles?"

He tried to convince me I should have sex with him. However, I refused.

After begging and me refusing, he left the living room and went into the bedroom. I just sat on the sofa listening to the music until the music stopped. I got up from the sofa went to the other room, and he was asleep. I stood there with my mouth wide open and eventually yelled, "Charles, are you going to take me back to my dorm?"

Charles rolled over in the bed and said. "No, not tonight. If you want to go to sleep, get in the other bed. I am tired." He never said another word.

REASON

I could not believe his ass was asleep. I went back in the living room and sat on the sofa. Finally, after several hours had passed I got into the other twin bed. I wondered why he had twin beds in a one-bedroom apartment and living alone. I was mad as hell, but eventually fell asleep.

The next morning he got up and took me to my dorm as if nothing was wrong. When he returned me to Whitley, I cussed him and slammed the car door of his raggedy, rusted blue Nova. It was about ten or eleven on a Saturday morning. When I entered my room, Monica and Cynthia were sitting on the beds across from each other. They ran to me, questioning where I had been. I was always the first one in the room. This was out of character for me to stay out all night. I was pissed off at Charles and refused to talk to them. I walked passed them as if they were not even talking to me.

They had stayed up all night worrying about me. They did not know whether to call the police or my mother. Monica had realized she did not know much about Charles that she painted this great picture. Monica called Cynthia over and the two of them called other friends but no one knew Charles. They kept giving me one more hour to come home before they would call the police. They treated me as parents do saying "Why didn't you call?"

I screamed, "The nigga had no phone. I could not walk from the middle of nowhere. Anyway, why are yall mad at me? I am the one who went on the date from hell. Who does he think he is anyway? This was our first date. Now I was down for the kissing, listening to jazz, and of course talking. But, he wanted to hit it on the first date. I guess he thought he was Teddy Pendergrass begging some chick to "Come On Over To My Place." I couldn't stand that begging Teddy. I thought Charles was the one, but he is a jerk."

Later that day, I was eating in the cafeteria. I looked up and noticed Charles staring at me through the plate glass. I gave him the finger and mouthed "Fuck You." I continued eating my food.

He smiled and walked away.

For the next few weeks, he was MFs and SOBs. He kept calling me, and I hung up in his face. Eventually he talked me into coming back over to study but Monica warned me not to go. I went anyway. I was a good student and decided a little studying would not hurt. We sat at the kitchen table both studying and we did not talk to each other. After a few hours of studying, he took me back to my dorm.

Shortly after that, Charles' apartment complex burned down and he moved into a house with some guy. He continued to invite me over to study at that house. First, we studied in the dining room. Eventually we studied in Charles' room not to bother his roommate. Charles tried to get some again, but I would not. He got mad and called me a tease. He did not understand me and said he did not like to play games with little girls, so he took me back to the dorm. As I got out the car, he asked, "Are you gay?" I was offended and slammed the car door in his face.

Somehow, we went back to studying again. I had never studied that much, so this started getting old. One night, I started playing with Charles. He told me to stop because he was trying to graduate in a few weeks. He was taking a sex education class and I read the book and wanted to try out the massage techniques. I was persistent and eventually convinced him to put the books down. Since I was a free spirit and did not care about love anymore, I had sex with him.

One night at a basketball game, I saw Charles sitting in the stands. I was just waving, but he was acting strange. So, I walked right up to him and said, "What's going on Charles?"

"Nothing," he said fidgeting in his seat.

REASON

I noticed he seemed odd, but I turned and walked away, sort of puzzled.

***

Monica was pledging all semester, so we did not see each other much. Charles and I were dating, and I was having a great time in college. However, my grandfather was sick. Every time I talked to my mom, I asked her about him. I wanted her to say he was okay, but she never did.

***

One weekend, I decided to go to North Texas State University (NTSU) with some friends for a Greek show. We went to the Greek show, and it was *all* of that. The guy driving, however, decided he wanted to stay the night. I was mad that I was stuck in Denton with no way back to school. I ended up staying with two girls I had never met before. Their roommate had gone home for the weekend, so I slept in her bed. I realized that coming to Denton with these guys had been a mistake. My roommate set this trip up, but she backed out at the last minute so I was the only female. I swished my legs all night long. I had this dream that my grandfather died, and they could not find me anywhere. I woke up ready to go home. I went looking for my ride and ordered them to leave.

Once back on campus I was so thankful to be back at school. I would never leave the campus again without somebody knowing exactly where I was. I had that same dream every night for the next two weeks.

About two weeks later, on a Thursday morning, I came to my room and my roommate was looking out the window. I spoke to her but she would not look at me.

REASON

Monica whispered, "Your mother called and called and called. Your dad will be here this afternoon to look for you." She raised her voice some and turned to face me. "Where have you been?" She paused before continuing. Your grandfather died two days ago."

I said nothing. Was this another dream? This could not be happening. I plopped down on my bed and I thought back to the last time I saw my grandfather. He was in the hospital. I had the feeling I would never see him again. I wanted to give him a kiss, but he would have known that I was giving up on him.

When I was about twelve years old, I got in my grandfather's lap and said to him. "Poppaw, I am going to kiss you tonight for the last time in this life. I have gotten too big to get in your lap and give you a kiss. I am a big girl now. So, always remember this last kiss. Okay?"

Poppaw chuckled out, "Okay, big girl." He hugged and kissed me one last time.

So, that day at the hospital, instead of kissing him I said, "You will be okay, Poppaw."

He whispered, "No Angela, I will not."

"Poppaw, please don't give up?" I begged trying to hold back the tears.

"Angela, I will be okay. My time is up here. Always remember, I love you very much."

I left the room and cried in the hallway of the hospital. I knew that was it. I wanted to go back and give him a kiss, but instead I sat on the floor in the hallway crying in silence.

It was the week before finals and I went to class to ask my professor if I could take an incomplete. He said I would be fine and encouraged me to take the final. My father showed up around three. I was packed and ready to go. He was not happy.

"Where the hell have you been, Angela?" Daddy yelled throwing my luggage in the trunk of the car.

I never said a word. When we got home, everyone had the same question.

REASON

"Where have you been?" Each family member asked.

I never responded. I wanted to talk to my grandmother, but they would not let me. I needed to hold her. No, I needed her to hold me.

This was the first funeral of anyone close to me. I cried. I screamed. My dress came up. Aunt Grace tried to hold me. My cousins told me I kept saying my heart was hurting and I hurt all over. I was crying, "Lord, help me! Please Jesus, help me." I grieved harder than I ever have in my life. Every part of my body hurt with pain. I felt all alone. Mama, Mommee, Grandmother, daddy, my brother, Aunt Grace, or Serena could not help me.

My brother, Gary, kept saying "Shut up. You are embarrassing me. If you don't shut up, I am going to tell Mama to make you move. Be quiet." All the while, he was pinching me.

I could not stop crying. I was screaming to the top of my lungs. Serena kept patting me on the back. My dad's mother tried to talk to me but I was crying too much. All of my cousins on my dad's side were looking at me in a sad way. I was consumed with pain. I never stopped crying.

I cried for months as if it were only yesterday. Then one night I was crying and an angel told me to stop crying. She said I would be okay. At that point, I realized that God had not put more on me than I could bear. I prayed thanking God for blessing me and never felt that anguish again.

After returning to school, Charles had got it in his head that I was pregnant. "Angela, are you pregnant?" Charles asked me not looking me in the eye.

"No, I am not pregnant and why do you think that?" I said trying to get eye contact with him.

REASON

"Well, I have been thinking this for awhile and pondered over whether I really wanted to know. I decided to ask. You told me you have a son when I first met you so I assumed you were on birth control pills."

"I did not tell you that." I said very matter of fact.

"You did too. You even showed me a picture of him, Jansen. I wondered why you never acted as a nurturing mother."

"Oh yeah, Jansen is my buddy. He is my friend's son. I was just playing. I was trying to get you to tell me if you had any children and it worked. That is when you told me about Tiffany. I am sorry. I didn't realize you believed me." I said with disbelief that I had a child.

Charles asked, "So you are not pregnant?"

"No, I am not." I shook my head from side to side.

"Okay then, are you coming to my graduation?

"Yes, I decided to come." I said with excitement.

"Don't come." Charles put his head down.

"Why not?" I asked.

"Because my parents and my daughter's mother will not understand you being there."

I was pissed at this point. I put my hand on my hip. "Well, you cannot stop me from coming to a public event." I paused and remembered how he acted at the basketball game that night. "Were you with your baby's mama at that basketball game that time?"

"Yes, she and I are dating again." He seemed ashamed to tell me but relieve that I was not pregnant.

REASON

"Oh really? You make me sick. Anyway, fuck you Charles Jeffrey." I slammed his front door hard as I left. I went back to the dorm and packed my bags. Cynthia and I left school later that day. I would never see Charles Jeffrey's ass ever again.

On the way home, Cynthia and I had a flat tire. All of our stuff was in the trunk. We took all of our stuff out just to get to the spare. We tried to change the flat but did not know what we were doing.

This white guy stopped and said, "You young ladies need to stand back. You have the jack on upside down. I will change the flat for you."

We had no money, but I asked him what we owed him anyway. All he wanted was a grammar book he saw lying on the ground amongst our stuff. I picked the book up and noticed that Charles Edward Jeffrey, II was written all around the edges of the book. It was the book that I had written on the first night we had talked all night.

I said to him, "Take it; it's yours and thank you so much." *Good riddance, Charles Jeffrey.*

REASON

SEASON

Papa Don't Take No Mess

The summer of 1975, I enrolled in Richland Community College because I failed history the previous semester. My history professor said he could not give me a passing grade because I did so poorly on the final. I was pissed at him, because I asked him for an incomplete when my grandfather died, but he said I would be fine. Three A's, two B's, and an F, I was devastated. My dad was pissed. He argued I was not going to class. But, I never missed class. That day, I vowed never to fail a class again.

It was the first day of summer school and I was sitting on the floor of my bedroom reading my history book and wondering why I was not celebrating my birthday. The telephone rang and interrupted my thought. I answered and it was Charles Jeffrey. He had looked me up in the telephone directory. We talked for only a few minutes. He had graduated and ended the relationship with his daughter's mother. He wanted to start over with me. I agreed and again, we started talking.

About one week later, I met a popular guy at Richland Community College. Since Charles and I were not a couple yet, I agreed to go on a date with him. He was average height and average build with a lot of personality. I noticed that all the girls on campus would talk to him so when he asked me out. I was flattered. We had planned to go bowling. However, we decided not to go bowling, and went to his apartment to watch the basketball playoffs. We did not hit it off though. He was too cocky and aggressive for me. We never went out again.

SEASON

That Fourth of July I was depressed. Project Boy had asked my friend Joyce, to talk me into spending The Fourth of July with them as we had done the year before. Joyce begged me to go to the lake on a picnic with her and her boyfriend one last time. I told her I did not want to go because he and I were no longer a couple. I tried to tell her it would not be fun but agreed to go.

Actually, I had a good time, but they were all miserable. They were relieved to get me back home and out of their presence. I thought it was funny. Project Boy had convinced them we would all have a great time. Just like old times. He was wrong.

Once home, I began to feel depressed and decided to call Charles.

"Hello." A female voice answered.

"Hello, may I speak to Charles?" I responded.

"Who is this?" She asked with disbelief in her tone.

I looked at the phone and said matter-of-factly. "This is Angela."

"You want to speak to Charles, my husband?" She questioned me.

I stuttered, "No, uh no, your son."

"Okay. I will get him." She said in a different tone.

She put him on the phone, and I begged him to come to Dallas. I told him I was depressed and lonely.

The next day, Charles came to Dallas. I was glad to see him and was immediately in love. I took him to meet both of my grandmothers. We went to meet my mother's mother first; she was just like my mom. She liked everybody and seemed to like Charles. My dad's mom would be tough. However, surprisingly, she liked him. Charles promised to take her fishing. My brother, Gary, liked Charles and he didn't like anybody. Sometimes I thought he didn't like me. Gary was tall well over six feet and lighter in complexion tone than me. He had an

SEASON

infectious smile with a slight gap in his teeth. His hair short and wiry, but long enough to hide

his football shaped head. He was a drummer, guitarist, running back, track star, and an excellent

swimmer. Gary was good looking if I do say so myself. Older women always commented about

his great legs. His build was perfectly in proportion.

Charles and I stopped and talked at a park. We talked about our future. It was so nice.

By Sunday, my parents were back and my father liked Charles right off. My mom liked him too,

but my mom loved everybody.

A few weeks later, Charles' cousin Charles, got married. Charles came to Dallas for the

wedding. We were standing outside my home getting ready to leave for the wedding, and

Project Boy sped by almost hitting Charles.

Charles yelled, "Did you see that? He tried to hit me."

I said getting in his car. "Yeah, that was my old boy friend. He was trying to scare you.

Just ignore him. He tries to act crazy but he is not that crazy. He harasses all my male friends. I

thought about having a contract put on him, but he is not worth it. Let's go. Ignore his ass."

The wedding was in the church my grandfather had been funeralized in earlier that year.

All through the wedding, I had an eerie feeling. It reminded me of the last time I had been in

that church. I do not remember anything about their wedding. I was sure it had been nice and

probably pink and green. However, I remembered the receiving line and how the bride kissed

everyone. I could not wait to get married, so I could kiss everyone and be the center of attention.

***

Over that summer, Charles came to Dallas about every two weeks. He was working at a

steel mill factory in east Texas. The factory was about sixty miles away from his home. It was

dirty, long hours, long commute, and not at all, what he had planned to do with his college

SEASON

degree. He decided to make some changes in his life. He began talking about getting married

and moving to east Texas where I would transfer to a junior college. But, why would I want to

get married? Why would I transfer to a junior college in my second year at a university? My

father was paying for me go to school. I did not work during the school years, and I knew Bernie

would cut off the funds, if I got married. This I knew. My father was nobody's fool. So, I

ignored Charles marriage talk.

Late summer, Charles decided he was going to take a teaching job in Houston. He

wanted to marry within the next two weeks and move to Houston. I had mentioned this to

Monica who told my parents. About two weeks after she told my parents, my father went off on

me. We were sitting in the kitchen when daddy said. "So when are you going to tell us that you

are leaving and moving to Houston?"

I started stuttering. I was stuttering because I had to be careful with my response. It had

to be the truth, without question, but I knew if I said something stupid, he would be all over me.

I said, "What are you talking about?" This would give me a little time to see exactly

where he was coming from. Now my father was fun, loving, street wise, smart, strict, great

father, and a get in your shit kind of guy. You know like James Brown's "Papa Don't Take No

Mess. He was the oldest of eight, five brothers and two sisters. He was short, very pigeon toed

and wore his haircut close. Actually, his hair did not grow fast, but he was not going bald. He

was dark skinned, a big guy, with nice hands. He had beautiful teeth but had loss one from a

severe car crash. He went without a shirt and wore shorts with dress socks. He had two large

scars one that went ¾ around his mid section and the other went 2/3 around the other side of the

mid section. One from a Kidney stone removal the other from an esophageal surgery. As a

young man, he was very handsome. He was a shade tree mechanic, fisherman, cook, great

SEASON

domino player, good at poker, craps, and comedian. My dad was a machinist by profession. He

had a magnetic personality, just an all around great guy. I knew he was going to come at me

hard with some words I didn't want to hear. But, I explained to my dad that Charles had asked

me to marry him, but I never agreed. I never considered getting married. Finally, I smoothed it

over with my dad, and he eventually stopped grilling me. However, I was going to KILL

Monica when I got back to school. I was glad we were not going to be roommates for the next

semester.

***

One night late that summer, Charles, his cousin Charles, some friends, and I went to this

new nightclub. As we entered the club, I was carded. They would not let me in, since I was only

nineteen and you had to be twenty-one. The men of the group were cruel. Charles told them he

should leave their asses since he was driving. Charles and I sat on the steps several feet from the

entrance and had a great conversation, while they got their party on. Sitting on the porch,

Charles asked me. "Are you going to Houston with me?"

I looked down at my hands and said in a soft voice. "No, I am going back to school."

Charles lifted my head and held my hands. "Angela, I need you with me and want you to

go as my wife."

I looked into his eyes and spoke. "Charles, I am not ready to get married. I want to get

my degree. Also, I do not believe you want to marry me for the right reasons. I think you feel

like it is time for you to get married since all of your friends are. You want someone to help you

raise your daughter. When I get married, I want to know my husband is marrying me because he

cannot stand to be without me. Not because of convenience. We have plenty of time to get

married. You are not being fair. You have your degree. I am still trying to get mine. I will not

SEASON

give up my dream for you. You are asking too much." I let his hands go and shook my from side to side.

"Angela, it is important for you to get your degree and I will help you get it. It will just have to be done on a part time basis. I have got to get custody of my daughter and need a wife."

I interrupted, "See that is what I mean. Just any old wife will do. I do not want to go to school part time. I am not ready to be a mother for your child. I am going back to school. If this were reversed, you would do the same thing. All I can commit to doing is taking more hours and graduating early."

"I don't know if I can wait Angela." Charles said with his head bowed. We both sat there on the curb not saying anything to each other.

I thought about what Charles said and believed he felt he gave me options. *One, get married, move to east Texas, transfer to some junior college, help him raise his daughter, and last but not least, get a job. Two, get married, move to Houston, transfer to some school part time, help raise his daughter, and get a job. Thirdly, get married, live in Dallas, go to ETSU part time, help raise his daughter, and get a damn job. What the hell was I getting out of the deal?*

I did not want to get married and surely did not want to help raise his daughter. I said I could do it, because I was in love. But, I was only 19 and he wanted me to go to PTA meetings. The thought of going to PTA was almost as bad as the thought of living in the projects, just kidding. Living in the projects was not an option for me. The projects are a place you only want to visit, but you wouldn't want to live there.

After a long period of silence, I came up with an alternative. I said to Charles, "Why don't we get married, you commute to Dallas from Commerce, I go to school full time with you

SEASON

paying. Because it is no way in hell, Bernie Hue will continue to pay. I will help raise your daughter, and we live in married housing." Charles was not willing to compromise and neither was I.

SEASON

The Truth

It was the fall of 1975. Charles had moved to Dallas and he was working the night shift at a battery company in the suburbs. He loved running with his crazy cousin Charles and the rest of his college boys. He even moved in the same apartment complex where his cousin lived. I teased him about moving directly above the woman he was with at the homecoming carnival the first night we met. He assured me they only dated for a short period and were not even dating the night we met. The truth was I didn't care. I was too fly to care.

A few weeks later, Charles took me back to school. I tried to convince him I would get my degree soon. I had decided to take twenty-one hours each semester and go to summer school to graduate in two more years. Charles did not seem as convinced but I was happy to be back in college. I was dating a great guy and had a private room. That was going to be a great year. Monica had moved into her sorority house. I was a sophomore, well almost a sophomore. I had it going on, sort of fly.

One of my classes that year was accounting, I thought accounting would be a piece of cake. I was a whiz in mathematics, so how hard could it be. Real hard.

A few weeks later the teacher handed me my first test results with a large red 67 marked on my paper. I cussed under my breath knowing that I had vowed never to fail again. I shook my head in disbelief. Then I noticed the grade of the young brother sitting in front of me, high A. I thought to myself, we are going to be friends. I leaned over and touched him on the shoulder. "Excuse me, my name is Angela, you are?"

"Michael, Michael Everette." He responded smiling showing his beautiful teeth.

SEASON

"Why don't you call me so we can ace this class together?" I said.

He replied, "Sure, what's your room number?"

"Room 1221, Whitley Hall."

"Cool, I will call you later tonight," he grabbed his test paper, book, and left the room.

Later, Michael and I became study partners. Three times a week, he explained our homework, Sundays, Tuesdays, and Thursdays. Accounting just did not make sense to me. Just when I thought I had it, I did not. I wanted to equate credits as bad and debits as good and that theory only worked some of the time.

Michael was a junior that transferred from Mountain View Community College of Dallas. He was from a small town, about eighty miles south of Dallas. He had a lot of brothers and sisters and a lot of confidence in himself, but he was very quiet. Not shy, just quiet. He was skinny, with a lean nose to match his body, and pigeon toed like me. He was about 5 feet 10 inches tall and weighed about 140 pounds with broad shoulders and long arms. His eyes were dark brown with long eyelashes that had the slightest curl, which touched his thick perfectly arched brows. He was thin with a large afro, which made him look like a black q-tip from a distance. His complexion was espresso with the nicest smile and perfectly straight teeth that looked like thousands of dollars had been spent on them.

I offered to braid Michael's hair since he was doing all the tutoring. His hair was long, real long, wavy, and a nice grade that was very thick. However, his girlfriend did not like me braiding his hair. The truth was I did not care because I was not interested in him except for accounting tutoring. I had to pass accounting.

"Michael, your girlfriend does not like me." Without hesitating I said, "Tell her I have a man, Charles Edward Jeffrey, II."

SEASON

"What is so special about him?" Michael asked in a tone as if he was only making conversation not really interested.

I answered with enthusiasm. "He is smart, good looking, educated, working, and he loves me. You know, a BMW."

"A what?"

"A BMW, a black man working."

"You are a trip." Pausing for a minute, he continued. "I bet he is cheating on you."

"I don't care. As long as he treats me, well. Everyone knows I am Charles Jeffrey's, woman. As long as he treats me like the queen that I am. I am happy. I am not jealous at all and he is not cheating."

"Do you really believe that?"

"Absolutely." I said.

***

Our first football game was against Prairie View A & M College, my mom's alma mater. I came home to go to the game. Everyone would be there. A lot of my friends were attending Prairie View. My homeboy, Dewey who saved me on the first day I arrived at ETSU, was a running back for ETSU. All of Charles' friends would attend the game. I wore the cutest 3-pieced peach pants suit to the game with the tightest afro around. I looked good. I was unusually quiet at the game with Charles and his friends. All of them were loud, all about me type of people. They all had a great time at the game, but I was pre-occupied with my own thoughts.

SEASON

I returned home the next weekend for the State Fair of Texas. I met Charles' mother the morning before we went to the fair at his apartment. Needless to say, his mother was not impressed.

Mrs. Jeffrey said, "I wanted to meet the woman that got my son to move to Dallas, he hates Dallas. Then she turned to him and said, "She ain't all that." She said that as if I was not sitting there.

I laughed to myself and thought, *I don't care if you like me or not, as long as he likes me, that's all that matters.* But, I just kept smiling at her.

That night Charles and I went to the state fair. I loved the state fair. I went every year about five times. I went on Richardson School day, Dallas School day, the last day, and any other time I could get somebody to go with me. Some times I rode all the rides, some times I went in all the exhibits, sometimes I played all the games, but each and every time I went to the Automobile exhibit and ate corny dogs, corn on the cob, and a candied apples.

Charles parked at a school parking lot a long way from the fair. We walked hand in hand. I was in love and happy to be with my man. He won a nice teddy bear for me. We had such a nice time.

The next day, Michael called me and asked if he could ride back to school with me. I agreed to pick him up. Since, I was driving my parent's car back to school for a few weeks. He was about twenty-five miles southeast of where I lived. Cynthia, Monica, and I went to pick him up.

Cynthia kept asking, "Who are we picking up?"

I replied, "The guy that is going to make sure I get an 'A' in accounting."

SEASON

We passed the street about fifty times. It was dark and each time we came down the service road we did not see his street. We kept on looking until we finally saw the turn. He came right out and the three of us made him sit in the back by himself. We did not know him well enough for one of us to sit in the back with him.

***

One day, while studying, Michael told me he had another woman, his high school sweetheart. She was attending college at Texas Tech University way out in West Texas. My girl Joyce was also a sophomore at the same school. I kept asking him when he was going to visit his girlfriend, because I wanted to ride with him so I could visit Joyce. Michael agreed that we would ride out there one weekend.

A few weeks later, while we were studying, Michael seemed distracted but nothing serious. While working a problem I asked. "So Michael, where were you this past weekend?"

He was hitting his pencil on his closed book and said, "What?"

I repeated. "Where were you this past weekend? Are you listening to me?"

"Yeah." He replied not looking at me.

"Yeah what, Michael? You are not listening to me and you have not opened your book. Are we going to study or what?"

"Yeah. Sure." He opened his book and pulled his shirt up in the back. This was something that my dad did when he has something on his mind.

I put my pencil down trying to make eye contact. "Earth to Michael. Are you okay?" I asked.

"Yes, I am fine."

I repeated. "Then where were you this past weekend?"

SEASON

"Well, I went to Lubbock."

I threw my pencil down and snapped. "You went without me?" I was about to put my hands on my hip.

Michael closed his book and stood. "Angela, we will have to study longer tomorrow. I have got to go."

"Alright, if you must. We will talk tomorrow and then you can tell me why you went all the way to Lubbock without me."

"Sure, whatever you say Angela." He left abruptly.

The next day while studying, Michael was looking real sad. He was not concentrating on Accounting. I went on and on about him going to Lubbock without me. But, Michael didn't seem to be listening. He had not opened his book nor had he responded to any questions that I asked him. That was odd because he was always a good tutor.

"Are you okay?" I asked.

"Not really."

"What's wrong?"

"Nothing." He said.

"It's something. You can tell me. I am a good listener." I folded my arms and turned to face him.

Finally, Michael spoke in a soft voice. "Well, I went to Lubbock to give my girlfriend money for an abortion."

I stopped turning pages. I put my pencil down and folded my arms. I noticed tears began to fall from his eyes. I was quiet for my own reasons, but I tried to think of something to say. I

SEASON

looked down and crossed my legs at both the top and the bottom like a gymnast might. I never looked back up.

Michael turned to me and said. "I begged her not to do it."

I think, I flinched a little but did not respond. I had never seen a grown man cry, but Michael was crying, "How could she kill my baby? How could she do that to herself and how could she do this to me?"

I wanted to console him. I wanted to hug him. But the more he said the more I started slipping away from the conversation. I looked away as the tears began to fall from my eyes. Michael did not notice my tears for he was blinded by his own. I stood up from the sofa and walked to the window. I looked out across the campus as I often did when I was lost. I did not know what to do or say.

After what seemed like hours, I started to speak, never turning to face Michael. "It was two summers ago right before my senior year of high school. I got pregnant by my high school sweetheart. I did not know what to do. He was happy and I was not. I believed he felt that this would be a permanent hold on me. I decided to have an abortion. I never told him. My mom told me it was my decision and only I could make the decision. He and I talked about getting married but I did not want to get married. My dream was to go to college. It was a difficult decision, but I decided to have an abortion." I paused and then continued. "I went to this clinic to have the procedure done. There were about fifteen other women there for the same thing. All of them were with their boyfriends, fiancés, or husbands. I was the only one alone and they all said that their mothers did not know. They took us all in a room together for group counseling. I remember every one talking among themselves and to the counselors, except me. They were crying on each other's shoulders. I was so alone. It seemed the room was only dark where I

SEASON

was. Nobody was holding my hand, no shoulder to cry on, and I never shed a tear. I was the only black person, the youngest, and the only one without a man.

After the initial counseling, two of the couples changed their minds and left. The next process was to determine how far along we were in our pregnancies. One by one, we were taken into a room to have our blood drawn. My veins were so small, the nurse decided to take blood from my thighs after several attempts from my arm. I was so afraid of needles and doctors in white coats. We were sent back to the group room. One young lady was five months pregnant. She was crying uncontrollably when they told her she had to have her baby since she was too far along.

The whole setup was as if we were only there for vaccinations or something. It was not set up for something so personal, so final. All of our personal business was being discussed in front of everyone. Three women left. At this point, they asked the men to leave. After they left one by one, they came and gave us a shot and they took us to a room. I was one of the last ones.

When they got to me I felt as if they were about to take me to the electric chair. They gave me a shot first, and then two nurses one on each side helped me to walk to the surgery room. I remember white coats, white walls, white sheets, and white faces all within the darkness that was upon me.

They described the process as a vacuum type suction that would be a short procedure. They said we would receive a local anesthesia, but would be awake during the entire procedure. The process was not real long but the pain was excruciating. Afterwards, they took me to a room with several beds where you were to sleep for several hours. I did not sleep, just stared out of the high-rise window looking over the city of Dallas. Everyone else in the room slept and talked when they awakened. I was empty, no baby, and no words.

SEASON

You had to eat before you could leave. I threw the soup and juice up each time I tried to eat. They finally let me go with a bag of books. I had a prescription for Valium and Birth Control pills. I did not tell my boy friend for two days." A tear ran down my face as I continued.

"He was so angry with me. He cussed me. His mother even called me a murderer. There was nothing I could say. I had no words. I could not explain to him that I did not want to get married. I could not explain to him how I felt about disappointing my dad."

I shook my head. "My dad and I had dreamed and talked about me going to college since I was a little girl. How could I disappoint my dad? He could not even look at me."

Swallowing hard I continued, "I was sick for the next two months. I kept hemorrhaging and I was all alone. My dad had no sympathy for me and Ricky was mad as hell. Who could I talk to? Who would help me?" I paused for a moment.

I prayed for forgiveness, but I could not ask God to help me through this. I knew it was wrong to have pre-marital sex and I knew it was wrong to have an abortion. So, I believed all I could do was confess my sins and ask for forgiveness."

Raising my voice a little, "What should have been the best year of my life was not. Ricky was a jerk but I still loved him. He was not even happy for me when I graduated from high school. He hated I left and went to college. I had no one, but I was determined to get my college degree, determined to make my dad proud of me."

I looked into Michael's eyes. "Michael, I am sorry I stopped listening to you and I hate I dumped all of my stuff on you. I never meant to tell you any of this, but forgive her, grieve for your child, and try to let it go. I know it was hard for her and she did not want to do it. I have

SEASON

asked for forgiveness from God on more than one occasion. Talk to God about it and try to forgive her."

Michael stood and came over to where I was standing. He wrapped his arms around me. We held each other not saying anything for hours. Michael and I bonded that night, but we never discussed this again. I felt better though because Michael was the only person I told how I felt. I let some of the guilt go that day.

***

The next few weeks I did not go home too often. I was having the time of my life in school. That year was even better than the first year. Everything seemed to be so much fun. I was happy and content with my life. Charles on the other hand was not so content. He wanted me to be with him. He needed a mother for his child. He complained it was hard for a man to come home after working two jobs with no one to come home to. But, I felt like India Arie's song "The Truth." *If I am a reflection of him, then I must be fly.*

***

One Saturday night I was getting my party on at the civic center. I had danced up a sweat and decided to go outside to get some air. When I got on the porch, I plopped between two guys. I complained to the guy on the left about the heat inside. The guy on the other side said something that I did not hear. So I turned to ask him what he said. To my surprise, it was Charles. He stomped off the porch and got in his car. I ran after him. I got in the car and said, "Hey baby, what's going on?"

He looked at me with disgust. He had been looking for me all over Commerce. Charles stared at me with anger in his eyes. "Angela, you were flirting with the guy on the porch and I have been watching you for awhile and you were not acting like you have a man."

SEASON

I responded, "I was not doing anything wrong except having a good time. I was not flirting and was only talking about how hot it was in the party." In the next breath I said, "Let's go to Dallas?"

I convinced Charles that I would get back to school the next day, somehow. So, he agreed to take me to Dallas. I spent the night with him.

The next day, Charles took me to my parent's house to get a ride back to school. Now, why I thought my parents would be glad to see me was a mystery to me. My dad said, "It is no way in hell, I am taking you back to school."

I called Cynthia and asked her how she was getting back. She needed a ride herself. So I went to my grandmother's house to find my mother and ask her to take me back to school. She agreed to take Cynthia and me back.

Charles offered to ride with her and she let him drive us. We dropped Cynthia off at her dorm and then they took me to Whitley Hall. They helped me bring all my food and stuff back to my room. My mom was nice enough to go and get in the car so Charles and I could say our goodbyes. I felt bad, getting my mom to take me back, though.

When I got back to my room, Cynthia called me. "Angela, who was that guy?"

"You remember the guy from the cafeteria last year? The one that I told you I loved."

"Yeah, I remember." Cynthia said.

"Charles Jeffrey is his name. He is the one, girl."

Cynthia chuckled and responded, "He seems really nice."

A few weeks later, Charles came for Homecoming. We stayed over at his friend's apartment. The game was uneventful but the carnival was nice. We played the dice game where

SEASON

we met the previous year. Charles complained that I had not been coming home enough so I agreed to come more often.

After Charles left, I was back to my study routine. My grades were looking pretty good in accounting. However, Michael and I continued to study. Michael's girlfriend was pledging the same sorority as Monica. He was tasked with taking pictures of her at the Greek show. Michael talked me into getting high off of marijuana with him before the Greek show. He and I were laughing the whole time he was trying to take her picture. She was in the lead and not at all amused at us. But she could not laugh which made it even funnier to us. She was mad at him saying we made spectacles of ourselves. She was convinced we were messing around, but we were only good friends, not just study partners anymore. We both knew each other's secrets.

Although, I had agreed, I still was not going home much after the last fiasco. So, one Saturday night, Charles came to Commerce right after he got off work. Neither of us wanted to go back to Dallas so I asked, Monica could we stay at the sorority house. She agreed and we spent the night in her room.

Sunday morning, Charles let me use his car so Monica and I could go to the Baptist Church. Church was good as usual. The pastor's subject was "Detection, Infection, Conception." He spoke on pre-marital sex. His sermon was powerful and hit me hard. There is a saying, "If you can't say amen, say ouch." I had to say ouch several times. That sermon moved me to tears. As the doors of the church were opened, I went up for prayer and watch care. It should have been the first thing I did when I got to college.

***

SEASON

One Friday night, Charles showed up at Whitley Hall expecting me to go to his hometown with him. I packed and we drove about an hour down some back roads to his parent's home. It was late. We parked in the back under a carport and went to the back door.

His mother opened the door. She had been asleep. She took me to the back bedroom and told me to climb in the bed with her daughter, Teresa, and granddaughter, Teliah. I climbed in next to the wall because they were sound asleep.

The next morning, I was awakened by a two year old playing with my lips. It was Charles' niece. She was the cutest little girl. She was talkative but I was not my talkative self. Later that morning, we went to pick up Charles' daughter, Tiffany, to buy her a coat. His daughter was cute too. She loved her dad but was not feeling me.

Later that night Charles and I went by his friend's house to play spades. We hadn't been playing long when his daughter and her mother came by. Tiffany was all over me. Now, we had been together all day and she did not want to have anything to do with me, but that night she wanted to sit in my lap. Tiffany's mother sat behind Charles. He seemed irritated, but I could have given a rat's ass about her. She did not bother me in the least but I was not thrilled with Tiffany and her new attitude either. I knew her mother put her up to all of that. I would never do or say anything to hurt someone else's six year old, at least not intentionally. So I played along with whatever she wanted. Tiffany's mother was whispering stuff in Charles' ear. He got angry and had a couple of leave me alone replies. Finally, he was ready to go. His friend went off on his wife for inviting Tiffany's mother over. We left but we could have stayed all night as far as I was concerned. I was good at spades. Normally, I liked to talk a lot of noise, but I was very quiet that night. We left and Charles drove me all over town.

SEASON

Eventually, we went back to his home. I met his father and grandmother. I liked Mr. Jeffrey right off and believed he liked me. We had a nice conversation. You know the questions, who are your people? What are you doing with your life kind of thing? Charles' grandmother was nice too. She was talkative and lived right across the street.

Late that afternoon, Charles took me back to school. He went to my dorm room and shortly, after we got there, the phone rang. It was Mac. I got Mac off the phone abruptly. Charles was not amused. I told Charles that Mac had some personal problems and wanted to discuss them with me. Charles still was not amused. Mac called again. I didn't want to be rude, but got him off the phone as quickly as possible.

A short while later, Mac knocked on my door. That was what I hated about open house on Sundays. Guys could roam around the dorm, no escort was required. Mac came to my room uninvited. He had only been to my room once in the two years I had been in college, which had been the year before. Charles was livid. I told Mac, that I had company and would talk to him later.

He left but the mood was gone. Charles said he had to go, but not before getting on my case for cheating on him. I was not cheating and began telling him all of Mac's business. Charles was not interested in what I said. He left abruptly and I followed him.

Charles' car was parked across the street in front of the dorm. As I hurried to Charles' car, some female yelled, "BITCH! Hey Bitch, Angela Franklin, Bitch."

I turned to see who could be yelling at me. This was a twelve story building so I could not tell where this was coming from. So, I turned back around and kept walking as if I did not hear them.

"It's me BITCH, on the fourth floor, Marilyn." A female voice yelled.

SEASON

I thought to myself who in the hell is calling me a bitch named Marilyn. I only knew one Marilyn, a friend from South Texas.

"I know you hear me Bitch, the one that is going over to Charles Jeffrey's car." The voice repeated.

I kept walking and wondered what that had been about. I had forgotten that Charles was mad by the distraction. I got in the car and Charles was laughing. I snapped at Charles. "What in the hell is so funny and who was that?"

Still laughing he said. "Marilyn, you know Marilyn Barnes."

"Why is she calling me that?" I questioned.

Charles was laughing and wiping the tears from his eyes. "Do you remember that time I took you and Monica to the cafeteria from church?"

"Yeah," I nodded, "Last semester?"

"Marilyn and I were dating at the time."

"What the fuck?" I said.

"She got mad at you for making her get in the backseat."

I turned in my seat to face him and raised my voice. "You mean to tell me, you were trying to kick it with me and dating her at the same time? Why did she get in the back? Why didn't you tell me that she was your woman? You and I were just." I paused for a second. "Hell, we were just nothing. It's no way I would have let some bitch put me in the backseat of my man's car. Stupid, Heifer." I folded my arms and faced the front not looking at him.

Charles snapped, "Let's get back to the subject. You need to get your shit together." He put his hands on the steering wheel before continuing. "Next weekend and every weekend here

SEASON

after you had better be in Dallas by one, on Fridays. I am tired of coming home with no woman. I need you with me."

I turned to face him and sheepishly asked, "What do you mean get my shit together?"

"You know what I mean. I expect you to come home next week."

I agreed to come home the next week. I asked Charles again what he was talking about. His response was the same.

The next week it was hard to get a ride home. Nobody was going home. My home girl, Cynthia was going home but not until six. That meant I would not get home until seven. I needed to get to Dallas before three. I had no other options so I rode with her. I was antsy all the way home. As soon as I got home, I took a bath, dressed, and jumped in the car to go over to Charles' apartment.

I drove straight to Charles' apartment. His car was not in the carport behind his stairway. I drove around to the front and his apartment was dark. I drove over to the mall where he worked part time. He was not working that night. I was frantic he had left town for the weekend. I went inside the mall where his cousin, Charles, worked and asked him if he knew where he was. He said Charles was gone out of town to a party. I did not want to believe he had gone out of town. At least I hoped he had not left town. I hoped his cousin was wrong.

Charles had made it clear the week before that I needed to be home before one o'clock. Did he think I decided not to come home, when I was not home earlier? I was hoping he would show up soon.

I drove back to his apartment. I entered the complex from the south entrance instead of the north. To my surprise, his car was parked, on the far end of the complex between two cars. Now, I thought, why would he park down there? It did not make any sense to me. But, I parked and walked up the back steps slowly. Wondering all the while, why was he parked way down there? I did not know why everything seemed strange to me, but I proceeded to knock on the door. Charles opened the door and stepped outside.

"What's up baby? I said.

"Nothing much," he responded.

I said to Charles, "Where have you been? Why are you parked way down there? And why are we standing out here in the cold?" I raised the collar on my coat and waited for his response.

He mumbled, "You have to leave."

"What?" I yelled in disbelief.

"Yeah, I am busy, so I will to talk to you later." Charles said with a strange look on his face.

Smiling I said, "You are not letting me in?"

He responded, "Just go, I'll talk to you tomorrow."

I looked at him not understanding and slowly turned and walked away. I was thinking as I took each step that he was going to stop me. I was puzzled. *What was he doing? Why did I have to leave? What had happened?*

I went home and tried to sleep. I could not sleep because I did not know what had happened. My mind would not even let me imagine what had happened. I was totally clueless.

The next morning I got dressed at dawn I needed to ask Charles what happened the night before. He did not have a telephone and I wanted to talk to him before he went to work Saturday morning.

SEASON

His car was parked in the same spot as it had been the night before. *What did that mean?* I stood at the door before knocking, hesitant for some reason.

Finally, I knocked on the door. Charles opened the door and I entered. I sat in the chair nearest the door and he sat on the adjacent sofa. I looked at him. He could barely look at me. His bedroom door was closed.

"What's going on?" I asked with my arms folded.

"Nothing," he said rubbing his head.

I crossed my leg at the knee and said. "Are you sure?"

"Nothing is going on." Charles folded his arm and leaned back on the sofa.

"Why did I have to leave last night?"

"Well." He leaned forward.

"Well what?" Then the light bulb went on in my head. "Charles, do you have a woman here?" About that time, a woman said something from the bedroom. I totally got it then. "What the hell are you doing?" I said in a stern low voice.

"Angela, I love you."

"Oh, really, you love me but you have another woman in your bed?" I said just staring him down, watching every move, he made.

His eyes were filling with water. He rubbed his hands together. "It's hard to explain."

"Try." My leg was rocking slowly up and down.

Stammering and looking at his hands Charles said. "Oh, uh, I I…"

I interrupted gritting my teeth, "Charles, don't lie."

"Angela, you know I love you, but…"

I interrupted again, "But, nothing you sorry Son of a Bitch."

SEASON

"I, I, I…" Charles ran his fingers through his hair.

I stared at him and said. "I hell, kiss my black ass, Mother Fucker. I thought you were a better person than this." I felt my eyes bulging.

Charles leaned forward on the sofa and whispered, "If you will just let me explain."

I raised my voice, "Explain what? You cannot explain this shit to me Mother Fucker."

"But, But . . ." A single tear fell from his eye.

I had not blinked my eyes. "But my ass, you Bastard, I deserve better than this."

"But..."

I leaned forward and held my hands out in my lap. "Charles, help me to understand how you could say you love me but just got through fucking another woman. I do not understand. Please, help me with this?" Still not closing my eyes.

"Well."

"Well, what, Asshole?" I said with anger in my tone.

Charles stood and said to me. "Just, forget you ever knew me."

"What?" I uncrossed my arms and legs. I wanted to understand.

He came closer to where I was sitting. Charles extended his hand to me. "Angela, just forget you ever knew me, I cannot explain it where you can understand it. So just forget you ever knew me."

"No, you don't mean that." I said sitting to the edge of my seat.

"Yes, just go and forget you ever knew me."

"Okay, I am leaving." I stood directly in his face and announced, "Now, I will never forgive you for this and when I leave, I will never come back." I stared him in his eyes and did not see any glimmer of hope. I wanted him to say something, anything. *Say you don't mean it.*

SEASON

Say you fucked up. Ask me to forgive you. Say something. Don't let me go. I walked to the door and opened it. I turned to him. "Bye," I shouted and slammed the door.

I walked down the sidewalk and then down the stairs in a trance. I went back to my house, got in bed, and went to sleep.

Sometime later that morning, I was awakened by the telephone.

"Hello." I said.

"Good morning, Angela. What are you doing?" Charles said.

"Trying to forget, I ever knew you." I said.

"You can't forget me that easy."

"It may not be easy, but I will forget you, Mother Fucker."

Charles insisted that he would take me back to school on Sunday and we would talk. I slammed the phone down in his ear. I couldn't believe that Bastard called me asking what I was doing. What the fuck did he think I was doing? Trying to forget yo dog ass, that was what I was doing.

Charles called Sunday night to inform me he would not be taking me back to school. I responded, "Okay. Bye dog." I slammed the phone in his face. But I thought we would get to talk on the way back to school and both of us would be able to explain exactly what had happened. What was I going to do? I had to go and ask my parents to take me back to school late on a Sunday night. But, they must have known something was wrong. Neither of them complained about taking me back.

I got back to my dorm late Sunday night. The telephone rang.

"Hello." I said in a whisper.

SEASON

"Hey, this is Michael. Where have you been? It is late and we need to study for the test."

"I don't care. I want to die. I am not studying. Bye." I hung up.

Crying for the first time, I began to pray. "Lord, I don't know what to do. I loved him. Please Father, help me to get through this. I know I should be studying. Lord, help me. Amen."

SEASON

Let Me Down Easy

Monday morning I went to accounting looking like death warmed over. I was wearing jeans, a sweatshirt, and a black doo rag.

Michael greeted, "What's wrong? You look like shit."

"I know." I sat and took the test and never said anything else to Michael. When the test was over, I went to take another one.

That afternoon, the telephone rang in my room. I answered.

"Hey, it's Michael. Are you okay?"

"No, and I will never be okay again. Charles and I broke up."

"What happened?"

"He was cheating on me like you said. I am hurting and don't want to go on. Can I borrow your car to go to Dallas?"

"Why?"

"To go to Dallas and talk to him."

"Do you think that will help?

"Yes, if I could only explain."

"Tell me what happened."

"Well, he was with another woman."

"Then what do you need to talk to him about?"

"I don't know. I just need to try."

"No, you cannot borrow my car."

"Why, Michael?"

SEASON

"Because it is stupid and if you had any sense you would see how stupid this is. Anyway, forget his ass. How did you do on the test?"

"Who cares? I don't."

"You should. You said you would never fail again." He paused before continuing. "I thought you said you were not a jealous person."

"I am not jealous. I am not jealous of her. My issue is with him. He is the one that cheated on me, not her. I was in a relationship with him, not her. She is insignificant in this situation. It is all him. I am not jealous. I am mad as hell, but I still have to get him back." I never took a breath. "How can he drop me like this? Only last week I was meeting his parents. We were going to get married. Maybe if he had let me down easy, I could take this. You know like that song?" I began singing with tears flowing from my eyes. "Let me down easy, to get over you baby. Break it to me gently. If this is goodbye, please say it slow. You taught me to love you, so come on boy teach me not to love you before you go." I stopped singing and asked. "Do you remember that song?"

"I guess. You got it bad girl. I will talk to you tomorrow when we study. Bye and take it easy."

***

It had to be the Lord, because I made an "A" on both exams. Michael and I began studying again, but I could not get through one session without tears falling. Sometimes I asked Michael to borrow his car. His response was always the same. "No!"

I went home for the holidays, which we always spent with my grandmother who lived around the corner. All of my cousins would be there. We would have lots of fun. My grandmother would do all the cooking, and she could cook anything.

SEASON

My mom's mother would be there also since my grandfather had passed. Oh, how I missed him. Poppaw was funny, the best storyteller I ever heard. He was very smart but uneducated. As a matter of fact, Poppaw could not read, but he was a hard worker who knew the importance of an education. He sent all of his children to college.

Anyway, while home for Thanksgiving, Charles called. He told me he was still buying me a watch for Christmas. I told him not to bother. He gave me some foolishness about him being a man of his word. But, secretly I was hoping he was calling to kiss and make up. I knew I was not going to get him anything. I didn't have a job or a reason to buy anything for him. However, he had the nerve to tell me he wanted some type necklace made of wood. *Whatever,* I thought.

My grandmother was glad to see me. I knew I was her favorite. She asked me about Charles.

I said to her, "I don't know, grandmother. We are no longer friends."

"Well, tell him I still want to go fishing."

I thought to myself, what part of we are not friends do you not understand. I wanted to remain her favorite so I responded, "Sure, I will tell him grandmother."

My dad also asked me how was his friend Charles, stating he had not been over for dinner in awhile. I responded, "Daddy, we are no longer friends."

Other than thinking about Charles, it was a great Thanksgiving. By final exams, I was so depressed, but through much prayer, I made it through. I did well in all of my classes and received an 'A' in accounting. Michael asked if we could go out over the holidays. I agreed to show him Dallas.

SEASON

That was the first Christmas without my grandfather. My grandmother spent Christmas with us. She seemed so sad. I wanted to help her but I was no help. I was a mess over my breakup with Charles.

Charles called a couple of days before Christmas wanting to schedule time to bring me my present. I didn't know why, but I bought him a necklace made of wood, from Sears on my new credit card. It was ugly, but the best of their selection.

Charles came by with the gift. I asked for a Mickey Mouse watch with a leather band. Well, he did not buy a Mickey Mouse watch, but it did have a leather band. He opened his present and he hated it. I thought, good I don't care. Now take the ugly thing and go.

A few days after Christmas, Michael called to see if I would still go out with him. I told him sure, thinking, this would get my mind off Charles. That Saturday night, Michael and his friend, Stanley, came by and the three of us went to several clubs in Dallas. Michael was wearing an outdated tan leisure suit. We all had a good time. I danced with both him and his friend.

Each day Project Boy drove by my house real fast. Sometimes he called and I cussed him out and threaten to tell my daddy. Then he would stop calling.

Soon the holidays were over and I was glad, no more seeing Charles Edward Jeffrey or Project Boy.

SEASON

In My Mind

It was January 1976 and Earth, Wind, and Fire were holding a concert in Dallas at Southern Methodist University (SMU). Serena and I went to the concert. It was a bitterly cold January night. The concert was fantastic! The music and the visuals were great. After the concert, Serena and I were standing in the hallway of the coliseum and across the way stood, Charles Jeffrey and his new lady. I noticed she was staring at me, but he and I were staring at each other. I felt drawn to him, wanted to walk up and speak but something held me back. I knew he wanted me and believed he would walk away from her and we would just kiss and make up. *In my mind, I would always be his lady.*

Serena finally said, "Let's go, Angela." We walked to the car. It was raining outside. It was so cold the rain was freezing on the windows. We scrapped the ice off the windows and went on our way.

The next weekend, while home, Serena and I decided to go to the movies. As we left the movies, I saw Charles and his new lady. He was sort of arrogant that night.

A couple of weeks later, I returned to school to get on with my education. It was beginning to look like Charles and I had truly broken up. I was taking twenty-one hours again that semester. Accounting was one of my classes again, and Michael was in my class. This semester we were taking Accounting II, Business Math II, and Introduction to Management together. We continued studying that semester. However, I was not doing all of the receiving. I was helping him in some of the classes.

Michael and I talked everyday for one class or another. He was still dating the same girl from the previous semester and I was still talking about Charles Jeffrey.

SEASON

Mac had married over the Christmas holidays and they were the proud parents of a son. I didn't care because he had not been my man ever since I met Charles.

The whole semester, I kept telling Michael I needed to get Charles Jeffrey back. He kept saying I was crazy and to get over him.

***

One weekend, while in Dallas, Michael and I went to a party together. Charles Jeffrey was there and asked me to dance. Michael gave me those don't do it eyes, but I danced anyway. It was a slow jam. He held me in his arms. I was so sad a tear fell from my eye. Charles commented on how good I looked and asked about school. All I could say was thanks and fine.

After the dance, Michael asked if I was okay. I tried to act as if everything was fine, but he knew better. Michael consoled me while we danced to another slow dance.

Michael said, "I hate it when you see him, because he treats you like a yoyo. Let him go. He has moved on. You deserve better."

I wasn't ready to let go.

***

One spring day, I saw Charles washing his car at the car wash in my neighborhood. I could spot that gold Grand Prix out of a thousand cars. I stopped at the car wash and got out of my car.

"Hey Charles."

"Hello, Angela."

"How have you been?" I asked.

"Good." He said continuing to wash his car.

"Well, do you think we could…"

SEASON

Charles interrupted, "Angela, you need to go back to school and get on with your life."

"But, I could quit school and move back to Dallas to be with you and we could get married."

Charles looked at me with the spray wand in his hand and said. "Angela, you will be fine without me. I have moved on. You need an education and I know it is important to you. You will have a good life. We are not going to get back together and I am sorry about that."

I wanted to plead with him but he did not seem interested at all. A tear ran down my cheek. I wanted to go back to school, but my heart was breaking. I turned and walked away.

I cannot describe how I felt. I did not cry a lot but sometimes the tears fell. I think if I had not wanted a college degree so badly things would have been different. I asked God to ease the pain and remove the love I had for Charles. Sometimes I felt like I hated him. Often even singing the song, "It's a Thin Line, Between Love and Hate. "

***

One day, my dad asked me what really happened with Charles and me. I said, "You should ask him."

"I will the next time we have lunch." He replied.

I said to my father, "Daddy, Charles and I are no longer dating. When I break up with someone, you need to break up with them too. It is a rule or something. I am your daughter. Drop that dog."

Daddy looked at me as if he finally got it. He never asked about Charles again.

Each night I prayed to God asking for some divine intervention in fixing my relationship with Charles. I would lie across my desk and look out the picture window facing the campus. I looked out at the stars and imagined the life Charles and I could have had. The life we should

SEASON

have had. I dreamed up scenarios of what I could do to get him to come back to me. Would pregnancy, sickness, fame, or another man lure him back? Could I talk his cousin into convincing him I was the better woman? Could his mother or father convince him he should have chosen me? Would my father talk to him about taking his only daughter back? What could I do to get Charles back?

I dated several guys, none of which ever meant anything. I sank so low once that I dated a married man. The worse part was Project Boy was the one that told me. I had no clue the guy was married. They must have been separated at the time. But, when I confronted him, he admitted to being married. I stopped talking to him that very day. He gave me some crap about it being okay for me to be the other woman, because all men have another woman.

I said to him, "Leave me the hell alone and if you need another other woman then you better find one, because I am not the one." Why did Project Boy have to be the one to tell me about the guy? I was numb; no feelings only love/hate feelings for Charles.

***

Charles' cousin and I became friends. He told me Charles cared about me. I told him I still wanted him back. Charles, the cousin, had a party and invited me. Serena and I went to the party together. It was awkward. Charles was there with his new woman. But, we partied as if Charles was not there. I was sad though and stayed on the opposite side of the party from them. The guy from Richland College was at the party. I could not stand him. So, I said to Serena, "Let's go, girl."

Finally, the semester was over and I had done well. By then, I was the tutor and Michael was the student, except in the love department.

***

SEASON

That summer I met Faye. Faye was average height with a sharp auburn stacked haircut. She had a bubbly personality that you noticed as soon as she spoke. Faye was a really cute girl. We hit it off right away. We went to concerts together and spent the night at each other's houses. We were both college students and having a great time. I told Faye about Charles Jeffrey. We talked about our college lives all summer. We talked about how we did not want to be like the young women at our job. They were men crazy and appeared to have no dreams. Faye and I had big dreams. We were going places and were going do great things. We had our whole lives to live for.

"Faye, I think Charles and I made a perfect couple."

Faye responded, "Really?"

"Yes, we had a good relationship. I was totally into him. I wanted him back and did not know how to get him back. Sometimes, when I ran into him I would be mean to him. I wanted him back, but I wanted it to be as it was before. I wanted him to want me as much as I wanted him. I needed him to be finished with the new lady."

***

That summer Michael was doing construction work with his brother in my community. One afternoon before I went to work, I decided to stop by. I went around the back of the house, where they were doing a room addition. I was wearing some tight blue jeans with angular orange top stitching up and down the legs. I had on a bright orange body suit all of which was a junior's size five and complemented my dark skin tone. I thought I was all that.

"Hi, Michael, I told you I would come by."

"I am glad you did. You look nice." Michael said.

"Thanks. I can't stay, I have got to go to work."

SEASON

"Alright, I will talk to you later."

A few weeks later he was doing brick work on the people's house that lived across the street from my parents. All of our neighbors talked about how good his work was, and he was attending college with me. They were impressed by Michael. He was the talk of the neighborhood.

SEASON

You Got Me Going In Circles

In the fall of 1976, Monica and I decided to room together again. We moved into West Hall. Michael and I were taking Introduction to Marketing, Business Etiquette, and Business Law. Michael hated when I ran into Charles Jeffrey, because for the next three months I cried on his shoulders, talking about what could have been, asking him if he thought there was anyway we could get back together.

Michael would say, "Just because he calls you every six months does not mean he loves you." Sort of like Luther's song "Just because he wants to make love, doesn't mean that he is in love with you."

I did not realize that Michael was interested in me. He wanted to get with me, so my irrational behavior was starting to annoy him.

***

One weekend while in Dallas, Serena and I did a drive by Charles' apartment. He was in the parking lot working on his car. I was so embarrassed he saw me driving through the parking lot. I did not understand why I felt compelled to do such irrational things. All I knew at the time was one day we would kiss and make up, but it wasn't going to be that day. Of course, I went back and told Michael.

***

One Saturday night, a few weeks into the semester, there was a basketball game that my friends talked me into attending. I was tow up from the flo' up. I had on a purple printed headscarf, with a blue oversized sweatshirt, jeans, and some pink house shoes. I did not want to go out and see people, but they convinced me to go.

SEASON

The game was boring, so we decided to leave. Who did we run into as we were leaving? Charles Jeffrey, II, his cousin, and two former students that were professional football players. There I was looking like who did it and what for. How could I have let Charles see me looking like that? He was looking good, and I was out there looking like an orphaned child. So, what did I do? I went straight to my room and regrouped.

I put on a pair of black velvet jeans with a black velvet print vest and a silk blouse. I took that scarf off my head and hooked up the afro. I put some makeup on too. I looked good and it was to the after party for Monica, Cynthia, and me.

It was an Omega party off campus. I was chatting with an Omega, but really was waiting for Charles to walk through the door. I was sitting on a long table with others and then a short thick guy decided he wanted to put his big butt on the table. My legs were crossed and locked up under the legs of the table. I felt the table falling. I tried to unwrap my legs to jump off. But the weight and force of the people on the table took us to the floor fast. Most of the people were not expecting to fall so they fell flat on their butts. But I landed face down with about 30 people sitting on top of the table with my legs underneath.

They were all laughing while I was trying to scream for them to get off my legs. I could not scream, so I just laid my head on the floor and cried while beating the floor with my hand.

Finally, someone realized they were on my legs and they all got up to see if I was okay. Of course, I was not okay. Makeup running down my face, and all the while I was thinking Charles couldn't see me like that. An Omega picked me up and took me to Monica's car. My leg was bleeding. I was hysterical. Monica sped off in the car to take me to the hospital. She drove around the corner and stopped the car. We looked at each other and started laughing uncontrollably.

SEASON

Monica screamed with laughter, "I know you aren't hurt that badly, only embarrassed. You look like a raccoon with that mascara running down your face." She pointed to my face still laughing. "You better act like you are hurt for the next two weeks."

We went to the store and bought bandaging. I wrapped my leg and hopped around for the next two weeks. Every time Monica saw me, she laughed. She made me so mad, always knowing what I was thinking. Everyone was concerned I had been hurt. Everyone, but Charles, he never even came to the party.

A few weeks later, Monica, Cynthia, and I, all who had been dumped by our men, decided we were going to call them up and tell them off. You know like the scene in "Waiting to Exhale," where Bernadine was going to call her husband to tell him off. Well, in the movie, her friend Gloria stopped her from making that call by telling her it was childish. Well, my friends did not stop me. I called information and got his telephone number. The information lady said she had a new listing for Charles Jeffrey. I took the number and called. Now it was late on a Saturday night.

"Hello." He answered the phone sounding as if he was asleep.

I had him on the phone but did not know what to say. "Hello, Charles this is Angela."

"Yeah, what is it?" He asked annoyed but concerned.

I mumbled, "My mom is sick." I could not believe I said that. She had the flu but that was all. "Never mind, bye." I hung up the phone.

We all laughed at ourselves and said how stupid we had been to call those guys that didn't want us anymore. I prayed to God asking Him not to let my mom get sick.

SEASON

That semester Michael and I had several classes together again. We each sat together by choice or because the teacher put us in alphabetical order. He was Everette and I, Franklin. We were always right next to each other.

It was ironic that since Charles and I were no longer a couple, I was going to Dallas more often. One weekend while in Dallas, Charles Jeffrey called me and asked me to come over. He told me he cared about me and maybe we should get back together.

I was thinking it was time, kiss and make up time. In fact, we did kiss. He had a picture of me I hated on his dresser. He had a new stereo system that was complete with an eight-track tape player and turntable. He played the Spinners Live album with "How Could I Let You Get Away."

It was a nice day talking with Charles. While sitting on the floor, my hand was behind me under the bed. Somehow, a pink house shoe ended up in my hand. I was livid.

Charles had fed me lies all day long. I went to the restroom where he had an alcove. In the alcove was his new ladies drivers' license. I looked at them and to my surprise were two things. We were born on the same day and both of our last names were Franklin. That was the first time I actually thought about her and who she might be. Could we be related? Could we be twins? How could we be born on the same day? Who *was* she and what was she to me? I gave Charles some excuse, and left abruptly. I was tripping. Charles' new lady had never bothered me before. However, that day she became a real person. One that was possibly connected to me. That made me think she was more special than I had thought before. I never told Charles that I knew he was still with her. I just left. I realized that day; we would never kiss and make up.

Over time, I often wondered if I ever really wanted Charles back. We had not been a couple for an extended time. I wondered if I only wanted revenge on him because no guy had

SEASON

ever broken up with me. I was the one that did the breaking up. Was this punishment for the way I broke up with Project Boy? Was this what I was reaping? But, I didn't understand why I could not get Charles out of my head.

***

One night while at a party, I hooked up with this guy. Michael was at the same house party. I was sitting on the stairway in a lip lock with a guy. Michael passed by and almost knocked me down the stairs. I thought it was an accident until he called me on the incident later.

Michael did not understand how I could be kissing on that guy, when I wouldn't give him the time of day. I admitted I was just messing around and at least I wasn't talking about Charles Jeffrey, anymore.

***

Michael called everyday for one class or another. Usually right before the telephone rang, I had a sudden urge to go to the restroom. Monica would tell Michael I was in the restroom and for him to call me back later.

One day she said to me, "You know, I think you are going to marry Michael."

I laughed at her, "You are crazy. We aren't even holding hands, and he is not my type."

Monica said, "Your stomach never hurts until Michael calls. Mark my words, you two are going to get married."

I repeated, "You are crazy. I don't like him like that and neither does he."

SEASON

If Only For One Night

It was the spring of 1977, Michael and I were again taking several courses together, but he was acting different. He was not sitting next to me anymore, nor was he calling to study. I was bothered that we were no longer as close.

One afternoon, I called Michael to ask him if he wanted to study, but as soon as he started to talk, my stomach started to churn. I had to call him back.

Monica laughed uncontrollably saying, "He's your husband."

I thought she was totally insane. He was not my type and he had a girlfriend.

***

One Sunday, when I got back to school I told Michael I had seen Charles over the weekend.

Michael responded, "I don't understand you. How can you be so together and at the same time act so stupid? The guys you like are no good dogs."

"Michael, I don't like Charles anymore. In fact he makes me sick."

"Well, it is about time but the jury is still out on that."

I listened to him go on and on.

That day as we were leaving math class, Michael was going on and on about how I liked guys that would use and abuse me. He said a good brother didn't have a chance with me.

I disagreed.

He continued, "I am going to show you what I mean. As we walked across campus, I will pick out the guys you would like. You only like dogs."

SEASON

I did not say a word.

"No, you wouldn't like him," he paused to point out someone else. After spotting the next guy, he turned to me and said, "Not him."

I thought to myself, *he would never figure that I would like this brother coming here.*

"Now, that brother there, you would like. He is definitely your type." He pointed to another brother and said. "You would like that dog, too."

I was thinking to myself *here comes Butch, everyone loves him except me. I know he is a dog.*

"No, you don't like Butch even though he is a dog."

Next, we passed a fine white boy. Now I am not into white boys, but he was fine.

"You would even like that white boy there. He's a dog too."

We passed at least one hundred guys and Michael was 100% on target. *How did he know who I would like?*

"I bet you want to know how I could do that." He paused before he continued, "I know men and I know you and what you like. Just like, I am not your type. But, I would treat you right. We are already friends. What a wonderful way to start a relationship. Oh, but you don't want a good relationship." Michael said in a sarcastic tone.

Michael gave me a lot to consider. Did I really like dogs, guys that treated me badly? How could he pick out all the guys that I liked? *I will give him some and his curiosity will be peaked.* We will then be able to go back and be just friends.

The next time he came over, I gave him some. Actually, I whipped it on him. After he left, I thought, now we can go back to being friends.

I was wrong. Michael did not go away.

SEASON

LIFETIME

A Dance Turned Into Romance

One winter night in February, Cynthia and I went to a party at the Kappa house. Michael was there. I was already bothered by the lack of communication between us. So, I decided to ask him to dance on a slow song, so we could talk. "Michael, lets dance?" He never said a word, but we began dancing. I said to him, "Are you mad at me? You don't like me anymore?"

The music was dying down and Michael said in a loud tone. "I don't like you, I love you!"

I was surprised by his statement and I knew Cynthia heard him. I was touched and embarrassed all at the same time. It looked as if a tear was about to fall from his eyes.

He said. "I can't be your friend anymore. I love you and you don't want me so, I must move on."

It was at that moment, I thought, maybe he was the one. I felt the love coming from him, and I wanted to be loved. I needed to be loved. That dance turned into romance.

We decided to leave the party and walked back to West Halls. It was so romantic. It was snowing. We talked all the way to my place and into the night.

"Michael, how do you know you love me?"

He reached for my hands and looked into my eyes before he spoke. "I knew when I could not get you out of my head. When I starting thinking about you night and day. I do not want to be just friends anymore."

I knew then I loved him. We spent the rest of the weekend together, and I was in love. We became a couple. But, I was afraid to ask him about his girlfriend. By the end of the weekend, I decided to ask.

LIFETIME

Michael said, "She broke up with me; because she was convinced we were messing around."

"What is she going to think now?" I asked.

"She is going to think she was right. I am glad she was right. She told me, you were who I wanted and for me to go get you. She also said we might as well be messing around because we were both into each other. I could not argue with her. I knew I loved you. We let each other go. I knew she was right."

***

By spring break, I had a man and not just any man. I had Michael Anthony Everette who was also my good friend. The first day home on spring break I called my grandmother to tell her about Michael. She had so many questions about Michael that we planned to get together during the week to finish discussing him. The very next day March 12 my grandmother died. She fell ill through the night. My mom took her to the hospital. I didn't know they were at the hospital, until my mom called late on Saturday afternoon. I heard my grandmother moaning in the background. She must have been in a lot of pain. Before we could get to the hospital, my grandmother had passed away. How could it be? She was fine the day before. I went into the room to see her. She had a tube in her mouth and her mouth was twisted. Her dentures had been removed. I knew she would be upset about that.

"Oh God, I can't take this. Mommee is my grandmother, my idol, my mentor, my friend, my special person. Oh Lord, what am I going to do?"

Michael offered to take me to the funeral, but I declined. We had just begun dating and I knew I was going to be pitiful. Serena was right there with me, helping me all the way. My grandmother's funeral was extremely sad. One of my young cousins asked me if she was going

LIFETIME

to see my slip again as she had two years prior at my grandfather's funeral. Everyone was looking at me waiting to see how I was going to react at my grandmother's funeral. My brother was sitting next to me pinching me saying, "Don't start."

I did cry a lot but I did not fall out.

My brother put his hand over my mouth so he would not have to hear me. Pinching my leg with one hand and holding my mouth with the other. No one could see what he was doing though, because they were all looking straight ahead, including him. I tried to tell him I could not help it. He said the same thing to me. "I can't help it either. So shut up."

***

I was a different girl when I returned to school. It was time for the Zeta Ball. Monica wanted me to go with her. I told Monica I would not be attending. Michael and I had just started dating and his old girlfriend was in that same sorority. It did not seem right to throw Michael up in her face. Monica was disappointed with me leaving her holding two tickets.

However, the night of the ball, I saw Michael drive by on his way to the ball. I was livid. I started looking for a date. I asked a friend to escort me to the ball. He agreed, but I did not have anything to wear. After going through all of the drama of getting a date and then not having anything to wear, I decided I was being childish and let it go.

It was nearing the end of the semester and my academic advisor, called me to his office. I wondered what he wanted. Normally, I had to wait weeks to get an appointment with him. He was the head of the business department and we never agreed on anything. He said I was taking too many hours.

I went to his office. "Hello Dr. McCuin, you need to see me?"

"Yes, come in and have a seat. What are your plans?"

LIFETIME

"Pardon?" I asked with a puzzled look on my face.

"Are you planning on graduating this summer or this fall?

"Excuse me?"

"Miss Franklin, you have been taking an overload every semester and only need thirteen hours to graduate. However, you will have to take all of your remaining hours on this local campus. But you must obtain my approval to take 13 hours in summer school."

I had no idea I needed so few hours to graduate. I couldn't even remember why I was in such a hurry to graduate. It was Charles Jeffrey. Michael had another semester. I did not want to graduate and leave him there without me.

The professor said to me, "Excuse me Miss Franklin? What are you going to do?"

"Dr. McCuin, this is all news to me. I did not know that I could graduate this summer. Is there an actual graduation ceremony in the summer?"

"Yes, it is just as large as the December graduation."

"Do I have to give you my answer today?"

"No, but don't take too much time. The classes you need should have been taken by your sophomore year. You need health, information systems, economics, and statistics, which is a four-hour class. Why have you not taken statistics? Your mathematics grades are all high 'A's. You have an emphasis in mathematics with your course work. What is the problem?"

"I don't know. Scheduling I guess, it is a four hour class. I could always take two classes to this one."

"Think about it and get back with me by the end of the week." He said sort of dismissing me.

LIFETIME

I stood, thanked him and left. I walked back to my dorm in disbelief. It had caught me off guard. Michael would not graduate until December. I did not know what to do. Should I have signed up for the Masters Program? Could I pass statistics in the summer? I knew the summer session would be very aggressive.

I called my parents when I got back to my dorm.

"I have a collect call from Angela. Will you accept?"

"Sure we accept." My dad responded.

"Hey Angie. What's going on?" My dad said.

I responded, "School."

"Don't take no wooden nickels?" He said with a chuckle.

"I won't Daddy. But I can graduate this summer, if I stay here, go to summer school, and pass statistics."

"How much?"

"About $700 dollars." I said.

"Cool, do it."

"But daddy, I want to get in the Masters program and go an additional year."

"Girl, you can do what you want after you get a job. This will save me about $3000 and will give me one year to prepare for Gary to go to college. Do it. Do it. Bye."

I heard the dial tone and looked at the phone in disbelief. I mumbled to myself, "Daddy makes me mad; all he thinks about is the mighty dollar. I wished Mama would have answered the phone."

The next day I told Dr. McCuin I was graduating in the summer. He signed the papers allowing me to take the hours required. I thanked him and left. As I was walked back to my

LIFETIME

room, I realized I had to find somewhere to stay for the summer. Everyone I knew was graduating in May, including Monica.

That night while studying with Michael, I told him I would be graduating in the summer and needed a roommate and an apartment.

Michael said, "Cool, I am going to summer school also, but I am not graduating until December. I think my next door neighbor needs a roommate for the summer."

In a few weeks, I moved into the apartment right next door to Michael. I was excited about summer school except for statistics. My new man was attending summer school with me. It was going to be a great summer.

Why Does It Hurt So Bad

It was the summer of 1977, I would be graduating that summer, classes had started and it was my birthday. The professor Bernie Bidway began as soon as I sat down, "Good morning, I am Bernie Bidway; this is my last semester here. I have turned in my resignation and will be teaching at University of Mississippi in the fall. The administration here wants me to give more 'A's and reduce the amount of failing students. I told them, no can do. I will not grade on the bell curve for statistics. For those of you who do not know what the bell curve is; ten percent A's, twenty percent B's, forty percent C's, twenty percent D's, and ten percent F's. There are 65 students in this class. The probability of one getting an 'A' in this class is one percent. How many of you are first time Statistics students?"

Michael and I both raised our hands.

Bidway said, "The probability of you passing this class is forty percent."

He must be crazy I thought. I am passing this class.

Bidway continued, "How many of you are taking this class for the second time?" About eighty percent of the class raised their hands. Their probability was good.

"How many of you are taking this class for the third time?" Their probability was lower than the second time students, but higher than the first time. "How many of you are taking this class for the fourth time?"

He was being ridiculous. Nobody had failed that class three times. Wrong. Our friend Miami raised his hand.

"How many of you are graduating seniors?"

I raised my hand again, high doing my happy dance.

He looked at me and said, "And this is your first time taking this class?" He stacked my books on top of each other and said, "Pack your books and drop this class now. You will not pass or graduate and I will not waste my time telling you the probability of that."

I got vocal, "Oh yeah, I am going to pass this class and I will graduate this summer. You don't know me, man."

He laughed and asked, "Why, are you taking statistics as a graduating senior and this is a sophomore level class?"

I replied. "I never had time."

"Too bad for you, because you will not graduate. You should have made time."

Bernie Bidway looked at Miami and said, "You need to drop now and change your degree plan. You will never pass this class." He clapped his hands. "Now, enough of that. For those of you taking this class in the summer because you think it is easy. Drop now. We cover all of the material in the entire book. This is how my class will run. I give homework everyday. I do not look at the homework, but you must do the homework to pass the class."

"Do we get credit for doing the homework?" I asked.

"No," he continued, "I will give six tests; Introduction to Statistics/Descriptive Statistics, Probability, Estimates and Sample Size/Testing Hypotheses, Inferences from Two Samples: Correlation and Regression, Multinomial Experiments & Contingency Tables/Analysis of Variance, and Nonparametric Statistics/Review."

I raised my hand again, thinking I had to pass that class. "Do you give extra credit for participation?"

"No!"

LIFETIME

"Well, do you give partial credit for starting a problem and are doing it correctly but don't finish?"

"No," he chuckled. "I give credit for having the correct answer with a diagram and the answer must be stated in a full equation."

I asked, "What do you mean by that?"

"Glad you asked. If the answer is 3.456 you must graph the answer and say the probability of me passing this class and graduating as a first time student is 3.456%."

"Okay, then how accurate do we have to be?"

"I can see you have some intelligence. This is going to be fun," he rubbed his hands together and continued. "Your answer must be within one 1000th of a point."

"Excuse me?" I asked knowing he did not mean what he had just said.

"Yes, darling you are excused and you heard me, one 1000th of a point."

"How is that possible? I would have to use the same calculator that you use."

He looked directly at me, "That is correct. Do you have any more questions?"

"Yes, a couple. Do we get credit for going to lab?"

"No, you don't even have to go. But, I suggest you do. The lab assistant can answer any questions that you have. Anything else?"

"Yes, you said we don't have to turn our homework in."

"That is correct."

"Then what incentive do we have to do it?"

He got right in my face and said, "Passing the class should be incentive enough. The only way you will pass this class is you must do the homework. Trust me. As a matter of fact I will know who is doing homework based on the questions they have the next day."

LIFETIME

I raised my hand again, "Back to using the same calculator as you, what did you mean by that?"

"Glad you bought that back up. I use a TI SR55-A calculator. Each day before class, you will need to go to the department office to check out the calculator. They will require your student ID. After class you must return the calculators for the next class."

"May we take the calculators home?"

"No, you heard what I just said."

He thought he had me. But, I was determined to pass his class. "How much does the calculator cost?"

"$150 dollars," he said so matter-of-factly.

Now at that time $150 dollars might as well have been a million, but I still had a plan.

"Miss Franklin do you have anymore questions?"

"Yes, one more. Do you grade on the curve?"

"No. It is either right or wrong, and remember right is within one 1000th of a point. No partial credit, no extra credit."

"One more."

"Sure."

"What will be on the test?"

"Ninety percent of work we have covered with homework, five percent of give away questions, and five percent of problems that I know you don't know."

"Okay, I promise, this is my last last question."

"It needs to be because I have got to start teaching for today."

"Can you be bribed?" I asked and the entire class laughed.

LIFETIME

"Yes, but no one has met my price yet and I will not tell you what it is."

"For real one last question." I said to him, "Do you give the same test each year?"

"Absolutely not!" He raised his voice. "Let's begin."

I thought at least, I knew all of his rules. I knew what I was working with. My dad told me to know your enemy. Bidway began explaining the lesson.

The bell finally rang. *Thank you Lord.*

"Don't forget to bring a calculator to class tomorrow. You have one hundred problems for homework, chapter 1, sections one and two. The answers are in the back of the book for the odd number problems." He looked at me and said with a smile, "Miss Franklin, I am going to love failing you."

I picked up my book, stood, and said. "In your dreams, I am passing this class."

He laughed aloud as I was leaving. Everybody was mad at me because he had not completed the lesson.

I didn't care about them being mad at me. I was going to pass statistics. I had to know my enemy. Michael and I walked away. I went to the office to get a calculator and he went in another direction. The lab assistant was my homeboy Richard. He stressed the importance of attending lab and keeping up with the homework.

I knew this was going to be a long summer, but I was going to prove to that white teacher that I was smart. Red neck jerk, going to Ole Miss, I could tell he would love to fail a sister and I was not the one, "Not this summer!" I said aloud.

I headed back to my apartment, dragging from the first day of classes on my birthday. I sang, "HAPPY BIRTHDAY to ME!" I decided to call home to get that calculator. I went next door and used the phone.

LIFETIME

"Operator, I would like to make a collect call."

"I have a collect call from Angela. Will you accept?" The operator said.

"Yes, I will accept."

"Hi, Mama, I was calling because I have got to have a TI SR55-A calculator. That calculator you bought me is throwing up. I have never seen a calculator do that. My teacher says it costs $150."

"$150 dollars! What?" My mother said with disbelief in voice.

"Yeah, how much do you think it will cost you at work?"

"I don't know." She replied.

"Angie, can't you use the calculator you already have?" My dad said from the other line.

"No daddy, I have to get a TI SR55-A."

"I will check tomorrow," Mama said.

"Mama, write it down, SR55-A not the SR55. Buy it tomorrow and over night it to me.

"Can't you wait until the weekend?" She asked.

"No, I am having a test on Friday and I need it as soon as possible. Don't y'all want to see me graduate in August? This man is crazy. He hates me. He wants to flunk me. He even jokes about it."

"Okay, I will do my best." Mama said.

"Thanks. Love you. Bye." I hung up the phone.

I went to Michael's apartment and we started on our homework. I still had the school calculator. They must have been crazy, if they thought I was going to turn in that calculator before I got mine. We did most of the homework; but it was impossible to do all one hundred problems.

LIFETIME

The next day, Michael and I had a lot of questions.

By Wednesday afternoon, I received my calculator. My mom paid thirty-five dollars for it on her employee discount. I turned in the calculator the next morning, because I needed my student identification card. Once in class, Bidway began, "Any questions Miss. Franklin?"

"Certainly, would you explain how to use this calculator to do factorial?"

"Sure, do this." He spouted out the instructions. He stood in front of me and asked, "Anymore questions?"

"Yes, I am having a problem recalling the memory. Would you be so kind to show me how to work this calculator?"

He took my calculator in his hand, punched a couple of buttons and said, "Miss Franklin that is how you recall the memory. Anything else?"

"No. Thanks." I said with my head down working a problem.

Bidway continued, "This is your freebee. The median is the middle value when the scores are arranged in order of increasing magnitude. This will be on the test. Mark this down. This will be on the test."

I got it! I put down the calculator and wrote down what he said. That was the five percent give away.

Michael asked a couple of questions about the calculator.

"Anymore questions?" Bidway paused, "Test tomorrow."

I asked, "How long do we have to take the test?"

"Three hours, class time and lab time, the test will be given in the lab. You can use your notes, book, and calculator. Bring plenty of paper. By the way you have one hundred problems tonight for homework."

LIFETIME

I shouted, "Are you crazy? Are these review problems?"

"I've been called that before. No. All new stuff the remainder of chapter 2.

Bastard. That meant we had to do the homework, before we could review. Class was dismissed and I went straight to the lab.

I had been going to lab everyday by myself but the whole class went that day. This pissed me off. I normally had the assistant all to myself. I wanted him to ignore them and only help me. He was helping everyone. *Just screw them.* "Richard, will you help me, please?"

That night Michael and I did our homework as we had done every night. Miami dropped by. Miami kept talking about his schemes to pass the test.

Michael said, "Man we are going to have to study to pass this test. We have one hundred new problems of homework, tonight."

"Man, I am not doing that," Miami said.

Michael said. "That's why this is your fourth time taking this class? You should know by now there are no short cuts. Did you hear the man?"

Miami asked Michael, "Do you think we can pass this class?"

"Hell yeah! I am passing whether yo ass passes or not. Quit trying to find a short cut and do the work. He already told you no one has ever stolen his test before he administers it and he has not been offered enough for a bribe."

Miami was tripping. He left after a couple of hours. Michael and I did homework from 3:00 Thursday afternoon until 7:00 Friday morning.

It was Friday morning 9:00 a.m. and we were exhausted. We did not have time to review previous homework and not allowed to ask any questions before the test. Bidway was passing out the test, singing a hymn and whistling. He was such a trip. I mumbled, "Shut up."

LIFETIME

"Begin." Bidway said.

I read the questions, only ten problems. I skipped around trying to find the easy ones.

Problem #10.   There are 65 students in Bernie Bidway's class. It takes the

average student 20.457 inches of rope to hang themselves in this

Statistics class. How much rope does it take you, to hang your

neck in my class? Remember to graph.

I knew how to work the problem, but that fool was crazy. I wrote, diagramed, and

underlined. "It will take me, Angela Franklin a graduating senior, 12.467 inches of rope to hang

myself in Bernie Bidway's class. I continued on to problem number 7. It was the freebee. Find

the median of the scores 7, 2, 3, 7, 6, 9, 10, 9, 9, 10. I answered, "The median is <u>8</u> for the above

scores." A*t least I will get this right*.

Three hours later, I had 26 pages of legal paper. Bidway, knocked on my desk with his

hand extended, "Miss Franklin, time is up. I need your paper."

"Hold on, I am in the middle of this. Please give me more time." I yelled.

"No." Bidway stood over me with his hand on my papers.

"Well if I had more time I could have aced that test," I flipped him my papers.

This was going to be a long summer and I had to spend the entire weekend catching up in

my other class.

Monday morning Bernie had jokes. "Some of you are making this class out to be way

too difficult. You need to read the question before you start because some times what I am

asking is simple. I may put a lot of information that has nothing to do with the problem. There

were others that surprised me." Bidway then handed me my 93.

I said aloud. "Yes. That's what I am talking about."

LIFETIME

Bidway stood in front of me smiled and said, "Miss Franklin, do you have any questions?"

"Yes, Mr. Bidway, how do you work number 9?"

"Oh yes, number 9." With that evil grin, he showed us how to work the problem and moved directly to probability. Now, I thought I was pretty good at probability. I was a great black jack and poker player. Therefore, it was going to be a piece of cake. Wrong.

The following Monday, I received my test results, 67, a 'D'. I was devastated. Miami made a 33 and Michael an 88. I was worried that Bidway was going to fail a sister. I decided to bring out my 'A' game.

Bidway was quite cocky as if he had won round one. He smirked and strutted, with his sloped footed walk. "Probability is what separates the men from the boys."

I was glad I was a female. "Jerk," I mumbled as I crumpled my failing test papers.

"Any questions, Miss Franklin?" He asked as if he had heard what I mumbled.

"Yes, are we finished with probability?"

"Yes, and that's the good news. The bad news is everything from this point forward builds on the previous chapter. Let's begin."

I had to pass that class to graduate and show Bidway that I was not an equation in his class. But, I was already doing all I could to pass and I remembered, "Don't take no wooden nickels."

Each week was more of the same with test on Fridays. By the end of the six weeks, Michael and I were crazy. We lived and breathed statistics. By the last week of class, I was going into the finals with a high B average.

Bidway began, "Miss Franklin, do you have any questions?"

LIFETIME

"Yes sir, after class."

"Sure." He said with a smile, but his smile was different.

After class, I lingered to ask him my question. I stuttered, "I have a high 'B' average right now. If I make an 'A' on the final are you going to give me an 'A' in this class?"

"Miss Franklin, Miss Franklin, Miss Franklin. You already know the answer to that question, because you are a bright girl. I do not give you anything. You will get what you get." He laughed. "But I will say this. You are an excellent statistics student. It has been a pleasure having you in my class and yes, the probability was incorrect. You will graduate in a few weeks. Congratulations!"

The jerk was about to hug me. I was not expecting that, we were not friends. I responded, "Thank you Mr. Bidway, coming from you that means a lot to me."

I received an 89 in statistics and jumped for joy when I saw my grade posted in the statistics office. I went straight to Mr. Bidway's office where he was packing.

"Mr. Bidway, do you have a few minutes?" I asked.

"Certainly." He never stopped packing.

"I want to thank you. You have made this class challenging and fun. You are the best teacher I have ever had anywhere. Although, you could have given me an 'A'." I paused and laughed before I continued. "But, a 'B+' from you is an 'A' in anyone else's class. I will cherish the memories. This school is losing out by not keeping you. I have never worked this hard in my life for anything. It's been a pleasure."

"Give me a hug, Miss Franklin. I wish I had just one Angela Franklin in every class. Because I enjoyed your, one more question, please. You are a great student." He gave me a big bear hug.

LIFETIME

I hugged him back and said, "Thank you, sir." I smiled and walked away doing my happy dance.

No one had seen Michael or me all summer. There were intramurals, sports, barbeques, parties, concerts, NBA basketball playoffs games and all. We were always at Michael's kitchen table doing statistics homework. We both received 'B's in the class, and yes, Miami failed for the fourth time. Therefore, that weekend, we celebrated by watching the basketball playoff games. I was sitting on the sofa in between Michael and Miami and the next morning I woke up on Michael's sofa, wondering how I had gotten there. I could not remember anything from the night before except watching the game.

Michael came in the living room about that time and started going off on me. "Why were you so rude last night?

"What are you talking about? What day is this? What did I do?" I rubbed my hand across my head.

"You know, we were sitting on the sofa watching the game. Then, all of a sudden, you stretched out as if we were not sitting there. You pushed Miami off the sofa, rolled over and went to sleep. I was so embarrassed."

I said to Michael, "I am sorry. I was tired. I haven't slept in six weeks, thanks to that damn statistics class." I was free, two classes and graduation. Michael on the other hand was taking statistics 2 all by himself. I felt sorry for him because he had to study alone. Michael had Dr. Weisman because Bernie Bidway was gone. Dr. Weisman knew statistics well, but he could care less about you. Michael did not have any fun in class. He got a 'D' in the class and was happy to get it.

LIFETIME

I had Dr. Gross for economics. Michael had been in his class before and had already warned me, he was crazy. Well, the first day of class Dr. Gross had jokes. I could not take another Bernie Bidway so soon.

Dr. Gross said to me, "Miss Franklin, why are you taking freshman economics as a graduating senior?"

I thought to myself, *here we go again*. "Well, I didn't do well in the first part of economics so I put this class off until now."

He listened and continued teaching.

After a couple of days of classes I observed that he only used two analogies; the cost of pot in Commerce (supply and demand) and the cost of Orinase for type 2 diabetes (supply and demand). Now pot, I could not get with. However, diabetes, I understood. My dad was taking Orinase for his diabetes. That was perfectly clear to me.

Economics was boring as hell so into the second week I had sleeping in class down.

"Wake up Miss Franklin." Dr. Gross said as he tapped me on the shoulders.

I raised my head and apologized.

"Tell me how is it that you are acing my class and sleep everyday while everyone else is failing?"

"Do you really want to know?" I questioned.

"Yes, enlighten me. What are you doing?"

"First, as you so pointed out on the first day of class. I am a graduating senior majoring in Business Administration with a minor in Computer Science. I have completed all of my business course work. Therefore, economics is common sense to me. When I took the first part of economics, I was a freshman and I had never had economics before, never heard of Gross

LIFETIME

National Product, I had nothing to pull from just like these freshmen here. In addition, all of

your analogies are about pot, marijuana, a lid, ten-cent bag, diabetes, Orinase, or Insulin.

Everyone in my family is a diabetic; they control it either by diet, Orinase, or Insulin. So, I

totally get where you coming from. I do not do drugs, but I still understand what you are talking

about. Maybe the school should look at making economics for upperclassmen or start offering

economics in high school."

"Hmmm, that's interesting." He said.

I ran my fingers through my afro and said, "Thank you very much. May I ask you a

question?"

"Yes."

"Since, I am acing this class, according to you, why don't you give me my 'A' and let me

go? So you can focus on the freshman."

"Thanks, I will consider it."

Sure, I bet you will. Crazy man, dope headed diabetic.

To my surprise, two days later, Dr Gross told me to take my 'A' and good luck in life.

"Thank you, sir." I grabbed my books and left doing my graduation dance. The

freshmen were looking at me with envy. But, I was graduating and all I had remaining was save

Lucy's life and I was out of there.

I was so blessed. I did not have to save Lucy, the doll for practicing mouth-to-mouth

recitation, was broken. I received 'A's' in both health and economics. *Graduation here I come.*

Monday afternoon the week of graduation. I got a letter in the mail that stated I owed

five dollars and would not be able to participate in the graduation ceremonies until all fees were

paid. All fees had to be paid by 3:00 Thursday, August 10. "Oh hell no, I will participate." I

LIFETIME

went next door to use the telephone. I knocked on her door. "Oh, I am sorry. I did not know you had company. I will come back later."

"No problem. What do you need?" My neighbor asked.

"May I use your telephone?"

"Sure, there is it is." She said pointing to the telephone in the midst of a room full of company.

"Thanks, this will be quick." I said. I dialed the operator. "Operator, I would like to make a collect call." She connected me.

"Yello." My daddy said as he answered the telephone.

"Would you accept a collect call from Angela?" The operator asked.

"No, you got the wrong number." Click. Dial tone. He hung up.

I looked at the telephone in my hand convinced that it had been my father. I replied. "Operator that was the right number, Try again."

"Yello." Daddy said again.

The operator asked, "Sir, will you accept a collect call from Angela?"

"NO, I do not know her?" Click. Dial tone. He hung up again.

The operator said to me, "Maam, he hung up again."

"Okay, thanks, operator." It was too many people in there for me to find out what was going on with him. Therefore, I asked if I could use the telephone in the bedroom.

She agreed.

I went to her bedroom and called again. "Operator, I would like to make a collect call. Tell him it is an emergency, from Angela."

"Yello!"

LIFETIME

"Would you accept an emergency collect call from Angela?"

"Hell no." Click. Dial tone.

"Thanks operator." I hung up and left my neighbors apartment.

I went to Michael's apartment and asked him to walk up to the pay phone with me. He agreed and we walked the couple of blocks together. I told Michael that I needed five dollars for graduation fees. And, my father was tripping.

I arrived to the pay phone and called home again, "Operator, I would like to make a collect call from Angela. Now operator, my dad likes to joke, so he may say that he does not know me. Don't let him hang up." I insisted.

"Yello!" My dad answered again.

The operator asked, "Sir, would you accept a collect call from Angela?"

He shouted, "Now, I have told yo ass three times that I do not know her."

"Daddy, stop playing?" I cried on the other end of the telephone.

"Sir, she says that it is an emergency and she is your daughter," the operator said with a chuckle in her voice.

"Well, if she is my daughter what the hell does she look like?" He asked.

"Sir, I don't know what she looks like, but…"

Daddy interrupted her, "Don't call my house no mo." Click. Dial tone.

I shouted, "Operator, please don't hang up on me. This is an emergency. I need to talk to him." I was crying. "Operator, allow him to hear me talk? I have to talk to him. He sounds like he is drunk."

"Okay, but I can't make him talk to you. Are you sure you are his daughter?" She asked in a questioning tone.

LIFETIME

"YES, I told you he likes to joke."

"Ring, Ring."

"Yello!"

"Sir, this girl name Angela, is begging you to accept this collect call. Will you accept?"

"No, operator, I keep telling you I do not know her."

"Daddy, quit playing. Are you drunk? Daddy, please! You know I am you daughter, your only daughter." I pleaded.

"Operator, what does she look like?"

She snapped, "Sir, I don't know."

"Daddy, please it's an emergency. I need five dollars for graduation. I don't have any money and they say I cannot graduate on Friday without it."

My dad said in a cocky tone, "You see operator, why I didn't want to accept. I am glad her Mama aint here. She is a push over. I aint giving her shit, she has gotten her last dime from me." He paused before continuing. "Anyway, did she say she was graduating from college on Friday and she can't come up with five dollars? What in the hell kind of degree, is she getting anyway? Shame on her, she is on her own. Now pass that to her operator." Click. Dial tone.

The operator said to me, "Angela, I am sorry but he hung up. Your father is funny."

"His ass ain't funny." I snapped.

"Good luck and goodbye, Angela." Click. Dial tone.

I was balling when I hung up the telephone.

"Your dad would not accept your call?" Michael asked.

"Hell no, his ass is going to come up here Friday for nothing." I slammed the phone on the hook. "What am I going to do?"

LIFETIME

Michael replied, "I will give you the five dollars."

"Do you have it?" I asked.

"No, but I can get it."

"Thanks, I appreciate it Michael. However, my dad makes me sick. I am never going to ask him for another dime. As a matter of fact, I am going to figure out exactly how much money I owe him and I am going to pay him every single dime. I probably owe him about one hundred forty thousand dollars and fifty cents." I wiped my face. "He makes me sick. I am going to figure out how much when I get home. I know I owe ten thousand dollars for my degree. Why is he being so mean?"

Michael and I walked all over town together with me crying and confused. Michael tried to assure me that everything would work out.

The next day, Michael gave me the five dollars and I went to the office and paid the fee. I was still going to pay my father back.

***

Friday morning, my entire family came to my graduation except my brother. I didn't know what his problem was. My father was grinning from ear to ear as if he was the one getting a degree. I ignored his ass the whole day. But, I was happy all my family and friends came to my graduation.

I arrived at the staging room with my five-dollar receipt. I would put it under my mortarboard, once they checked me off. A girl standing next to me asked if we had to have our receipts. I replied, "The letter said we had to have proof of payment."

"I don't have mine." She said.

LIFETIME

I said to her, "Oh well. They said they were going to make you get out of line without it."

A professor said, clapping her hands to get our attention. "Alright, listen up. I need to see the following people."

I got in line with the others and showed her my receipt. Then I returned to my place in the graduation line. I do not know what happened to the young lady. I never looked back to see what happened to her.

We marched into the auditorium. They did not even play "Pomp and Circumstances?" I just loved that song. That was the best part of graduation. I was pissed but I put on my good face and continued. I was looking around for my family; they were on the opposite side from me. The professors were in the middle as if they were the ones graduating. I took my seat and looked at the program. I spotted my name, Angela Renee Franklin, Bachelor of Science. I continued reading and saw Angela Renee Franklin, School of Education. I thought to myself, *I ought to participate in the two o'clock graduation.*

It was finally time for them to call the graduates. I got ready to step on stage. I straighten my gown and mortarboard.

Someone announced, "Angela Renee Franklin, Bachelors of Science."

I took a step and listened to the applause. My family members were loud. I loved it.

"Angie, Angie turn around." Serena and Aunt Grace both yelled.

Oh yes, I turned and posed. I did not know why the professor and school photographer were looking at me. I was not moving until all of my family got my picture. Michael got two. I waved to everybody before I walked off stage. You know the professors were even standing and applauding for me. It was my stage. I had done it, graduated, and in only three years.

LIFETIME

After the graduation, we were taking pictures. My father was standing there grinning. He was in every picture. I was going to cut his ass right off the picture when I got them back. And pay him back $140,000 and fifty cents. I never did the calculation though. That would be enough to pay him back. He would be more than happy with that.

We had a wonderful dinner. My grandmother cooked all the food. She made all of my favorites. We had chicken and dressing, ham, fried fish, greens, black-eyed peas, potato salad, peach cobbler, sock-it-to me cake, and tea. Everyone sat around all afternoon but I continued ignoring Bernie Hue. Although, I could tell he did not care.

I was hoping Aunt Grace bought me an aquarium. She would not tell me what she got. I told her what I wanted. I knew she had it. Aunt Grace loved me so much, maybe more than her own children. Well, just as much. She prayed for me to be born on her birthday. Aint that special, for someone to ask God to allow you to be born on their day? I loved me some Aunt Grace.

***

Michael and I packed up our stuff and headed to Dallas. On the way home, it dawned on Michael that his GPA was too low to receive his grant. Michael slammed his hand across the steering wheel. "Damn. I am not going to be able to come back next semester."

I was happy about that, because Michael would not be there without me. Then all of a sudden, I remembered why I had graduated early, Charles Jeffrey. What was wrong with me? Why was I tripping about him, with Michael sitting right next to me? Michael was taking me to Six Flags later on that night. Why did I still believe that Charles was the man for me? Babyface said it best in his song, "Why Does It Hurt So Bad." I needed to do what Charles asked me to do

LIFETIME

all those years ago and forget I ever knew him. I turned to Michael, "So Michael, what are you going to do about school?"

Michael replied, "I guess I am going to take two classes at El Centro Community College and work. You see since I am a transfer student, I only need fifteen hours, but the last nine have to be taken in Commerce. I sure hate to stop, but I can't afford to come back without the grant. My parents are not sending me to school. I am paying my own way."

"Do you need help from me?" I asked.

"No, just your love and support."

"You got it baby." I replied.

That night, as we were leaving for Six Flags, Project Boy sped by in his mother's car. I looked at Michael and said. "That guy is crazy. Just ignore him. If he doesn't stop, I am going to have him shot."

All Michael said was, "I see."

Although, I never paid my dad back the money that I owed him. I grew up the day he refused to give me five dollars. I was angry at first for a long time, but in time, I started to pay my own way. I started by paying my own telephone bill, then my car insurance, and then my life insurance. At some point, my dad told my mom to ask me to pay the rent. My mother let me decide how much. She hated to ask me, but my dad said that if she did not he would.

I paid her $40 a month and never minded paying her the money, because I was planning to pay my dad back all of his money. She used the money to pay off my school loan. Little by little, I was learning responsibility.

LIFETIME

My dad and I never discussed that call and I never told my mom about it. From that very day, I have never expected anyone to pay my way. I thanked God for my dad not giving me those five dollars. It made me a much better person. I loved my Dad. He was so smart.

LIFETIME

Living for the Weekend

I was a college graduate with no job or plan. I went from company to company looking for a job; you name it I was there. I didn't have a clue of how or where to look for a job. Finally, I took a job at a local department store. I figured that would be a good job until I could land me a real job in my field of study. Once on my day off, I went to a job fair that sent me on an interview in Lubbock, Texas. My friend was no longer living in Lubbock. It was a dreary looking town and I was not excited about the job being in West Texas. I was not offered the job, which made Michael happy. He said he did not want to lose another woman to the West Texas plains.

I returned to the department store to sell Christmas decorations. The book department was next to ours. One day, a middle-aged white couple needed help with purchasing a calculator. I went to get a key for the calculators, since they were in a locked cabinet and when I returned, the sales person for that department was helping them. I observed him showing the calculators, obviously ignorant of the product. I interrupted. "Excuse me; before you buy that calculator, what are you going to use the calculator for?"

The man answered, "It is a Christmas gift for our daughter."

"What I mean sir is what type of calculator is needed? Is it for a class?"

He responded, "Yes, she's taking a class."

The sales associate interrupted, "Excuse me, but I am helping them. " He continued showing them the calculator.

He was on commission sales and wanted me to go away, but I thought that I knew more about calculators than he did and said. "If you sell them the wrong calculator they will return it."

LIFETIME

I turned to the customer and said, "I am sorry to be a bother to you both." I turned and went back to selling Christmas cards and ornaments.

In a short time, the man came over to where I was and whispered. "How do you know so much?"

I smiled and told him that I was a recent college graduate that had to have a specific calculator for a statistics class.

The couple turned to leave and the guy stopped suddenly and said. "Our daughter is taking statistics next semester. Where can we get one of those calculators?"

I smiled and whispered, "Do you know someone that works at Texas Instruments (TI)? If so ask them to get you a TI SR55-A. They are thirty-five dollars. Otherwise, you can buy them at any TI store for $150. All of the calculators here are over a hundred dollars and are junk. All they do is add, subtract, multiply, and divide. You don't even need a calculator for that."

The middle-aged man extended his hand and said. "Let me shake your hand. Quit this job tomorrow. Do not stay here. Promise me you will not stay here."

"I promise." I shook his hand and nodded my head in agreement.

A few weeks later, the white couple returned to the store. They pulled me aside and said, "Our daughter needed the exact calculator that you said. We paid thirty-five dollars like you said. She sends her thanks. In addition, remember, what I said. Quit this job." He pulled his wallet from his pocket, removed his business card and handed it to me. "Here is my business card call me if you ever need me."

The next week I quit my job. The man was right. I would look for a job after Christmas. During the holidays, I took Michael to meet my grandmother. She seemed to like him, but as we were leaving, Michael noticed Charles' picture on the wall right by the door.

LIFETIME

Michael turned to my grandmother and said. "Mrs. Franklin, may I ask why you have Charles Jeffrey's picture hanging up here?"

My grandmother replied. "Now, look Michael, you seem like a nice young man. However, Charles is my friend. Now, if you want to give me a picture of yourself, I will consider hanging it up, but do not touch my stuff. Okay?" She smiled and pushed her glasses up on her face.

"No problem, Mrs. Franklin. I would never bother anything in your home. It was very nice meeting you." He hesitated for a moment. "I think I will pass on possibly having my picture hanging next to Charles Jeffrey's. Take care." Michael said as he exited the door.

Once in the car I said to Michael. "My grandmother likes you and it was good that you did not mess with her stuff. Why don't we go by Mrs. Thompson's? She lives right around the corner."

As soon as we got to Mrs. Thompson's house her first question was, "So Michael, what are your intentions with Angela?"

Michael replied with confidence, "Mrs. Thompson, all I can say is my intentions are honorable."

Mrs. Thompson folded her arms and said shaking her head up and down. "Well Michael, be assured. I will be watching you." She extinguished her cigarette.

***

After the New Year, I began looking for my new career. I called everyone except the white guy.

I was referred to Computer Incorporated (CI) by a friend, but I was not interested since I heard that was where Charles Jeffery worked. Somehow, this brother got my number and called

LIFETIME

me for an interview. He kept asking me to come on the interview, but I declined. The thought of seeing Charles Jeffrey everyday was more than I could take.

I ran out of ideas so I took my last resort and went to an agency where you paid them to find you a job. I filled out the contract and left. While leaving I noticed the bank next door and decided to see if they were hiring. They had an opening and gave me an interview for a file clerk in the bookkeeping department. In the interview, I realized they were not going to hire me. That pissed me off. They wanted someone with more of a math background. They implied I didn't have any experience, and in the next breath, they said I was over qualified.

I went off, but oh so eloquently. "I thought you have an opening that has been vacant for a month. It is my understanding that you are an Equal Opportunity Employer. Therefore, based on the job posting I do not need any experience. Since, I do have a college degree; filing should be something I can do. Also, what basis are you making the judgment that I do not have a mathematics background? How do you know that I don't have any experience? You have not asked to see my resume." I raised my resume up. Then continued, "The best qualified is the one that should be hired. If I am over qualified, you cannot discriminate on me for that. It is up to me to decide whether this job is beneath me, not you. And yes, I will move on if I get a better opportunity. You would too." I crossed my leg over the other and sat back in my seat. "However, if you discriminate against me, you will see me in court. Now, do you have any questions for me?"

"Yes, do you have a math background?" The white male interviewer asked.

"Yes, I do." I said un-crossing my legs as I sat straight in the seat.

He said. "Well, Miss Franklin, I am a graduate of ETSU also. Are you familiar with Business Math 175?"

LIFETIME

"Yes, I am familiar with that class. I took that class."

He asked, "What did you make?"

"I received an 'A' as a freshman and tutored football players that were taking the class. And, by the way, I made an 'A' in business math 218, 'A' in College algebra, 'B+' in statistics. What else would you like to know? Would you like to see my transcript?"

"No that would not be necessary. We will review your application and get back with you."

I was mad when I left but surely didn't want to file checks. However, I accepted the job to file checks on a daily basis for $550 per month.

After months of check filing, the Minority Women's Placement office called asking me to go on a job interview. It was scheduled for the next day. The next morning I called in sick. The interview was scheduled for 10:00 in the morning. I went downtown to the placement office first to pick up the referral sheet. I went back to my car and it would not start. Therefore, I had to catch a taxi to arrive to the interview on time.

All I had was five dollars and the fare had reached $4.75 a block from the interview. I screamed for the driver to stop and I got out of the car. I needed to ask for my quarter back but the cab driver looked as though he would fight me if I did. It was about nine forty-five when I arrived and there were at least three other minority women waiting. We tried to chitchat, but it was all so phony. We all knew we were competing for the same job.

They were called before me and were only there for a few minutes. Then, I was called. This again was going to be short. I could tell this was definitely a quota job. They didn't care who it was, as long as it was a minority woman.

LIFETIME

The interviewer glanced at my resume and stated that it was in order. He went on to say they would review my application and select the best three for a follow up interview. He said my resume was not any better than the others and he ended the interview. He stood up to dismiss me. I sat back in the chair and said. "Oh, I have a few questions." I was not going to let him throw me out that easily. "Exactly what is this job?"

"Sales," he said as he sat back down.

I nodded my head and said. "I see, what type of training will there be?"

After he answered that question, I continued, "Is there any travel?"

The guy said there would be two months of training in Atlanta and the job would be selling mainframe computers. There was a base salary with commissions. I was very interested. After he answered all my questions the interview was concluded, but not before, I made him shake my hand and thanked him for the interview.

When I left, it was about eleven. I went to the cafeteria; I didn't know why, because I didn't have any money. I asked a cashier was there a bus stop close by. She wasn't sure. The interview was over, but my car was downtown and I had no money. I walked to the bank next door to cash a check.

It was July and over 100 degrees. I was wearing a three-pieced navy blue suit, crisp white shirt, with three inched heels. The bus stop sign was leaning as if someone had started to take it down.

I waited for what seemed like hours for the bus to come and finally, a black guy in an old beat up pick up truck stopped at the light and asked me if I wanted a ride downtown. I agreed and got in. Just as I was closing the door, a voice said, "Get out." I immediately jumped out of the truck and waved for the guy to go on.

LIFETIME

In a couple of days, they called for me to come back for a second interview. I returned, took a test and proceeded with the interviews. Anyway, it was just me and another sister. What was funny, as I was leaving, I heard her ask the lady in the cafeteria about the bus stop outside. I thought DeJa Vu. I went back to work, back to filing checks.

***

A few months later, Monica my old roommate from college came to Dallas and spent a few days with me. We went by my grandmother's house for a visit. As we were leaving, Monica noticed that Charles Jeffrey's picture was on a shelf by the door.

Monica had the nerve to turn Charles' picture down and replied. "You need to take this picture down."

Now why she thought she had it like that I did not know. I knew grandmother was going to let her have it.

My grandmother said to Monica, "Now, what you need to do is get out of my house and never come back. Do not touch my friend Charles' picture." My grandmother stood the picture back up not looking at Monica.

"But grandmother," Monica replied. "Angela has a new boyfriend now, Michael."

My grandmother snapped, "I don't care. Charles is my friend and you are no longer welcomed in my home. And I am not your grandmother!"

My grandmother was walking toward her and I stepped in between them and said. "Bye Grandmother. We are going now. Just ignore Monica. She is crazy." I kissed my grandmother on the cheek and turned to push Monica out the door.

"I know she is crazy and I never want to see that ugly girl again."

LIFETIME

"Okay, Grandmother, but remember it was Monica that touched your picture and not me. Love you." I said.

"Love you too, but watch the company you keep." Grandmother said.

I said to Monica, "Let's go, girl, before you get me killed."

"But I don't understand why she is mad at me?" Monica had a questioning look on her face.

"Why did you touch her stuff?" I asked.

"Well, I I . . ."

I interrupted, "Well, you messed up. She is through with you. Now shut up and get in the car."

My grandmother told the whole family what Monica did. I knew she would. She was truly hurt. It was if Monica had physically cut her. I tried to tell the dumb girl that my grandmother was a piece of work. But no, she thought she could go in her house and do whatever she wanted.

***

A few weeks later, I got another call from the Minority Women's Placement Office to go on a job interview. This time it was for a systems analyst trainee, in my area of education, at a major retailer. The interview was intense and I was nervous when I left. While standing at the elevator, this black chick approached me. She was wearing an orange two-pieced designer suit above the knee that showed off her great legs. Her shoes were matching tapestry pumps. She was smoking a cigarette with perfectly manicured orange polished nails. She made my navy three-pieced Casual Corner's suit look shabby standing next to her, but at least my shoulder

LIFETIME

length layered cut was flawless. I wanted her to go away. I did not want to start fraternizing with her in the hall before I could even be hired.

"Hi, what's your name?" She asked.

"Angela." I said as I pushed the elevator button again.

"I'm Diahann."

Not looking up I said, "Hi, Diahann."

Diahann said, "Girl, calm down. You got the job."

I looked around to see if any of the interviewers were looking and said. "I hope I did, but I don't know." I kept pushing the elevator button but the elevator would not come. I thought she had done something to detain the elevator. I did not want them to see me talking to her. The elevator finally came, I got on and she extinguished her cigarette and followed me. During the ride, she asked me where I was from and stated that she was from Houston. As I exited the elevator on the first floor Diahann shouted, "Angela, I'll see you in three weeks."

"I hope so." I shyly said as I rushed away.

Three weeks later, I was a professional. Diahann came to personnel to welcome me on the first day, this time she was dressed in a red two-pieced designer suit, with matching nails, shoes, and lipstick. Her shoulder length hair was flawless. My salary had doubled, but I had to pass the 13-week training. I wasn't worried, until the first day they told me to read an entire book in less than a week, plus two case studies, and eight utilities.

A few weeks later, Michael had a party at his apartment clubhouse. I invited Serena, Cynthia, Faye and my new friend Diahann to the party. The party was on the same night as my cousin's birthday and I decided I could do both. But, what happened was, I kept drinking, and drinking, and drinking. When I left her party, I knew I was too lit to drive so I called Mac who lived close by. I spent the night at his house. He was divorced. And we kicked it every now and then.

I knew that Michael would never bust me, because he was at his own party. What I didn't know was how pissed he would be that I didn't attend his party. Michael and all of my friends were mad at me.

***

By Christmas 1980, I decided that if Michael and I didn't get engaged for Christmas I was going to start dating other people. Christmas day, Michael gave me a gorgeous diamond watch. I was hurt, but I loved the watch. I told Michael that we had been dating for four years and I was ready for a commitment. He said that he was not ready to get married, but he did love me. So I told him that I was going to date other people and stop wasting my time with him exclusively. Michael never responded, but it didn't matter, I was moving on.

By January, my grandmother was ill. She had surgery and was not doing well. I went to the hospital to see her. She was talking out of her head.

"Hello, Grandmother." I said as I entered her hospital room.

She did not respond.

So my mother said. "Mrs. Jewell, Angie is here and said hello."

Grandmother said. "I don't care. I don't want to see her."

I was devastated that she was not happy to see me. Additionally, at that time I didn't do hospitals. How could my grandmother say that to me? I was so hurt. I sat in a chair at the foot of the bed just looking. I had this latch hook rug kit with me and decided to start hooking the rug. All day I was bothered by what my grandmother said earlier. I kept hooking. I sat in that

LIFETIME

chair for hours wondering why she did not love me. Finally, I asked, "Grandmother you don't want to see me?"

She said, "Yes, baby, I want to see you. You know I love you Angie."

I said to her, "But you said that you didn't want to see me earlier."

"I didn't say that. I would never say that." Grandmother replied.

I was so happy knowing that she loved me, but I didn't move. I was smiling and hooking away. I was stuck to the chair, afraid to move. I needed help to get out of the chair before my grandmother changed her mind about loving me again. She was talking out of her head. She talked to her mother and stepmother, both had died many years before. I was scared but could not move. Therefore, I kept hooking.

Later that night, Uncle Jr. came to the hospital to relieve my mother. Somehow, Grandmother got Uncle Jr. in a chokehold. She had him by the tie and arms in a full nelson.

Uncle Jr. was begging me to help him. I was sitting there latching away. He gasped, "Angie, help me?"

I answered while hooking, "I wish I could help you, Uncle Jr."

"Help me?" He was trying to say.

However, Grandmother had him and she was choking him to death. I was in shock. With bucked eyes I was hooking away. Not able to move to help him. I wanted to get up and run out of the room. I was petrified, but I had comfort in knowing my grandmother loved me. That was all that mattered. I didn't move.

About that time, the nurse came in and helped get him loose. He was so mad at me. He ran over to me rubbing his throat. "Angie, why didn't you try to help me?"

Looking down at the yarn, all I could say was. "Sorry, Uncle Jr."

LIFETIME

She was really about to choke him to death. They put my grandmother in a straight jacket but I never moved. Sitting there as if everything was okay and hooking all the while.

Finally, my cousin realized that I needed help. She helped me out of the chair and took me to the waiting room. I was so thankful for her. I had been stuck there all day, numb and helpless.

The next day my grandmother died. I left work immediately when I got the news. As I was walking to my car, I thought, I saw Charles Jeffrey going into the parking lot. But, I decided it could not have been Charles Jeffrey.

Michael drove my cousins and me to the funeral. It was a sad day but I had some comfort in knowing that my grandmother loved me. After the funeral, I heard my cousins whispering about how well I had done at our grandmother's funeral. I was looking out the window. I turned and said. "Are yall talking about me?"

They tried to ignore me at first and finally Paula said. "You did real well today Angela."

"What?" I asked a little pissed with them.

"Well, we just knew you would be falling all out and stuff but you did not." Paula replied.

I looked at them and said, "Aint nothing but God and He aint through with me yet."

About one week after the funeral, I saw Charles Jeffrey working as a technician, in the computer room. He approached me. I hated his ass. Cheating on me and then breaking up with me. Who did he think he was? I ran and got Diahann, to show her the dog. "Remember that face. We don't like him. He is the dog that broke my heart." She agreed to hate him also.

The following month, Michael helped me move into my first apartment. It was a nice place. I was apprehensive about telling my parents about the apartment, but they were cool with

LIFETIME

it. They did not want me to move when I was working at the bank. I asked my dad why he didn't wanted me to move earlier.

Daddy said, "You were not ready and you would have come back home. You are ready now. I feel confident that you will stay gone."

I felt good about my move.

Let's Get Married Today

I had been in my apartment a few weeks and Michael had been coming around a lot. One night during the middle of the week, Mac came by my new apartment and we went a movie. It was his turn to pick the movie. He wanted to see a Japanese western film. The movie was full of subtitles not one word of English. He went on and on about the cinematography and this and that. All I could say was "What the hell were they talking about? The whole movie was in Japanese."

We laughed about the movie and went back to my apartment. We could not agree on where to eat dinner. We argued over steak, chicken, or fish. He liked breakfast, but I was not a breakfast person. I hated eggs. So while we were in my apartment discussing what we would eat. There was a knock at the door. I thought to myself, *it had better not be Michael.*

"Who is it?" I asked.

"Michael." The voice from the other side of the door said.

Damn! Why was he here? I should have let him stand outside. But, I opened the door and said. "What?"

"What the hell is going on here?" Michael asked as he stepped inside my apartment.

"What do you mean? I am on a date. I'll talk to you later." I said as I tried to block him from coming any further.

"Like hell you will." Michael said with arrogance.

What was I going to do? Mac was violent sometimes. I knew he had a 357 magnum somewhere close by. He had a black belt in karate and was crazy.

LIFETIME

Michael on the other hand was 5 feet 10 inches and weighed about 135 pounds soaking wet. He was strong, but coming in there talking crazy was out of character for him. I did not want any trouble. I said, "Michael, we are getting ready to leave do you mind?"

He took his jacket off and threw it on the sofa. "Hell yeah, I mind. Man, why are you here with my woman? Do you have a woman?"

"No, because I don't want to be in any shit like this." Mac said as he looked at me with disgust.

What was I going to do? I could tell Mac was not only irritated with Michael, he was pissed at me.

"Man you got to go," Michael said as he stepped toward Mac.

I stepped closer to Michael and said, "Michael, you can't come in here and put my guest out. You need to leave."

"I am not going no damn where." Michael replied.

Mac spoke up, "I tell you what, I am going to leave before someone gets hurt." He handed me Stevie's new album and a bottle of wine.

Michael snatched the album out of my hand and put the album in Mac's face. "Take this shit with you?"

I snatched the album from Michael and shouted. "Shut up Michael." Michael stared at me, and Mac looked at me with disgust. I didn't know what to do. I wanted Michael to leave.

Mac shook his head and said to me, "I'll call you later." He turned to go to the door.

"Macias, I am sorry. You don't have to leave, Macias." I only called him Macias when I was very serious.

Mac opened the door and turned to me, "I must. Take care." He was gone.

LIFETIME

I closed the door and never turned around. I did not want Mac to leave, but I didn't want any trouble.

Michael said. "Angela, why was he here? Who is he anyway?" His voice started to rise. "All this time, all I have ever heard you talk about is Charles Jeffrey. Who the hell was that?"

I still had not turned around. "Why? He was my guest."

"If anybody had ever told me you were cheating on me. I would not have believed it. Just put a knife in my heart and turn it. I never thought you would cheat on me. Not you." Michael said as he walked away to sit on the sofa.

"I am not cheating. I told you I was tired of wasting my time on you and that I was going to see other people. Just go, Michael." I turned and walked into my bedroom. He was taking every step I took. "Just go."

"No, make me understand, why he was here. Tell me he was a figment of my imagination. Tell me something. Please!"

"Tell you what?" I raised my hands questioning him.

Michael said, "I was sitting out in the car and the lights were off in your apartment and then…"

I interrupted him, "You were spying on me?"

"No, but why did he have wine? Have you two been fucking? Come here let me smell you?"

"Stop, Michael. Go home."

"No, and anyway, why is it I busted you, but I am the one doing all of the explaining?"

"There is nothing to explain. Leave me alone. Go home!"

"I am not going home until you make me understand." He kept rambling.

LIFETIME

"You understand. Go home. You have been hollering at me all night. I have to go to work shortly. Leave!" I cried.

Michael pleaded, "No, baby, I love you. Mac, Charles, and no other nigga is taking you away from me. If you want to get married, I am ready."

"Oh hell no, don't pull that married shit on me now."

"I do love you, and I realize that now. I am ready to get married. Marry me baby."

"No."

"Baby, please, marry me." Michael kneeled and reached for my hands.

"No and since you will not go home I am going to bed." I went into my bedroom and slammed the door. I was so tired. I could not believe he had behaved that way.

"Lord, Thank you for this day. Forgive me for my sins. Thank you for there not being too much trouble here tonight. Amen."

The alarm went off at seven, I was so tired after only getting a few hours of sleep. I stumbled into the kitchen to make coffee and was startled to see Michael sitting on my sofa. I questioned why he was still there.

Michael never turned to face me but responded, "Because we did not finish talking last night."

I ignored him and continued with my coffee. My head was hurting, no sleep and no dinner. I rubbed my head and then my stomach.

Michael stood and approached me in the kitchen. He looked into my eyes. "Angela, have you ever loved me? Be honest."

"Yes." I whispered and looked down.

"Then marry me. You wanted to get married just three months ago."

LIFETIME

"I did, but…" I stuttered.

Michael interrupted, not letting go of my hands. "But, I told you I was not ready. When I saw you with another guy, I knew, I didn't want to lose you. I love you. I have loved you from our first study sessions. I love your dirty drawers. You are my horse if you never win a race. Marry me, Angela?"

"I will." I said in a whisper. A single tear fell from my eye.

"I love you." Michael smiled, "Come straight home so I can buy you a ring tonight. I love you, Angela Renee Franklin." Michael said with wide eyes and a smile.

I went to work wondering if I should marry him.

The next day, Michael purchased me an engagement ring. I loved my ring. We were a happily engaged couple by the weekend. I only had one regret; I had not apologized to Mac. I should have called him.

I could not wait to tell Faye and Serena that Michael and I were getting married. However, Faye surprised me with her reaction.

"Angie, why are you marrying him?" Faye said to me over the phone.

"Because I love him and he loves me." I replied.

"You don't seem to love him like you loved Charles Jeffrey. I never actually met Charles, but you loved that man with all your heart. I think you still do."

"That's just it Faye, I never want to hurt like I did when he left me. I did love him and never want to love anyone more than they love me. Michael loves me so much I can't help but love him back."

"Are you sure?" She asked.

LIFETIME

"Yes, I am. I really love him and I know he is good for me. We will be fine. Michael helped me see it is irrational to keep hoping for something that will never be. He helped me understand that love does not hurt. I am not hurting anymore. This is real love. I went to God and asked him for someone to love me for me. He sent me Michael. Michael is everything I want in a man. I now realize that even though I loved Charles, he is not the one that God put here for me. I have gotten over Charles and know my treasure is in Michael. Faye, I am happy and I am sure this is an everlasting love."

Faye said. "I am happy for you then. I love you and wanted to make sure you were not getting married just to get married."

"No, I would never do that. I love you too and want you to be my maid of honor in my wedding."

For some reason it was several months before I called Mac.

"Hello." Mac answered.

"Hey, it's Angela. Are you busy?"

"No, Angie. How are you?"

"I am good. I am calling to apologize for the incident that happened when you came over to my apartment."

"No problem." Mac responded.

"I didn't want you leave that night." I hesitated for a second. "But, I am also calling to tell you I am engaged."

"What? I didn't think you wanted to get married. Had I known that, I would have asked you a long time ago." Mac said with a chuckle.

"That's sweet, but I love him."

LIFETIME

Mac responded and said, "I really care for you, Angela. You are good for me."

"You will be fine, Macias. I know you care for me, but that is not enough for me. I need you to love me. I need to love you. We don't have that. What we have is a mutual admiration for each other and we enjoy each other's company. The fact that we have not talked for five months is an indication that we are fine without each other. I am sorry for what happened, though."

Mac said, "You know we just may get together again." He paused and said. "Have you ever seen the movie, Same Time Next Year?"

"I don't think so." I said trying to remember if I had seen the movie.

"Alan Alda and some actress are both married to other people and they meet every year and have a one week affair." He laughed. "Be happy. You are special. I hope he makes you happy."

"Thank you, I am happy. Bye Mac."

"So long, maybe I'll see you the same time next year."

"You are funny. Take care." I said.

***

It was September 12, 1981 the weather was overcast on my wedding day. I wore my hair in an up-do with curls in the front and curls hanging down in the back. It was quite simple. Not too much, make up. My dress was white. The dress had a high yoke with a boat cut lace neckline. The bottom of the dress was layers of chiffon. It had a long train. The sleeves were long with a tapered 'V' at the wrist. The 'V' went down to the middle finger. There were eight buttons on the sleeves. The inner sleeve had lace cut diamonds and the outer sleeve was puffed and sheer.

LIFETIME

I didn't know how hard it would be to come down the aisle with my father. We both were pigeon toed and walking on that aisle runner was next to impossible. My dad had been drinking and I had taken so much medicine I was not feeling any pain. We finally made it to the altar.

The pastor did not say what we were expecting him to say. It sounded to me like I was marrying my dad. All I could think of, was he was reading from a book so it must be in there. Finally, he got to who gives this woman away. My dad did his thing and kissed me. Finally, we were getting married to each other. My pastor was long winded. We had an altar prayer and finally to the good part. "You can now kiss your bride."

Michael laid one on me. It was a great kiss. I think we forgot for a moment we were at the wedding. People were laughing and clapping. The pastor blessed our union with prayer and we went outside to the recessional.

I begged my mom not to cry as she always did. She didn't, but I did. By the time she got outside, I was crying uncontrollable. Michael was asking what was wrong with me. I tried to explain that everyone was looking at me saying God bless you child. As if it was the worse thing, you could have ever done. I got myself together, and we took a lot of pictures. When we finished we left for the reception. We arrived at the reception, which was held at the community center in my neighborhood. It was nice. There were so many people.

I loved the receiving line. I didn't want the night to end. Michael kept telling me to quit kissing all of the men. I told him he must be out of his mind. That was what brides did at their weddings. I did not understand why he was tripping. I totally ignored him and enjoyed every moment of the evening.

LIFETIME

That was the best day of my life, my wedding and all of the attention on me. How could I ever have that again? That was the only sad part. It would never happen again. I asked God to let the day go by slowly. *Thank you for the blessings of this wedding.*

Memories

About one month after our wedding, Michael and I went to our college homecoming. While at the game, I literally ran into Charles Jeffrey as I ran to the restroom.

"Hello, Angela." Charles said to me.

"Hi." I said as I rushed into the ladies room.

When I returned to the stands, Charles was standing in the breezeway. It appeared he was waiting on me. Charles said, "Angela, how are you doing?"

I smiled and said, "I am fine and I got married."

He smiled and said, "Congratulations."

I appreciated his well wishes and went on my way. I was truly over him. I knew it and I believed he knew it too. I returned to join my husband in the stands. Charles sat a few seats behind us. Michael never said a word.

***

Michael and I were living in our first apartment and every time someone came over, Michael pointed out I had a picture of Charles Jeffrey in one of the family albums. The picture came from my grandmother's house after she died. Michael could turn straight to Charles' picture. I thought he was paranoid.

One night, after we were married a couple of years, Michael came home late after being at some club. He woke me up out of a deep sleep and asked me how I could have loved Charles Jeffrey? He was ranting and raving about having seen Charles Jeffrey. I told him to quit tripping and go to bed. Michael was normally very quiet, but that night he was out of control.

LIFETIME

He went to the closet and got the album with Charles' picture. He told me he had all he could take and tore up my picture of Charles.

I was hurt and did not understand why he would want to tear Charles' picture. He knew I loved pictures and that it could not be replaced. Therefore, I got out of bed and picked up the pieces of the picture out of the wastebasket, clutched the pieces to my heart and got back in the bed.

Michael reached across the bed and snatched the pieces from my hand. He picked up a lighter from the dresser and burned the pieces. He sang, "Burn, baby, burn."

I was devastated. I started crying uncontrollably. He looked with questioning eyes. I cried all night long as if he had physically abused me. In trying to console me, he offered some pictures of old girlfriends for me to destroy. I slapped the pictures from his hands and screamed, "I don't care about those pictures. But, you know how I feel about my pictures. You have cut a whole in my heart tonight. They were my memories that I cherished. How could you do this to me?" I continued sobbing well into the morning. Michael began to rub my back that was turned to him. He apologized for hurting me. But, he was not sorry for burning the pictures. I never understood how he could have done that to me and he never understood how I felt.

***

One February, Monica was in town and she asked me to meet her at a fraternity party. I arrived only to see Charles Jeffrey as I entered. He approached me as soon as I walked through the door. I was short with him because the sight of him irritated me. While he was talking, I was looking at him trying to determine what I had seen in him and why had I loved him so much. I couldn't see the attraction and still wanted to hurt him. I could not understand my feelings

LIFETIME

because I loved Michael and knew he loved me. I looked for Monica and told her that I was not feeling well and I left. I went home to make love to my husband.

It was the spring of 1984 and I was pregnant and had been spotting. I had a sonogram, which showed the fetus was not viable. I had to have a DNC. I didn't even cry. I didn't feel anything. Michael tried holding me in his arms, but I did not want to be held. I was so empty.

A few days after my surgery, I went to the hospital to visit my grandfather, my dad's father. He and my grandmother divorced a while before. He had cancer. Grandpa was a tall, lean, dark skinned man and handsome. He was somewhat quiet. He always seemed to enjoy talking to me. We were close. When I came to the hospital, he started consoling me for the loss of my baby. I tried to convince him I was okay.

My grandfather lived about six weeks longer. He died two days before my birthday, on Diahann's birthday. At the cemetery, I was standing next to Gary and he asked me. "Are you okay?"

I nodded and said yes, as we stood at the back of the tent.

Gary said to me in a muffled voice. "Mama told me you lost your baby. I am sorry."

I thanked him.

Gary said as he put his arm around my shoulder, "I love you."

We were holding our conversation at the actual burial. While everyone else was in heavy grief, I smiled at my brother and said, "Do you really love me?"

He hugged me and said, "Yes, you are my only sister." My brother smiled, with that infectious smile that he had.

I put my arm around his waist and we rocked from side to side, in our own little world. Not hearing a word the minister said. It was a special moment. My brother loved me.

LIFETIME

The following month we had a birthday party for my dad. Gary bought him a weed eater. Weed eaters were relatively new at that time. That was the first time my brother had purchased his own gift without me paying and picking the gift. Gary was so anxious to show our dad how the thing worked. He went to get gas for it. I told him to calm down there was no hurry but I did not know this would be the last time I would see my brother alive.

Gary was killed Saturday, just three days after my dad's party on July 21, 1984, from a car accident. They say he went to sleep. How could that be, my younger brother dead at 24? I knew my mom was glad he accepted Christ and was baptized a few months prior to his death.

At Gary's funeral, I did not shed one tear. During the whole funeral, I heard Gary saying. "Angie, please do not embarrass me? Please don't cry? I hate it when you cry at funerals. Remember, I love you. Make me proud."

I prayed, "Lord help me to be strong. I do not want to be an embarrassment to my brother. He loved me and never asked me for anything." I held my head up high and I prayed my dad would not cry. *Lord, give my dad strength today.*

When my dad and mom went to view his body, my mom looked so pitiful. However, my dad got strength from somewhere. My dad said, "Lord, thank you for loaning him to us for a little while."

I thought to myself. *Look at God work. I can do all things through Christ Jesus who strengthens me.*

***

A few months later, I was pregnant again, still not over the deaths of my baby, grandfather, or brother. One day, while I was working and talking on the telephone with Serena, I felt a change in my body. I got off the phone and went to the restroom. It was if my entire

LIFETIME

insides came out. It felt as if my baby had been flushed down the toilet. I called the doctor and was told to come to the hospital immediately. They did an emergency DNC.

Michael and my parents arrived before the surgery began. My dad was crying, but I didn't cry. The hurt in my dad's eyes was all I could take.

After I went home, I thought I would never be able to have a baby. I asked Michael, if we should adopt. He did not want to adopt. I wondered if this was my punishment for having had an abortion. I was so sad, but I couldn't cry.

The following Sunday, I woke up knowing the Lord had a word for me. I called Faye and asked her to go to church with me. She agreed and came to get me.

At church, my pastor got up to preach his text, "When a woman cries in the midnight hour." He repeated the text, "When a woman cries in the midnight hour."

It was midnight when I looked at the clock the night before. I had gotten out of the bed and went in the living room to cry. I did not want Michael to know I was crying. I was crying and praying, real quiet like.

My pastor preached, "When a woman cries in the midnight hour. She doesn't want anyone to know that she is crying. She is having a serious talk with the Lord. A woman crying, at other times mean different things. A woman crying in the morning is with joy. Oh, but at the midnight hour, she is hurting in her spirit."

"Oh my God, speak, Pastor!" I cried out.

He broke it down on why a woman cries in the midnight hour. He spoke on God's promise to Abraham. How he promised Abraham that Sarah would give birth to a son. He talked about how Sarah did not have faith in God. She was an old woman and thought it would be impossible to conceive. Therefore, she tried to fix it on her own. Sarah gave her maidservant

Hagar to Abraham, her husband, and they conceived Ishmael. Sarah despised Hagar. He went

on to say that, we try to fix things ourselves, just as Sarah tried to do. However, if we would just

let God do His work we would be better off. God promised Abraham a son with his wife Sarah.

Sarah did conceive and gave birth to Isaac.

Thank you Lord. I get it. This is your business and I need to step back and let you do

your work. I shouted all up and down the aisles that day, because I truly got a word from the

Lord. "Ouch."

***

Four months later, I was pregnant again and my dad was so happy on becoming a

grandfather. My dad immediately called his sister, Grace, to tell her about the pregnancy. He

told her my mom was doing laundry each week. Diahann was cooking twice a week and then

asked her what was she going to do.

Aunt Grace said to my dad, "Boy I have already been going over there every week

cleaning her apartment. The question is what are you going to do?"

He laughed and said. "I am her manager and my job is to make sure whatever she needs

gets done."

They both laughed. However, for the next several months Michael, my mom, dad, Aunt

Grace, Diahann, Serena, and Faye would not let me do anything.

Three months into my pregnancy, I was doing well. Michael decided he was going to

Houston with some friends. He told me this in front of Aunt Grace. I wanted to discuss this trip

later, after Aunt Grace went home. Aunt Grace agreed with Michael that it sounded like a good

idea. They kept saying that I had been to Houston without him after Gary died. It was not the

same.

LIFETIME

Everyone got in on this. My dad said that I was wrong. Even Faye said that I was wrong. I could not tell any of them the real reason that I did not want him to go. The real reason was that I had the strangest feeling that he would not survive the trip. I thought that if I said what the reason was that would somehow make it come true. I couldn't tell anybody why he couldn't go. I tried making him feel guilty, leaving his pregnant wife. So finally, I just told him he could not go. I thought he understood that I was serious about him not going.

He obviously, did not understand because he went to Houston, anyway. I did not know with whom and he had not left me any money. My fear of the trip turned into anger. I was so mad that he went without my approval. Michael called late that Friday night saying that he had arrived in Houston. He told me the hotel they were staying in and gave me the telephone number. I was so pissed that and I did not write down any of the information. It was a long weekend. My mom wanted to hang out with me, but I wasn't having that. I wanted to be home alone in my misery.

The following Sunday, around four the telephone rang. It was my mom saying that my dad had been in a car wreck and that he was being transported to the hospital by helicopter. I went straight to the hospital. My dad's neck was broken. He was paralyzed. He was in good spirits except he was cold. All of my uncles started showing up to the hospital. They all had the same question. "Where is Michael?" Before I could answer the question, they would respond. "Oh this is the weekend that he went to Houston."

Why did they all think this was funny? But, my dad was hurt and I decided to be mad at Michael later.

My dad was shivering, so the nurses brought him several thermal blankets. Finally, about eight that night he was in intensive care in a Striker Rotary bed. By then Michael, had returned and come to the hospital. I was in the room when Michael entered. My dad laughed with him and they discussed the trip. I was furious with Michael and did not like it that my father thought it was funny.

I could not even look at Michael I was so pissed. I kept pushing the thought of anger back. It seemed so petty to be angry with him. I was pissed off at him because I was wrong about my fears. It all seemed so stupid. *Let it go Angela. Pray for your father's recovery.* But, I could not let it go.

I went back and forth from the hospital to work. I went to the hospital before work. I went at lunch and after work. I wanted to be there to feed my dad. Finally, by Wednesday, I told my manager that I was going on a leave of absence. He did not understand. I told him that I could not explain it, but I had to go.

By Thursday, my dad was moved to a private room and I stayed the whole day. We talked all day long. Friday morning, my mom called and asked me to come to the hospital. My daddy was dead. It had to be a dream.

It was not a dream. Bernie was gone. Bernie Hue, Uncle Bernie, Deacon Franklin, Fat Daddy, my daddy was gone. It seemed to me, that everyone was trying to make me see what my daddy was to them. They said stuff like, "He was my best friend. He was my domino partner. He was my fishing partner. He was my favorite uncle. He was our big brother. He was like our mother and father." All I could think was, he wasn't like a father, he *was* my father. My dad was gone.

When my brother died, I thought of my own mortality. He was my baby brother he was healthy, and strong. I could really die. But now my daddy was gone. I was his baby, his pride

LIFETIME

and joy. He was my hero. I was not thinking about my own mortality, but about my own grief. What was I going to do?

I only remembered some insignificant things from the funeral. I saw Project Boy standing outside my parent's home between where I needed to be before we left for the funeral. I went out of my way to avoid acknowledging him. I wondered why he was there. Why was I so insensitive? I was usually very sensitive towards people's feelings. But, my dad was dead and this was only happening to me. I could not deal with Project Boy at that time.

I was about three and half months pregnant. I felt all alone. Michael was there and my mom. Serena, Diahann, and Faye were there as well. Serena sat on the left side with the minister's wives. She got up several times to console me. The eulogy was "Bernie said."

Uncle Nate cried like a baby. My cousin Buck screamed out loud and my cousin, Rhonda, screamed out "Uncle Bernie" several times. I got angry with my Uncle Jr. for telling Rhonda to stop crying. Aunt Doris was crying out "Big Bern. Oh Lord what am I going to do?" When my dad died, part of me died, I think the best part of me. I changed. I wanted to drown in my sorrow.

***

Weeks later, Diahann tried to get me to go the movies with her. I couldn't do it. People would say let's do something to take your mind off it. I didn't want to take my mind off it. I couldn't understand how my relatives could go on with their lives. Mother's Day, Father's Day, Memorial Day, Fourth of July, Labor Day why were they getting together as if everything was okay? Everything was not okay. I was not okay. I lost Angela and wasn't even looking for her.

Serena, Faye, and Diahann were there for me. But, Angela was not there so I don't know how they helped me. They must have prayed for me. I was very selfish, not really concerned

LIFETIME

with anyone else's grief. The only thing that I cared about was my unborn baby. So, I tried to remain calm for my baby to thrive. I was in such bad shape and didn't even know it. I was sure that was one of the times the Lord was carrying me, "His Eye is on the Sparrow and I know he watches me."

LIFETIME

Isn't She Lovely

By my fifth month of pregnancy, my blood count was low and I had lost twenty-five pounds. Down to only eighty five pounds. Most said that I looked well and had hardly gained any weight. But, the doctor was quite concerned. Each month I went to the doctor's I was down by another three pounds.

My doctor prescribed me a multi vitamin, calcium tablets, and iron tablets. He informed me that I had to gain the twenty-five pounds to avoid a transfusion. HIV could not be detected in blood so I could be exposed to HIV. He was concerned and sent me to an Internist to determine my problem.

When the doctor came into the room, he looked at me and said. "I thought Dr. Childress said you were five months pregnant."

I confirmed that I was and he asked me to remove all of my clothes and he left the examining room. The doctor had not left a robe or anything. I removed my clothes and was standing there butt naked, ass out. He came back in the room and started to poke, pinch, and pull on me. I was just standing there. No nurse, just me and him. He touched my back, my legs, my stomach, my shoulders, and my arms. He told me to turn, stoop, and sit. All while he was feeling on me.

The doctor asked, "What did you have for breakfast?"

"Bacon, grits, fruit, and water." I replied.

"What did you have for dinner last night?" He continued poking me and looking over my body.

LIFETIME

I replied, "I had pot roast, mashed potatoes, fried corn, green beans, wheat rolls, and water?"

He never looked in my eyes, "What did you have for lunch on yesterday?"

Why? I wondered but I said. "I had meatloaf, wheat rolls, salad, broccoli, yams, black-eyed peas, and water. I know; what did I have for breakfast on yesterday?"

"Yes." He answered.

"Bacon, grits, oranges, and water."

"Do you drink milk?"

"No, but I am taking eight calcium tablets a day." He hit my knee with a small mallet.

"Do you drink coffee?"

"No, I crave it but I have been avoiding caffeine."

"Do you drink juice?"

"No, I don't like juice."

"Do you drink soda?"

"Normally I do, but the smell of sugar makes me nauseated."

The doctor sat in a stool and said, "Well, I had you take off all of your clothes, because I thought you were anorexic. I can see you are not and you eat like a horse. You would not have been able to hide an eating disorder from me with all of your clothes off. An anorexic or bulimic person would not have any muscle tone. You do have muscle tone. All we can do is monitor your progress. I am going to tell you something I never tell pregnant women. I want you to eat a minimum of five meals a day. Eat liver and beets at least three times a week."

"But I don't like liver or beets." I said wrinkling my noise in disgust.

LIFETIME

"Too bad, eat liver and beets a minimum of three times a week. Eat whatever else you want. Increase you caloric intake by five thousand calories a day. You have to gain weight. If your blood count and weight does not increase, you will have severe problems with delivery. Continue to eat like a horse. Never let yourself get hungry. You can get dressed now." The doctor stood and left the room.

Finally, by my seventh month, I started to gain weight. I gained the original 25 pounds back. I was not only eating, I had a huge appetite.

Six weeks before the baby was expected, I was feeling bad and left work, to go home and lay down. The space shuttle "Challenger" had exploded that week and Rock Hudson had died of AIDS. It was a Thursday. I felt bad all day. I knew eating before the baby was born was not a good thing. I called the doctor and told him how I was feeling. I wanted to know whether I should eat or go to the hospital. The doctor said it sounded as if I had pulled a muscle and that was normal at my stage of pregnancy. He said it was okay to eat and if I wanted to take two Tylenols it would be okay. He then said I could go to the hospital if I wanted.

I asked Michael to get me some pot roast, mashed potatoes, fried corn on the cob, and wheat rolls. He dropped off my order and left to go across town to a club. That made me unhappy and I silently vowed to have the baby while he was gone.

After I ate, I laid down in my bed. I felt horrible, so I decided I would take the Tylenol. But, I only had extra strength and decided against taking them.

I called my mom and asked her to bring me some regular Tylenol. It took her a long time to get to my place. By the time she got there, I had decided to go to the hospital. I knew the Tylenol was not going to help. My mom was relieved to take me to the hospital. She drove the short distance to the hospital. She pulled up to the emergency room and helped me out. Once she helped me inside, she left to move her car.

As the nurse was leading me to the examination room, suddenly Michael was holding my other arm. I was disappointed he made it to the hospital. That was going to be one of those things I would hold over his head for the rest of his life. He had changed his mind about going out and was going home when he saw us turning into the hospital.

The nurse took us to the room and examined me. She said I was dilated only one centimeter. She called my doctor.

The doctor advised the nurse to monitor the baby and admit me to the hospital. Due to my history, I would remain in the hospital until the baby came.

My husband went to admissions. The nurse hooked me up to the monitor. I heard the beeps on the machine and then all of a sudden Nurse Sharon ran and got another nurse. The other nurse was calm. Nurse Sharon showed anguish on her face. She called the doctor again. She gave me oxygen and the calm nurse, Ann, rubbed my arm.

By this time, my mom entered the hospital room. I had oxygen and tubes. There was sheer horror on her face. She started to ask questions. I told my mom everything would be okay. I asked her to pray.

Nurse Sharon was beating on the monitor and talking to calm nurse Ann. However, calm nurse Ann kept rubbing my arm. Nurse Sharon asked me to stretch my legs. It hurt so badly. It felt as if my insides were being ripped slowing and deliberately. She had the nerve to tell me it was going to hurt worse than this before I had the baby.

Michael came back and looked white as a sheet.

LIFETIME

My doctor arrived. He came in running and said he had been stopped by the police, but they escorted him in. He touched my stomach and said. "Angela, that's tender isn't it?"

"Yes, very," was all I could say.

He told the nurse something and turned to me and said, "Your placenta has ruptured."

I did not know what that meant.

Nurse Sharon was still tripping and I still didn't know why. Calm nurse Ann said everything would be okay.

Michael kept saying breathe.

I said to him, "Michael, breathing will not stop the pain. This was nothing like they had talked about in class." I heard screams down the hall. I was hurting but it wasn't excruciating but the pain never stopped. They moved me to the labor and delivery room. They kept looking at the clock, in the surgery room. They were all in a huddle and the baby stopped breathing.

That is when Nurse Sharon said, "I told you the baby stopped breathing. I know you all didn't believe me." She sounded happy.

The doctor said, "If I had not believed you, I would not be here."

She seemed relieved my baby had stopped breathing. About that time, the anesthesiologist ran into the room and said. "I am going to put you to sleep, good night."

The next thing I remember was someone was saying, "You have a beautiful baby girl." Calm nurse Ann said to me, "I am talking to you Mrs. Everette. Wake up?"

"What do you mean you are talking to me? I have a boy, right?"

"No, you have a beautiful baby girl and she is beautiful."

"Of course she is beautiful, but is she okay?" I said in response.

Michael came to my bed and said, "Nicole is so beautiful."

LIFETIME

I grabbed him by the shirt and pulled him close. "Tell me the truth, is she okay."

"She is fine, except she doesn't have the Everette nose. She has your nose."

I could barely see and was paranoid. I believed everyone was lying to me about the baby.

Aunt Grace was standing by the door, whispering my name. She was not supposed to be in the room. "Hey Angie, she is beautiful." She whispered.

I turned my head in the direction of her voice and I started whispering too. "Aunt Grace, come here and tell me the truth. What's wrong with her?"

"Nothing, she is beautiful." Aunt Grace replied in a whisper.

I was so frustrated. Why did they keep saying that? "Mama, is she okay?"

"She is so beautiful." My mother said with a huge smile on her face.

Finally, the neonatalogist arrived. "Mrs. Everette, you have the most beautiful baby girl."

I repeated, "Doctor, I know she is beautiful, but is she okay?"

"She is fine, although her heart is not functioning properly."

I raised my voice and sat up, "What? How can she be fine if her heart is not functioning properly?" I was out of control. "Please, take me to my baby."

They rolled me downstairs to neonatology. I saw babies that were small enough to fit my hand, some had tubes, and some were in incubators. They rolled my bed right next to hers. I looked at her for the first time. I rubbed my hand across her entire body singing to myself, "Isn't she lovely, isn't she wonderful, isn't she precious, less than one minute old." They were all correct. She was beautiful. She had long black slick hair, with an olive complexion, and a cleft chin. She was exceptionally beautiful.

LIFETIME

I didn't know until later that a ruptured placenta was such a serious thing. God had truly blessed us, *Thank you Lord, for blessing us with Nicole.* She was perfect. Her smile melted every heart she came across.

My mom held Nicole before Michael and I did. Mom kept going to the intensive care to check on her and they finally asked if she wanted to hold Nicole. I hated I didn't get to hold her first. But, the nurses thought I might be sick since my placenta ruptured. I was glad my mom could shower my daughter with her love though.

Michael held her next. That was probably why she was a daddy's girl. Maybe that was it, or maybe it is a rule; daughters are going to be daddy's girls.

The next day, the nurse said she needed to be held by me. The nurses came and took me to hold her. Nicole was so precious. She was five pounds and ten ounces, large compared to the rest of the babies in there. I held Nicole and rubbed her head, smelled her, kissed her, hugged her, and said a prayer thanking God for her. I never doubted she was less than perfect. I never worried for a moment she had any brain damage, as the doctor predicted.

***

About a week before I was to go back to work, I discovered the daycare person I set up was not going to work out. I went by another ladies house that was referred to me by a friend's mother. The lady wore a duster and her hair was not combed. She was nice but she talked to me about twenty-minutes while the children were in a back room.

Some of the babies were sharing a bed. The house smelled like mothballs and I was fanning flies like crazy. It was a few days before Thanksgiving and finally I asked myself why I was wasting my time with that lady. I was constantly fanning flies and my Nicole would not be able to keep the flies away.

LIFETIME

I abruptly thanked her for her time and went on my way. I decided to wait until after Thanksgiving to look for another daycare provider because I was not leaving my precious gift with no flies and mothballs.

We had a great Thanksgiving our family had a program for every occasion. So I gave my testimony about how, I was so blessed to have been born in my family. I started to cry, because I had friends that had so many problems. I thanked God for my family.

Monday morning, I started looking again for daycares. Everyone I called had no vacancies. I decided to call some of the people I called in the beginning, who told me they did not have any vacancies.

I started with my friend's mother who had given me the name of the lady with the flies. She said she would love to keep my baby, but she was full and did not want to lose her license. She asked about the lady. I told her everything. She said she was so sorry and would never recommend her again.

Serena had recommended Sonja Williams. She said Sonja was perfect. I had called her before but she did not have any vacancies. I called her again. I knew of Sonja and she was very nice. I said a prayer before I called.

"Hello," she answered the telephone in a soft singing voice.

"Hi, my name is Angela Everette and I am looking for someone to take care of my daughter. Do you have any openings?"

"Praise God, someone quit Friday afternoon and did not give a notice. If you had called on Friday, I would have told you no." She said.

I said to Sonja, "I am starting work in three days. May I come by to talk to you?"

LIFETIME

"Sure, if you can come now. My babies are resting and I like to be prepared for the parents when they arrive."

I asked for her address and was surprised to find out she lived right around the corner from me. Nicole and I went straight over.

When we arrived, Sonja was dressed in some slacks with a matching top, and nice shoes. Her hair was in a nice style. Her home was nice. We entered in the front and walked through the entry past the living room, into the kitchen, then family room. Across the back was a fully glassed room. There were three swings in one corner, three walkers in another corner, and three baby beds up against the wall by the door. There were large green plants and a desk on the other side of the door.

Sonja offered me a seat at her desk. I had it in my mind, I was going to be interviewing her, but she interviewed me. She was organized. She gave me a ten-page contract of her rules. There was nothing for me to ask, except will you provide daycare for my daughter? *Thank you Lord, for a good, clean, Christian woman.*

Six months later, on Michael birthday and the date his grandmother was buried. We purchased our first house. We thanked God for blessing us with our home.

LIFETIME

Can't Take My Eyes Off Of You

Two years after Nicole was born, I was pregnant again. This pregnancy was more normal than the first. I was gaining weight at a normal rate and the baby was active. About six months into the pregnancy I was going to work and decided to take a different route, down Arapaho instead of Campbell. I was eating a grilled cheese sandwich while driving to work with Nicole who was in her car seat. I was sitting in the left turning lane at Greenville and Arapaho, and began to feel sick. I thought to myself, I was going to have to stop at the bus station around the corner because I was getting sick. I turned at the corner. I was in second gear. As I started to turn, everything started to spin and get blurry. Then nothing. I do not know what happened next. I must have passed out. It was about a mile between Arapaho and Belt Line. When I came to, about a mile down the road, men were running everywhere. I was headed towards a building. I was so paranoid. Where was I? Why were they running towards me? What was going on? I let my window up and turned the key off. I didn't seem to know how to drive. They all ran up to the car, some were bracing the car. I wanted to scream.

"Are you alright, Ma'am?" A strange man shouted at me.

"No. Where am I? Did I hit anyone?" I replied.

"Yes, you hit the city bus." Another man shouted.

I said. "Call my husband." I turned to check on my daughter. "Nicole, are you okay baby?"

"Yes, I am fine, mommy." Nicole said jumping up and down in her car seat.

"Oh Lord, what is going on?" I said as I looked around to determine where I was.

LIFETIME

"Ma'am, let us help you out of the car?" The strange man said to me.

I shook my head and said, "No, I am afraid." They were screaming and running. The only one that seemed okay was Nicole. She was sitting there in her pink car coat looking like it had been a joy ride. She loved rides. I decided to get out and use the phone.

"May, I use your phone, sir?" I asked the man while still sitting in my car confused.

"Sure, come inside." He said as he opened my car door. I got Nicole out of the car and we went inside the building. I picked up the telephone to call home.

Michael answered. "Yello,"

I shouted to him, "Michael, come get me. I had a wreck."

"Where are you?" He asked.

I looked around but nothing was familiar and screamed. "I don't know."

"What do you mean you don't know?" He asked with his voice raising some.

I screamed. "I don't know. Hurry and come get me, before the police gets here."

"Baby, where are you?" He insisted.

I looked around again and said, "All I know is, I was going to work and I turned on Arapaho. Hurry, before the police come and take me to jail. Hurry, I am scared."

"Okay, are you and Nicole okay?"

"I don't know. Hurry! I see the police coming." I hung the phone up and held Nicole close.

About that time, the officer walked in. "Good morning, I am Officer Smith. What happened?"

I stood up and said in an excited voice. "I am not on drugs, nor have I been drinking. I am pregnant. Please don't take me to jail."

LIFETIME

"What happened?" The officer asked again.

"I don't know. I am pregnant." I responded.

The man in the shop said, "Officer that car was coming down the street with no driver. She was slumped over." He pointed to me. "Then the car crossed the three lanes of oncoming traffic went up the hill and hit a parked car at a transmission shop." Standing by the window, he pointed across the street. He continued. "Then the car came across all six lanes and turned up into this parking lot. She was headed for that building when she came to."

I screamed and pointed at my husband's truck driving down the street. "There is my husband. Stop him. He does not see us. Please stop him."

The officer kept talking to me, "Ma'am, did you say you are pregnant?"

"Yes." I said in a timid voice.

The officer was standing in front of me. He said, "This happens a lot, but usually people get hurt very badly. I am going across the street to assess the damage." He left and walked across the street to the transmission shop.

About that time Michael entered the building, I said to him. "Baby don't let them take me to jail, take Nicole. I am scared."

He rushed to us and took Nicole, putting his arm around my shoulder. "Nicole, are you okay?"

"Yes, daddy, I am okay. Everyone keeps asking me that. I am okay." Nicole said with excitement.

The police officer returned. "Mrs. Everette, you are truly blessed. You hit a car that is in the shop. The shop owner said the car is broken down and the owner will probably not bother with getting it fixed. You did not hit the bus. The car is on private property, so I cannot give

LIFETIME

you a ticket. The police officer turned to Michael, "I suggest Mr. Everette you take both of them to the hospital for examination."

Michael stood Nicole on the floor. The officer approached her and said to her. "Young lady, you are so cute and I am glad you are okay."

Nicole smiled at him and said, "Thank you Mr. Policeman." Then she pointed and said to him. "Is that a real gun?"

He took a couple of steps back and said. "Yes, darling it is real."

Michael took me to the doctor. I had an EKG and an EEG. Then I went back to Dr. Crazy, the one that thought I was anorexic. All day I was at one doctor or another.

My car had damage in the front. Michael said to quit telling people that it was only a fender bender. I had been in a major wreck, but by the grace of God, we were spared. This was my testimony. At that point, I knew God was and is in control, not me not the doctors, but I had God's grace.

***

About four weeks later one Wednesday night, I went to bed rather early. I awoke through the night to use the restroom. I was still half-asleep so I had not paid much attention to the gas pains I felt.

My husband had been in the garage building cabinets for some job and I noticed he was getting his coat to leave. I looked at the clock and it was past midnight. I asked him ever so sweetly. "Where in the hell are you going?"

"I am running to South Dallas to pick up a saw from my brother. I need to install these cabinets by eight tomorrow morning. So I need the saw tonight." Michael said to me.

"Yeah right. All I know is you don't need to go anywhere at this time of night."

LIFETIME

"I have got to go, it won't take long."

Well, I thought to myself, this would be the perfect time to have this baby, while he was gone.

He probably was not a mile away when I felt another pain. It felt like gas, but this time it hurt a little longer. I was only seven months. My baby was not due for eight more weeks. Another pain hit. Therefore, I called the doctor's office. I got the nurse; they said it sounded as if my water had broken.

I always thought when your water broke it was a big gush and then it was over. Mine was like a slow faucet, drip, drip. She said I had to come to the hospital right away.

Well, Michael was gone and I did not have a way to reach him. Therefore, I called my mother. She was there in no time. It was early February and cold.

My mom drove real fast to the hospital. They took me to the labor room to examine me. I was prepared to have a C-Section.

My son Brandon Michael Everette was born at 4:44 am and weighed 5 pounds and three ounces. He was so precious, a carbon copy of Nicole. Michael made it to the hospital before he was born.

Michael said to me, "Thank you baby for giving me a son, but he doesn't have the Everette nose."

***

When Brandon was eight weeks old, he had a second well baby check up. He was doing well on the check up until the nurse measured his head. She measured about three times and then the doctor measured. They kept measuring, but then eventually let us go. The doctor

LIFETIME

commented his head had grown a considerable amount, but since he was premature by eight weeks, they would not have seen this growth. We left the doctor and went on our way.

The next day I returned to work. I had been at work about an hour when I received a call from the pediatrician's office. I was instructed to take my son to Medical Center Hospital within the hour for an appointment with a specialist. They said Brandon might have to be sedated so not to feed him.

I called Sonja in panic. "Sonja, the doctor called and said to bring Brandon to the hospital. Do not feed him anything else. They think they will have to sedate him. Pray for my son."

When I arrived, Sonja had prayed and anointed my son with oil. Sonja said. "Don't worry those are brains in his head. I had a talk with God. He is fine."

I was crying and taking him at the same time. He was screaming all the way to the doctor because he was hungry. We went to this doctor's office not far from her home. They sent us to the main hospital for a CAT scan. My son was crying. I was crying too. I kept putting his pacifier in his mouth but he would spit it out. I rocked him and held him, but he was hungry. They would not even let him have water.

Finally, they called us in. They took my baby and put him in a radiation protection suit, strapped him down, and slid him in the enormous tube. He was looking all around and sucking on the pacifier. I watched from the glass window. It took about forty-five minutes to complete the test. They didn't even have to sedate him. The doctors and nurses commented on how good he was. As soon as they gave him to me, I fed him. He was so happy to eat.

We returned to the doctor's office in the adjacent building to the hospital. The doctor was dressed in a fine Italian suit. His office did not look like a doctor's office. This doctor was only at Medical Center one day per month. His regular office was at Children's Hospital in Dallas. He was throwing Brandon up in the air. I tried to warn him he had just eaten. It was too late. Brandon threw up on his nice suit. But, he sent me a bill for one thousand dollars.

He said Brandon had some fluid on his brain, but he did not have hydrocephaly. Brandon's head had grown five centimeters in a two-week period. There was nothing we could do about the fluid at that time, but a shunt was a possibility to drain the fluid. He tried to assure me not to worry, and made an appointment for us to return in six months.

I never reached Michael that day. He did not answer my page. Since he was a self-employed contractor, he would have had to leave the job site to call me. I did not talk to him about Brandon until that night. I told him everything that the doctor said. Michael picked Brandon up and said, "Son, your head is big just like the rest of the Everette's." He laughed and laid him back in his crib. "Call my mother. She will tell you, he is fine. Don't worry."

But, I was so worried. I said a prayer.

Six months later, we went back to the neurologist, and the fluid sack was smaller. The doctor said Brandon would grow into his head. He measured my head and commented that my head was a tad large also. We both laughed.

***

A few years later, I was watching television and recognized Brandon's Neurologist as a world renowned Neurologist. The show was about children with hydrocephaly. Hydrocephaly was usually fatal by age five. I was so thankful my child had been spared of this disease. About seventeen years later, the same physician successfully separated Siamese twins. We were blessed our son only had a large head with no problems. I thanked God, for my son.

LIFETIME

Sonja kept Brandon and Nicole until they were three and five. We all loved Sonja. God had truly blessed us by putting so many loving Christian people in my family's lives.

LIFETIME

Whip Appeal

A couple of years later I thought seriously about getting a divorce. I was so sad. I would lie in bed and think about all the things that I was going to do to Michael when I left him

One night I heard Oprah on television saying that other people cannot make you happy or sad. I sat up in bed and said, "I get it Oprah." Why was I spending all of my time and energy thinking about sticking it to him? I totally got it; I decided to find myself and my happiness. I realized Michael was not doing anything to me to make me unhappy. I was unhappy on my own and did not know why. I got busy. I learned to quilt, decorate cakes, planted a garden, and gradually began to feel happier.

I had pushed my feelings deep within myself because it was so difficult to be angry with him and grieve for my father at the same time. I was not really sure why I had been so angry with Michael. Had I been angry because my premonition was not his death but my dad's? I talked to Michael about my anger and fears. I told him I was sorry for being so hateful, mean, and selfish. I loved him and I didn't want him to die. I was sorry. I loved him still.

He held me and said, "Baby, we are going to be okay. I really love you, always have, and always will."

***

One night Cynthia called and was disturbed. "Angela, you are not going to believe this but, Ricky is on the sex offenders' list for our neighborhood."

I could not believe what she said and could not talk to her anymore. I went into immediate prayer. It was quite selfish on my part, but I thanked God for removing me from that situation.

LIFETIME

Four years after my dad's death, the old Angela was coming back. I had been lost in depression. I did not have a lot of confidence and was very needy of Michael. However, Michael could not do anything right. If he came into the room, I left out. If he wasn't home, I was mad. If he wanted to hold me, I pulled away.

One of the things that I did to get myself together was to start a new job. To celebrate, I treated my friends Faye and Cynthia to the annual Kappa Casino night. The night of the party, I could not decide on what to wear. I had not been out in awhile and didn't have a clue on the latest fashions. I called Diahann to ask her what to wear. She insisted that I wear a dress. I described a gold dress that I had. But, Diahann said it sounded ugly. Then, I remembered I had a black dress my cousin let me have. It was a basic black dress, pretty simple. It had a rounded neck and it was fitted down to the hips, with layered taffeta at the bottom. I didn't really like the dress because it emphasized my behind. The back of the dress had a strap across the back and was very low cut. I tied a flowered scarf around my shoulders to hide the back as the doorbell rang. It was Faye at the door.

As she entered the house she said, "Angie, that dress is bad, but the scarf has got to go. Your makeup is flawless and that asymmetrical haircut is laid. You look good, lose the scarf and let's go."

I whined, "I am about to take this dress off. I don't like it. I look fat."

"You look good, not fat. But take off that scarf." Faye commented as she sat on the bed.

I took off the scarf and turned to show her the back of the dress.

Faye stood and looked through my closet. She found a black jacket that had a 'V' cut. She handed me the jacket. I put the jacket on to cover the low cut back." I turned to Faye and said, "This is better but I still look fat."

LIFETIME

"No you don't." She paused and asked me if Michael was home.

"Yes, in the kitchen." I said.

Faye waved her arms for me to go show Michael. "Go let Michael see how you look. He will tell you how good you look"

I went in the kitchen reluctantly. Michael was sitting at the counter. "Baby, how do I look?" I asked in a timid voice.

Michael dropped his fork and said. "Take that shit off."

"Why Michael?" I asked in a sheepish voice.

Faye interrupted, "Michael you know she look good. You go out and you know that's what they wear."

My mind wondered off, as the two of them were having words.

Michael bucked his eyes and yelled. "I don't care what those bitches and hoes wear. The mother of my children, my wife, is not wearing that shit out."

Faye replied, "Michael, I wear this kind of stuff. Are you calling me a bitch and a ho?"

Michael stood and raised his voice walking toward Faye, "I don't give a damn what you wear Faye you are not my wife and you are single."

I was listening to what they were saying and I thought to myself. *He didn't just tell me to take this dress off. We have been married for almost ten years and he cannot tell me what to wear. If he wanted me to take the dress off, he should have said I looked fat or like a clown. I would have taken the dress off, but to tell me to take the dress off. I thought he must not know who I am. Actually, I was thinking the Angela that had been living here for the past four years was not me. I didn't recognize that bitch myself. But, wait a minute, Angela was back. She was*

LIFETIME

back with a vengeance. All while I was working this out in my head the two of them were going at each other. Finally, I said. "Excuse me. What's wrong with the dress Michael?"

He looked me up and down before answering, "All of your breasts are hanging out."

I looked down at my non-chest and thought, he was full of shit. Not, all of your ass was hanging out, but all of your breasts are hanging out!! I thought to myself that was the weakest thing he could think of. So, I looked at both of them as said. "Faye, let's go." I walked out the door and went to the car.

Faye followed me to the car and before opening the door she said, "Angie, I am so sorry. Go back in the house and apologize to Michael."

I waved my hand across my face, "Girl, let's go. I have been married too long for him to start telling me what to wear. My dad warned him when we got married to never make me feel like he was telling me what to do. However, since my father died, I needed him to tell me what to do. But, no more, Angela was back.

Faye drove away not saying a word. We picked up Cynthia. She wanted to change when she saw my outfit. She wore a black herringbone business suit with black pumps. Faye had on a long black leather skirt, black leather boots, and a red sweater. We all looked good, but we looked like we were going to three different events.

We arrived at the event and everyone was raving about how good we looked. We went inside and saw a lot of Kappa's we knew. No females had on pants. I was glad I was in a dress. I was glad I was looking good when I ran into Charles Jeffrey. He spoke but didn't have too much to say. I did not care, because I had long stopped wanting him. He looked sort of lonely. I had a great time at the party. We stayed until the party was over about two in the morning.

LIFETIME

On the way home, we decided to get breakfast. We laughed and talked about how much fun we had and about who attended the party. We had been out of college for ten plus years and talked about how well everyone looked.

It was late when I got home the next morning. I removed my makeup and showered. I noticed when I got out of the shower that Michael was not only awake, he was reading Essence. I thought he must have been trying to figure women out. I laughed to myself, prayed, and got in bed totally exhausted.

Before I dosed off Michael got in my face and said, "Don't you ever disrespect me in front of your friend again. How dare you leave in that outfit when I told you to take off? You didn't even ask me to go or say where you were going."

That crazy man went on and on for two hours all up in my face. I was so tired. Every time I would even think about yawning. He would say "Oh no, wake up and listen to what I got to say."

I said, "Can't we discuss this tomorrow when I am awake."

Michael yelled, "Oh hell no, I got to get this off my chest."

Finally, I interrupted. "You have been going on and on for the past two hours. I am tired and I am going to sleep. Let's get this straight. Don't you ever again tell me what to wear. I don't even like the dress. I only wore it because you told me not to. You should know better than to tell me what to do. I don't ever want to discuss that dress again. Good night." I pulled the covers over my head, turned my back to him, and fell asleep.

A few weeks later, I was getting dressed for the play "Beauty Shop." I was putting on a winter white blousy pants suit that I loved.

LIFETIME

Michael said, "Please don't wear that too big pants suit. I hate that outfit." Before I could respond, he continued. "And don't even think about wearing those black leather Guess jeans."

"You bought them." I said to him.

"But do you have to wear them every where we go?"

I stood in the closet just looking. Then Michael thumbed through my clothes stopping at the black dress. "What about this dress. The one you wear with your friend Faye."

I snapped, "I thought you didn't like that dress?"

"I never said I didn't like it. I simply did not want you to wear it without me. You always wear pants when we go out. You seem to dress up more for other people than you do for me. If you don't mind, wear it for me?"

I laughed to myself and put the dress on. I knew that breast thing was pure B.S. Michael told me I looked real good that night. He said I had that "Whip Appeal."

***

By April, I gave Michael a birthday party. A lot of our old friends came to the party. Miami and I were talking and all of a sudden, Michael interrupted and said to me. "You didn't tell me you went to the Kappa Casino night."

I looked at Miami and said, "I guess you told him?"

Michael said to Miami, "You saw her there, man?"

"Yeah, man and she was wearing that black dress." Miami said shaking his head from side to side.

LIFETIME

"Oh man, we can't talk about that dress." Michael turned to face me before he continued. "But anyway he didn't tell me he saw you. I never knew where you went that night." Michael paused and then insisted on dropping the conversation.

Later on in the party, Faye approached me, "Angie, will you get the black dress?"

I looked at her puzzled and asked. "Why?"

Faye said, "We have been discussing whether it was appropriate for a married woman to wear a dress like this without her husband. Everyone wants to see exactly how the dress looks."

I found the dress in my closet and handed it to her.

One of the guests at the party said with a surprised look on his face. "You wore that dress?"

Miami responded before I could say anything. "Yeah she wore it and looked good too."

Michael took the dress from Faye and said in a matter of fact voice. "We have decided never to talk about this dress again." He put the dress away and we continued with the party.

I think Michael realized his Angela was back and could not be pushed around. She had that "Whip Appeal."

LIFETIME

My Boo

I had been at my new job for a couple of years, and I got into a conversation with friends Tommy and Howard. We were talking about that one person that made you say, "Oooh Baby, please take me back. I'll be good. That one person that still had your heart even though you were no longer a couple." I asked each of the guys if they had an Oooh Baby.

Howard starting smiling, but Tommy said he didn't have one. I told Tommy he was probably someone else's Oooh Baby. I talked about my Oooh Baby. But, I never said what his actual name was. From that day forward, I referred to Charles Jeffrey as my Oooh Baby, except with Michael.

In the next day or two, the three of us went to lunch and as we entered the restaurant, I was running my mouth with Howard and Tommy listening quite attentively. Then all of a sudden, they were distracted by something or someone. So, I turned to see what they were looking at. I smiled at the guy, turned back around, and continued talking.

We chose a table and went to the buffet to get our food. When we returned the guy came to the table and sat beside me. It was Charles Jeffrey and he looked great. The two of us began a conversation but I never introduced him to Tommy or Howard. So, the two of them started talking to each other.

Howard said to Tommy. "Do you think this is Oooh Baby?"

Tommy replied with a snicker. "It must be. She has not bothered to introduce us."

I heard everything they were saying, but chose to ignore them.

Howard said, "I should say Hi, Mr. Oooh Baby, I am Mr. Howard Baker."

LIFETIME

I pretended not to hear them. Charles eventually left the table but not before getting my telephone number. The two of them teased me from that day forward about, Mr. Oooh Baby.

The next couple of days, Charles and I met again at the same buffet for lunch. Charles was driving a nice ride and looked good. I was looking good myself wearing a size eight. We talked about our lives over the past fifteen years. I was happily married with two beautiful children and was gainfully employed. Charles was divorced with two children.

"You are divorced?" I questioned.

"Yes, my son's mother left me. I am raising my son, Devin, alone. I am Mr. Mom."

Instantly, my heart went out to him, "I am sorry, but you were always a good father."

"Yeah, it's just me and my son." He said with a smile on his face.

"Do you think you will get married again?" I asked.

"I don't know if I ever will."

I began to feel sorry for him. He had been through so much. But, I thought to myself he should've picked me. Charles said he heard of my brother's death. I put my head down for a moment sighing some then said, "My dad died eight months later from a car accident."

Charles said, "I didn't know. Why didn't you call me?"

I looked at him with disbelief and said. "We are not friends. Charles and it never occurred to me."

We had a nice lunch and departed on a good note. I felt sorry for him for all he had been through. I thanked God for giving me a husband that loved me and for my remarkable children. I felt blessed.

When I got home that afternoon, I said to Michael. "I love you, Baby."

Michael turned to me and said. "You know I love you more."

LIFETIME

As I got closer to Michael, I said. "I had lunch with Charles Jeffrey today."

"And why are you telling me?" He asked as he held my hands looking into my eyes.

"No reason. Except seeing him lets me know how blessed I am to have you. I love you. I am happy we chose each other. I love your dirty drawers." I kissed his lips softly.

Michael kissed me back, and as he turned to walk away, he said. "I still do not see what you saw in him." He ran his hand across his hair and said. "He surely doesn't look as good as me and he talks too much." He turned to face me again, "But you know, you are my horse if you never win a race girl."

LIFETIME

Jesus Be A Fence

A few years later one Sunday morning, I was getting dressed and heard the strangest noise coming from our bedroom. However, every time I stepped into the bedroom it stopped. Finally, Nicole stepped in the hallway and asked, "What is that?"

Then Michael said, "That's me singing my favorite hymn. It is an old one, "Jesus Be a Fence." He was beating on the headboard, singing the lead, the chorus, and whistling the melody. It sounded real strange. He asked, "Don't yall know it? Listen." He sang, "Jesus be a fence all around me everyday. Jesus I want you to protect me as I travel along the way. I know you can. Yes, Lord. I know you will. Yes, Lord. Lord, be a fence all around me everyday."

Nicole and I looked at each other and laughed. We got dressed and went to church smiling about Michael and his singing along with his instrument playing.

About two Sundays later, we were at the Hamilton Park Church Drill Team Annual Day and they began singing "Jesus Be A Fence." Nicole and I turned to each other and smiled.

The next week we were in Waxahachie at their annual day and someone sang the song there. Again, Nicole and I smiled at each other.

That summer was the first time our church drill team attended the National Sunday School and BTU Congress (Congress) in Houston. When it came time to go to Congress, I asked the bus owner who would be driving the bus. He responded a nice white man would be our driver.

I said to him, "Rev. Jacobs, I don't think I can deal with a white man for a week. Do you have any good brothers that could drive us?"

LIFETIME

He hesitated with his response. "Well. I do. But, do you know Raymond Jones?"

"No, I don't think so. Is he a good brother?" I asked.

"Well, yes but . . ."

I interrupted and said, "He sounds good to me. Now, I don't have a problem with white people, but this trip will be a family trip for us so I need someone I can think of as family."

He agreed to ask him.

"Tell him what I said. He will like us."

"Alright." Rev. Jacobs said with a laugh.

It was finally time to go to Congress and the good brother was late. The only number I had for Rev. Jacobs was at his church, I did not know how to contact him at four in the morning. It was ten minutes after four and I started praying. I did not tell anybody I was worried. I had everyone gathered in a big circle on the parking lot of the church and had a powerful prayer meeting. We finished the song and prayer and the good brother arrived two hours late driving a bus that looked liked something from 1970. I was a tad bit upset. He got off the bus and said. "Who is Mrs. Everette?" He was a tall thick brother. He was wearing a baseball cap with a blue short-sleeved shirt with dark slacks. He appeared to be in his mid thirties.

"That would be me." I responded looking at my watch. "You are two hours late."

He removed his cap before speaking. "I know. I am sorry. The bus yard was robbed. I had to take care of that first." He said very matter of fact.

"Why didn't you call me? You have my cell." I asked.

"Again I say, I am sorry." He turned and started loading all of the stuff on the bus.

I was ticked. But, I would break him down. However, I would do that later.

He then turned to me and said. "I thought you were going to Houston for three days.

LIFETIME

"That is correct." I responded.

"Then why do you have all of this stuff?" He asked.

"We want to be prepared for what ever we need."

The good brother stopped loading the bus and said. "Well, I noticed on your itinerary you are planning a barbecue at the hotel on Thursday night."

"That is correct." We cannot afford to go out eat for each meal so we will be cooking. I got the barbeque taken care of. Anything else?"

"No, that would be it."

"Cool, Mr. Jones." I replied.

"You can call me Raymond, Mr. Jones is my dad." He said with a smirk on his face.

"Suit yourself." I responded.

I heard the kids complaining about the dump of a bus. I asked them to be quiet.

Our pastor gave the youth a talk. "I am leaving Angela in charge and I expect a good report from her. I will be Houston on Wednesday. Anyone not obeying will be sent back home and dealt with when I get back. Be safe. Stay together. Obey Sis. Angela. Remember whose child you are. You are representing Solid Rock Baptist Church. Do not embarrass your parents or me. Let us pray..."

We were finally on our way. As we left the parking lot of the church, Raymond took LBJ heading east. When we got to highway 75, he kept going instead of taking the south exit. So I asked. "Raymond, where are you going? We are supposed to be going to Houston?"

With a chuckle in his voice, he said. "Oh, I didn't know that." He kept driving in the wrong direction.

LIFETIME

Rev. Beaux, the youth pastor and the drill team director, started laughing and said. "Raymond, I like you. You shut her right up."

I just looked at both of them thinking. You got jokes. That was one more thing that I would get him back for. So I sat back to see how he was going to get us to Houston. Eventually, he got on interstate 45 south and we were headed to Houston. I put on my headphones and did not say anything else.

When we got to Centerville, Raymond pulled up at MacDonald's and said. "Mrs. Everette, is this where you were planning on having breakfast?"

I looked out and said. "Yes." We had prayer for safe arrival to our first stop. I reminded the youth that they were responsible for their own breakfast. My mother was traveling with us to attend a class and to help watch my son who was not in the drill team. I turned to my mom and asked her to join Raymond and me for breakfast. This was my first plan to break him down. I approached Raymond and said. "Raymond, let's sit together and talk about the trip."

"Sure. Mrs. Everette." He responded back to me.

We blessed our food and the three of us ate. My mother was doing a lot of talking just as I wanted her too.

Finally, Raymond looked at me and said. "Mrs. Everette, I could not wait to meet you. I have never in all of my years as a bus driver seen an itinerary as detailed as yours. Rev. Jacobs told me that you insisted on a good brother to drive you. But, I took your church on a trip before and it did not go well. And, I said that I would never drive Solid Rock Baptist Church anywhere again. He begged me to drive you saying that you were a piece of work."

I looked at Raymond and smiled knowing that I was breaking him down.

LIFETIME

Raymond said. "I was amazed at what I saw when I got to the church. I was the only one late, which I truly do not believe in. You guys had those green garment bags all laid out with two boxes of food for each room. I thought to myself what kind of people are they? I could not say anything to you about being late, because I was embarrassed. However, you were very professional. I thought to myself, this must not be the Solid Rock Baptist Church or maybe I had been wrong before. I am glad to be driving for you."

I was smiling by then and then my mom said. "Raymond, I was on that trip with you before. Now, you say it was us, but you were not so nice yourself."

"Mrs. Franklin, you were on that trip?" Raymond asked her.

"I sure was Raymond and I thought that was you when you drove up. You are not acting like the same person that took us on that trip. Maybe, it was you and not us?"

"I don't know Mrs. Franklin. But you all are very nice people today."

We finished breakfast and headed to Houston. We went straight to Astroworld Park. I purchased all the tickets and everyone headed inside except Rev. Beaux and me. We had to attend orientation at the convention center and planned to come back later.

We were only at the convention center for a short time. The two of us decided to go by the hotel to check in then head to the park.

When we got to the hotel, the manager said to us. "Oh, I tried to call you, Mrs. Everette, this morning because we do not have any rooms for you."

I thought she was joking. So I said. "Excuse me?"

Then she repeated the information again with an attitude. I put my brief case on the floor and put my hand on my hip. That was when Rev. Beaux said, "Let me go pray."

LIFETIME

I thought to myself, yeah you better go pray, because I am about to go off on this lady and I don't want you to have to witness this. Therefore, he stepped out in the hall. He was praying. I heard him.

God stepped in and ordered my words. They already had our money. I asked what they were going to do to remedy the situation. She gave us a couple of alternatives.

I called Raymond on his cell and informed him of the situation. Raymond begged me to come and get him. He said, "Come get me, because you two will not lay down your religion and we will be sleeping on the bus. Come get me."

"No, Raymond, we got this." I said to him over the phone.

We went to a hotel across the street, but they did not have kitchens in the rooms. All of the rooms were smoking rooms and were very small. We passed and went to the next hotel. The hotel was nice enough but the previous hotel had already sent over another church that wanted the ten rooms that we needed.

While at the front desk, I was able to see the telephone number of the area manager. I called him on my cell. I told him the situation and he arranged for us to move to a new hotel that was just outside of Houston.

About six that evening, Rev. Beaux and I were on our way back to pick the youth up. They followed us to the hotel where they changed for dinner. We rushed to get to the local cafeteria before it closed. Everyone laughed when they heard what Rev. Beaux and I had been through.

Rev. Beaux said. "I had to go pray because she was getting ready to work that neck. But, I tell you what. This girl got skills. She got the cell of the director in Florida. He has

LIFETIME

already called her checking on us. We are at a hotel that opened three weeks ago and we are the only people staying there. AND we are getting a refund."

Everyone had a story to tell, including my sisters. I asked, "Raymond did you see baby sister fall?"

He busted out laughing and did a hand gesture to describe how Janice slid down the hill trying to get out of the rain. We all laughed and had such a great time.

Since we were staying in Katy, we would have to be dressed and on the bus by 4:00 Wednesday morning. I came to the bus bearing a hot breakfast for Raymond and orange juice at 3:55. I knew it would blow him away. Roll call was re-scheduled for 4:01 a.m. Raymond had the bus ready and all were accounted for on time.

That afternoon in the drill team session, someone led devotion with "Jesus Be a Fence." It seemed that all of a sudden everyone was singing that song. I had grown up in church and could not recall ever hearing the song.

We had a great first day at Congress. That night, I knocked on Raymond's door whose room was across the hall from mine and said. "Do you like iced tea?"

"Yes." He said.

I handed him a tall glass of tea and went back to my room. A couple of hours later there was a knock on my door. It was Raymond.

He was standing there with his empty glass looking pitiful. "Do you have any more tea?"

"Sure." I stepped back into my room and got a full pitcher out of the refrigerator. "Why don't you take a whole pitcher?"

"Thank you so much. This is the best tea I have ever had." He said with a big grin on his face as he left.

LIFETIME

I knew it would be, because I can make some tea. I don't leave home without it and I still had another pitcher in the refrigerator.

The next night we had our barbeque. The hotel was filled with the smell of Texas barbecue. I had tables from several rooms on our floor and made a long table in my room. We placed tablecloths and decorations on the tables. We invited our pastor, deacons, and others attending Congress to come and fellowship with us. We served grilled hamburgers, hot dogs, chicken, potato salad, baked beans, fruit cocktail, watermelon, soda, and tea. We had a great time.

The youth marched in the parking lot of the hotel. We had enough food for the entire hotel staff. Some of our former church members came to the hotel as well as family members that lived in Houston, including my cousin Paula, to share in our fellowship.

Sometime that night, Raymond came up to me whispering, "Do you by chance have any bubble bath? I know you do. You have everything and I am so tired and want to take a bath."

I looked at him under my glasses, "I imagine so."

"Can I come by and get it from you when you go back to your room?"

"Sure." I said.

Raymond came by and my sisters were in my room making sandwiches for the next day. I tried to give him the bubble bath but he shook his head so fast saying no don't say it in front of your sisters. I laughed to myself. After a few minutes, he took the bubble bath when no one was looking and eased out of the room.

The next morning, he gave me the bubble bath back and said he really appreciated it. I laughed to myself.

LIFETIME

By noon on Friday, the air conditioner was not working on the bus. Raymond said it was the big air conditioner. He would fix it after we went inside the convention center.

That afternoon, Raymond called me and said. "Mrs. Everette, I have bad news." He paused, "The air conditioner is just part of the problem. But do not worry; I will have it fixed by ten tonight when you are ready to leave."

I understood.

That night at the closing of Congress, Raymond came inside and said to me. "Mrs. Everette, I have good news and bad news."

"Okay, let me have it." I said.

"The good news is, I have a bus for you all to return to Dallas on. The bad news is you will have to change buses at the bus yard and take your stuff off of the original bus. I will drive you to Huntsville. You will have to take all of you stuff off that bus and put it on a bus coming from Dallas. I will not be able to return with you. The alternator is out on the bus and I cannot drive the bus at night with no lights also there is still no air. I am sorry."

"No problem." I said.

We left the convention center and did all of the bus changes. I was so tired I could hardly move. I had not slept the entire week. I did not care how we got home; I was just ready to go. When we got to Huntsville, the older white guy came to pick us up. I thought I was going to scream if he didn't shut up. He talked non-stop, and he stopped every half hour to get his smoke on. We left Houston at ten at night and did not get to our church until seven the next morning.

Michael had been waiting since one in the morning. We were glad we had made it back to the church.

LIFETIME

The day after we returned from congress was Father's Day. Michael's mother was rushed to the hospital. By, Monday she was very ill. His mother passed away three days later.

Michael was like a zombie. I helped him walk, drive, and even told him to breathe. I never saw him shed a tear. He did this random talk about how he wasn't ready for this. He was so helpless. I wanted him to cry. I did not know what to say, so I said nothing. The tears rolled down my cheeks.

At the funeral, I held his hand as if he was a little boy. Every now and then, I said, "Exhale. Breathe, Michael." He would do it too. He needed me to help him. I prayed for strength. I had never helped anyone through grief. I was always the needy one. When his mother died, I believe I lost part of Michael.

A few days later, I went to a furniture store. Charles Jeffrey was there working. He had aged. We talked for a few minutes and then I went on our way. When I got back to work, I saw Howard, Gabe, Don, and Tommy in the cafeteria. I said to them, "Guess who I saw today at lunch."

They all guessed Oooh Baby.

***

It was about six months before Raymond tracked me down. He sent me a thank you note with his telephone number by one of my church members. From that point on, Raymond and I were good friends. We talked often about our trips and began to talk about other things, just as real friends do.

LIFETIME

The Beginning of My End

June 8, 2002, I went to the salon to get my hair done. While at the shop, the new manicurist offered to do my nails. I agreed and my nails turned out great. I could not wait to get home to show Michael. He loved for me to keep my nails up, but I had not since Nicole was born.

When I got home from the salon, I called Raymond to tell him I was having a birthday party that night. Raymond thought that was the funniest thing because we had been through that the week before. He questioned, why I thought I was still having a party. I assured Raymond I knew I was, but had to admit there were no clues. He laughed at me and I got off the phone to rest for the party. Soon as my head hit the pillow, the telephone rang. Brandon, my son, yelled for me to pick up the phone. I rolled over and took the receiver off the hook. It was my mom.

I heard fear in her voice. "Angela, something is wrong with Michael. Can you come over here?"

"Where?" I responded.

"At mothers."

"Is he okay?"

I don't know was all she said.

"I will be right there." I hung up the phone. I leaped from the bed grabbed my keys and was out the door on my way to my grandmother's house. I called Rev. Beaux on the way. I didn't know what to say to him. I just started to cry. I told him I was going to my grandmother's house in North Dallas because something was wrong with my husband.

LIFETIME

He said, "I am on my way." However, he had no clue of where my grandmother's house was. I had known him for about ten years but my grandmother died ten years before we ever met.

When I arrived at the house, my mom was with two strange men. Michael's truck was there but Michael was not. "Where is Michael?" I cried.

"They took him to the hospital." My mom said.

"Take me." I demanded.

We jumped in my mom's car leaving my car and Michael's truck in the driveway. In ten minutes, we arrived at the hospital. My mom drove to the emergency room door and I ran into the hospital. I ran up to the desk and asked for Michael Everette. The nurse looked at the computer and said he was in room one. I went straight back. As I entered the room, Michael was lying on the table. Two nurses were in the room both keying into the computers. They were not doing anything to help him. I screamed. "Help him!" They looked toward me and returned to what they were doing. I cried, "Please help him." The female nurse faced me and I said to her "He is okay, right?" She turned away. Then I said, "Is he dead?"

The nurse turned toward me and looked into my eyes, "Yes Ma'am and we are very sorry for your loss." She lowered her head, turned and walked away.

I ran to the male nurse, fell to the floor and grabbed his arm. "No!! Help him. Don't leave." I started to cry. No, I started to scream.

I was startled by my mom's crying outside the room. My body was spinning uncontrollably. My play brother Rodney entered the room. He held me and tried to console me. I kept looking at Michael lying on the table. They had removed his pants and underwear only covered by a sheet. His t-shirt was cut off and on the table. Paint was all over his face and arms.

LIFETIME

He seemed to be resting. I rubbed his arms. I rubbed his legs. I wanted to put his clothes back on him. He seemed stripped of his dignity. I screamed. I rubbed. I sat down. I stood up. I cried out, "Oh Lord." I thought I was dreaming. I tried to awake myself. I remembered lying down. "Wake up Angela." I said to myself. This had to be a nightmare. I could not wake up.

My mom, Rev. Beaux, and his wife Deanna came in the hospital room. I was pacing and sitting and sitting and pacing. I could not be still for a single second. Beaux was consoling my mother. Rodney was saying something to me but it did not register. I felt like I was going through what G. C. Cameron sang, *"Why oh why? I heard her mother cry. As I rushed to the scene with a tear in my eyes, somebody asked who the next of kin was? Oh, Lord! It was the beginning of my end."*

My mom said she would tell the children before someone else. She left with Beaux. Rodney went upstairs. His mother was in the same hospital. He went to break the news to her. He left me with Deanna, Rev. Beaux's wife. Deanna was crying and trying to console me. She was several months pregnant and had to leave. I was alone with Michael. I was crying. I looked at my nails and wept because he would never see them. Everything was running through my mind so fast. So many things left unsaid. I did not get to say goodbye. I did not say I love you today. What was I going to do?

I called my dear friend Diahann. Diahann could not understand what I was saying. I hung up with her and called Aunt Grace. She started to pray. I tried calling Michael's brother, but could not reach him. I tried his sister, no answer. I tried his sister Ann, still no answer. I tried his sister Rose, again no answer. I tried his brother Evan. His wife answered. I couldn't remember her name. I called her Shirley, my other sister-in-law. I called her Katrina, my ex-sister-in-law. I told her I was sorry but I could not remember her name, but Michael was gone. I

LIFETIME

cried repeating that my husband was dead. I called my pastor. I called Raymond and could hear the excitement in his voice when he answered. We were to leave for Phoenix in two days. He could not understand what I was saying.

He said, "Sister, what's wrong?"

I wept whispering. "My husband is gone, Raymond. What am I going to do?"

He said nothing.

I thought somebody could help. Therefore, I kept calling people. No one was any help to me. I looked at my husband lying on that table. I couldn't believe it. This had to be a dream. Why had they taken his clothes? He had no dignity. I called my hairdresser she said she was on her way. I called Johnnie, my matron sister. I could not stop crying. My son called me. He wanted to come to the hospital. I told him I would call him back. I could not bear to deal with my son then. I had to go. "Oh Lord, this is the beginning of my end."

What do I tell our children? My 'Baby' was gone. I had no feelings. I was sinking into myself fast.

My family and friends started showing up. Serena came. Diahann came. Faye and Kenneth came. Renita came. I couldn't even look at Renita. Her husband who was Michael's best friend had died about eleven months before. He was killed in an automobile crash. My hairdresser came. Patricia, Rodney's wife came. Baby sister Janice came. I was concerned she had missed her son's graduation. She said she didn't. Dorothy Fields came. Toni and Vincent came. Michael's brother came. His sisters came. His nieces came. Forty-five people arrived in a short time. Eventually, the coroner came and they made all of us leave.

Diahann took me home. I cried all the way home. I called my friend Gabe who worked with me. He couldn't understand what I was saying. When we got to my house, a lot of people were there Uncle Jr. in his wheel chair. My cousins, Aunt Grace, my matron sisters, and so

many others were there. I went straight upstairs without acknowledging anyone, only asking for

my children to be sent upstairs. We cried together.

I told the kids it was going to be hard for us. Nicole was crying but Brandon did not. He

needed his mother. I could not help him. I needed my husband. I needed my baby. I had no

warning. I didn't get to say goodbye. *Oh Lord, this is the beginning of my end.*

By Sunday morning, I was getting real antsy because I had not heard from the funeral

director. I wanted to make the arrangements while church was going on so when our church was

out I could provide them with the details for the funeral. By afternoon, I was livid. Because I

had not heard from the funeral home. I called Raymond and told him that I was ready to make

the arrangements. Raymond said for me to be patient. I said to Raymond over the phone.

"Raymond, I tell you what; if I don't hear from them soon I will be calling someone else. You

guys suggested them to me. They better call soon!"

About five minutes later Raymond called with the funeral home owner on the line.

"Angela, I have Mr. Robertson of Oak Cliff Funeral Services on the other line."

I said hello and he began speaking.

"Mrs. Everette, I am sorry for your loss." He paused for a second and continued. "I

understand that you want to have your husband's services on Tuesday morning. Where is the

body?"

I said, "At the county coroner. They have not released the body yet."

"Okay, I will contact them." Without taking a breathe he continued, "What I need you to

do is bring a clean suit, underwear, tie, shirt, and socks to the funeral home in the morning and

we can make all of the arrangements there."

LIFETIME

Quite abruptly, I replied. "I don't care what you want. I am the one that has lost my husband. You need to be asking me what I want."

"I am sorry Mrs. Everette, but I thought you wanted to have the services on Tuesday and I was trying to expedite this. I am so sorry. How may I help you?" Mr. Robertson asked.

"First of all, I am not coming to Oak Cliff tomorrow. If you can't come by my home this afternoon, then I can contact someone else. Secondly, I have never buried anyone and I have a lot of questions. I refuse to be treated in any manner. So if you cannot come to me today, then I will contact another funeral service."

"Again Mrs. Everette, I am so sorry. I will send Anthony over shortly. Do you need anything else?"

"Yes, I need to be walked through the entire process and this need to occur soon or ..."

Mr. Robertson interrupted, "No, Mrs. Everette. I understand. I am sorry I miss-understood the situation. Anthony will come by soon."

"Thank you and goodbye." I said and hung up the telephone.

Diahann was standing near. She looked at me and asked. "What's wrong Angela?"

"That guy pissed me off. Where is the list of funeral homes?"

"I will look for it, but calm down." Diahann said.

"No, you calm down. They want me to pay them and they treat me poorly. If he thinks I am driving forty miles across town to pay him he is out of his mind."

"Yeah, you are right." Diahann said.

"You better believe I am right."

The telephone rang and it was Miami. Toni answered the phone. The conversation went like this. "Hello, this is Keith Whitfield, who I am speaking with?"

LIFETIME

Toni knew who Keith was. "Oh hey Miami, this is Toni."

"How are you doing Toni?"

"Oh as well as can be expected." Toni replied.

"Well, I was calling to see if Angela had any life insurance?"

Toni asked sarcastically, "And that is your business because if she doesn't you will come over bearing cash?"

"Yes." He replied.

"Then be here within the hour. The funeral director is expected anytime."

Well, he has not shown up with that cash yet. However, about forty-five minutes later, Anthony and Raymond arrived at my home. They came into my bedroom to make the arrangements. My friends Serena, Diahann, and Toni were all in the room with me. It was obvious to me that Anthony had been informed about me. He said something light hearted to break the ice, but he only put a dent in the ice. This was serious business and he was dealing with Mrs. Everette, not Angela and certainly not Angie. I still had to determine if he would handle my husband. Anthony gave his sympathy and put on his glasses as if he came to be professional. I was thinking come on with it, then.

He said Michael's body had been released and he could be picked up later that night, if I agreed to use their services. He gave me an overview of the Oak Cliff Funeral Services. Anthony started with, "We are a full service funeral home. We pride ourselves in being the best morticians in the city. We have several new 2002 limousines. We are professional and can handle all of your needs."

He handed me a catalog of caskets. I thumbed through the book and asked about one casket in particular. I pointed to the casket and said to Anthony. "What type of casket is this?"

LIFETIME

"Ah yes, that is a full couch." Anthony said as he looked at the catalog over his glasses.

"What is a full couch?" I asked.

Anthony responded saying, "With the full couch the entire top opens up so you can see the legs and feet. You will have to supply shoes."

"Oh, I don't like it." I frowned and shook my head.

Raymond mumbled sarcastically, "Good because it costs $9000."

"Are you sure, you don't like it? It is very nice." Anthony asked.

I continued thumbing through the catalog not looking at him. "Yes, I am sure." Finally, I stopped turning pages and said. "I like this one here in the color of a tiger's eye. And, I want him buried at Peaceful Valley, because I am not going to Oak Cliff."

"That is fine. I will call Peaceful Valley and make an appointment to find a plot. At Peaceful Valley, you will be required to buy a vault. The minimum cost is $750 and the most expensive is $1500. A vault is not a requirement of the city but is a requirement for that cemetery. It allows for easy maintenance of the grounds."

"I understand. I want the $750 vault."

Anthony did not open his mouth but he wrote something down. Then he continued. "The plots range from $3000 to $6000."

"That seems quite pricy."

"Well, we can take him somewhere else that is more reasonable."

"That would be NO!!!." I said as I rolled my eyes at him.

"Okay, then that is what it is going to cost?"

"How many limousines do you need?

I folded my arms and said. "Two."

LIFETIME

"They are $270 each."

"Okay."

"The casket sprays run about $250."

"I will pay for the spray." Raymond replied.

I turned to Raymond and like a robot said, "Thanks." I turned to Anthony and asked. "Is that everything Anthony?"

Anthony took his glasses off and began again. "Programs. We charge . . ."

Serena interrupted, "I will handle the programs." She was writing everything that was being said.

I uttered, "Thanks."

"Then there is the announcement for the paper. That will run about $350 with a picture."

"Okay." I whispered looking down at my manicured nails.

Anthony said to me, "Then I need you to write up what you would like to say, unless you want me to do it."

"No, I will do it." I responded still not looking at him.

"Mrs. Everette, do you still want to have the services on Tuesday?" Anthony questioned.

Looking down still I responded. "No, I am not ready yet. Let's move it to Wednesday.

Anthony added up the total and said we were done. I asked to use his calculator. He slid the calculator toward me and gave a chuckle saying, "Don't you trust me?"

Everyone laughed except me. I said to him, "This is not about trust. This is about business." I added up the figures to find they were incorrect.

After Anthony corrected the figures, he said to me, "As for payment, how are you going to handle it?"

LIFETIME

I folded my arms, "I don't know, because I don't have any money." I said in a matter of fact tone. I stood and walked toward Diahann.

Anthony was returning all items to his briefcase, "I am not worried; you went straight to the Cadillac section of the casket book. Therefore, I know you got some money. We can discuss that tomorrow."

Raymond interjected, "Well, I would like to say this Angela. Let Anthony do what they do. Let him handle everything. If you have insurance let him take the policy."

"I will think about it, Raymond."

"Like I said, Mrs. Everette I am not worried." Anthony repeated.

I said. "You should be. Thanks for coming over and walking me through everything." I was standing at the bedroom door, dismissing him at that point.

Monday morning Diahann came by. She discarded her cigarette as she entered my home. She and I were alone. Brandon and Nicole were shopping for clothes to wear to the funeral. Diahann was concerned from the night before and what she said shocked me. "Angie, I went to the bank and cashed in a CD. Here is fifteen thousand dollars for you to have for the funeral."

I covered by hand to my mouth and looked at the stack of bills. "You did what?"

Diahann was handing me the money and she said. "You said you didn't have any money so I want to help you."

"Girl, I love you for this but, I have insurance." I reached for her to give her a hug and whispered in her ear. "You must really love me."

Diahann wiped the tears from her eyes and said. "I do and I will do anything to help you." She paused and wiped more tears. "I loved Michael too."

LIFETIME

We embraced each other and cried. After we both had a good cry, I told her to take that

money back to the bank. Diahann left to go to the bank. I got my insurance policy out of the file

cabinet. About that time, Serena came by for us to complete the funeral arrangements.

We went to a one-hour cleaners to get Michael's clothes cleaned. Michael wanted to buy

a new suit a few weeks prior from our income tax refund, but I talked him out of it. While we

were riding around, Serena said. "Angie, it is obvious that Raymond likes you."

"No, he is just a friend." I said.

Driving along, Serena said, "I can see that, but he really cares about you a lot. I noticed it

last night."

I looked out the window of the car so she would not see the tears in my eyes. Finally, I

said, "I have a lot of friends and I am glad you are my friend."

We stopped and purchased some good quality paper. Then we went by the church where

Serena's sister worked to drop off the paper for the programs. I reviewed the program draft

while we were there. We stopped to pick up the suit from the cleaners. Serena and I completed

our errands and we returned to my home. Serena prepared the newspaper announcement, while I

located a picture for the newspaper.

Later that afternoon, Anthony came to take my mom, Aunt Doris, and me to the cemetery

to select a plot. I gave him Michael's clothes, the newspaper picture/write up, and the insurance

policy.

Anthony took us to the cemetery in a limousine. A friend of my mother wanted us to use

her daughter at the cemetery. I did not tell Anthony until we arrived at Peaceful Valley.

Anthony explained that it was a problem to change directors in midstream. He already had an

appointment with Loretta White. He was a colleague of the lady we wanted and did not know

LIFETIME

Ms. White. However, he agreed to make the request. Ms. White refused the request, as Anthony suspected. But I was not bothered by her refusal, for I did not know the other lady anyway. But, Anthony still wanted to know who we knew in the funeral business. I would not tell him.

As we were going in the door of Peaceful Valley cemetery Anthony said, "It must be William Broughton."

I did not respond. I ignored him as if he had not said anything.

Ms. White would not agree to change with the other lady, and she seemed offended with Anthony for asking. After that, Ms. White refused to let Anthony accompany us in her office. She asked him to sit in the hall, which sort of irritated me. No, it pissed me off.

As Ms. White was closing the door, Mr. Broughton's daughter entered the room. She hugged my mom. I could see Anthony sitting in the hallway facing me. He had a smirk on his face, indicating he knew he was right about Mr. Broughton. I shook Ms. Broughton's hand and said hello. As she was leaving, she said to Ms. White, "Treat them well."

The lady seemed nervous, but I wasn't sure why. It could have been that black people were in the room. I was not sure. Anyway, she drove us around the property and gave us prices. Anthony had been correct about the prices. The lady showed us a lot that had signs in Chinese or Vietnamese or some other language that I could not read. She said the lot was reasonably priced.

I looked at her as if she was out of her mind and said. "Now why would I want to bury my husband in an area where I can't read any of the signs? I looked out of the window of the van and said. "What else do you have?"

"Well, there is a lawn crypt but..." She paused in mid sentence.

I turned to her and said, "But what?"

LIFETIME

"Well, I usually don't mention it to African Americans, because some people are offended by this concept. It has two graves in one."

"Show me." I said.

She agreed and drove around the cemetery to show me a lawn crypt. "Here is one." She parked the vehicle and we got out. "The cost is $4957, but it is two graves, one on top of the other. The vault is already there so you save on that." She paused before continuing. "If you purchase two plots it will be $6000 for the plots, plus $750 vault, plus, $1055 for the opening and closing of the grave for a total of $7850. With this, you get two plots and will be saving about three thousand dollars."

I said to her very matter of fact. "That is what I want."

She asked me about the headstone and I said I was going to wait. We returned to her office and she wrote up the paper work. Ms. White then said. "If you let Peaceful Valley provide the headstone and it is damaged in anyway, we will repair or replace it at no cost to you. Additionally, we will put a temporary headstone on the grave the day of the funeral."

I crossed my legs and arms and asked the price.

Ms. White replied, "$1500."

I leaned forward, uncrossed my legs, and said to her. "If I buy it from my funeral director, will you fix and repair damages?"

"No." She replied.

"Okay, I will take it." I said as I stood to leave.

Ms. White picked up a brochure and asked, "What color would you prefer slate or rose?" She handed me the brochure and said. "I think rose is much softer."

LIFETIME

I looked at the brochure. "I don't know. That looks sort of feminine." I said scratching my head.

Ms. White shook her head from side to side. "No it is not. Do you want me to show you the day of the funeral."

I put my right hand on my hip, cocked my eyes, and said. "Are you crazy?" I waited for a second or two and said. "No. I'll take the slate and I do not want my name on it." I handed her the brochure.

Ms. White said, "What we do is we put your name and your birth date."

I was ready to go off, but my Aunt Doris did instead. Aunt Doris said as she stood. "Did you hear what she said? Do not put her name on it."

"No problem." Ms. White responded.

I started for the door and said. "Are we done?"

Ms. White stood to shake my hand and said. "Yes, at Peaceful Valley…"

I shook my hand like a referee saying it's no good. I said, "Save it. I am not interested."

She had a look of disbelief and uttered, "Well . . ."

I looked at my mom and aunt and said, "Well nothing let's go." I opened the door and gave Anthony the cue that I was ready to go. We walked to the limo and I explained to Anthony what we agreed to.

He looked at the paper work and said, "Our funeral home is not paying for a headstone. We have to pay the cemetery in full the day of the funeral, but we will not get our money from the insurance company for several months."

LIFETIME

I reminded Anthony that I wanted the headstone before he went inside to discuss this with Ms. White. We came to an agreement that I would pay for the headstone the following week and the cemetery would still provide the temporary headstone.

That was done. However, Anthony was still asking about our connection to William Broughton. I would not discuss this. Later, I found out both Raymond and Anthony had worked for Mr. Broughton at another funeral home. Neither of them would discuss him with me, only saying he knew who they were.

William Broughton told my mother he was not familiar with the Oak Cliff funeral home the day Michael died. I think they were all lying for whatever reason. It must be a rule or something. It seemed there are a lot of rules and protocols in the funeral business.

The next day was very busy. I don't know what all I had done that day, but it was 3:00 when Anthony finally reached me. He needed me to come and view the body before we could have the wake.

Diahann drove the kids and me to the funeral home. I went in alone to see Michael. Michael looked nice. He had gotten a hair cut a few days before he died. Anthony shaved and trimmed his beard nicely. He was wearing a beard in remembrance of his best friend Jimmy who died the prior year.

I noticed Michael's nose had something in it. The attendant had me leave and he cleaned Michael's nose. After he finished, Nicole, Brandon, Diahann, my mom, and I went inside. No one said a word. Everyone seemed to be having his or her own private talk with Michael.

We left, returned home, and got ready for the wake. Traffic was horrible. I was worried about being late for the wake. While in traffic, I wondered if Michael's barber knew about his death. I called the barbershop. His barber, Dimple, was very sorry for my loss. Someone had told her of Michael's death.

Many people attended the wake but it was not too sad. My hairdresser came by before she went to her own brother-in-laws wake. Kayron was what I call "Throwed off." You know crazy. She had never met Michael before. When she viewed his body, she backtracked to where I was sitting and said "Oh Angie, he is real cute." I looked at her and just shook my head. As I said, she was throwed off.

Serena's husband, Brian was the officiator of the wake. My mom spoke. Michael's brother Lawrence spoke. Don one of the Dreamz team spoke. The Dreamz team were VIP members of a local nightclub. Michael was a Dreamz team member, also. Not too many people spoke. Some thought that they would get the opportunity to speak at the funeral. A lot of college friends came.

We served food in the Chapel. People always bring a lot of food to your house when someone dies. I decided that day, never to take a box of chicken to someone's house ever again for their bereavement. Eating was the last thing on your mind when you have lost a loved one. I did not eat for three months. I just was not hungry.

That night, in the bed I began looking at the ceiling. I was numb so I laid there and listened to the ticking of the clock. Each tick of the clock intensified my anxiety. I knew what time it was, but I rose up to look anyway. It was 11:35 a.m. I dialed Aunt Grace.

Aunt Grace answered as if she was expecting me to call. "Hello."

With a whimper I said, "Aunt Gra" not able to speak her name. "I can't sleep."

She responded, "It's okay, baby."

"But what am I going to do?"

LIFETIME

"Angie." Aunt Grace said.

I did not respond.

"Angie, Baby, it's going to be okay."

I began crying louder. She let me cry.

Every now and then, she said, "It's going to be okay."

"It's so hard." I whimpered.

"I know baby."

I continued crying.

She asked me, "Do I need to come over?"

"No." I said in a soft whimper.

Aunt Grace cried out, "Oh Lord give her strength."

Still crying, I said, "Goodnight." I must have known Michael needed to talk to me because I hung up abruptly.

Michael said, "Baby."

I was not afraid. I stopped crying and listened to what he had to say.

"Baby, now I will be looking good on tomorrow so you better be looking good."

I smiled and said, "Okay." I turned to pick up the telephone to dial Diahann.

Diahann answered as if she was not asleep. It was 1:15 in the morning.

"Diahann," I sobbed.

"What do you need, Angela?"

"Well." I blew my nose before continuing, "Michael just told me that I need to look good on tomorrow."

She responded, "You will."

LIFETIME

I whimpered, "Will you bring me some jewelry?"

"Yes." She paused for a second. "Do you need anything else?"

I did not respond other than sniffing my nose.

Diahann said, "Angela, do I need to come over?"

I sobbed, "No." We held the phone. Occasionally she said something. I just cried and eventually I let her go. The clock was louder than before. I counted the ticks, after 2825 ticks, I called Diahann back at 3:02. She answered on the first ring.

"Hello."

"Will you bring me a diamond watch?"

"Okay, I will bring it."

"Thanks." Then I just held the phone crying.

"Angela, I think you should get some sleep."

I agreed and said goodnight.

After I hung up I did not notice the clock ticking so as I rose up to see the time. Michael said, "Baby."

I wiped the tears from my eyes and listened.

He said, "Baby, why did you get two limousines? That will not be enough room for my father, sisters, brothers, and their spouses. You know I never made a difference between them. Either all of them ride or none of them ride."

I whispered, "Okay." I picked up the telephone and called Raymond, who was in Phoenix with my drill team. "Raymond, I need another limousine. Call Anthony so he can bring another one."

Raymond responded, "Hold on." After a few seconds, he clicked Anthony into the call.

LIFETIME

Anthony said, "Good morning, Mrs. Everette, how may I help you?"

"I need another limo."

There was a pregnant pause before he responded. "That will be real hard."

In a soft yet firm voice I said, "Work it out."

"I will do my best." He replied.

"Do better than that." I paused for a second and said, "I will see you at ten with three limos. Goodnight."

"Goodnight, Mrs. Everett." Anthony hung up but Raymond and I stayed on the phone.

Raymond asked, "Do you need me to do anything?"

I began to cry again and sobbed out, "No."

"I need to be there, Man."

"No, you need to be with my drill team kids." Raymond a former funeral director himself thought he would be of more help to me in his former profession.

Raymond said, "I have talked to the funeral home and have told them they better treat you well. Anthony is good and he will take care of you." He paused before continuing, "Boy, I need to be there."

I did not respond for a while. Then I asked him what he was doing before I called.

"Sleeping." Raymond said in dry voice.

"Oh." I sighed and said, "I am not sleepy."

"Really?" He responded very sarcastically.

I decided to let him sleep. "Raymond, I am going to say goodnight so you can sleep. Goodnight."

"Try to get some rest, Angela. Goodnight."

LIFETIME

I hung up the phone and the clock was just as loud as it had been earlier. I laid there not sleeping wide-eyed only blinded by my tears. Then I called Aunt Grace again.

"Hello, Baby."

"Is Aunt Doris asleep?" I asked.

Aunt Grace answered, "Let me check."

Aunt Doris chimed in from the other line. "Yes, Angie."

"Aunt Doris, tell the pastor that I don't want anyone to touch me on tomorrow."

"Okay, Baby girl, but you need to get some sleep."

I started stuttering, spitting, and crying. She did not respond. Eventually, I heard her tell Aunt Grace that Angie needs you. She got back on the, Aunt Grace and I held the telephone. I cried. I must have fallen asleep crying to Aunt Grace, by 7:00 in the morning I awakened with the phone still in my hand. Aunt Grace was still holding on. I said, "Goodnight, Aunt Grace."

Aunt Grace responded, "Goodnight, I love you."

My mom and Diahann had arrived, at my home. They were in the kitchen cooking breakfast. I went to the kitchen poured myself a cup of black coffee and sat in Brandon's chair. I sipped with tears flowing from my eyes. I did not speak to anyone just sat, sipped, and sobbed. It didn't seem like I had been sitting there long, but at 9:00 my mom said. "Sweetheart, you need to shower and get ready."

Like a robot, I did what she said, showered and dressed. Once dressed, in my bedroom I noticed Diahann was dressed somewhat different. She was wearing an oversized paisley top and a black skirt. I looked at her somewhat puzzled and questioned, "Are you wearing what you have on?"

LIFETIME

Diahann replied, "Well, let me show you what I am wearing. She pulled the top to her suit from her garment bag. It was a black two-piece St. John's. It was in her words "Nasty" and quite expensive too.

When I saw it I said, "Oh, I am wearing that." I took the top out of her hand.

Diahann removed her skirt. I removed my black dress, went in the restroom, and put on the suit. I thought I looked good. I came out of the restroom and asked for the jewelry. Diahann showed me what she had, but the jewelry was somewhat small. I wanted big jewelry.

Diahann said, "Now remember you were wearing that dress." She pointed to my black dress on the bed. "So I brought jewelry for that dress."

I looked at her nodding my head up and down as if I understood and asked. "Well what were you going to wear with this suit?" I paused with my hand extended. "Give me that."

She looked at me with sadness, took of her jewelry, and gave it to me. I went back into the restroom to make sure I was looking good. This time when I came out of the restroom, I asked Diahann for some black panty hose.

Diahann stood there looking frustrated and said. "I gave you a pair yesterday. What happened to them?"

I stuck my leg out and said. "Well, I got a run in them."

Diahann sat on the bed and took off her panty hose. All she was wearing was a blouse and panties. I stripped her of all her jewelry, except her rings. My hands were much smaller than hers are. But, she had the nerve to say that she was thankful for that.

About that time my mom came in the bedroom and in a startled voice said, "Diahann, where are your clothes?"

LIFETIME

Diahann raised her arms like a little girl to talk to my mother and said. "Mother, she has all my clothes and if she wants anything else she can have it. I love her and will give her all I have."

My mom said to her, "But Diahann what are you going to wear?"

"I don't know." Diahann replied with her palms up.

About that time, I pulled something out of my closet. But, all my clothes were too small for her. It was funny that I could wear her clothes but mine were too small for her. My mom was worried Diahann didn't have anything to wear.

About that time, Anthony was knocking on the bedroom door. I left the room and said, "I'm ready to go."

"I got a third limo." He said.

"I know, let's go."

"Well, Angela we need to wait on your pastor." Anthony said as he followed me into the living room.

"Why?" I asked.

"Because it is the right thing to do."

"Well, I am ready and I am not waiting on anybody. Any Everette' that is late today will be left. I will call the church to see if he is there and then we will leave."

After I called, Anthony asked. "Was he there?"

I responded, "No, he will be there soon. Let's go." In all actuality, they did not know where he was. There was no way in the world that I was going to tell Anthony that the pastor might be on his way to my home.

LIFETIME

On the way to the church, the young brother limousine driver was chit chatting about what he was going to cook for dinner. He talked about his kids and one conversation after the other. Mrs. Everette, who doesn't meet any strangers talked right back to him, on the way to her husband's funeral.

Anthony called from the lead car, asking where the programs were. I told him my friend printed the programs and not to worry. He was worried because if the programs were not there the funeral home would be blamed, not my friend.

I said to him on the limo driver's cell phone, "Don't worry. If my friend said she would be there with the programs, then she would be there with the programs." I hung up.

We got to the funeral and I saw a white girl, Emily, from work rushing inside, I was pleasantly surprised that she thought enough of me to come. The parking lot was full. As we entered, I noticed there were a lot of flowers. I wore dark shades and did not give anyone eye contact. My cousin from Mississippi escorted me in. Most people did not know who he was. He sat next to me for a while until I told his wife to take their baby outside. He jumped up to go outside with his baby. Although, I said it in an abrupt tone, everyone was glad that I had said it.

Nicole said that she thought his wife was relieved when I told her to leave.

It was if I was having an out of body experience at the funeral. There were a lot of people at that affair; people that I hadn't seen in awhile. Everyone was trying to look at me for some reason. But, I had on shades so they could not see my eyes.

The choir sang "Jesus Be a Fence." However, I sat there with no expression or movement. A friend of Michael's sang a solo. I had never seen the man before. As he got up to sing, Nicole and I both wondered, could he sing? We looked at each other with a concerned look. As he prepared to sing, my sister-in-law's ex-husband went to the piano. I wondered if he

LIFETIME

could play. A little woman jumped up with her short legs and went to the organ. I was worried. Nevertheless, they turned it out. The man sang, "Yes, God is Real." He could sing too. One of our choir members sang his heart out, "I Really Love the Lord." The church was spirit filled. But, I kept wondering why I was there.

My aunt Doris officiated the funeral. Brian, Serena's husband, spoke really nice. He was comforting and mainly talked to me. Faye's husband, Kenneth started talking and talking and talking. Rev. Brian Kendall and my Aunt Doris were getting up to pull his coattail. I looked at Kenneth and rolled my arms and mouthed, "Wrap it up and sit down." He did just that, shut up in the middle of the sentence. Kenneth abruptly took his seat. My pastor did the eulogy and had a powerful message.

Finally, it was time to view the body. As soon as they opened the casket, my pastor told everyone not to touch the family. I wanted to have an open casket so I could see who attended the funeral. But, I did not want anyone to touch me.

Some people were upset that he said that. Some people thought my pastor was not talking to them. There were about 700 people attending the services. But, twenty people decided they *just had* to touch me. I remembered who they were, too.

The first one was Lynette. Lynette was a tall slim co-worker and a friend from south Texas. She had so much compassion for people. She was taking care of her 94-year-old aunt and raising her nephews along with her own 14-year-old daughter. She was the type of person you wanted to confide in. She loved to read. Lynette was a member of my book club. I worried about her sometimes because she neglected herself for others.

Ryan, on the other hand, also co-worker, was an all about me kind of person. Ryan heard the pastor, but he did not believe that was meant for him and touched me anyway. Each time

LIFETIME

someone touched me I had to regroup so I missed the next ten people behind the person that touched me.

My former hairdresser touched me. It took so much out of me. Dimple, Michael's barber, touched me. My uncle Lee winked at me, as to say 'Duck-a-Lucking' you can make it girl. It gave me strength. I appreciated him for that. One of my co-workers whispered in my ear to be strong. He was Ryan's cousin and a minister. He was encouraging because he did not touch me. I knew the people that touched me wanted to help and really cared about me, but I was trying to make it through.

I do not remember my children viewing the body. It was finally my turn. I stood slowly and walked to the casket. I looked at Michael and he looked good. Just as he said the night before. I took my shades off to get a good look and say goodbye. I touched his chest and after a few seconds, it seemed that my hand was pushed away. As if to say, "Let me go girl." Therefore, I turned and walked away.

As we exited the door of the church, Brandon reached for me. He almost fell over. I grabbed him and the both of us almost hit the floor. He started to cry. I held my baby. I thought my poor baby finally broke down.

The processional to the cemetery was very long. We had two escorts but could have used four. Michael was buried in a lawn crypt, a double grave at Peaceful Valley cemetery in North Dallas. The cemetery delivered the courtesy grave marker as they promised. They had a water cooler by the gravesite. It was hot, over one hundred degrees. My kids were socializing with everyone after the burial. I went straight to the family car. I was not in a socializing mood. Eventually, they all got in the car and we went back to the church to eat. A lot of family

LIFETIME

members came back to the church, but most of my co-workers went back to work. We ate and then returned to my home.

I fell asleep on the way home. It had been a long day. I was not in a talkative mood anymore. As I was getting out of the car, that jerk handed me his home telephone number. He wanted to get to know me better. I thought to myself, I just bet you do. Why would I want to get to know him that day, after having just buried my husband? It made me want to throw up. I didn't like the fact that he knew my deceased husbands name, my address, and all. I thought his conversation was interesting on the way to the funeral as small talk. I never saw his 'push up' coming. It is sad that people will prey on you when you are most vulnerable.

Late that night I called Raymond and talked to him for a couple of hours. I told him about the limo driver and he assured me that he would not call directory assistance to get my telephone number through my deceased husband. He said that men did not think that way. If he called, that meant he went through your records at the funeral home. Raymond said if he does call for me to report it to the funeral home. He asked me what I was going to do the next day.

"Sleep." I said.

Raymond had a silent sigh of relief. I said goodnight so he could sleep. I still had to get packed.

The next morning, we arrived at the airport real early. It was post 911. First, they said we had too many pieces. We had a lot of stuff for our return trip, which would be by bus. I had to put my pillow and purse inside Brandon's garment bag. Brandon beeped as he went through the scanner.

As we boarded the plane, Nicole's ticket was scanned a red light went off that said "Random Search." My ticket did the same thing and so did Brandon's. The airport security went through all of our things.

Nicole was first. They frisked, wand, opened, and went through her luggage. When they finished they told her to board the plane.

I said to the security personnel, "She is my daughter. Can she wait on us?"

The security guy said, "No, she has to get on the plane." So, she walked down the runway slowly. "Speed up young lady." The security guy said to Nicole.

Then they searched my things. They told me to board immediately after they finished. I lingered. They noticed me lingering and they stopped searching Brandon.

After we got to our seats on the plane, the flight attendant came to me and asked for my identification because they did not have a record of me boarding the plane. My purse was still in Brandon's garment bag. The reason that we had such a hard time was we were all flying with one-way tickets that had been purchased just two days before. The three of us were the only people that were searched. The plane could not take off until we were seated. Nicole and I slept the entire way. Brandon did not sleep. He held my hand.

When we got to Phoenix, I called Raymond. He answered the phone as if he was wide-awake. "Hey! What are you doing?" I said all bubbly.

"Sleeping." Raymond said.

"Quit playing, you are not sleep. Nicole wants to talk to you."

Raymond said, "Let me talk to my girl." I handed Nicole the cell that was on speaker.

"Raymond, what did you have for breakfast today?" Nicole asked.

LIFETIME

"We had pancakes, eggs, bacon, fruit, danish, and juice. It was good. If you want me to, I'll come get you."

"Okay, come get me, now." Nicole said to Raymond.

"I can't come, now." Raymond said.

Nicole begged, "Please?"

"Nicole, don't make me cry. You know I can't come get you now. Next time."

"No, this time. Please?" She was still pleading.

"Baby, don't cry."

I took the phone from Nicole and said. "Raymond, come down here and get us?"

"Now there you go." Raymond said to me.

I said to him, "We are at the Phoenix airport, come get us."

"Quit playing, so I can go back to sleep. You told me you were sleeping in today."

"I did sleep on the plane." I said with a chuckle. Brandon and Nicole were standing there laughing at Raymond. We were all three listening to the whole conversation.

"Quit playing so I can go back to sleep. I am going to cut my phone off."

I said, "Before you cut it off your phone, come and get us."

Raymond raised his voice, "I tell you what. If I do come, you better be there or else somebody is going to pay."

We grabbed all of our stuff and went outside the airport. We knew he would leave us if we were not visible. Raymond was in shock. He gave all of us a big hug. He was in a compact car and we could hardly fit. He borrowed one of the bus driver's rentals. He rushed us back to the hotel. It was almost lunchtime and the drill team would be coming back to the hotel to eat.

LIFETIME

My matron sisters, one by one tried to break my neck with their hugs and kisses. I took a seat and when the 80 drill team members filed in, they were all surprised to see us. They slobbered us down. I was glad to be there among family. They told me that our family had been lifted up in prayer at the National Baptist BTU and Sunday School Congress.

Everyone that knew me gave me a hug at the convention center. It was encouraging. Our drill team performed that night.

Friday we received an elite rating. Nicole and Brandon collected the trophy. Then it was time to go home.

It was a long ride back home. When we got back to the church, my mom was there to pick us up. Michael had always picked us up. The reality of him not being there was evident. I cried when I got home. I was so empty.

The next day was Fathers Day. I cried all through church service. I cried some more. *Oh Lord, it was the beginning of my end.*

About four in the morning, the day after Fathers Day, the phone rang. It was Faye. Her father had passed away. My friend needed me. I called Raymond to ask him what to do. He said to call Anthony later in the day.

Faye wanted to use Oak Cliff Funeral Services and Anthony. I called Anthony later that day and he handled all of the arrangements.

The following Saturday I was faced with attending my best friend's father's funeral. *Oh, Lord I need you.*

Raymond took me to the wake. Less than two weeks had passed since, my husband's body had been at the same funeral home. I was so weak, but it was not about me. I showed Raymond the guy that had 'pushed up.' I had to stop Raymond from saying anything.

LIFETIME

My long time childhood friend, Serena, took me to the funeral. It was so sad. But, as Faye's best friend, I had to go. It was my turn to be a friend to her. I had to be strong for her. I lost my father twenty years prior and it almost killed me. I thanked God for my friends. I know this was a time the Lord carried me.

LIFETIME

Stand

I was off work for several weeks when Brandon complained that I needed to return before the bank stopped paying us. Brandon stood at my bedroom door and said. "Now that daddy is gone somebody has got to go to work up in here, and I am not ready to go to work. Just get back in there and go to work. I promise you; you will feel better." His eyes were so sincere, but I did not respond.

The following Monday I went to work early but could not get out of the car. I listened to Donnie McClurkin's "Stand." I listened and wondered if I could even stand up. I didn't think I could. I listened to that song again. It repeated about five times before I had the strength to get out of the car. Finally, I opened the car door. I placed one leg on the ground then the other. I stood up humming, "…when you've done all you can."

I walked inside the building and went to my desk. I plopped my purse on my desk; that was when I noticed our family photo. It was Michael, Brandon, Nicole, and me sitting on our living room sofa. I rubbed my hand across the picture touching Michael's face. I was still standing. Still standing and looking around. Everything was so prominent. There was a small picture of Michael in the corner of my desk. It looked as though he was winking at me. The message light wasn't highlighted on my phone. I thought that was odd. No one had called me in the month that I had been out. I stood in the small 6 x 6 cubicle. Eventually, I sat down and hit the power button on my computer. It took a good ten minutes to boot. I had over twenty five hundred new emails. I thought to myself a lot of work but no phone calls…hmmm.

The whole day I had to remind myself to just stand. My friend Don sent me an email.

> **To:**   Angela Everett
>
> **From:** Don Woods
>
> ## LIFETIME

Angela, I saw your car. Can I come down to see you?

Don Woods, Vice President

The reply.

> **To:** Don Woods
>
> **From:** Angela Everett
>
> No don't. Also, do not tell anyone that I am here.
>
> Angela Everette, Assistant Vice President

His reply.

> **To**: Angela Everett
>
> **From:** Don Woods
>
> Are you okay?
>
> Don Woods, Vice President

My reply.

> **To:** Don Woods
>
> **From:** Angela Everett
>
> Not really, but I will be.
>
> Angela Everette, Assistant Vice President

He replied.

> **To:** Angela Everett
>
> **From:** Don Woods
>
> Send me an email if you need me.
>
> Don Woods, Vice President

LIFETIME

We emailed each other every day for about two weeks. Then one day, Don sent an email.

> **To:**   Angela Everett
>
> **From:** Don Woods
>
> Let's have coffee.
>
> Don Woods, Vice President

Reluctantly I replied.

> **To:**   Don Woods
>
> **From:** Angela Everett
>
> Okay. I will meet you downstairs in five minutes.
>
> Angela Everett, Assistant Vice President

I stood from my chair. I paced from my chair to the opening of my cubicle. I stood there for ten minutes before I took the back stairway to the cafeteria. There were a lot of people that I knew in the cafeteria. Some spoke, others tried to act as if they had not notice me. Some said, "I am so sorry," others asked about the kids.

Each day I listened to Donnie McClurkin before I got out of the car. This went on for months. Some days it repeated five times, others three times, eventually only one time. I was always preoccupied with that song.

***

A couple of months later, Michael's barber, Dimples, called me at home. She told me how sorry she was for my loss. She talked about how she told Michael three days before he died that he needed to go to the doctor to see about his cough. She laughed at how one of her customers asked her for a haircut like Michael's. He had real thick curly hair. Dimples told the guy he could not get Michael's hair cut with his hair. She was going on and on.

LIFETIME

I thought the call from Dimples was odd because we had never been friendly. In fact, I was often bothered by the way, she stared at me when I was at the barbershop. One day a couple of years before Michael died, she confided in me saying. "Mrs. Everett, I need to tell you something. Every time I look at you, I want to laugh. I never knew that Michael was your husband until he brought your son in the shop one day. After I realized that you were his wife, I knew you were the one who's dirty drawers he loved."

That night, Dimples went on to say that many years ago when she worked in South Dallas, a guy asked Michael. "Man, do you love you wife?"

Michael said, "Hell yeah. I love her dirty drawers."

Dimple said she thought to herself. "Now that's love. Many years later, I came to the North Dallas shop. You always brought your son to the barbershop. Michael found out I was on this side of town and he started coming too. When Michael brought Brandon in the shop that day and I realized who he loved, I could never look at you without laughing." Dimple paused and then continued. "But why did the preacher say not to touch you?"

I said to her, "Dimple, because I just could not take people touching on me." I paused and then said. "I do not know what I am going to do without Michael. I really loved him."

Dimple said, "I know you did. You two had been together a long time and I am sorry that I touched you." She raised her voice a little. "But all I could think about was the man that loved her dirty drawers is dead. What is she going to do? I touched you to let you know that I cared. I did not mean to hurt you."

I told her it was okay and I knew I would be fine.

LIFETIME

Several weeks later, I received a voice mail. It was a familiar male voice. "Hello, Angela. This is Charles Jeffrey. I am sorry to hear about your husband. You can call me back. Here are my numbers... Take care."

I smiled and said, "Oooh Baby." I dialed the number. Charles answered. I said, "Hey Charles, this is Angela. I got your message. How are you?"

Charles responded, "I am fine, but I am so sorry about your husband."

"Thank you." I replied.

"I called you at work after I heard about your husband, but the secretaries said I could not leave you a voice mail. They said I had to call you at home or wait until you returned to work."

I remembered not having any voice mails, but did not respond.

"Is there anything that I can do for you?" Charles asked.

"No, I don't think so." I said.

"Well, I better let you go."

"Okay." I replied.

"Call me if you need anything. I want you to know you can reach out and I'll be there for you."

"Okay thanks, bye." I hung up the phone, relaxed in my chair for a few minutes and began to reminisce. I got up and went to the cafeteria to tell Big Daddy, Tommy, Don, and Gabe that Oooh Baby had called. They were all sitting there together. I walked up to their table and said. "Guess who called me?"

"Oooh Baby," they all said in unison not even looking at me.

"What did he want?" Big Daddy asked.

"Nothing, just to give his condolences," I said.

LIFETIME

"Sure." Big Daddy said.

"It was." I insisted.

Big Daddy picked up his sandwich in his hand and said. "Okay, if you say so." The rest of them just had smirks on their faces. Gabe and Tommy could hardly hold in the laughter.

***

Each day I went through the motions at work as if I was doing okay. But, what I really wanted was to go home and get back in bed. I climbed in my bed and stared at the ceiling. All I wanted to do was count the popcorn on the ceiling directly over my head. There were six hundred and seventy three bubbles of popcorn. I laid in bed each evening not saying anything, not crying or anything, only counting over and over. I tried to see if I would come up with the same amount of bubbles each time. I could not wait to go home and get in bed each day. I did not eat, sleep, or go to the grocery store. Nicole and Brandon would get in bed with me sometimes. I would turn my back to them wishing they would think that I had fallen asleep and leave so I could get back to counting the bubbles on the ceiling. After I counted the bubbles, a number of times I would call either Lynette or Raymond one of them would take my mind off the ceiling bubbles for a while.

***

A few months later, my matron sisters, Janice, Gwen, and I were at Rev. Beaux's preparing for the homecoming of his wife and new baby. We were cleaning their home and preparing dinner for Deanna. Deanna had requested beef stew which none of us knew how to prepare. We called Irene who was at home sick. Irene could cook anything and she gave us step-by-step instructions on making stew. While we were discussing the stew, my cell phone rang. It was Raymond. I could hardly understand what he was saying.

LIFETIME

I stopped cooking and said. "Raymond. Raymond, what's wrong?" He was crying really hard. He cried out his sister died. I imagined him rolling around on the floor from the sorrow that I heard in his voice. I fell to a seat and just held the phone. It had only been four months since Michael's death.

Gwen walked over to me and said, "What's wrong Angela? Who is on the phone?"

I looked at her with a tear running down my face and cried out, "Raymond's sister is dead." Gwen sat in a seat close by. Rev. Beaux heard me and removed the telephone from my hand. Rev. Beaux began to speak to Raymond. He walked out of the kitchen with the phone. I had nothing in me to give, nothing to say. I looked at Janice and she was washing dishes.

Janice never said a word. She shook her head from side to side in disbelief. She never wiped the tears from her eyes. I knew she was still grieving from her mother. Her mother had died only one month after Michael. Raymond took me to her wake. She was so happy that we came.

Gwen turned her back to me. Her mother died just a couple of months after Michael. We all sat there and grieved. Not saying a word, not looking at each other. We were in shock. We were empty, just silent in our own grief. We could not help Raymond or each other for that matter. We said silent prayers for our brother and silently encouraging ourselves.

***

The next day, Charles called again. This time, I was not having a good day. "Hello Angela, this is Charles."

"Hi." I said in a dry voice.

"How are you?"

"Not good, I am having a bad day Charles."

LIFETIME

"What's wrong?" Charles asked.

I responded quite frustrated, "Everything. My toilet is broke, my daughter's brakes need replacing, and my garage needs cleaning, just everything." I gave a big sigh.

"Is there something I can do to help?" Charles asked.

"Yes, you name it and I need help with it."

"What do you have in your garage?"

I said. "Paint, wiring, tools, compressors, it is knee deep in stuff."

"Do you have any electrical wire?" Charles asked.

"Probably." I said.

Charles replied, "Well, I can come by on Saturday to take a look and get the wire. I will pay you for the wire. And I can look at the toilet and your daughter's car."

We exchanged numbers and Charles was scheduled to come by my home the following Saturday.

As soon as I hung up with Charles, Raymond called. He said his sister's funeral would be on Saturday. I thought about calling Charles back and telling him not to come by on Saturday, but I did not want to talk to him. We were not friends and I did not want to be a bothered. Each day I said I was going to call Charles back, but I did not.

That Saturday morning I went to Raymond's sister's funeral. It was about 1:00 that afternoon when I realized I had never told Charles that I was not going to be home. I pulled over in the car, looked up his telephone number, and called him.

Charles said, "This is Charles Jeffrey."

"Hey, this is Angela. I forgot you were supposed to come by today."

LIFETIME

"Yeah, I called your house and I guess it was your daughter saying you were not there. She sounded just like you." He sounded like he didn't believe my daughter.

"No, it was not me. I had to go to a funeral. I am sorry."

"Well, I had to go back to work." Charles said.

"Don't worry. Another time." I didn't want him to come over anyway.

"Alright, if I get off before it gets too late I will call you."

"Okay, Thanks Charles. Bye." I was relieved since I did not want him to come over anyway. The garage was a mess and it was nothing he could do about it that day. It was raining and I was no longer as concerned about the garage as I had been earlier in the week.

When I got home I looked for the wire, but it was just too much stuff. I hoped he would never call. Because, I didn't want to be bothered.

Although, Charles was my Oooh Baby he was the last person I wanted to see. He got on my last nerve. He broke up with me and I never forgave him for that. That was why all my friends knew him as the dog that he was.

About 6:00, that same day Charles called. "Hello Angela, this is Charles."

"Hi." I said in response to him.

"I can come by now." Charles said.

"That is fine, but you don't have too." I said very nonchalant.

"Well, I am on my way. You can show me the garage and I can look at the wire. My sister needs some. I will pay you for it."

Charles knocked on my door thirty-nine minutes later. I took a deep breath and opened the door. I had been cleaning and was wearing a jogging suit. I didn't care and would not have dressed up for him, anyway. "Hi," I said stepping back.

LIFETIME

He stepped toward me as if he wanted to hug me.

I took another step backwards. *Hug the air you dog.* He was bald on the top with salt and pepper hair. He had a beer belly, but basically looked the same.

"Hello, Angela." Charles said stepping inside with his arms outreached to give me a hug.

I did not hug him but said. "I didn't find the wire, but come on, let me show you the garage." I showed him the way to the garage.

"Okay."

"Here is the garage."

"Oh, this is a job." Charles said looking around in disbelief.

"Do you see any wire that looks like electrical wire?" I asked.

Charles looked around for a minute. "Well no, but . . ."

I interrupted, "Well I guess I don't have any then." I was ready for him to go.

"Let's go back in the house."

Once in the kitchen Charles asked me. "When do you want me to help you with the garage?"

I was standing in the kitchen ready to walk him to the front door. "I don't know." I was ready for him to leave, but he was lingering around the kitchen table?"

Charles said, "Let me look at the toilet."

I showed him to the bathroom where he was able to fix the toilet with parts he found in the garage. He checked Nicole's car and said the brakes were not as bad as I thought. After he finished he returned to the kitchen.

At that time, I wasn't eating so all I could offer him was coffee or water. My cupboard was bare. But, I offered him something to drink.

LIFETIME

Charles said, "Sure, what do you have?"

"Water or coffee." I said in a dry tone.

"I'll take water. It's too late for coffee." Charles took the water and a seat at the kitchen table.

I wanted him to take the water and leave but he was sitting down.

"I am so sorry about your loss." He paused but not long enough for me to respond. "How is your mother?"

"Fine." I said, since he had sat down. He was at the kitchen table. I was over by the bar, still standing. "You know you really hurt me." I said as I ran my finger around the rim of my coffee cup.

Charles took a drink of water and said. "I am sorry. I realized a long time ago that I was wrong. I should have stayed with you. I realized too late that you were a good woman from a good family."

I said very cocky. "Sure was. Your loss." I sipped my coffee.

"Do you think we could have been happy?" Charles asked.

"Hell no!" I snapped.

"I think we could have been good together. But you were so mean and talked so bad." He took a drink of water and crossed him leg.

"I was never mean nor did I talk bad."

"You did to me, and maybe I deserved it."

"I am sure you did deserve it." I snapped.

Charles smiled and said, "How old are your kids?"

LIFETIME

With pride in my voice I said, "Nicole is 16, a junior at Berkner High School and Brandon is 14, a freshman at Apollo Jr. High."

He sat up in his chair. "Your daughter attends your alma mater?"

"You remember that?" I asked in a surprised tone.

"Yes, Angela. I knew everything about you. You were my woman. The oldest child of Bernie and Autrice Franklin, your brother was Gary. Both he and your dad died from car accidents. Your dad's mom was Mrs. Jewell. But, I don't remember your mother's mother name, but she lived on Church Road." He paused for a second. "What do you remember about me?"

"Like what?" I looked at him puzzled and was ready for him to go.

"I bet you don't remember my parents or my sister's names."

I was trying to be funny and said. "Well, since you are a named after your father, your dad's name is Charles. You have several sisters and I think your youngest sister's name is Nedra.

"That is correct but I cannot believe that is all you remember about me."

"Why? Are you finished with the water? Are you leaving?"

"You want me to leave?" He asked.

"Well, we are done here." I stood up.

Charles leaned back in the seat and said. "Do you ever sit back and think about us?"

I had my arms folded. "Yeah, I wondered how could you have loved me and treated me like you did. You hurt me. You hurt me badly." I went to the coffee pot and poured myself another cup since he didn't seem to be ready to leave.

"I am sorry. I promise I will never hurt you again."

LIFETIME

I took a sip of coffee and snapped. "You are damn straight, because you have no power over me. I can't be hurt by you again."

"Angela, I am sorry. I promise." Charles replied

"Don't promise me anything. You don't owe me shit. I am over you. Been over you. I have had a good life, a good husband, a happy marriage, and some wonderful children. I don't need your apology now and since you brought it up." I took my seat at the bar and then continued. "But, my dad really liked you."

"Did he like Michael?"

"Hell yeah, M.F. Do you think we sat around here wondering about yo ass? Hell no. You are the one that lost out. I loved you with all my heart and you stomped on it." I stirred my coffee.

I was quiet for a moment then I said. "I used to say I would never forgive you but God showed me that He provided me with a husband who loved and adored me. I am thankful for all of the blessings that God has given me. Although, my husband is gone I know God has great things in store for me, so nothing is required of you. The Lord is my strength. I can do all things through Christ Jesus who strengthens me. Believe me when I say God has great things in store for me. I don't know what, but I know it is so. Please, stop apologizing and sympathizing for me. I will be okay. I count it all joy." I sat down and sipped my coffee with a new attitude.

Charles looked at me but didn't say a word. "Well, I guess. I can go now. I will call you when I can come back and finish helping you."

I got up to walk him to the door. "Goodnight Charles."

LIFETIME

I felt so much better. Even though he pissed me off, I did get to say things to him that I never got to say in 1975. I called Lynette as soon as Charles left and recapped the whole conversation.

Lynette said to me, "Girl, if he makes you talk this bad, don't let him come by again."

I replied to Lynette, "I know, but I want my garage cleaned."

"Do you think it is worth it?" She paused before continuing. "Anyway he was pushing up." Lynette replied.

"You think he is pushing up?" I asked totally clueless.

"Yeah, it sounds like it to me. You have been married way too long and you don't have a clue."

"I don't think he was pushing up." I said scratching my head.

"Well, don't let him make you so mad. He had you cussing and you never talk like that."

"I know. He makes me so angry. Goodnight, Lynette."

LIFETIME

Somebody Prayed for Me

It goes with out saying that my mother prayed for me. My mother had been the best mother anyone could have hoped for. All of my friends always said the same. My mom was very humble and sincere. She was generous and loving. My dad died when my mother was in her early fifties. She had been a strong praying woman. I knew my Mama prayed for me. I dedicated Boyz to Men's "A song for Mama" to her.

Aunt Grace, Aunt Grace, Aunt Grace. My aunt prayed for me even before I was born. Aunt Grace was a mighty prayer warrior. She loved me so much. It had been evident. Everyone knew she loved me. Aunt Grace prayed to God asking Him to allow me to be born on her 13th birthday. I always loved when she told me that story. It just reinforced that someone other than my parents was praying for me before I was born. It always made me feel special to know that Aunt Grace loved me that much. Aunt Grace prayed for me on many occasions, not just in grief. Six years prior, I was scheduled to have surgery. Everything went wrong that day. The doctor told me the wrong time, it snowed that morning, traffic was bad, and I was over four hours late for the actual time and two hours late for the time I was given. When I arrived, I should have already been in surgery. My blood pressure was too high and had to be lowered before surgery.

Aunt Grace stepped in and said, "Let us pray. Father God we come before you as humble as we know how. Thanking you for all that, you have already done and all that You will do. Lord, I want to ask YOU to bless the hands of those that will conduct this surgery. Lord, bring Angies' blood pressure down to a normal rate and Lord; I want YOU to remove all pain from this surgery. You are God Almighty and You said to ask and you shall receive. In Jesus name, we pray. Amen."

LIFETIME

At that time I said to myself, *now, you know there will be pain. You did not have to ask for all of that.* To my surprise, when I came out of surgery, I had no pain.

The nurse asked, "Why are you not asking for drugs for the pain?"

I said to the nurse. "I am not hurting and do not need it."

Her response was, "You will."

She was wrong. I did not. I told my aunt. "You know I didn't have any pain."

Aunt Grace said. "Angie, I know, because I prayed for that."

"But why did you? A little pain is okay." I said.

Aunt Grace said. "Because God is a great God, a merciful God, and I knew He would not allow my Angie to be in pain, if I asked and believed."

"You know Aunt Grace, I already knew that God had everything, but in my mind I was trying to rationalize how that could be possible. But, if I ever doubted, I know now that ALL is possible for them who love God and call on His name in faith. You asked and you had faith. I thank God for you." *Thank you Lord.*

I knew Aunt Grace prayed for me. Without a doubt, she was praying for me, and I was grateful she did.

***

Raymond and his family prayed for me daily. One day, I was at work feeling really low. Raymond called and said, "The Lord put it on my heart that you needed this prayer." He began to pray over the telephone. "Father God, Lord, and Savior I offer up this prayer to YOU for Angela and her family. Lord, YOU already know how many strands of hair she has on her head. You knew her even before she was born. Father God, have mercy on her and these children. Give her the strength that she needs to make it through the day. Father God give her what she needs right now, just to make it through this day. Father, we thank YOU for the blessings that YOU have and will bestow upon her family. Bless them collectively and bless then one by one. Bless Angela, Nicole, Brandon and Mrs. Franklin. We thank YOU for these blessings. Amen."

I really needed that prayer that day and *I am so glad Raymond prayed for me.*

***

Kenneth, Faye's husband, called me every three days to have a short prayer with me. He would call and say "Good morning, sister. I called to offer up this prayer to God. Father God, thank you for this mother. God, thank you for this daughter and thank you for this son. Give them the strength to trust in you and continue with the love in their hearts for YOU. These blessings I ask of YOU. Amen. Love you. Talk to ya."

I am so glad Kenneth prayed.

***

I knew people were praying for us, my pastor, Rev. Beaux, Serena, Diahann, Faye, Aunt Doris, my uncles, the Ambassadors for Christ Drill Team, Sonja, Lynette, Don, Tommy, and Big Daddy. Gabe was in constant prayer for me. He said he was so worried about me. I thank God for all of the prayer warriors in our lives. *I know somebody prayed for me and I'm so glad they did.*

LIFETIME

They Say You Needed Me

It was the winter of 2002, Charles called and asked if it was a good day to come by and hang the sensor light. I agreed for him to stopping by. He arrived a short time later. I escorted him to the garage. He decided we needed to go to Home Depot to get some materials. I tried to give him the money for him to go alone. But, he wanted that to be a group project. I wasn't at all happy with that idea. I had no intentions in helping, but we went to Home Depot together. Charles commented that he lived in the area. I could have cared less but the thought that we lived in close proximity and never ran into each other was odd. Charles lived right around the corner from my friend Renita. Maybe that was why Michael would come home sometimes and ask me what I saw in Charles Jeffrey. Michael was probably seeing him in Home Depot. When Michael was living, I never had a reason to go into Home Depot. He was the carpenter, not me.

While we were at Home Depot, Raymond called. It was his birthday. He was excited. He had been teasing me about the birthday party that I did not have on my last birthday. I was trying to talk to him without letting Charles know who I was talking to. Raymond kept asking who I was with; but I didn't want him to know it was "Oooh Baby," so I just talked about his birthday and ignored his question.

We gathered the items and returned to my home. I went in the kitchen to get a cup of coffee. Charles stood at the garage door looking funny.

I poured my coffee, turned to him, and asked. "What?"

He was standing by the door when he said. "I need you to come and show me where you want the light."

"Can't you figure it out?" I said to him as I took a seat at the bar.

LIFETIME

"No, I want you to tell me exactly where you want it."

I wondered what was wrong with him. Just put the light up and go. I got up and went into the garage. I opened the garage door, walked outside, and pointed to the only place the light could go, right above the address numbers on the garage door. I pointed and said. "Right here is fine."

He smiled and said. "Okay, but stay out here."

"For what?" I asked in total disbelief.

He placed the sack on the ground and looked at me, smiled, and said. "I need you to help me and keep me company."

I wondered what was wrong with him. I did not want to keep him company. However, I sat on the truck and thought to myself maybe he would not talk to me.

As soon as I had the thought he would not talk to me he said. "Well, Angela it's been a long time."

"Umm huh." I said folding my arms.

He started working. "You know we could have been good together."

"You think?" I rolled my eyes at him for trying to make me talk.

"Yes, I do. I really cared about you."

"Whatever." I unfolded my arms and legs not believing a word he said.

"If you had not been so fast, we could have..." Charles said.

I interrupted. "I was not fast."

"Oh yes you were." Charles said as he put another screw in the light.

What was wrong with him? He cheated on me but he said that I was the one that was fast.

LIFETIME

"You were messing around with Mac."

"No, I was not." I thought to myself, hurry up, jerk, and go.

"Everyone said that you were." Charles insisted.

I snapped, "That was your problem, you believed everyone, but me." I started talking to Michael. I told him he was right about Charles Jeffrey being annoying.

"I know." Charles said.

"Obviously you did not know. I do not lie. You never trusted me and in fact, you were the dog. Just shut up. It's over." I leaned on the truck with my arms folded and wondered was it all worth it.

Charles stopped working and looked at me. "But I feel bad for the way that I treated you. It wasn't all, my fault."

I said, "Yes it was. I loved you with all of my heart, you cheated on me, and then you told me to forget I ever knew you. Are you almost finished?" I never looked in his direction.

"No, I am not almost finished."

I moved from the truck and started for the kitchen. "Charles, are you working or are you strolling down memory lane?"

"Both."

"Well, are you hungry?" I asked to avoid going down memory lane.

"No."

"Well, I am. I am going inside to get some coffee." I went toward the kitchen.

He turned toward me and said. "I thought you were hungry and you are talking about drinking more coffee."

LIFETIME

I mumbled, "Shut up and finish working." I went inside the kitchen to have a cup of coffee. After about twenty minutes, he came in the kitchen.

"Are you coming back?" Charles asked.

"Yes, when I finished my coffee. Do you want some water?"

"Sure." He said.

I gave him the water and he asked me to return outside with him. I really did not need the light. Charles was torturing me. I uttered to myself, "*Michael, you were right he is annoying.*" I went back outside and said to Charles. "Do you know what you are doing?"

"Yes, I do and everything has got to be right."

"This is not an all day job. I am glad I am not paying you by the hour."

Charles snapped, "I am not charging you and I am having a good time reminiscing."

"Humph." I sighed

"You are still mean, Angela."

"Still? I've never been mean." I put my hand on my hip and looked at him.

He stopped working and looked at me. "You were to me. But, I guess I deserved it. You would look at me with those big eyes of yours and talk bad to me."

"Only when you deserved it. But, I was never mean and I did not talk bad."

"I used to think all city girls were mean and fast." He laughed out loud.

"I keep telling you I was never fast or mean." I paused and scratched my head, then asked. "But, why were you so cruel to me Charles?"

"Well, when you busted me, I knew from the look in your eyes that you would never forgive me. Therefore, I decided to be with her instead. She was on me real hard and you had Mac on the side anyway."

LIFETIME

"Quit saying that. It is not true." *Why does he keep saying that?* Charles was getting on my nerves. That was what I loved about Michael. He loved and trusted me. "Are you done?"

"Almost."

"I hope so. You have been here all day." I thought for a moment. "But Charles, didn't you know that I loved you and wanted you back?"

"No, I did not." He shook his head and looked directly at me.

"Didn't I say Oooh Baby, please don't leave me?"

"No, you did not. You cussed me bad."

"Did I cry?"

"No, I wish you had. I thought you did not love me and even more you were disappointed with me."

"You should have known how I felt. It hurt that you didn't seem to care."

"I did care, but you don't know the whole story." He shook his head from side to side and looked away.

"Neither do you." I said, as I looked at the truck that I was leaning on.

"Tell me the whole story." Charles insisted.

"No, it is over. It does not mater."

"Angela, I believed that you did not love me. You never said that you did. I believed that you were messing around."

"But why?" I said throwing my arms in the air in disbelief.

"Just forget it. One day I will tell you the whole story."

I just didn't understand him. He should have known that I loved him. I thought, I begged him to come back. I wanted him to let her go and love only me. Why didn't he know? I

LIFETIME

mumbled, "Humph." I sat there for a while not looking at him. But, I knew why he did not trust me. But, it wasn't my fault. I did not do anything wrong. Finally, I said, "Charles, one day I will tell you the whole story."

"What about today?" He asked.

"Not today." I said in a barely audible voice. I looked out across my yard. Finally, Charles finished and went into the front yard to put up another light. It was almost dark when he finished.

 I appreciated the lights because it was so dark on my street. After Michael died, certain things that I took for granted bothered me. That was why I wanted the sensor lights. When he finished we went inside and I thanked him.

He said, "You are welcome. I don't mind and I feel like I owe you something for the way…"

I interrupted, "You don't owe me anything, Charles."

"But, I have always hated that I broke up with you. I believed that you would not forgive me for cheating."

"Charles, get over it. I did. I have had a good life. God has blessed me so much." I said as I handed him a glass of water.

"But, you have been through so much, losing your husband and all."

"Yes, but God will see me through. Again, don't feel sorry for me. God has great things in store for me." I paused before continuing, "But, I really miss my husband."

"Are you going to counseling?" Charles asked as he took a seat at the kitchen table.

I was sitting by the bar when I said. "No, I don't need it. I will be okay."

"You should think about going." Charles replied.

LIFETIME

I wanted to scream when Charles finally left at seven in the evening. He had been over since ten that morning. But, the lights were up. What did I ever see in him? Who knew? I sure didn't see it.

I was happy to have my lights up. My neighbors finished painting the outside of my house. Something Michael started before he died. It was strange that he replaced the rotten wood in the entryway. He started painting both sides of the house as if he was in a rush to do everything. Michael was planning to start on our bathroom as soon as he finished working at a friend's house. After he finished he kept saying he didn't feel well. He didn't seem to be sick to me. The plumber down the street replaced my tub with a jet tub. He also replaced the four by four ceramic tiles with ten by ten tiles. It was really nice. Cynthia and my brother-in-law painted and wallpapered the bathrooms. Everything was so nice and I had my sensor lights in the front and the back. The next big thing was to get that garage cleaned. If I could stand Charles a few more hours then I would probably get it done.

Later that night before going to bed, I called Lynette and recapped the entire day. Lynette asked, "Why did you let him come over again? It is obvious that he gets on your nerves. Don't let him come over again."

I responded, "I know, he gets on my nerves and I don't understand what I saw in him. He was mad at me as if I did something to him. He kept saying I was cheating but I was not. We both kept saying the other doesn't know the whole story." I paused and then began to cry.

Lynette got excited and started talking fast as she sometimes does. "Angela what's wrong? Tell me. Tell me. What's wrong? Do I need to come over there?"

"No, I'll be okay." I said.

"What's wrong?"

LIFETIME

I stuttered. "Rape. I was raped." She did not say a word. "Lynette, I was raped back in the day. I got an STD from the rape and gave it to Charles."

In a hushed voice Lynette said, "Did you just tell me that you were raped?"

"Yes I was." I have never told anyone this before, not even Michael. In fact this is the first time in my life that I have admitted it to myself."

"What happened?" Lynette asked.

"Well, Charles and I broke up after my freshman year of college. I thought I would never see him again. Therefore, I came home that summer and enrolled in Richland Community College. After being there for a short time, I met this guy. He asked to take me on a date, bowling. He came to my parent's home and picked me up. Then, he said he left something that he needed to pick up at his apartment. Casually he said I could get out with him. No sooner than we entered the apartment, he raped me. It was awful. I thought he was going to kill me. The sad fact was his roommate came home with a woman and they did nothing to help me. He was raping me on the stairway when they came into the apartment. He drug me upstairs to his bedroom, the shag carpet burned my legs. His room was nasty with smelly clothes everwhere. He told me he would kill me if I didn't do everything that he wanted me to do. He slapped me and threw me down repeatedly. No one came to help me. I prayed that he would just let me live. Since, I was not a virgin; I thought I should just do whatever he said so he would not hit me again. When he finished, he ordered me to get dressed. My clothes were downstairs and on the stairway. I had to go down the stairs, naked, to get my clothes. You know he took me home as if nothing even happened. My dad was across the street. I ran in the house and scrubbed my body. I prayed that my dad would not come inside until after I was in my room. I believed that he would be able to look at me and know that something was wrong. That was in June of 1975,

LIFETIME

at that time I had never heard of date rape. It was not until this instant that, I have put this into words. And I can't believe I never told Michael and I told him everything."

"Angela, you have to tell Charles. Have you told your mother?"

"No. I have never told anyone."

"And you decided to tell me. I don't know what to say to help you. You need to call Margaret for counseling. Angela, you have to tell someone. Have you told Nicole?"

"No. I have not told anyone and I don't think I can ever tell anyone. Lynette, the other night, Rodney was over here doing some work on the house and a "Lifetime" movie was on. It was about a date rape. I was sitting on the floor wrapping a present. We were watching the movie and Rodney asked Nicole and me how we felt about the movie. I could not say anything. I was fidgeting and felt as if Rodney knew my secret I got up and went in the bathroom until I thought he forgot about the movie."

Lynette responded. "Well, I promise you, I will never tell a soul. I do think you need counseling about this. And Charles needs to know. That is why he is mad at you. You burned him and have always treated him as if he was the one that did you bad. He probably thinks that you are either crazy or a big liar. You have to tell him."

"Maybe." I didn't say anything for a second. "I better let you go."

"Angela, are you going to be okay? I can come over there."

I said. "No, I will be fine."

"Goodnight Lynette. Call me tomorrow?"

"Okay I will call you. Are you sure you are okay?"

"I am sure. Goodnight."

LIFETIME

A few Sunday mornings later, while lying in bed wondering what the day had in store, Charles called. "Good morning Angela, how are you doing this beautiful Sunday morning?"

"I am okay." I replied sitting up in bed smiling.

"Are you getting ready for church?"

"Not yet." All the time pulling the rollers out of my hair as if he could see how I looked.

"Well, I am getting ready to go to east Texas and then to Oklahoma for work. I will be gone about two weeks. Maybe I can take you out to dinner when I get back. Maybe you will be ready to tell me the whole story then."

"Maybe." I responded holding my knees to my chest.

"Well, I hope you have a blessed day. Talk to you later."

"Bye." Now, that was nice, I thought to myself.

***

A few days before Thanksgiving, Charles called and said he would come by and clean the garage the day after Thanksgiving. I agreed. Our conversation was short.

That was our first Thanksgiving without Michael so I chose to cook at home and start a new tradition. I invited Johnnie and her family, my mom, and Tommy over to the house. Cynthia came by too. I cooked turkey, ham, pig feet, greens, dressing, fruit salad, pecan pie, sock-it-to-me cake, German chocolate cake, buttermilk pie, broccoli and cheese casserole, and yams. I stuck my foot in it if I do say so myself. But, all I had was coffee.

We had a real nice time. Tommy was talking about me and the kids getting passports. Over dinner, I causally mentioned to Tommy that Oooh Baby was cleaning the garage on the next day.

LIFETIME

The next day Charles came by about 2:00. I didn't expect to get much done since it was so late. Charles was on a mission though. I knew I would have to help. He told me to pull everything out of the garage. If it was trash, take it to the front curb. If it was recyclable, put it on the right side of the driveway. If in doubt, put it on the left. Home Depot returns went in the back of the truck. Some items we could not pull out until we cleared the items on top of them. So we got started.

"Angela, take this to the front."

"Okay Charles."

"Let me have that over here, Angela."

"Sure Charles."

"My dad can use some of the paint."

"That's fine, Charles."

"Angela, help me move this?"

"Just a minute Charles."

"Take this to the front, Angela."

"I got it Charles."

"Move faster."

"Alright, Charles."

"Get with the program, girl."

By 6:00, the front curb was five feet tall with trash. Charles had a trunk full of old paint to take to his dad. I had roughly one hundred dollars in returns to Home Depot in the bed of my truck.

We stacked everything else back in the garage neatly.

LIFETIME

There was probably two hundred gallons of old paint, most of which Michael had brought from someone's paint store about ten years earlier. Some blue paint had exploded in the garage probably five years earlier. We were able to shovel it up. It was hard as a rock.

There was ash wood, plywood, two by fours, four by eights, two by twelve's, siding, trim wood, and more. I tried calling Habitat for Humanities to donate some stuff, but the guy never returned my call.

I had saws, hammers, and every type of nail that you could imagine. I had roofing shingles, roofing nails, roofing felt, roofing plywood, roofing staples, and several roofing staple guns.

I had paint by the pint, quart, gallon, five gallon, and spray cans. I had paintbrushes, rollers, stilts, kneepads, sand paper, masks, scrappers, flashing, sprayers, mixers, sawhorses, stepladders, eight 8-foot ladders, and one 30-foot ladder.

I had five toolboxes, golf clubs, fishing rods, battery charger, hoola hoops, volleyball set, car seats, strollers, sleeping cots, levelers, two compressors, and kites.

I had four bicycles, lawn mowers, three weed eaters, edger, trimmers (electric, gas, and manual), chain saw, and grass blower.

I had ten shovels, twenty rakes, five pitch forks, two post hole diggers, garden hoes, two wheel barrels, cement, sand, rain slickers, about thirty umbrellas, thermometers, and three dollies.

I had every kind of light kit that you can imagine, propane heater, electric heaters, oscillating fans, ceiling fan in the box, and an assembled fan.

I even had the same stuff that Charles and I had bought the first time we went to Home Depot. Charles calculated how much money I had in that garage each time he picked something

LIFETIME

up. I didn't care I just wanted it cleaned. If you think I have named half of the stuff on one side of the garage you are wrong. The garage was a mess only on one side. I always had enough room to park my car.

While we were cleaning, Tommy came down the alley to bring me the passport information.

Cynthia came by to see how much work we had done. She was impressed. She remembered Charles from college and he remembered her. Cynthia always liked Charles.

After we finished I gave Charles some German chocolate cake. He took some home for his fishing trip he had planned for the next day with his dad.

My mom came by later that night. She was in total shock. She kept asking, "Who did this? Is he a professional?"

Nicole kept asking, "Who was that guy?"

"A friend from college," I responded.

Diahann came by too. "Dang. I thought it would take us at least three months to clean the garage. I think I love Oooh Baby."

I called Lynette and told her that Charles got on my nerves but my garage was clean.

"You mean he cleaned your garage?" Lynette asked.

"Yes." I replied.

"Girl, you better keep his ass around. I am coming over this week to see that garage."

***

Later that night, I was so happy, that I wrote Charles a thank you card.

LIFETIME

11/25/02

Dear Charles,

Thank you so much for helping me with my garage. I appreciate it more than you can imagine. I just want you to know that you have always been special to me, and I will always hold a special place in my heart for you. Others talked about helping me, but you actually did. I pray that you have a blessed life. Please accept this small token of my appreciation. It is not intended as payment, but just a little something to say, thank you again.

Sincerely,

Angela

I finished the letter and put it away. I decided to have a garage sale the next week to get rid of some items still left in the garage.

***

Monday morning after the holiday, Tommy told Gabe, Big Daddy, and Don about the garage being cleaned. Tommy had actually seen the garage, since he was in a wheel chair, he normally entered my home from the garage.

Big Daddy said, "I told you when he called the first time he was 'pushing up.'"

I replied, "No, he was just being nice, Big Daddy."

Gabe said, "I am glad he cleaned the garage. That means we don't have to do it. I think I like Oooh Baby."

"Me too." Don responded.

"You guys make me sick," I whined.

"Don't get mad at us. Get mad at Oooh Baby." Big Daddy said.

"Big Daddy, be quiet." I said hitting him in the arm.

The next week or so, Charles called to put cable in my upstairs game room and replace Nicole's brakes. I wanted to take Charles out as a thank you for cleaning the garage. He ran a cable line upstairs, replaced the brakes, and we went to lunch. I had my usual, coffee. While we were at lunch, I handed Charles the thank you card.

"Should I read it now?" He asked.

"It is up to you." I couldn't remember what I said in the letter. I remembered that I had put a one hundred dollar bill inside but not what I said. It had been a few weeks since I'd written it. Charles continued to eat.

When we left, I was driving. Charles decided he would read the card. He read it and said with such sincerity, "You did not have to. I wanted to help you." He paused. "Can I have a kiss?"

I wondered what I had said in the card. I hunched my shoulders and said, "Sure, I guess." He kissed my lips while we were sitting at the traffic light. His lips were soft. But, I wondered why he wanted to kiss me.

We went back to my home and watched Tyler Perry's "Diary of a Mad Black Woman." Charles seemed to enjoy the play and asked if he could take it with him to show someone. I let him take the tape home.

Brandon came home from school before Charles left. As Charles left, he gave me a kiss. I didn't want him to kiss me in front of my son. However, it was just a friendly kiss.

Soon as he left, I called Lynette and told her about the cable, the brakes, and the kiss.

***

Charles called on Wednesdays, the night we had drill team practice. I found myself racing home to see "Soul Food" and checking the caller ID. Some Wednesdays, he called and others he did not. I found myself hoping that he called. I had no problem returning his call, but I

LIFETIME

did not want to call him first. I still had that I can't stand you attitude. We were just friends, not even good friends. Our conversations were always short, but long enough.

One night he asked me what I was getting my kids for Christmas. I told him nothing, because I was not buying anyone anything. Charles suggested that since my kids had lost their father I should try to give them a nice Christmas. He also suggested that I should get counseling.

I told Charles that I did not need counseling. Charles kept telling me that he had been to counseling when his wife left him. He said he was so messed up that he had to go to counseling and it helped him. He said, "Angela, I know my loss was different from yours, but the only way I could deal with the situation was get counseling."

I agreed to think about it.

***

Each night I called Lynette and told her the whole conversation. Lynette said, "I think Oooh Baby is right you should go to counseling. Angela, I go. I have a great therapist, Margaret. As a matter of fact, her office is right by your house."

"Girl, I don't need therapy. I will be okay." I shouted.

"Okay then, but do you think Oooh Baby and I are crazy because we went to therapy?"

"No, but . . ."

Lynette interrupted, "But nothing. Here is Margaret's number. It will not hurt you to talk to her and the job will pay for it."

"I will think about it." I responded

"Please." Lynette demanded.

***

LIFETIME

Don and I talked almost every day at work. Some days we sat and had coffee in the cafeteria and neither of us said a word. Don assured me that I could tell him anything or we could just sit and not talk. Some times, I cried. He was always comforting.

One day out of nowhere, I told Don that I had been raped. Don sat up in his chair and listened attentively. He suggested that I get counseling. I ignored him and knew he hated that I had confided that information to him.

Only a handful of people knew, but each time I shared the information I felt a bit better. That secret was no longer in control of my life. I didn't even have that love/hate feeling for Charles anymore. I considered him a good friend. I was free from my past.

***

One night, Charles telephoned and told me that he cared about me. He asked me to tell him the whole story. I did not want to tell him what happened on the phone. However, he insisted. I took a deep breath and told him the whole story. For a while neither one of us said a word.

Then Charles asked, "Did you go to the police?"

"No."

"Who did it?"

I said to Charles. "It has been so long ago and this was something that I never wanted to remember. I don't remember his name. But, you know, after he did that to me, I saw him talking to girl after girl. I wanted to tell the women to run, but I never did. I was petrified of him. I could not even look at him. I felt like I had to slide by him, hoping that nothing on him touched me. I knew he did the same things to other girls because he would never talk to one girl very long."

LIFETIME

Charles sounded as if he was crying, "Why didn't you tell me?"

"Charles, I was young. I did not know what happened. Remember when I called you that Fourth of July frantically asking you to come see me; it had been about three weeks after the incident. I did not think of it as rape. I had no idea that I had a STD. I went to the infirmary at school on more than one occasion. They treated me for gonorrhea and syphilis but nothing worked. The weekend that we went to east Texas, you told me to go doctor and take care of myself. That was when I realized that I had given you what I had. Remember, I was only 19 not very knowledgeable. Back in the day you said, we could get married and move to the next level if I got my shit together. I asked you what you meant. Your response was you know what I mean. But I didn't. It was not my fault. I am sorry."

Charles was quiet for a few minutes and then said. "I don't know what to say. I wish you had told me. I could have helped you."

"I thought it was nothing, it was over, and I could move on without anyone ever knowing. I am so sorry; I made you not trust me. All these years I have hated you and now I realize that you thought I was cheating. What else could you think? I am so sorry."

"Angela, I am sorry for what happened to you. I would have helped you."

I was very quiet.

Charles asked me again who it was. But, I could not discuss the details of what happened with him.

I stopped talking. We both held the phone for hours not saying anything. I started counting the popcorn on the ceiling. Eventually, Charles said goodnight.

LIFETIME

That night as I lay in bed, I felt a burden had been lifted from me by finally telling Charles the truth. At that point, I knew I could go on with my life and not ever be sad or mad at him anymore. Because I was, free from my secret.

I called Faye and told her the whole thing. Faye was at a loss for words. I tried to assure her that I was fine and would be okay. She was very quiet.

***

The next week, was the first time I had seen Charles since telling him everything. He had a helpless questioning look on his face. He held me and looked into my eyes. His eyes were filled with tears. "Tell me what happened, Angela."

I tried to get out of his arms, but he would not let me go. I put my head down and started to explain. Charles loosened his hold on me.

"Charles, when you and I came back from east Texas many years ago, the last thing you said to me was to go to the doctor and take care of myself. I asked you what you meant. You told me that I knew. You said that I had given you a STD and that you had not been with anyone but me. You told me to take care of myself right away. You had been telling me for months to handle my business and I did nothing. You ordered me to come home the next weekend. You said that if I wanted to continue to be your woman, I must come home every weekend. The next weekend I came home and that was when you told me to forget I ever knew you. I went to the county hospital that Saturday and they gave me a prescription to cure Trichomonas. I thought that I would be able to explain everything to you when you took me back to school on Sunday. That day never came. I was young and I was not sure what was happening to me. Often times, after I realized something was wrong with me I would be distant and quiet. I think I was trying to work things out in my head. I remember thinking that I had not done anything wrong.

LIFETIME

Somehow, the incident was pushed way back into my subconscious. I needed you to tell me to go to the doctor. Although I had gone to the infirmary, nothing worked. When you came back around this time, I could not understand why you thought I cheated on you. This secret had been buried deep within me. I am sorry. All these years I thought I was the victim and had done nothing wrong. And now I realize you felt like a victim too."

Charles whispered, "You know Angela, I am so sorry for what happened to you. I wish you could have told me. I would have helped you. You know everyone says that I am pushing up, but I am only showing you kindness, because you are someone that was always special to me. I knew we would never get back together because you had given me a STD before. Moreover, I knew you knew. I often wondered why you acted as if I was the only one that had cheated. I wish I had known. She was on me hard at work trying to get with me. We had been on one date prior to that night. When you busted me, I decided my mind was made up. My cousin, Charles, had been telling me that I should choose one of you because his wife did not feel comfortable being around both of you. He said I should talk to you about the STD because he knew I loved you. I often felt I made the wrong decision but believed that you would never really forgive me. I tried to explain that I loved you but you looked at me and kept saying that you did not understand how I could do you that way. If you would have cried or said that, you loved me I would have chosen you. I loved you then and have always wondered what it would have been like with us together. I wish I had known then. Maybe things would be different. We could have been happy."

I did not respond for a few minutes. "Charles, I don't think we would have been happy. I did not have a degree and would have been hanging on your coattail. I had a good life, a happy marriage. It just wasn't meant to be. I am sorry that I hurt you."

LIFETIME

Charles held me and said, "I wish you had leaned on me. I am so sorry I was not there for you. I think things would have turned out different if you had told me."

***

About mid December, I was off work and wanted to go see the movie "Drumline." However, Charles had to work, but he thought he could at least meet me for dinner. I met him at a restaurant in Las Colinas. Oddly enough, I was hungry and ordered a salad, but I lost my appetite when a bug crawled out of it. Charles was not eating, but he was livid. He let them have it. The management staff apologized profusely. We left abruptly and went shopping for Christmas gifts. While shopping, Charles realized we had enough time to see "Drumline." We went to the movies next door and waited forty-five minutes before the next movie started. Nobody was there but us. Finally, two other couples came in as the movie started. Charles put his arm around my chair. I found it awkward. He leaned over and whispered something in my ear during the movie. I wanted to see the movie so I kept ignoring him.

I knew when we went to the movie that he would have to leave before it was over, but I forgot that we were riding together. He looked at his watch and had to go. It was about fifteen minutes into the movie. I wanted him to leave without me. Then it dawned on me that we were in one car. Therefore, we left. We gave each other a short kiss and I was on my way home. He called to make sure I made it home safely. I was beginning to like him. I could not wait to get home to tell Lynette about our evening.

Monday, the week of Christmas, I promised to cook dinner for Charles. I called Charles that day and told him that I had to renege on the cooking because I was ill. I was really sick, but I didn't want to cook in the first place.

LIFETIME

Somehow, I talked Charles into cooking for me. He fried fish and made a salad. I realized as he finished cooking that I was going to have to eat something. Since, I was sick I could not taste a thing. Basically, his cooking the food was the actual date so I didn't stay long.

As I was leaving, Charles kissed me. Although I liked it, I was sick and I was still in heavy grief. Charles asked me how long it had been since I had been made love to. I looked at him as if he was crazy. He kissed me again and I warned him that he would get sick. I decided to go home, sort of abruptly.

I called him on my cell phone when I got lost. By the time I called, I had no voice. I was sick and had to stay in the bed for the next couple of days.

On Christmas Eve, Charles came by to wish me a Merry Christmas. He brought me some beautiful fresh flowers. They were very nice.

I had not bought him anything except a Christmas card. Now cards were my thing but I doubt that I spent much time on a card for him. You see I was missing my husband. I was sinking back into myself.

Diahann invited us over for Christmas dinner. It was Diahann's husband, Harold, her son, my mom, Diahann's cousin, and me. We had a nice Christmas. Diahann's cousin was non-stop talking. Every time I opened my mouth, she would beat me to the punch. Diahann laughed at us all day. Brandon was real quiet. Nicole and my mom seemed to have a good time. The food was really good. Diahann prepared every thing except the deviled eggs and cake that I made.

We came home that night with nothing to do. The phone rang and to my surprise, it was Charles. "Good evening." He said in his sultry voice.

"Hey, Merry Christmas." I said.

LIFETIME

"Merry Christmas to you, too." He did not hesitate. "You will not believe what happened to me."

"What?"

Charles said, "My car caught on fire."

"Really. Is everything okay?"

"Yes, I am fine."

"Where are you?" I asked.

"At home. I packed my car to go to back home and my neighbors were running and shouting. I couldn't believe it. I know my blood pressure is up."

"When did this happen?"

"Yesterday."

I said to him, "You should have called me. I would have let you borrow my truck."

"Really."

"Yes."

"Well, I am going home tomorrow with my sister. We are having a party for my mother. Her 75th birthday is this week."

"That will be nice."

"I appreciate the offer. You are amazing." Charles said sounding surprised.

"I know. You see what you could have had?" We both laughed.

"Are you busy the Saturday after New Year's?" Charles asked.

"No, I don't think so. Why?"

"Will you go out with me? I have this invitation and I was wondering if you would go with me."

LIFETIME

I agreed to go, but he never really told me where we were going. I was sort of excited. That would be our first date. The Drumline movie did not count.

Charles came back to Dallas a couple of days after Christmas. He called me and asked me to come over. It was late. I asked him what I would tell my children.

Charles said, "If they ask, say you are going bowling."

I knew when I left that was going to be a booty call. I was sick and depressed so it was something to do. I got dressed in a red jogging suit, ran my fingers through my crimped bob and went over. On the way to Charles' I called Lynette from my cell phone so someone would know where I was.

Lynette asked, "How did you come up with the term bowling?"

"It was Charles' idea." I said, laughing all the while.

"I told you Oooh Baby was 'pushing up' when he cleaned that garage." Lynette laughed.

I replied, "He was not. He just knew that I needed him."

I arrived at Charles' home and he seduced me just like Winston (Taye Diggs) did to Stella (Angela Bassett) in How Stella Got Her Groove Back. Remember the tear that fell from his face in the shower scene. Oh yeah. It was quite seductive but again I didn't have any feelings for him. It was just something to do.

Before I left to go home, Charles handed me an email that he received from his friend. I sat down and read the email.

LIFETIME

To: Charles
From: Willie

Reason, Season, or Lifetime?
Pay attention to what you read. After you read this, you will know the reason it was sent
to you! People come into your life for a reason, a season, or a lifetime. When you figure
out which one it is, you will know what to do for each person.

When someone is in your life for a REASON. It is usually to meet a need you have
expressed. They have come to assist you through a difficulty, to provide you guidance
and support, to aid you physically, emotionally, or spiritually. They may seem like a
Godsend, and they are. They are there for the reason you need them to be. Then, without
any wrongdoing on your part, or at an inconvenient time, this person will say or do
something to bring the relationship to an end. Sometimes they die. Sometimes they walk
away. Sometimes they act up and force you to take a stand. What we must realize is that
our need has been met, your desire fulfilled, their work is done. The prayer you sent up
has been answered. Now it is time to move on.

Then people come into your life for a SEASON. Because your turn has come to share,
grow, or learn. They bring you an experience of peace, or make you laugh. They may
teach you something you have never done. They usually give you an unbelievable
amount of joy. Believe it! It is real! But, only for a season.

LIFETIME relationships teach you lifetime lessons; things you build upon in order to
have a solid emotional foundation. Your job is to accept the lessons, love the person, and
put what you have learned to use in all other relationships and areas of your life. It is said
that love is blind but friendship is clairvoyant.

Author Unknown

I read it repeatedly not saying a word. Finally, I asked, "What do you think of the email,

Charles?"

He came close to me where I was sitting at the bar. He held my hand and said. "I think

we met for a lifetime relationship."

I went home thinking Reason, Season, Lifetime and I wondered which one was Charles?

LIFETIME

Lean On Me

During that time of bereavement, I leaned on a lot of people. I leaned real hard on my matron sisters. Johnnie was one of the people that I called from the hospital, like calling your big sister for her to call the rest of the family. She did just that. Janice came to the hospital. Both Irene and Gwen were at my house in the kitchen doing what they do, when I got home. Johnnie was there organizing everybody. All of their children were there just like blood relatives. I can't say 'real relatives' because we were a 'real family.' We have leaned on each other many times.

***

The first Christmas after Michael died, Diahann called. She said that she noticed Brandon did not say anything on Christmas. She suggested I consider taking him to counseling. I knew that I would be okay, but didn't want to lose my son in the process.

The next morning I called Personal Assistance Services (PAS) and requested an African American family grief counselor. They referred me to an African American male minister counselor. I also called Margaret, Lynette's counselor; who was able to see me within the week.

When I told Lynette that I had gotten an appointment with Margaret, she was pleased. She said, "It definitely will not hurt you to go."

Don said to Lynette, Big Daddy, Gabe, and Tommy, "I tried to tell her to go to counseling. Lynette told her to go to counseling too. It took Oooh Baby to tell her. Ain't that something? You know that guy is a computer technician, an electrician (remember the lights), a plumber (the toilets), a mechanic (Nicole's brakes), maintenance man (garage cleaner), and now he is a therapist. That man is a jack-of-all-trades. Look at her. She does everything that he

says."

Lynette chimed in, "You are right Don. I asked her, "Do you think it is okay for your

crazy friends to get counseling? She did not want to have any part in it. I am just glad she is

going."

I said to them, "You guys make me sick. I am going to counseling for my children. Now

leave me alone."

***

I leaned on Raymond probably more than anyone. I called him every day for seven

months. We talked in the mornings, during the day, and for hours at night. I even told him about

Oooh Baby. He called Charles 'Ouch Baby.' I confided with Raymond about how we had

broken up, and I still wanted him back.

Raymond said, "Really, he must be your soul mate?"

"That would be a no." I said.

Raymond said to me, "If you still want a man after you bust him with another woman.

Oh yeah, he has got to be your soul mate."

The next time Raymond mentioned that Oooh Baby and I were soul mates. I said, "You

think?"

Finally, Raymond said, "I tried to tell you that he was your soul mate, but you didn't

believe me."

LIFETIME

It's So Hard To Say Goodbye to Yesterday

It was New Years Eve 2002, and I did not want to go to Diahann's annual New Year's Eve party. I mentioned it to, my hairdresser, Kayron and she suggested I get someone to go with me. Her first suggestion was Charles. But, I did not want Charles to attend the party with me.

Kayron saw I was adamant about him not attending so she suggested Cynthia. I called Cynthia and she agreed to go. We had a nice time at the party. After the party, we returned to my home. Cynthia and I were talking and I confided to her about my feelings for Charles.

Cynthia assured me it was nothing wrong with that. "You were happily married to Michael and he is gone now. Angela, Michael is not coming back. You have loved Charles from the first time you saw him. Angela, people change and he seems like a nice guy. I know you guys had a bitter break up, but you lived a happy life in spite of that. Be happy now. Don't worry about what other people have to say. Go for it."

Later that night while in bed, I thought a lot about what Cynthia said. I wanted to believe what she said. Eventually, I went to sleep with a smile on my face.

The next day or two I had my first counseling session with Margaret. I filled out some paper work first and cried most of the session.

Margaret let me cry and then asked me some questions. "Tell me about your husband?"

I sobbed, "Well, Michael and I had been married twenty years. We met in college. We were friends first. I was dating someone else, when we met. Eventually, he started to like me. I was still in love with the other guy but Michael made me realize he was good for me and we got married."

LIFETIME

"How did he die?" Margaret questioned.

I blew my nose and said. "He had a heart attack. He went to work at my mom's rent house and she found him lying in the floor." I looked at the tissue in my hand.

"How long has it been since he died?" She said.

"About seven months."

Margaret started asking me other questions. "Tell me about your family structure as a child."

"I am the oldest child of two. Both my parents were in the home. I had a happy childhood. Our family was quite functional. We all loved each other. Why do you ask?"

"Well, Angela grief is different for everyone. Some of the things you are going through are not from the actual death of your husband, but from other unresolved issues."

I shook my head from side to side. "Well, going back to my family life is not it. We were a normal happy family."

"Well, that is not normal; most people had a dysfunctional childhood."

"Not me, I was happy." I smiled a little and moved around in my chair.

"Well, Angela, from what you have answered on this sheet and what you have said to me. You are depressed. It appears your husband loved you more than you loved him."

I looked at her over my glasses and said. "Oh no, that is just not true."

Margaret stated, "I am only going on what you have said. At least in the beginning he loved you more."

"I have to think about that, because I really loved him." I was ready to leave at that point.

"I am not saying you didn't. He seemed to have loved you more. From what you have said, it sounded like you were very busy. A lot of times couples like you split up after the nest is empty. Anyway, what I want you to do is write a letter to your husband. You will read the letter to him at the cemetery and then you will destroy the letter in a ceremonious way."

"What should be in the letter?" I asked quite confused.

"Tell him how you felt when he died. Tell him about the funeral. Tell him what has been going on with you and the kids since he died. Lastly, tell him goodbye. This is your homework for the next week. I will give you up to two weeks to write the letter, but no more than two weeks. You will find it hard to write the letter. You will be all right. Our time is up. I will see you next week." Margaret put her pad down and stood to shake my hand.

I shook her hand and left. I called Lynette as soon as I left Margaret's office.

Lynette commented, "She just doesn't know you. You will whip that letter out in no time."

We both laughed. I was glad I had gone and thanked Lynette for encouraging me to go.

Charles called and asked how counseling went. I told him it went okay, but did not give him any details.

Later that night I wrote the letter to Michael. It was thirteen handwritten pages. Lynette had been right. It was easy to write the letter.

I completed the letter and called Faye. I told her what Margaret said about Michael loving me more than I loved him. Faye said, "Angie, remember when you told me you were marrying Michael and I asked you why you were marrying him?"

"Sort of."

"Well it was because I did not believe you really loved Michael. But you convinced me you did."

LIFETIME

I said to Faye, "I always said Michael tricked me. He became my best friend and then he got me to fall in love with him. He knew all my vulnerabilities. Faye, I loved him just as much or more than he loved me. I would have left Michael years ago had I not loved him with all of my heart."

"I know, Angie." She said trying to comfort me.

***

The next week at therapy, I had completed the letter. Margaret said, "Now I want you to go to the cemetery and read the letter to him."

"Do I have to destroy the letter?" I asked holding the letter in my hand. I thought I was going go have to read it to Margaret.

Margaret replied, "No, you don't have to, but you probably should. Does the letter have personal stuff in it?"

"Yes." I said.

Margaret said. "You should have a glass of wine and read the letter one last time and then burn the letter. You still feel married to Michael and you must let him go."

I cried at counseling that day, but not as much as I had the week before. I decided to destroy the letter because of the personal stuff in it.

A couple of days later, Brandon, Nicole, and I went to see the family grief counselor. Bro. Ngo was a minister as well as a counselor. He gave us some forms to fill out, while Brandon and I were sat next to each other on the loveseat. All three of us cried during the entire first session. Based on what we put on our sheets, he said Nicole and Brandon were going through normal grief, but I was depressed. He gave all of us homework and said he would see us in a week. Before we left, he had prayer with us. We were all very quiet on the way home.

LIFETIME

The following Saturday, I went to Peaceful Valley cemetery about seven in the morning
to read the letter to Michael.

Jan. 6, 2003

Baby,

*I am writing this letter to express my feelings since your death. You know I have written
you, many letters through out the years of our marriage and have mailed them to you but
the postman does not deliver here. Well, I hope you know everyone misses you, Nicole,
Brandon, Mama, Sister, Lawrence, Ann, Rose (big time), Leslie, Evan, and most of all
me. You were at one time my best friend and then my lover, the best I ever had. I know
you always seemed bothered that I was such a fool for Charles Jeffrey, but I got over him
and ... Over the years my love grew stronger for you, but I feel our friendship lessened
and ... I appreciated you letting me be me. I know you knew everything about me and
allowed me to be me. I loved you for that and this is one of the things I am having
difficulties with now. Everyone wants to manage me. They think they know what I want
and need, but how could they, when I don't know. I find myself angry with people for
trying to tell me what to do. Remember the black dress? Even the kids have expectations
on me that I don't want to fulfill.*

*Brandon has really become a man. He is much taller than I am. Since you died and he
seems to feel, as he must take charge. He is so serious that it scares me. After he was
told that, you died by Mama and Rev. Beaux, they said he stopped talking. He would not
say anything, just in shock. Sort of like you were, when your mother died, but worse. He
got a new suit for your funeral, his first suit from the men's department. James took him
to the barbershop and told Diane you died. It wasn't until after Brandon left that
Dimples was told you died. Since it was summer time, Brandon did not call any of his
friends to tell them you died. Not April or anyone. The drill team all came over all
eighty members on that Sunday before they left for congress. Nobody wanted to go
without us. They all wanted to stay. I encouraged them to go. I knew we would be okay.*

*The funeral was beautiful. Everyone said I put you away nicely. If I had been thinking I
would have buried you in a mahogany wood casket but I wasn't thinking. My church
choir sang your song, "Jesus Be a Fence," and they turned it out. Bilbo sang, "Yes, God
is Real" that man can sing. My pastor preached the funeral and Aunt Doris, the Rev. Dr.
officiated. Fred came, the Oklahoma cousins came, Steve Hicks and crew came, Uncle
Calvin, Trina, and Ressa came, and Cheyenne. Miami and Grant were pallbearers with
your nephews. I later found out ... was in jail and did not make it. The church was
packed for the wake and the funeral. All of Dreamz came. I didn't know half of the
people there. Roy, Joey, Bubba, John O, and a lot of other ETSU people came. Anyway,
we went to Phoenix the next day to congress.*

LIFETIME

Nicole, your baby girl, is missing you. She prays a lot and seems to be doing well. Her friend is still coming over. You know the one you didn't want to meet. She worked at the Richardson Hospital all summer and worked hard in the band. She is on the school paper as a reporter. She is a good student. She dropped AP Physics this semester because she had a 'C.' I am sure she will do better next semester. I talked to her history teacher. She is crazy. Anyway, I let her know I don't play. She has a 'B' average in her class now. Nicole was inducted into the National Honor Society and Who's Who among American High School Students. She is such a beautiful girl. She is the highest-ranking officer in the church drill team.

I sent a picture of us to everybody for Christmas. Everybody cried when they received it. I told them the kid's grades and their many accomplishments. Oh yeah, Brandon is first chair saxophone player in the Symphonic II band. He has a new private lessons teacher, a woman. Don't know her much.

*Well, we are going to therapy now with an African guy. He seems pretty good too. Brandon said he felt **SAD** on his paper in big letters. I couldn't read what Nicole wrote. I put that I was angry with people for trying to manage me. I am grieving, sad, and do not know what to do with my life. What I did say was my feelings about Charles Jeffrey. Before I get into that, I recognize and appreciate you coming to me. First, you told me to look good at the funeral, because you would be looking good. And baby, you looked real good. I never realized you were such a handsome man until you died. Some things you just take for granted. The next time was the same night you asked me why I had only gotten two funeral cars, because you have a large family and you have never made a difference. If one rides, they all ride so I decided to get another family car at 3:00 a.m. Anthony Hurst, the funeral director said he would try and he showed up with three family cars. Baby, they had three brand new limousines. Fred said all the other funerals had mix matched Cadillac's on that day. Steve Hicks said, "Cuz, you really put ole boy away." Your brother, Lawrence, said people were commenting for weeks about the funeral. The lady came that taught you the song "Jesus Be a Fence." They said, Stanley Chatman cried like a baby during the whole funeral. Several of your classmates came. George Jenkins was there but I did not meet him because the pastor told everyone not to touch me. Joel Farley, could not come because his van was in the shop and he is in a motorized wheel chair now. Leonard Rowe was there and the entire Dreamz team. Kasey and Don spoke they gave me $700. I did not cry at the funeral, but I looked good. I made Diahann take off her dress so I could wear it. I had on big girl jewelry and looked good. Faye's sister, Daphne, said I was Jackie O. She told her sisters, "Will you look at Jackie O?" You see I was wearing shades. The next time you came to me you got in the bed and held me. I appreciated that. And most recently, you held me and told me I would be okay.*

I have been wondering when you were going to ask me why Charles Jeffrey was helping me in your house. Charles put up two motion sensor lights in the front and back yards, cable in your former office, and he cleaned the garage. After he cleaned the garage, I wrote him a letter thanking him and gave him one hundred dollars. He was touched and asked to kiss me. He kissed me lightly and I was in shock. So after that he kissed me

LIFETIME

whenever we were departing. I was supposed to cook for him the Monday before Christmas, but I got sick. He wanted to cook for me at our house, but I said no and asked him to cook for me at his place. I went to his house and he cooked fish and salad. It was good. He showed me pictures of myself from back in the day. Of which he said he was going to show the kids. Anyway, he eventually kissed me passionately and I kissed him back. He wanted to know when was the last time I had made love… Kissing got pretty hot and then I went home. Well, he caught my cold. The day after Christmas, Charles was sick. The kids kept asking who he was and I kept telling them he was a college friend. I felt I had to lie or avoid the kids to be with Charles. Eventually, I had to tell them that I had dated him before I dated you. I told them he was not their father and would never be. They seemed to be okay with that. I think you are okay with it too. I feel God has placed Charles in my life for whatever reason. I know God has great things for me. I know I will survive the grief, but it is so hard for me to let the kids grieve with me. I believe you always thought I had feelings for Charles, but I was really over him twenty plus years ago. I told Charles I should tell him to call me in two years from now but my emotions want to be with him. I don't want to be a silly woman. I can't afford to be a silly woman, but you always knew this man makes me crazy.

I pray I am a good mother to our kids. I know I tried to be a good wife to you even though I was not perfect. I loved you. I loved your dirty drawers. Thanks for being my friend, my lover, my husband.

Peace be with you.

Love,

Angela

Rest in peace.

It took me an hour and a half to read the letter to Michael. I kept trying to read it but the tears kept flowing. I fell to the ground. It was drizzling rain and I was a mess. I had a hard time finishing the letter. But, when I left the cemetery, I knew I had let Michael go. I believed that was what he was trying to tell me when he came to me the last time. I believed he was saying, "Angela, you will be okay. So let me go so I can have eternal rest."

It was the right thing to do. As I had told my children, "Life is for the living. Your dad has fulfilled his purpose in life, but God has a plan for us. We don't know why he had to die so

LIFETIME

young, but we must go on until God calls us home. It will be hard for us, but we will make it with Christ Jesus."

Michael came into my life for a reason that helped me get through the breakup with Charles. We developed a love for each other that lasted for a lifetime and now our season has past. It was really hard to say goodbye to yesterday.

LIFETIME

I Wouldn't Take Away the Rain

Charles never told me exactly where we were going on our first date. Initially, he said it was a formal affair. Therefore, I bought several outfits to wear.

Kayron was coming by to touch up my hair and make up before the date. I shared most of my secrets with her. She knew a lot about both Michael and Charles. When you are at the hairdresser, you tell them all of your business. I loved Kayron and I could tell her anything.

Nicole and Kayron talked me into the black swing type dress. It looked real nice. But, when it came time to go I was apprehensive. Nicole was laughing at me. She had her camera ready to take my picture.

Charles was right on time. Nicole let him in. She came back into my room and said I was over dressed. She was laughing so hard that Kayron went out to see what he had on. Kayron came back into my bedroom and said, "Change clothes you are over dressed."

I refused. They were laughing so, that I asked them what he was wearing. Nicole said, "He has on a brown suit, with a brown argyle sweater that is not working with a maroon shirt. You need to put on your brown pants suit." She fell on the bed trying to muffle her laugh.

I refused to change. I had asked the kids to go to the mall before he arrived and now it was time for me to go but I was afraid. Charles was in the other room asking what was wrong. I begged them to leave, again and to take Brandon with them. They kept saying they wanted pictures, but I just could not come out of my bedroom.

They finally left. I knew they were somewhere outside laughing at me. I didn't want my kids or friend to see me having a good time with a man other than Michael.

LIFETIME

It was so hard for me. I had never been single before with children. I never had people looking at every move I made. I felt as if I should have been a grieving widow. I found myself wishing it had been two years later.

We went to the Wyndham hotel up to the 21st floor. As we were riding, the elevator there was another couple going to the same location. Charles spoke to the guy. I thought I recognized him from somewhere. As we exited the elevator Charles said, "That was your husband's friend, Louis."

"Who?" I asked.

Charles replied, "Michael's friend Louis."

"Oh yeah, I met him at the Michael's wake. He told me he was Michael's friend."

As soon as we walked through the door, a photographer took pictures of us. After we got inside we both started talking to people we knew. It was a retirement party for one of Charles' friends.

Marsha, a neighborhood friend, was attending the party. The honoree was her older brother. She and I talked and talked the entire night. She was sorry about my loss but said I seemed real happy with Charles. She had dated Project Boy before I had. We laughed at some of the things we had experienced. She had seen Project Boy a few days before. Marsha did not know I called him Project Boy. However, she never mentioned his name either. Ironically, she said he was living down in the projects. I was not surprised.

I really enjoyed reminiscing with Marsha. She commented how it was no coincidence we had run into each other, how God had a reason for our meeting again.

Louis, the guy from the elevator, approached me and asked, "Do I know you from somewhere?"

LIFETIME

I smiled and said, "Yes, I am Michael Everette's widow."

"That's right. I remember you. How are your kids?" Louis asked.

"The kids are making it, but it sometimes hard." I said.

Louis said, "I can only imagine. I really miss my buddy."

I replied, "I think we will be okay." Louis introduced me to several people that knew Michael. Everyone had a different story of the impact Michael had on their lives. I had not realized so many of Michael friends worked with Charles.

Charles kept smiling at me from across the room and I returned a smile. Eventually we left. As we were leaving Nicole called, "Are you having a good time?"

"Yes." I said with a smile in my heart.

"Were you over dressed?" Nicole asked, with a snicker.

"Yes."

"Did it bother you?"

"No." I replied.

"I am glad you are having a good time. I love you so much."

"I love you too, Nicole."

The date was really nice. Charles and I laughed at all the people we knew in common. Many of the people at the party had been to my home. I kept thinking it was so amazing that Charles and I never ran into each other at our mutual friends social functions.

Later, I mentioned to Charles that I could not believe he and Michael ran into each other so often. "I never realized how Michael must have felt about you, him seeing you and wondering why I had loved you so. When Michael asked me about you, I would be irritated with him. I often said there you go again. I told Michael I had gotten over you."

LIFETIME

Charles said. "I used to see Michael around town and never knew who he was, but I could tell he did not like me. One night we were playing against each other in a pool tournament and Michael never said a word. After he beat me, I asked another guy standing there what was his problem. He said you know he is Angela's husband. That was when I found out who you were married to. From then on, we had a gentleman's stand off. Before then, I never knew why he did not like me."

"I never realized you bothered him that much." I replied.

Charles asked me, "Do you think he thought we were messing around?"

I snapped, "No, he did not think that. He would have called me on that. I think he wondered what hold you had on me. I believe he thought you had a piece of my heart that he never had. I hate we never talked about it. However, I did not know he felt that way. I am sure that is why he burned your picture. I wish I had realized how he felt."

***

The next week I went back to counseling. I told Margaret about saying goodbye to Michael. Reading that letter was the hardest thing, I had ever done.

Margaret asked about my date too. I told her it was nice, but I was bothered by something. I explained I was bothered with the fact my husband and Charles ran in the same circles.

I told her, "Michael often asked me what I saw in Charles Jeffrey? I never had a response. I never knew why I once loved Charles. However, it bothered me that I threw Charles in his face anytime I saw him. I believed Michael felt I loved Charles more than him. He must have believed that Charles had a piece of my heart he never had. I never realized until now he

LIFETIME

was jealous and felt I did not love him enough. He should have been able to tell me how he felt."

Finally, I understood why he tore up Charles' pictures. I could only imagine how he felt when I cried about it all night.

Margaret asked me more questions. I do not remember what she asked but I was talking fast and said I had been raped sort of matter-of-fact.

"Did you say you were raped?" She questioned me looking over her glasses in my eyes.

I responded, "Yes" and tried to talk about something else.

Margaret asked me questions until I told her everything. Before I left, Margaret said, "The reason you hated Charles all those years was he was your man and you had a textbook case of how a victim of rape feels about their protector. You needed him to protect you. You felt he had let you down. You blamed him for what happened to you. You were a classic rape victim. You could not love him because he had not protected you. You could not love him because you thought you were not worthy. You were young." Margaret paused, "You did not have any counseling. You hid this deep within yourself. You thought you had moved on but the rage was there for Charles when he broke up with you. You felt deep down you deserved it. You were not worthy of better treatment. All these years that's why you never let him go from your heart."

"Hmmn." Was all I said.

Margaret took off her glasses and stood up. "Our time is up. I will see you next week at the same time."

I left her office and dialed Lynette on my cell walking to my car. As soon as she answered, I told her about the session. "Lynette, all these years I have been angry with Charles thinking he had done me wrong. I thought it was his entire fault. I had a break through today."

LIFETIME

I paused before continuing. "But, I have known for many years I was blessed for having been with Michael. I am thankful we fell in love with each other and married. I even told Charles I don't believe we could have been happy together back in the day. We had too many issues. As Heather Headley sang in her song, *they say if you lost something, you have got to let it go. But, if it comes, backs it means so much more. But, if it never does, it was something you had to go through to grow.* Losing Charles made me grow. There is a saying, *what doesn't kill you makes you stronger.*"

***

I started to believe what I have been telling the children. Life is for the living. I don't think I would go back and change a thing even if I could. I have so many blessings I cannot count them all. *I wouldn't take away the rain.*

LIFETIME

Going to the Chapel

It was January 9, 2003 and I stopped by Lynette's desk to say hello. She was not in so I wrote a note. I reached for the paper and noticed "The Daily Word." I read it. It was about the divine order of things. It said we don't have to understand the things that are happening in our lives, but trust in God's divine plan. It touched me. I thought about my own life and how it had changed so much that year. In particular the scripture, "I can do all things through Christ Jesus." I read it over and over. I did not need to understand what was going on in my life. Just simply trust in God's divine plan.

I thought and thought about how Charles came back in my life after 28 years. How we both lived in Dallas less than five miles from each other and rarely ran into each other. How Charles and Michael ran in the same circles and Michael never told me. How Michael questioned me time and time again on what I saw in Charles Jeffrey. And, now here he was back in my life, in the midst of my grief for Michael. Could it be possible that Charles was in my life again for a lifetime? I decided I would simply trust God's plan for my life.

***

Valentine's weekend of 2003, Charles and I went to Las Vegas. My play brother Rodney was real upset with me when he heard that I had been out of town and not told him. He ranted and raved for days about me leaving town and not letting him know. I finally smoothed it over with him, by promising never to do it again. I really loved Rodney. No one really knew how close we were. He understood more about me than I did sometimes. I thanked God for Rodney.

LIFETIME

I Never Should Have Let You Go

Charles and I were talking every day by March 2003. Diahann complained of me being out of pocket. She wanted to be able to reach me at anytime. That was when I started answering my cell phone. Diahann was only relaying what she received from Nicole. Diahann also wanted to meet Oooh Baby. I agreed for them to meet. She insisted on meeting him immediately. It was around ten on a Friday night.

"Right now?" I asked.

"Yeah, bring him over now. I am home alone. Charles won't have to meet Harold." Diahann knew I had issues with Charles meeting her husband and the husbands of my other friends. I agreed to go by.

Thirty minutes later, we were at her doorstep. We went into the kitchen where I introduced Diahann to Charles. I don't remember anything about what was said.

Diahann told others later the two of us were into each other so much that we never noticed when she left the room. She had a good feeling and she was happy once she met Charles.

Diahann initially thought I was using 'Oooh Baby', because he hurt me so. I told her, as bad as I did not want to; I was falling for him. Charles passed Diahann's test. I felt good about that. One down two to go.

A week or so later, Harold, Diahann's husband, wanted to meet Charles. So we agreed. As soon as we walked in, Harold said he knew Charles from somewhere. Eventually, Harold remembered Charles had been the pitcher for their softball team about twenty years before.

LIFETIME

They reminisced about softball. I sat back and tried to remember if we (Michael and I) had even gone to any of Harold's games. I never went to any of the games but Michael did. I don't think it was meant for me to see Charles back then. I had gone to see Charles play intramural softball in college. Just like I hated Charles, I hated softball.

A few weeks later, Faye decided she needed to meet Charles. Therefore, she invited Charles and me over for her grandmother's 85th birthday party. That way everything would be centered on her grandmother and not Charles. I liked that idea.

As soon as we got there, Kenneth came to the door to greet us. I introduced Charles to Kenneth who had a strange look on his face. Oddly enough, he did not have a comedic response.

After most of the guests, left the party, Kenneth and Charles fessed up they had known each other back from the club scene. Faye liked Charles right off, which was not surprising to me.

All the way home, Charles commented about how he knew Kenneth. "You were worried about me meeting Harold and Kenneth for no reason. It would be funny if I already know Toni's and Serena's husbands. How has Serena been anyway? You do remember I worked with her?"

I smiled to myself, not responding to him.

***

One day at work, I decided to call Aunt Grace and tell her about Charles.

Aunt Grace answered the phone. "Hello."

"Hey." I said back to her.

"Hey, Angie."

"What are you doing?" I asked.

"Nothing."

LIFETIME

"Oh. Well, I have something to tell you."

"What is it?" Aunt Grace asked.

"Well, I have this friend and he is really nice."

"You do? Who is he?"

"He is the guy that cleaned the garage."

"I see. Well, are you happy?"

"Yes."

Aunt Grace said, "That is all I have ever wanted for you. Why were you afraid to tell me?"

I replied, "Because I thought you would not approve."

"Angie, I just want you to be happy. You know I loved Michael, but I love you more. I miss Michael everyday. I have been praying that God would bring somebody in your life to help you. You need somebody. You are a young woman."

"But I thought you would be sad."

"Angie, I would never be sad for you if you are happy. I love you. Always, remember, you can tell me anything. Even if I don't agree with you, I will never judge you. You are my baby. I am glad you told me and would like to meet him."

"Okay. I love you too. Bye."

"Did I call you or you call me?" She asked.

"I called you." I said. Aunt Grace had this rule that only the person that initiated the call could terminate the call.

"Okay. Bye then." Aunt Grace replied.

LIFETIME

When I hung up the telephone, I was balling in the phone booth at work. I was missing Michael and happy my aunt loved me that much. I knew she loved me, but I still thought she would not want me to be with Charles. I thanked God for my Aunt Grace; I thought she was my own special angel on earth. I knew God had sent her here for me.

A few days later, Aunt Grace was in the hospital. It was a Friday, our date night, so we went to visit her. Aunt Grace was having problems with her left eye. It looked real bad. She was almost blind in the right eye. She asked Charles to come close to her face so she could see him.

Uncle Nate did not say too much to him. He was not ready to get chummy with him. However, Uncle Nate's sister asked Charles a lot of questions. Her friend lived in his hometown. They hit it off real well. I guess, or maybe she was questioning him for Uncle Nate.

Later, Aunt Grace said he was very different from Michael. She commented he was talkative and large. She was expecting a small frame man. She said he seemed nice.

***

In March, Charles and I decided to go on another trip. We decided that time to go on a road trip to Tulsa, Oklahoma. We took the back roads to Tulsa. I had my camera and took lots of pictures. I took pictures of some large birds of prey. Of course, they were eagles. Charles pulled over and let me take pictures of them. I loved that.

While riding to Tulsa, I was listening to some music that Brandon had given me. High Five's "I Never Should Have Let You Go" came on. I was reading a book and listening to the music at the same time. I closed my book and sat up in my sit. "Oh my goodness, Listen to the words of this song Charles." I said.

LIFETIME

We listened together. "That is you Charles." We laughed about it for a while. He put in another CD. We listened to several Jeffrey Osborn and Luther Vandross songs. We had so much fun.

We arrived in Tulsa early afternoon. I was so excited. I started looking in every car I passed saying, "I know I am going to run into my cousin, Bridget. I can just feel it." We were on a main street running east and west through Tulsa. I wanted to stop at a hotel I saw, but Charles kept driving. I was looking for my cousin.

I did not have Bridget's telephone number or her address, so I called her sister. She was not home. I left a message for her to call me back.

Bridget's sister called me back later that night to say Bridget's phone wasn't working but she would call later to check on her niece. She would give her my message then.

I went to bed early that night. I was real tired. I always slept very hard and was not conscious of telephone conversations when asleep. Well, sometime that night my cousin called.

"Hello." I said sound asleep.

"Hey cuz, this is Bridget."

"Hi." Still sleep.

"What are you doing?

"Sleeping."

"Where are you?"

"I don't know?"

Bridget asked. "What?" She paused and then continued. "Where are the babies?"

"What babies?" I replied annoyed at her.

"Yours."

LIFETIME

"I don't have any babies."

"Where are your kids?" Bridget insisted.

"They are at home, I guess. We are…"

She stopped me, "Who are you with?"

"A friend."

"Where are you headed?"

"I don't know."

"You don't know?" She raised her voice some. "Where are you right now, Angie?"

I raised my voice, "I don't know. Some hotel."

"You don't know? Who is this friend? Can I talk to her?"

"No, it is not a her. I am sleep can I call you tomorrow?"

"No, wait. I can come to your hotel."

"No. I am sleep." I argued.

"Where are you going, Angela?"

"Here."

"Here? Girl talk to me. Nobody comes to Tulsa just to come. Where are you going? Talk to me."

"Bridget, I am sleepy. I will call you tomorrow."

"Wait, let me come by and see you?"

"No, I am sleep. I will talk to you tomorrow. Bye." I hung up, rolled over, and continued sleeping.

LIFETIME

The next day I wondered if I had actually talked to my cousin the night before. I looked on my cell phone and had a long distance number late. I hit the send button and called the number.

"Hello." A strange voice said.

"Hello, may I speak to Bridget?" I said.

The lady said, "Oh, this is not her phone, I let her use my cell last night. But I do not know her."

"Excuse me?" I said very confused.

"Yes, we were at a church convention and she came up to me and asked if she could use my cell to call her cousin."

I thought my cousin had to be crazy. She went up to a perfectly good stranger (a white woman) and asked to use her phone. Now that was crazy. But, the trip was the woman said okay. Therefore, since I had this crazy woman on the phone, I decided to ask her a crazy question. "Do you know how I can find my cousin today?"

"No, but she told you she would call you back today."

"Okay, then, thanks. I am glad you let her call me."

"Sure." The nice woman said.

Sometime later that morning my phone rang. It was Bridget. "Hey Angie, Bridget."

"Bridget, I am glad you called me back. I was asleep last night when you called. What did we talk about?"

"Well you were not making much sense. Where are you?"

"I don't know. Some dump of a hotel." I looked out the window and wondered why we had stayed at that dump.

LIFETIME

"Can you see the street name?"

"No, but I am not going to be here much longer. What are you doing today?"

"Nothing, but I need to see you." Bridget said.

"Okay, why don't we come by your place?"

Bridget said with excitement in her voice. "Okay, here is my address. When are you coming?"

"Oh, in a couple of hours." Pondering if I really wanted to see her.

"Okay, that is good. I can clean up by the time you get here." She paused for a second, "Are you coming for real?"

"Yeah. Sure."

"Okay, I will have Danesha meet you at the gate."

***

Charles and I went to the mall and shopped around. We went to Oral Roberts University and took a bunch of pictures. We rode around and looked at homes. We had a nice time but I was not as excited about seeing my cousin, as I had been when I first got to Tulsa. I did not want her to judge me for dating Charles so soon after Michael's death.

Eventually, we started looking for her apartments. Ironically, Bridget lived right across the street from the first hotel. The nice hotel I wanted to stay when I was looking in everyone's cars. Right where I had the feeling, Bridget was near.

We got to her apartments. I didn't know how Bridget called me earlier. We were at her apartment gate and rang her apartment, but no answer. I was beginning to wonder what was going on with my cousin. She had borrowed a cell phone the night before. Her sister said she did not have a telephone and now I could not get her to answer the apartment gate. We were at

LIFETIME

the gate trying to get in and then came Danesha her daughter. She was the spitting image of her

mother. Danesha got in the car and we drove around to their apartment. We went inside and

Bridget and I hugged each other. Bridget offered to cook for us but Charles wanted to take us

out. The four of us went to a restaurant and on the way there, Bridget was asking Charles

questions.

Somewhat randomly, Danesha said. "My mom used to work right there?" Pointing to a

building down the street.

I turned to face them in the back seat. "Where are you working now?"

Bridget said, "I am unemployed right now."

"Oh really?" I said and then asked, "Well, what do you do for a living?"

Danesha interrupted. "You haven't figured out what she does by now." Danesha

laughed, "She has been using it on you already."

I looked at Danesha, then back at Bridget, and asked. "Are you a therapist?"

"Yes, I am. I have a Masters in family counseling." Bridget said.

"Danesha responded. She used a lot of it on you last night."

I turned to face them in the backseat of the car again and said. "Really? You mean when

I was asleep."

"Yeah, tell her Mother." Danesha hunched her mother.

Bridget leaned forward and touched the back of my seat, "Well, Angie you were giving

me these crazy answers. You did not know where your babies were. You argued you did not

have any babies. You did not know where you were or where you were going. I thought this

was textbook suicidal depression. Your call to me was a last cry out for help. I knew the family

would not understand if I, a therapist, let you kill yourself. You were talking crazy. I had to keep you on the phone. I thought you were attempting suicide and had taken some sleeping pills. You could not tell me where you were or who you were with. I kept saying to myself, I can do this. This is what I do. My family is going to kill me if I let her kill herself. Girl, I was praying. The lady with the phone was praying."

I interrupted, "Speaking of the lady who was she?"

"I don't know. Some random lady. Nice though. Girl, I haven't worked in eight months. I only have a phone for so many minutes per month. I have run out of minutes. I call my sister every Friday because Rita is real sick and to let her know how we are doing. You guys being here are a blessing to us. I do not have a landline. That is why the gate cannot call our apartment. It is a blessing to see you. Last night I thought I was saving you and today you and Charles are feeding us. We have been so blessed. I haven't worked but we haven't gone hungry not one day. God is so good."

I said, "All the time." I smiled and then turned around in my seat.

"Well, Charles back to you. Where did you meet my cousin?" Bridget grilled.

"In college." Charles said.

"Really? You know Angela is special to us so we have to make sure that not just any joker tries to use her. Tell me more about yourself. Are you a Christian?"

"Yes, I am a Christian. I am no joker, user, or abuser. I am a country boy. I met Angela about 28 years ago." Charles looked at me while he was driving and asked. "Did I know Bridget's mother?"

I thought for a second, "I think she went fishing with you, grandmother, and Aunt Millie."

"That is what I thought." Charles said.

LIFETIME

Bridget sat up from her seat and said. "Wait a minute, you knew my mother?"

"I believe so. Miss Jewell and I went fishing every Friday and her sisters went with us sometimes." Charles said.

"Really? And you passed the sisters test?" Bridget asked.

I said, "Yeah, they loved him Bridget. When we broke up I had a hard time getting him out of their lives." I paused before continuing. "But he did not drop them cold turkey like he did me."

"Well, I have to pray on this because we loved Michael. I will have to talk to God about you." Bridget said.

The four of us had a nice lunch and talk. Eventually, we left on our way to nowhere. The concept Bridget never could understand. Since, I wasn't suicidal; she could tell the family she had done her job.

As we drove down the winding back roads, Charles kept saying. "I know Bridget."

After several hours, he asked, "Was she petite with a nice shape and worked at the City of Dallas?"

"Yes." I said.

Charles said, "I knew her back in the day. She dated a guy I knew. She was not the sweet woman she is now. She was bad. Real bad."

"Naw, not my cousin." I blew him off and started looking at the scenery. We passed farms and rivers.

Somewhere in Arkansas, we passed a creek with rocks along the side and rustling water. We decided to stop. We turned around and went into the wooded area. We walked back down a path and down a hill. It was beautiful. We skipped rocks. At least I tried. I got pictures of

LIFETIME

Charles skipping rocks. It was so relaxing. I had never been on a trip where I had no destination. No itinerary just going. Thinking about it, I understood why Bridget was worried. It was the best trip, ever. It was so relaxing. We listened to music we looked at nature and admired God's work. We lived in such a beautiful world. I needed that trip.

***

Some weeks later, one Wednesday night, my matron's sister started talking about dating and relationships. Someone asked me a question about Charles. Deanna, Rev. Beaux's wife, did not know about Charles. She kept asking questions until she got caught up. She said she must have been sitting at the children's table way too long.

The following Sunday morning, Palm Sunday, I saw Rev. Beaux coming toward me. I knew from the moment, I saw him, that Deanna had been talking to him. He was trying to look me in the eye, but I was avoiding eye contact.

"What's going on with you?" Rev. Beaux asked.

"What?" I said squinting from the sun.

"Where were you on yesterday?"

"Oh, I had to work." I said and looked at my watch.

"What about all the other days?"

"When?" I looked down at my shoes.

"Why are you not looking at me?'

"Oh, the sun is in my eyes," I paused and said. "But I have a friend."

"You do?" Rev Beaux asked trying to look me in the eyes.

"Yeah, and I know Deanna told you." I said.

LIFETIME

"But have you told me? I do not believe anything I hear about you from Deanna. We need to talk."

"Okay, but I have got to get inside before the Cantata starts. See you later." I walked away. I thought to myself, Deanna talks too much. That was why she had been over there at the children's table. I picked up my stroll to get inside the church.

A couple of weeks later we had the annual drill team workshop. I was planning to leave early, to go to Charles' fathers Mason banquet. Before I left, the national drill team leader came up to see how I was doing. He had not seen me since Michael died.

Rev. Beaux said to me, "Yeah, tell him how you are doing?"

"I am good." I said.

Rev. Beaux said to the national drill team leader. "I am not sure about her. She is getting ready to leave now. I will tell you about it, later."

I left and went with Charles to the banquet. While Charles and I were on our way to east Texas, Rev. Beaux called and started to get on my case. He said we had to talk.

I replied, "We will talk soon, as a matter of fact; Charles will cook fish for you soon."

"How soon?" Rev. Beaux demanded.

"Maybe next week."

"Is he with you now?" Rev. Beaux questioned.

"Yes, we are in the car." I said.

"Let me talk to him."

I handed the phone to Charles. Beaux questioned Charles. Charles was fidgeting and driving at the same time. After they finished, Charles said we would have to have that fish fry real soon.

LIFETIME

When we arrived at the banquet, it had already started. Charles' dad was at the door taking the tickets. People were in line getting their food so it was difficult to tell what seats were taken. Charles found us two seats facing each other. When the people returned, the lady sitting next to Charles looked familiar. Charles moved abruptly and sat next to me. While we were getting our food, he told me the woman was his daughter's mother. She looked like Charles' daughter, Tiffany.

The banquet was nice. I had not realized Charles' parents wanted to meet me. We went by their home afterwards. Mr. Jeffrey had asked Charles to wait until he got home. When his father came home, the questions began. "Charles tells us you lost your husband a few months ago." Mr. Jeffrey said.

"That is correct, he had a heart attack." I said.

"How are you coping?"

"It is sometimes hard, but I will be okay."

"How are your children doing?"

"They are doing pretty good."

"I am glad to hear that." He paused and then asked. "Which one of your parents is from Hooks?"

"My mother was born in Hooks. I understand you worked with my cousin." I said.

"Yeah, we did and he is a nice guy. You are from good stock. Now, I want you and Charles to take care of each other." Mr. Jeffrey said with a smile.

He was nice, but I was glad the questioning was over. Charles' mother did not say too much. However, I could tell he was the drill sergeant for the Jeffrey family. Charles' mother seemed to like me this time.

LIFETIME

On the way home, Charles and I decided to go hear Rev. Beaux preach the next day at a small church. The church was empty. Most of the members were gone with the pastor. Rodney, Patricia, Deanna, and the Beaux girls came in after we did. They did not see us, no one except my goddaughter. They never noticed she was reaching for me. It wasn't until Rodney decided to take her out that he noticed me. He brought her to me and he went outside.

When Rev. Beaux entered, he never looked up. He went to the rostrum with his head down. He began with, "Good morning. I would like to thank my lovely wife and beautiful girls for accompanying me today. I would also like to say thank you to my brother in Christ and friends Bro. and Sis. Monroe for accompanying me today."

At that point, Rev. Beaux held up his head and saw Charles and me. He almost lost it. With a chuckle in his voice, trying to keep from laughing out loud he said. "Well! I would like to thank God for sending other people." He put his head back down to focus on his sermon. He was real good, once he gained his composure.

After church, Rodney spoke to me. I tried to introduce him to Charles but he kept walking. Charles questioned me about Rodney's attitude. Rodney just needed time to get to know him. He would come around in time. I said to Charles, "Don't push him."

We decided to go to lunch together. The conversation was friendly and not to imposing on Charles. Rodney did not say anything. Deanna, Beaux, and even Patricia did most of the talking. However, they wanted to know when they were getting that fish dinner. We made an appointment for a fish dinner that day.

About a week or two later we had the fish fry. We invited my mom, the Beaux's (Deanna and Taylor), the Monroe's (Rodney and Patricia), the Preston's (Faye and Kenneth), and Johnnie and her children. Mama, Faye, and Kenneth already liked Charles. Everybody else was out to get him.

Charles fried fish. I made cabbage, potato salad, banana pudding, salad, and tea. We had our circle prayer all holding hands and then we ate. There was not too much talking, except for Kenneth. None of my church friends had ever met Faye or Kenneth. However, Kenneth kept the air in the room very light-hearted.

As soon as Rev. Beaux finished eating, he turned into a person I had never seen before. He pulled out a chair and told Charles to sit in it. He asked the big kids to leave and he started questioning Charles as if he was on trial. Deanna said several times he and Rodney were excessively hard on him. Beaux told Deanna to shut up. I couldn't believe it. Johnnie was laughing. Faye asked them to lighten up. Even Kenneth tried to take up for a brother. Charles said he had been expecting this so it was okay. Deanna wrote a sign and held it up that said, "HE IS IN."

Beaux looked at her with a serious look and said. "If you don't be careful, you will be out. We are not playing with this Negro. Now you stop interrupting or you will be asked to go to the children's table."

Johnnie was cracking up.

Rodney said, "This is serious stuff man. This is my family."

Finally, they decided the inquisition was over. I asked Rodney did he pass.

He looked at me and said. "Are you kidding? Do you think this is over? Well, it is not. The jury is still out. The verdict will not be given today."

Faye responded, "You guys are hard. You are going to run Charles off."

LIFETIME

Rodney said. "Well if he can be run off with our questions, then that is what we want. Good riddance."

Faye said. "Wow. Charles, I like you and if Angela likes you then I love you. Kenneth and I are for whatever they want."

"Well good for you, Sis. Preston," said Beaux. "Did I tell you, she is our daughter's god mother? I have to know any Negro that is going to be around my daughter."

I never said a word. What could I say? They said enough for us all. Charles was clear on their position when they left. We were glad that was over.

***

Almost everyone had met Charles, except Serena, Renita, Toni, Vincent, and my matron sisters. I wasn't worried about my matron sisters, but Toni would be tough. Serena probably would be okay with him, but if she wasn't I would be worried. Serena, read people real well. She knew Charles from before and she knew all he had done to me before. However, she said she would have an open mind.

It was Memorial Day when we had our next gathering. We invited a lot of people over to meet Charles. The main guests were Serena, Brian, Cynthia, Renita, my matron sisters, and their children. The whole thing was for Serena to meet Charles. Serena did not say much about Charles that day. As long as she did not take me to the back room during the party, I felt safe.

***

It was September before Toni and Vincent met Charles on Harold's birthday. It was supposed to be a seventies party. We were to dress up like an artist from the seventies and then we were to sing their songs. I forgot to dress up or tell Charles about the dress code. When we arrived, all the regulars were there.

LIFETIME

Charles knew most everyone, except Vincent and Toni. That pissed Toni off. She questioned why they were the last to meet Oooh Baby. Diahann told her we had played cards in the middle of the week once and they would not come. Toni complained that Diahann had not told her that Oooh Baby was there.

Everyone wanted me to do my song. I tried to act as if I didn't know what they were talking about. Harold kept saying, "Angie, I want my song."

I told them I had not gotten a song together. They did not want to hear it. So finally, Charles picked out a song. Harold put the song on. It started to play. It was Freddie Jackson's, "You are My Lady." I looked at Charles and said I could not sing that song.

At that point, Charles took the microphone and began to sing to me. It was as if no one was in the room but us. He crooned to me. All of the couples were shocked that Charles who did not know them was singing to their friend as if he could care less about what they thought. They could tell the two of us had something real special.

The men took Charles into the other room to question him. The women were questioning me. I told them, how I felt about him. They all knew the story about 'Oooh Baby' so they were puzzled as to when things changed. Diahann was the only one that knew all along that now we liked 'Oooh Baby.' We started to play bid whist. Charles came in the room to play. Toni sent him out. We were not finished talking.

Charles said, "Yall don't like me do you?"

Diahann responded never even looking at him. "If we didn't like you, you would know it."

"Well, why can't I play cards?" Charles asked.

Toni snapped. "Because we said so, now go on back in there with the men."

LIFETIME

Diahann said. "Now, Oooh Baby we like you because our girl likes you. However, if she stops liking you, then we will stop liking you again. So don't mess up."

Charles asked again, "Can I play cards?"

"No, go back and watch football." Toni said.

"The game is over." Charles replied.

"Too bad." Toni shouted waving her hand in the air.

I mouthed to him. "It will be okay. Go back in the den." He turned and went back into the den with the men. He looked sad, but I was happy. All of my friends were accepting of my new guy. My Oooh Baby. "Make that a five no trump." I yelled.

***

By June 2004, Lynette's husband had been killed. That Sunday in church, I had the feeling I should look at my phone. There were two missed calls from Lynette. My phone was on silent. It was a Sunday but no one would call me on a Sunday morning. I told Charles I better go outside and call her. I returned her call. Lynette said Robert was gone. I said something so stupid, "Gone where?"

"He is dead." Lynette cried.

I fell to the ground outside the church. I tried to compose myself to ask her what did she need. She said she needed to talk to me and asked to come over later.

That night Lynette came over to talk. The two of us were at my house. She was crying. My heart went out to her because I knew it would be tough for her. I found myself crying and then she was consoling me.

I often wondered did I lose my husband and leaned on Lynette so she could lean on me later.

LIFETIME

We're Going All The Way

One summer night, Charles and I talked well into the morning as we had been doing for months. We decided to meet for lunch the next day.

The next day turned out to be a bad day for me to meet for lunch, but he kept insisting. I got to the mall and we walked to the food court. I needed to get back to work. But, we sat down and ate. After we finished, I was trying to rush off but Charles started talking.

"Angela." Charles stuttered.

"Yes." I said.

He said, "I want to buy you a ring."

"A ring? Why?"

I folded my arms. "Well, the past few months have been wonderful and I . . . You know what this is. So what do you say?" A tear fell from his left eye.

I responded. "What do I say to what? What is the question?"

"You know what I am asking." He said looking in my eyes.

"Well, I may know what you are asking, but if you don't ask a question there is nothing for me to answer."

Charles got on his knees and said, "Will you marry me and be my wife?"

I sank back in my chair. I looked at my watch because I needed to go, but he had asked me to marry him. I did not answer. A tear fell from my eye. I did love him, but what about my children. I had always loved him, but what will people think. What should I do? I looked at my watch again and finally, responded, "Yes, I will marry you."

LIFETIME

He immediately, went into the jewelry store and purchased a beautiful engagement and wedding ring set for me.

By the time I got back to work, I had been gone for over three hours and was being paged by my manager. She was not happy with me. Everyone had been looking for me. I was in tears. I told her Charles asked me to marry him and she totally forgot about being mad at me.

***

My rings would be ready that Friday, so I needed to tell my kids before then. Charles asked me if I wanted him to be with me when I told them. I declined because I had to tell the children on my own.

Wednesday night of that week, my sisters were giving me a hard time about Charles. I wanted to tell them, but I had to tell my children first. That night when we got home, I called Brandon and Nicole into my bedroom for a family meeting. I told them Charles asked me to marry him and I agreed.

"Are we the first to know?" Nicole asked, with her hand on her hip.

"Yes, I wanted you both to be the first to know."

Nicole said, as she sat on my bed. "Okay, because I was going to be mad if your sisters knew before us. As long as you do not have a big wedding, I am okay. I want you to be happy. Mommy, you have always told us life is for the living. I love you so much and wish you all the happiness ever."

I was happy that she seemed to be happy for me.

Brandon said, "Well, I want you to keep Everette as your last name. This is my daddy's house. I love this house, but Charles has got to find us somewhere else to live. I do not want

LIFETIME

him to come up in my daddy's house. That would not be right. And, I am very happy for you. I love you and he seems to make you happy." Brandon came and kissed me on my cheek.

My eyes filled with tears. My children were happy for me and accepted the change in our lives. We embraced each other for several minutes. I had a big smile on my face with tears in my eyes. I was so proud of them at that very moment. The thought of their acceptance, made me think of their father. I felt happiness and sadness at the same time. I wished Michael was there to witness that moment and realized had he still been alive the moment would not exist. At that point, I needed to be alone.

***

By Friday, we were picking up the rings. They were absolutely impressive. We went straight to Diahann's house to show her. In all the years that Diahann lived in that house, what happened next had never happened before. I got out of the car and dropped my cell phone down the manhole in front of the house. I had never seen that manhole before. We tried to get the phone but gave up and went inside.

Diahann loved the rings. She thought it was funny my cell phone was in that hole. She commented that quite a few of our friends stuff was down there. Charles tried to get the phone out, but he could not reach it. We would need a key to the water meter to open it up. I could not think of one telephone number, they were all in my cell. Later that night, Harold found a water meter key and got my cell phone out of the water drainage hole. It fell on a rock and never got wet. I was so blessed.

That Sunday, we went to hear Jeffrey Osborne. The concert was really nice. He sang "We're Going All The Way." Charles held my hand, looked in my eyes, and said. "We are going all the way baby, you and me."

LIFETIME

I smiled and said, "I think you are right."

***

By the weekend, Brandon had us riding around looking at homes for sale. We looked at several houses but we liked one particular house that had so much curb appeal. We stopped and admired the house. As we were driving off, I noticed the house was listed by Everette Realtors. I asked if they thought that was a sign to us. We jotted the information down and drove away.

Eventually Charles and my kids were driving by looking at that house every day. I was not interested because the house was too pricy. One night, God spoke to me. *I am God all by myself. Trust in me. Step out on faith. Follow your husband. Don't take control as you always do. Follow your husband. I am God and I have everything.*

I wanted to be obedient but I was afraid. I knew as a believer that I should not have a spirit of fear. I knew, "Faith is the substance of things hope for the evidence of things unseen." I knew and believed, but I was afraid. *I would trust God. I would let my man lead me.*

***

We decided to have Rev. Beaux come and look at the house. Rev. Beaux came straight there one Sunday after church. He looked through the house and said, "This is it." Then, he asked us to join hands. The realtor asked could she join in. Rev. Beaux asked Charles to hold the front door and he began to pray. "Father God in the name of Jesus, we are here today asking you to Bless this house. Let it be a home where YOU reside. Father God I want YOU to touch the foundation, the roof, and all the bricks and mortar to make it clean. Bless it from the front door to the back door, from the foundation to the roof. Bless the yard. Lord, if there are any unclean spirits here remove them Lord. They cannot stay here, Father God. Bless this family

LIFETIME

and build up Charles as the man of this house. Lord bind them as a family. Love them as a family. In Jesus name. Amen."

The next day I called Gwen, my matron sister, and told her about the house. She said, "What is the address?"

I thought for a moment and said, "2004..."

Gwen interrupted, "Did you say 2004? Girl, that's a sign this is your house 2004 is your year."

"Wow, I hadn't even thought about the address." I said with surprise in my voice.

"That's right up the street I am going to go and pray over it right now." We hung up the telephones.

Gwen called me later that day to say she went up the street from her job, got out of the car, and prayed over the yard. She was convinced that was our blessing.

***

A few weeks later, Deanna threw us a nice engagement party and invited about 50 of our closest friends. Deanna prepared lots of great food. She served shrimp, chicken, champagne, and cake. Every one had great words of encouragement. Kenneth had everyone laughing. He said he told me when you get to be our age love does not matter, but can you change each other's diapers. He went on to say Charles could change mine, but I probably would not change Charles'. Everyone was cracking up laughing. However, Kenneth thought I would pay to have someone change Charles' diaper. He said he was going to buy us some 'Depends' as a wedding gift. Everyone was laughing except me.

After Kenneth finished speaking my mom said, "Good evening everyone. When Deanna asked me to speak at this engagement party for my daughter, I thought what should I say. I have

LIFETIME

never been to an engagement party before. Deanna wanted me to say something funny, but I am a serious person, so I will just speak from my heart. I am happy for my daughter, Angela Renee. She has been that special daughter since the day she was born. Some say I have really spoiled her." She paused for a moment. "If you mean I have spoiled her with my love then so be it. I love my daughter and I thank God for her. Charles, I like the fact you talked to me about my daughter and said you would never hurt her. I love you and am happy you have asked her to marry you. She is happy and she has been sad for a long time. You make her happy and I love you for that. May God Bless you both." She threw me a kiss and I threw her one back as we so often did.

My aunt Grace stood up next and began speaking. "Hi, I am Grace, Angela's aunt. Angela is just like one of my children. You see I prayed for her to be born on my birthday and God allowed it. When she told me, she had a new friend. I told her as long as you are happy I am happy. I love you both."

"Good evening everyone. I am Cynthia. Angela and I have known each other all of our lives. We grew up across the street from each other. We were classmates from elementary school, junior high, high school, and college. I told Angela not to be bothered with what others think about you and Charles. She has always loved him and he loves her. Be happy."

Standing there listening to my family and friends was unbelievable. I had long since gotten over the feelings that one day Charles and I would kiss and make up. I was truly blessed. God had given me a great husband that loved me for more than twenty years. Although God took him home too early for me, He sent me a second helpmate, Charles Edward Jeffrey, II. It looked like we are going all the way.

LIFETIME

I can't believe its real; I can't believe it is true. Sometimes I want to shout with excitement of getting my Oooh Baby, yet cry at the same time because I really missed Michael. I not only missed him because he was my husband and lover, I missed him because he was my friend. He was the only one that really knew how I felt about Charles Jeffrey.

I did not understand how and why things were happening. *The Lord giveth and the Lord taketh away. Thank you Lord for all your many Blessings!*

LIFETIME

We Will Understand it Better By and By

The next day, Nicole, Charles, and I flew to Baltimore, Maryland for Nicole to attend Howard University in Washington, DC. It was about a forty-five minute drive from Baltimore to DC. But, it took us four hours to arrive at Howard. We got lost. We had a two o'clock appointment with the band director to sign scholarship papers, but we did not arrive until six.

As we exited the elevator, Kelvin Washington was standing at a desk in front of the elevator. He yelled out, "Nicole Everette get over here. You are late. Read these papers and sign them. Look at me when I am talking to you."

"I am sorry for being late." Nicole said in a soft voice.

Mr. Washington yelled, "I don't want to hear it. Read the papers. I have to get these to the Financial Aid Office, they have already closed." He was rustling papers and said. "Look at me. Now, I am not giving you this scholarship because you are cute. You must maintain a grade point of 3.0 or above. Do you see those students down there?" He pointed to some students at the end of the hallway exercising. "They all have a 2.9 grade point average and will not receive their scholarships. You will need to work in the band office on a daily basis." He stopped speaking to look at a young lady that passed behind him. Then he turned back around to speak to Nicole. "You need to be out there marching so your hair would look like that young lady that just passed here. Read the paper, Nicole." Mr. Washington got up in Nicole's face and said. "Now I will not be like those white band directors you are used to. I will be in your face. Do not come to me talking about I am in love. Three point or better. Look at me. Do not look at your mother. She will not be here. I will get on your case and then call your mother. Do you understand, Nicole?"

LIFETIME

"Yes sir." Nicole replied in a soft voice.

"Alright, then. Welcome to Howard University." Mr. Washington said with a smile and opened arms.

Later that night we went to an orientation session. While we were there, a professor said. "Students look to the person on your left and then turn to the person on your right. Tell each of them that I am going to do everything that I can to help you graduate with me in four years."

I thought to myself now that was awesome. I was going to love that Historically Black College and University. I thought back to what they told us more than thirty years ago. The school was not concerned with whether or not we graduated. I sat back in my seat and smiled. I felt, they loved my baby. I had a smile on my face.

The next day Nicole moved into her dorm. By Sunday morning, Charles and I came to wish her well and say our goodbyes. We took a few pictures of Nicole in her new home. Nicole started straightening things in her room. Her eyes were filling with tears. Charles whispered it was time for us to go. I had given Nicole all of the advice I had so I gave her a big hug and said. "I am so proud of you Nicole. I know your dad is looking down on you smiling. I love you so much." Nicole was wiggling trying to get away, but before she started to cry, I whispered in her ear. "Don't take no wooden nickels."

She looked at me with a puzzled look and asked. "What did you say?"

I repeated, "Don't take no wooden nickels. My dad told me that every time he took me to college. Now, I will tell you the same thing." I turned and walked away. She kept straightening stuff on her desk.

LIFETIME

Charles and I walked to the car. Nicole did not follow us. I was proud. My baby was growing up. Charles had started to ramble. He thought I was going to cry. I never cried. We drove away. I had a smile on my face. My little Nicole was in college.

Monday morning, Charles and I were heading back home. Tuesday morning we were sitting in closing of our new home. By the weekend, we were moving.

***

I had forgotten how hard moving could be and therefore had not planned on that nightmare. It almost killed me. I had not moved in seventeen years. I never knew I had so much stuff. I did not pack or anything. That was the worse mistake I could have ever made. That move was a big test for Charles and me. I tried to kill him.

He kept saying, "Didn't you know moving was hard and why didn't you pack?"

Brandon started school and was moving a carload at a time. He had to be at school at six forty-five each morning for band not returning until 3:00. We were all extremely exhausted.

Nicole left her room a mess. She was so busy telling everyone bye. Charles' sister packed and unpacked her room. Her room and the kitchen were the only rooms in the new house that were totally organized.

Sunday morning following the move, I was in bed and realized I did not know where our new wedding rings were. I jumped up looking for them frantically.

The telephone rang. Charles answered. It was for me. No one was on the phone when I picked up. So, I hung up and continued looking for my rings. The phone rang again. I was running through the house looking for the rings, not wanting Charles to know the rings were lost. Charles called me to the phone.

LIFETIME

I was upset someone was calling me while I was trying to look for the rings. "Hello."

No response. "Hello," I repeated. I heard someone on the line but no response. "Hello," I said

for the third time. I heard whimpering. "Nicole, what's wrong?" All I heard was uncontrollable

crying. My baby sounded as if someone had hurt her. "Nicole what's wrong. Tell me." I

shouted while crying on telephone. "Talk to me. Tell me." I pleaded.

Nicole spit out, "I want to come home. I want to come home."

"Did somebody hurt you? Are you okay?" I questioned.

"I just want to come home. I want to go to my own church. I need a hug. Come get

me." Nicole cried.

"I am on my way, if you are hurt." I was getting ready to book a flight.

"No, I am not hurt. I just hate this place. I hate Sundays here." She whimpered.

I realized she was not hurt and I remembered the rings. So I said. "Can I call you right

back?" I felt her looking at the phone as if her mom had lost her mind. She did not respond.

"Nicole, I will call you right back, Okay?" I hung up.

Where were those rings? I remembered putting them in a box marked important items. I

started looking for boxes that were taped and had writing on the outside. I could not find them. I

had floor to ceiling boxes. I had at least fifty people helping me move. Anyone could have

walked off with my rings.

I was frantic. I sat down to think. Where could they be? Then, I remembered I decided

not to mark them important. I had put them in a non-descript box and threw all of my important

papers in the box with the rings. I started looking through the boxes again.

Nicole called me back two more times. I only talked to her a few minutes, before I told

her I needed to call her back. If I knew what box, the cordless phone was in or my cell phone I could have talked to her and looked for the rings at the same time. They were both lost. Once I found the rings, I called her back. She did not answer. I was worried about her then.

Nicole called me back that night about 7:30. She was acting as if nothing had happened that morning. She said they had gone to Chapel and it was very good. She was a totally different person that night and so was I.

The next day or so, I went to the mailbox totally exhausted from moving and working. I received a letter from Nicole. I opened the letter outside and started reading it at the mailbox.

August 27, 2004

Mommy,

Words cannot express how much I love you. I do not just love you because you care for me and provide for me but because you have always supported me. Whether it was through playing on the 'C' team volleyball, trying out for theatre in 9th grade or making contest block in marching band or even trying out for Ramblers, you've always supported me 110%. You have nurtured me and helped me grow into the lady that I am now. I sometimes forget to say thank you for the little things like the constant reminders about deadlines and for always making sure I sent applications on time. You have continually made a constant effort to make sure that all goes well with everything. You think of things before I can forget them and you always provide for me when I need you most. I definitely know that I am blessed to have you as my mother. I owe God about 10 billion thank yous for putting you in my life, not only as a mother but also as a friend. I know that the past few years have been hard for us, but I am thankful that we have made it through. Although I may not show it, but deep inside I am happy that you have found someone that you can trust and talk to when times get hard. Yes, life is for the living, and I am thankful that you have someone. I know these next few months will be hard to get through without your love and comfort present everyday. I do know that I will always have your love surrounded by me and in my heart. I know that God will provide me with everything I need as I venture off to college. Even though I will be gone, I will continue to hold the morals and values that you have instilled close to my heart. I promise to keep God first in my life and persevere throughout all the challenges that I will face. I promise to become a success in everything I do, even when failing seems inevitable. I know that through Christ, all things are possible and with that, I take on all responsibilities for myself. You have supplied me with everything I could ever need and want in life, and not just the material things, but love, trust, and understanding, and for this Mommy, I say THANK YOU.

Love always,

LIFETIME

Nicole Renee Everette

By the time, I got inside the house. I was rolling around on the floor screaming and hollering like crazy. It finally hit me. I had not cried at graduation. I had not cried taking my daughter to college. But, I was crying. Charles was trying to find out what was wrong, so I handed him the letter. I could not stop crying. I cried the entire evening. Everywhere I turned, something made me cry. I went through some stuff and cried. I found a letter from my dad. I never remembered my dad writing me. I cried. I found a beautiful anniversary card from Michael. I was just a mess. Charles checked on me and then allowed me to roll around in my sadness. It was all just too much.

***

By September, it was time for my first wedding shower. Faye was hosting it. She planned a shower before she started the retail Christmas season. She invited about twenty-five of my family and friends.

The shower was really nice at Faye's home. The best thing about the shower was the poems. Faye had everyone write a poem about Charles and me. They were only given five minutes and were told it must rhyme. I was supposed to choose one winner. The poems were so good that I declared them all winners.

My mom's poem read.

> Angela without Michael wasn't the same
> Along came Charles in the rain.
> Nicole and Brandon sad at first
> Now their feelings are reversed
> God worked it out to their gain.
> Now January 8th comes the wedding flame.

Diahann's poem read.

LIFETIME

Charles and Angela met thirty years ago
All of a sudden, they didn't talk no mo
She was down and Charles came around
Now you can't catch Angela, no mo
If you want to be with this lady
Your name better be Oooh Baby.
Love you girl.

Faye's poem read,

How they met was long ago.
How they got back together, we all know
Love is patience, love is kind,
All Charles said to Angela was
Will you be mine?

My aunt's poem read,

Angela met Charles a long time ago
Things do change this we know
Charles asked Angela to be his significant other
Angela said Charles I have to ask my mother
She called her mother and said, Charles asked me for my hand
I told Charles I will give you my answer, as soon as I can.
Angela asked, Nicole and Brandon what should I do?
They both said "mother," If you love him, we love him too.
She told Charles, yes I'll be your wife to be with you for the rest of my life.
Charles said, Yes that will be great, now we can set our wedding date.
He called the reverend and said I know in my heart.
I found my mate we will have a big celebrate on January the 8th.
I love you very much.

Toni's poem read,

Angela, this is your season of life
We've gone from Friday night Bid
To a grown woman's strife
Your strength has been my strength
Your plights have been my plights
As you, enter into your next chapter
I read your pages of life with great anticipation
Yesterday, I was proud of you
Today I rejoice in your self-pride
God has truly blessed you
So as you and Charles take this step of faith
I too, right beside you,

LIFETIME

And Charles
Step . . . step
Into your beautiful, spiritual filled
New season of life.
I love you both and wish you God's continued blessings.
Your sister,
Toni
Luv you mean it

My cousin wrote,

Charles and Angela sitting under their tree
K-I-S-S-I-N-G.
First came friendship, then true love
And a lifetime of happiness, Blessed by God above
A new start, a new beginning
A fairy tale start, but no ending
Continue to keep God first,
And the best is yet to come
The smile on your face,
Reflects the happiness in your heart
This union was blessed right from the start
You deserve all the happiness in the world
For you are a very special girl
Your love for Charles is just like fine wine
It will only get better in time
You know; a love like this still does exist
And we thank God for blessing you with it
Love ya,
Your cousin

My cousin's went like this.

Love Conquers All
Angela and Charles met many years ago
But didn't think that once again
They would give it a go.
The Lord already had set up the plan
But it was He who knew
When the time was at hand.
We never know what God has in store
But be assured He knows when to open the door.
There are many things in this life
That may come to call,
When all else fails or starts to fall,
When God set the plan;

LIFETIME

Love conquers all.

My sister Johnnie's read,

Once upon a time Charles said to Angela
I'll help you out of a bind
Angela said you are so kind
She thought another love I'll never find
She thought on Charles Jeffrey she'd never pine
He didn't have to give her wine
So after the Chinese line
He asked her will you be mine?

Big sister Irene's read,

I know a woman named "Angela"
Who met a man name "Charles"
He really put her to shame
When he told her, Baby you're my Thang
She laughed and grinned with glee and said
Oooh Baby you're talking to me
I love you too,
But your heart is the key.
Big Sister

Gwen's read

There was a couple from East Texas State
They are back together and not by fate
Through many years and different circumstances
God reunited them
And not by any chances
Angela and Charles are meant to be
So January 8th will be a happy day you see

Deanna's read

Charles and Angela went up lover's hill
To fetch a happy day.
Charles said, January 8th
But, Angela had something to say
You know it's all about me
And that's just the way
Seeing that Charles is so in love said
For you anyway, any day, is okay.

LIFETIME

My cousin Paula's read.

Charles has taken Angela to a higher plain
The only time she is blue
Is when she has the flu
No tears only smiles
Which to last for miles and miles
May their new marriage
Be like a ride in a horse driven carriage
I hope you and Charles have lots of love
And stay together for life, like two doves.

Renita's read

Angela and Charles were once upon a time
Winds blew and the directions changed.
They went their separate ways
And lived their own lives
Time passed on and their lives grew on
Some were fine and some were blue
Their paths crossed again and the time was right
And now again the new
Once upon a time.
Love you
Renita

The Banana Split

Charles and Angela, the big delicious banana split
He came and went from this banana split
She came and went from this banana split.
They came back together was the rich ingredient
Too sweet and creamy, a big banana split.
The banana, the cream, the topping and the cherry
For this banana split.
Time and love came with a twist
To tie together and make this
One big delicious banana split.
Your new sister
Nedra

LIFETIME

What wonderful expressions from my friends and family, they were all winners. They loved us so much that they were able to put such beautiful words into poems. I would cherish them forever.

***

It was Thanksgiving 2004, and we were having dinner at our home. It was the first time Nicole been home since she left for college in the fall. We did not have any furniture in our living/dining room, so we took three long tables and put them together to create a long dining table. We had patio chairs, folding chairs, and any other chair we could put our hands on. We served turkey, dressing, greens, ham, tamales, fruit salad, cherry marshmallow salad, fried turkey, potato salad, turnips, yams, rolls, and cornbread. Everyone had a nice time.

Charles' sister Barbara had a lot of questions about our upcoming wedding. She asked me about the flowers. She asked to see the dress. She asked me several questions and after seeing everything, she decided I should walk down our stairway with a dramatic entrance. An entrance to remember. She asked if she could use my tulle and make me a cape that would hang down my back like a train. She wanted me to drop the cape at the bottom of our staircase. You know as James Brown used to do.

Now all while she was describing this entrance, I was thinking 'ghetto.' No actually, a country sighting, most of all I was thinking, no way. I was hoping the look on my face was not saying, "Are you out of your mind?" I was hoping my facial expressions were not getting me in trouble with my new sister-in-law. I hoped I had pulled it off with her. Now, I knew Barbara had a marvelous voice so I asked her to sing at the wedding. She would sing "The Lord's Prayer." But, I had to figure out a way to get out of wearing the cape without hurting her feelings.

LIFETIME

All evening everyone asked what Barbara and I had been up too. I never said, since that was all part of her grand plan.

Every time I came down the stairs after that all I could think about was, I ain't going to be able to do it.

The next day, Charles and I went to purchase an artificial Christmas tree, a fourteen foot, pre-lit tree, green spruce tree.

Nicole and Brandon went off about the tree, because it had been an Everette' family tradition to get a fresh tree each year. However, I decided since fresh trees made me sick each and every year, I was starting a new tradition.

They whined and whined from the moment they saw the tree. They said they would never accept that artificial tree. I ignored them.

Charles put lights outside the house on the sidewalk bordering the yard. It looked really nice. To our surprise, our next-door neighbor did the exact same thing. Nicole loved the lights outside, but demanded we return the artificial tree. As if, she could tell me what to do. I was almost in agreement when we tried to set the tree up. It did not look full at all. It looked fake. I never knew you had to bend, fluff, and twist the tree to make it look nice.

The tree had been standing in the living room for two weeks naked. So, I called my girls, Renita and Diahann, to do magic. They turned that ugly tree into a work of art. They decorated the banister, the family room, and the kitchen. Everything looked really nice and festive.

LIFETIME

Reunited

It was the night before the wedding and we were getting everything in order. The ceremony would be held in our living room, which we turned into a beautiful wedding chapel. Renita was finishing the final touches on the decorations. Toni was going over her plans for the next day. Diahann and Serena kept questioning their attire for the wedding.

My response was always the same. "Wear whatever you like, but do not up stage me." That was not good enough for Diahann, so she kept asking.

Since, Charles had invited more than his eight guests it meant Diahann, Serena, and Faye would have to stand along side me as a real wedding party. "But I am the coordinator." Diahann yelled pointing to her chest.

"Yeah. I know." I replied.

Diahann turned toward Serena and said, "What do you want to wear Serena?"

"Well, I was planning on wearing blue." Serena said to Diahann.

"Do you have chocolate brown?" Diahann asked.

Serena said, "I have a chocolate brown pants suit, but I was planning on wearing a dress."

"Well, I have a chocolate brown pants suit too." Diahann looked at me and said, "Angie, call Faye to see if she has a brown pants suit?"

I called Faye about 1:00 a.m. telling her what Diahann and Serena wanted her to wear.

Faye was livid. She refused to consider wearing one of my brown pants suits saying I was too short. "I cannot believe y'all are over there coming up with bridesmaid's stuff at this late hour. If you had told me, I could have brought something from my store."

I said to her, "Well, they just came up with this. I told them to wear whatever. You still can."

"No, I will have to go by my sister's house in the morning. I am mad at all of y'all."

"Don't be mad at me?" I begged.

"But, I am." Faye answered.

"Love you." I said to Faye.

"I love you too. But I am still mad." Faye hung up the telephone.

"She is mad." I said.

"We are mad too. It is your fault." Diahann said and she turned to Serena. "Serena, have ever heard of anyone coming up with a bridal party a few hours before the wedding?"

I said to them, "Wait and see. It will be nice."

"It better be," Diahann said.

About 2:00 a.m., the doorbell rang. To my surprise, it was Barbara, Charles' sister. I had completely forgotten about the cape. Barbara and I went upstairs while the rest of them stayed downstairs. They would be much more critical than I of that country sighting.

Barbara was talking and unveiling the thing. I was speechless. The cape was breathtaking. She had hand painted calla lilies on the sides of the cape with spray glitter and sequins that popped up and down as the train unfolded. It was simply stunning. However, I was still concerned about wearing it as a cape and taking it off. I whispered, "How do I wear this cape?"

Barbara stepped back and looked down at the cape. "Well, I decided against making it into a cape."

Thank you Jesus, I said to myself.

LIFETIME

"Are you carrying a bouquet?" Barbara asked.

I responded, "Yes, fresh calla lilies."

"Can someone stand at the bottom of the stairs and hand you the bouquet?"

"Sure. My uncle is giving me away. He will be downstairs."

"Okay then what I will do is make this train into a bouquet that will follow you down the stairs and when you get to the bottom of the stairs you will lay it down. Then your uncle will give you the fresh flowers." She nodded her head up and down. "Yeah, that will work."

That was when I got the nerve to get the rest of them to show off my gorgeous bouquet train. They were taken away.

January 8, 2005, and I was descending the stairs on Kenny G's "The Wedding Song." I had a smile on my face. It was joyous.

Finally, I was standing there with Charles Edward Jeffrey, II my first love. I was thinking reunited and it feels so good. I was not listening to Rev. Beaux and was not ready when he asked me to say my vows. He had to prompt me twice.

I had to say my vows with feeling, you know like in the soap operas. I hoped every one in the room could feel the love. I looked into Charles' eyes and opened up my heart. I said to myself, *go for it girl.* "Charles." I sobbed. "Charles." More sobs. I did not want the tear to drop. I began again. "Charles, I do not know why God has blessed me with so much. I am not sure how you captured my heart with your smile. What I do know is I love you. You take my breath away. I never thought I could love or feel again. But oh, what an awesome God we serve. I was going through the motions watching life go around me with me looking from the outside. I was so empty that I could not feel, but God being God all by Himself sent you to me. He sent your smile, your soothing voice, your compassion, your friendship, your love that was

LIFETIME

built over 30 years ago. You know, I could never have imagined there was a purpose in our past and how the future could be impacted by a brief encounter. You once sent me an email entitled Reason, Season, and Lifetime. I now believe that 30 years ago you came into my life for a reason, that lasted for only a season, and now I can say my love for you will last for a lifetime."

***

I sat up from the back seat of the limousine and said to Mary. "It is beyond reason to me why I met Charles thirty years ago for him to be brought back into my life again. It is also beyond reason why Michael was there for me when I broke up with Charles all those years ago. God placed them both in my life to fulfill His lifetime plan for me. It seems ironic that Michael came into my life to help me through the break up of Charles. And, Charles came back into my life to help me to go through the grief of my husband Michael. I have stopped wondering what the reason is but simply enjoy the blessing." I rubbed Charles' leg and continued. "Initially when I read the email Reason, Season, Lifetime, I thought it only applied to the men in my life. As I pondered it and read it again and again, I realized that everyone we meet falls into one of these categories. Your family is a lifetime relationship. Your true friends are lifetime relationships and others come in and out your life for reasons and seasons. I know God's divine plan is evident in my life. It is beyond anything that I can understand. But I will understand it better by and by." I touched Mary's arm and said listen to this song. I sang, "Blessed assurance Jesus is mine. O what a fore taste of glory divine. Heir of salvation. Purchase of God. Born of his spirit. Washed in His blood. This is my story. This is my song, praising my Savior all the day long." Amen.

LIFETIME

Beyond Reason

It is funny how you can hear a song about a thousand times and know the words to the bridge, but have never really listened to the lyrics. One day while working, I heard Heather Headley's song "In My Mind." I was amazed at the lyrics. It was exactly how I once felt. At that moment, I decided to write this book

Beyond Reason is a story following the life of Angela, an ambitious Christian young woman from the South. She narrates her journey as she reminisces over her own life. Her strict parental upbringing impacts her life as she struggles with relationship problems, pregnancy complications, and death.

Beyond Reason is a story spanning three decades with moments of joy and sorrow. It will inspire readers to evaluate life and begin to appreciate its blessings. This poignant and comical story shows that there is a defining purpose for our existence.

I hope this story brings joy to someone and allows young people to persevere to achieve their dreams, keep their faith, and always believe in love.

Tell It Publishers
P. O. Box 850432
Richardson, TX 75085-0432
www.tellitpublishers.com

Biography of
Elaine Evans Johnson

Born and raised in Texas, Elaine Evans Johnson grew up in Hamilton Park, an African-American neighborhood in North Dallas. In school, she always liked to use her analytical mind. At a young age, she knew she wanted to pursue a mathematical career in the professional world.

Elaine graduated from East Texas State University in 1977 with a bachelor's of science in business administration/computer science.

Since graduating from college, Elaine always wanted to write a book about her life. *Beyond Reason* started out as a simple love story. However, she says writing the book was therapeutic and provided personal satisfaction.

Family-oriented, logical, and optimistic, Elaine takes an active role in her church. She has a passion for helping people, especially high school students applying for college and scholarships.

She has spent 28 years as a systems analyst in the information technology industry.

Elaine lives in Dallas with her husband, Frank. She has two children, Erin and James.

Tell It Publishers
P. O. Box 850432
Richardson, TX 75085-0432
www.tellitpublishers.com